NEW FAIRY TAL

Essays and Stories

Edited by

John Patrick Pazdziora *and*
Defne Çizakça

UNLOCKING PRESS
2013

New Fairy Tales: Essays and Stories
Copyright © 2013 John Patrick Pazdziora and Defne Çizakça

For information, contact Unlocking Press www.UnlockingPress.com

Unlocking Press titles may be purchased for business or promotional use or special sales.

Cover Design by Faye Durston Hanson

10 - 9 - 8 - 7 - 6 - 5 - 4 - 3 - 2 - 1
0-9829633-8-8
978-0-9829633-8-8

Table of Contents

Introduction
John Patrick Pazdziora and Defne Çizakça　　　　vii

Chapter 0 Galantha
Joshua Richards　　　　1

PART I Minatures　　　　3

Chapter 1 Glass, Bricks, Dust
Claire Massey　　　　5
Chapter 2 Robert Herrick's Fairy Epithalamium and
Natural Religion
Jesse Sharpe　　　　17
Chapter 3 Anti-Fairy Tale Taxidermy: The Animations
of Tessa Farmer
Catriona McAra　　　　41
Chapter 4 Gnomes
Katherine Langrish　　　　61

PART II Storytellers　　　　71

Chapter 5 Do Fairies Still Exist? Fairy-Tales in
Hebrew Nowadays
Hanna Livnat and Gaby Cohn　　　　73

Chapter 6 Deciphering the Ottoman Fairy Tale:
Tayyarzade Throughout the Centuries
Defne Çizakça 115
Chapter 7 Cloud Catching in the Realm of the
Drought King
Fiona Thackeray 137
Chapter 8 "On Fairy-stories" and Tolkien's Elvish
Tales
Christopher MacLachlan 147
Chapter 9 "Oh, You Wicked Storytellers!"
John Patrick Pazdziora 167

PART III Shadows and Reflections 195

Chapter 10 A Prevailing Wind
Elizabeth Reeder 197
Chapter 11 Not for Children: The Development of
Nihilism in the Fairy Tales of Oscar Wilde
Colin Cavendish-Jones 221
Chapter 12 Radiant Mysteries: George MacDonald,
G.K. Chesterton, and the *Claritas* of Fairy Tales
Daniel Gabelman 249
Chapter 13 The Land Without Stories: A Threefold Tale
Eric M. Pazdziora 269

PART IV Fairy Brides 279

Chapter 14 In the Midst of Metamorphosis: Yōko
Tawada's "The Bridegroom Was a Dog"
Mayako Murai 281
Chapter 15 A Gothic Fairy-Bride and the Fall: A Lecture
on "The End of the World" in Kenjirō Hata's
Hayate no Gotoku
Joshua Richards 299
Chapter 16 Dante
Joshua Richards 319

PART V Fairy Tale Pedagogy 357

Chapter 17 Footsteps in the Classroom: "The Little
   Mermaid" and First-Year Writing
   Kate Wolford 359
Chapter 18 Dragons in Hereville: Comics as a Vehicle
   for Fairy Tales
   Orlando Dos Reis and Emily Midkiff 371
Chapter 19 Little Sparrow
   Kirstin Zhang 393
Chapter 20 Beedle's Moral Imagination
   Travis Prinzi 399
Chapter 21 The Sea in the Hat
   Tori Truslow 421

Introduction

On Making New Fairy Tales

John Patrick Pazdziora and Defne Çizakça

In the preface to *The Lilac Fairy Book* (1910), Andrew Lang complained that many readers and writers "think that to write a new fairy tale is easy work. They are mistaken: the thing is impossible. Nobody can write a *new* fairy tale; you can only mix up and dress the old, old stories, and put the characters in new dresses."[1]

It seems altogether too likely that this delusion of ease continues. Ed Catmull, head of Pixar Animation Studios, said in an interview that "If you say to somebody, 'You should be doing fairy tales,' it's like saying, 'Don't be risky.'"[2] Catmull implies that fairy tales are safe, sheltering, unchallenging, that an author chooses the fairy tale form because it presents little risk.

Nothing could be further from the truth.

Finding

The fairy tale, as an art form, is far from the saccharine stories of happy endings. It is built from folktales and folk customs and forms a literary memory of an oral tale tradition. A new fairy tale, on the other hand, is neither a retelling of the old tales, nor a deconstruction. It is a new story told in the old manner; it appropriates motifs from the folkloric tradition, but remains recognisably the work of an individual author.

This form has proved a fascinating and fertile challenge for generations of writers. Lang himself was not immune, rearranging Scottish folk motifs in *The Gold of Fairnilee* (1887), and satirising the French conte tradition in his Pantouflia stories. Which bits and forms are available to the artist and the scholar seems an irresistible subject of conjecture—consider the pragmatic but poetic grandeur of such catalogues as Stith Thompson's *Folk Motif Index* (1955-1958), which arranges and interrelates the motifs by their tens of thousands. A wholly new tale may be impossible, but a new arrangement, though fiendishly difficult, has lured authors time and again in the past centuries—including the editors of this present volume.

From 2008 to 2010, a small online journal quietly restructured the nature of modern fairy tale discourse. The journal, *New Fairy Tales*, was created and edited by the Lancastrian author Claire Massey. She was later joined by Faye Durston, Andy Hedgecock, and Anna McKerrow. In the introduction to the inaugural volume, Massey wrote: "We don't believe the fairy tale canon is complete or that we should only retell old stories. We believe that there are many new fairy tales out there waiting to be written and read and loved."[3] This process of discovery, of providing a space for new fairy tales to flourish, provided the aesthetic and intellectual backdrop to the project.

New Fairy Tales was unique in online culture at the time. It shared a similar emphasis and aesthetic to Terri Windling's *Endicott Studio* and *The Journal of Mythic Arts*, and Windling has undoubtedly had some influence on Massey's work. But New Fairy Tales departed even farther than *The Journal of Mythic Arts* from the mainstream of speculative fiction and genre fantasy; rather than emerging from the conventions of fantasy, it took its place in the tradition of literary fairy tales themselves. Hedgecock, himself the editor of the prominent science-fiction magazine *Interzone*, explained the distinction:

Here was a site showcasing stories which drew on traditional tales of wonder to extend our imaginative response to the world in which we live. It offered highly original variations on the themes of traditional tales of wonder; or used their symbols and tropes to provide thematically and stylistically innovative stories.[4]

Massey, in fact, specifically related the stylistic innovation of new fairy tales to both the literary and oral tradition:

> Fairy tale bequeaths us a language rich in motifs which I believe we should feel free to plunder. Fairy tales have always belonged to the tellers, their listeners and readers; they belong to us all. And rather than stuffing them away in a cupboard we should play with the form, experiment with its language, make it our own, tell the stories that mean something to us, the stories that dance at the edge of our dreams...[5]

The present anthology evolved directly from Massey's online journal. But, though Massey has provided the inspiration for this volume, and contributed a new fairy tale of her own, it is not the same project. As with the fairy tale tradition itself, we have taken bits from Massey's original idea, rearranged and elaborated them. We are, quite simply, curious about the innovative use of the new fairy tale form which the *New Fairy Tales* journal showcased. The question behind this anthology is not only what a new fairy tale is, but perhaps more importantly how new fairy tales are made.

Making

J.R.R. Tolkien, in his 1939 Andrew Lang Lecture "On Fairy-stories," attempts somewhat fancifully to compare the process of rearrangement with soup: "Speaking of the history of stories and especially of fairy-stories we may say that the Pot of Soup, the Cauldron of Story, has always been boiling, and to it have continually been added new bits, dainty and undainty."[6] In other words the motifs and types of the folk and fairy tale tradition should not be placed on an ascending or descending scale from myth to history; everything, whether the loves of the gods or the Archbishop of Canterbury's tumble on a banana skin, roils together in a fertile imaginative stock.[7] Perhaps in tacit attempt to vindicate his own ambitious project of writing an English mythology, Tolkien argues for the importance of the individual author: "if we speak of a Cauldron, we must not whole forget the Cooks. There are many things in the Cauldron, but the Cooks do not dip in the ladle quite blindly. Their selection is important."[8] To some extent Tolkien is being demure, if not disingenuous; three years earlier he argued in "Beowulf: The Monsters and the Critics" that the role of the poet in reshaping the traditional material was of immense aesthetic importance, demanding "considerable [...] learning and training."[9] He calls the Beowulf poet "a greater man than most of us," and insists that "the author draws upon tradition at will for his own purposes, as a poet of later times might draw upon history or the classics and expect his allusions to be understood."[10] This is a different posture than saying that an author works "not quite blindly"; the individual will, and the discipline to learn both the tradition and the practice of the art, are of ultimate importance to the telling.

It is, perhaps, the idea of tradition which best informs the creation of a new fairy tale. T.S. Eliot argues that tradition "cannot be inherited, and if you want it you must obtain it by great labour."[11] Tradition, he says, involves "a perception, not only of the pastness of the past, but of its presence"; a writer understands not only the historicity of literature, but its immediacy, as the whole exists within his own time.[12] To speak of new fairy tale tradition, then, suggests not only a general awareness of literature, but the specific awareness of the folkloric roots of fairy tale, and the uses they have been put to—the soup, as Tolkien inelegantly puts it. Whereas retelling involves complex understanding of an individual taletype, and deconstruction requires a renunciation of the past, a new fairy tale demands knowledge of the breadth of folkloric and literary fairy tale tradition, and a recognition of how these interact.

Retelling the tales can too easily descend into rote, with the self-delusion that one has done something new; it is often better perhaps simply to tell the old tales, than retell them. These perils may be what Catmull had in mind. And deconstruction, sitting in haughty judgement on the past, is inevitably a cracked cistern, breeding both unhealthy contempt for the past and smugness about the present, failing in the storyteller's task of speaking judgment on his own age.

The work of the teller of new fairy tales is both like that of the poet drawing on tradition for his own purposes, and of the oral storyteller reassembling an old tale for immediate telling. He must love the past for its own sake, yet address himself fearlessly to the present; in his mind they are undivided. In this way the care, the discipline, and the transience of the cook's art are all apt metaphors for the work of writing a new fairy tale.

Yet Tolkien would later draw away from this image of the cook, or at least return to it more critically; the Great Cake cooked in *Smith of Wooton Major* (1967) began as an analogue to the craft of storytelling. Here the cooks are more ambiguous figures, alternately an adventurer, a charlatan, and an elf; the central figure of Smith, arguably Tolkien's self-portrait, becomes a craftsman—the village blacksmith—but never a cook. His wandering in Faeire makes his utilitarian craft unique, but brings the unresolved fear that when he grows too old for travelling his work will lose its uniqueness. The cooks with their Great Cakes—authors with monumental works—may have less or more vision than Smith, but he is ultimately not one of their number. The wanderer is an outlier, with no status in society; Smith's wanderings are only valued because of the aesthetic prettiness they give to his utilitarian craft. This tension is never resolved within the tale; Tolkien concludes somewhat wistfully that people benefit from the visions of the wanderers whether they are aware of it or not.

In light of all this, one could be forgiven for despairing of the new fairy tale as nearly unattainable, and unlasting when attained—impossible, as Lang suggested, and hopelessly ephemeral. But perhaps Tolkien strikes closer to the truth later in "On Fairy-stories" when he claims that there is "a mythical or total (unanalysable) effect" to the old stories, and the new stories drawn from them: "they open a door on Other Time, and if we pass through, though only for a moment, we stand outside our own time, outside Time itself, maybe."[13] And here we have come to the heart of literary tradition, and of the new fairy tale.

Eliot explains that "a sense of the timeless as well as of the temporal and of the timeless and of the temporal together, is what makes a writer traditional." Thus the distinction of new and old has no ultimate significance. By participating in tradition rather than simply responding to it, the new fairy tale attempts to re-discover and re-enter that Other Time, to stand "outside Time itself, maybe." Small wonder, then, that Lang and others like him would both judge the thing impossible, and find it irresistible. The timeless and temporal together create the frisson of the new fairy tale and the power of its inception. In Eliot's words:

> There is only the fight to recover what has been lost,
> And found and lost again and again; and now,
>   under conditions
> That seem unpropitious. But perhaps neither gain nor loss.
> For us, there is only the trying. The rest
>   is not our business.[14]

Arranging

A study of new fairy tales should pay homage to the fairy tale tradition as well as to the novelties present in the new form. But most of all it must allow readers to make their own discoveries in this relatively unexplored field. To this end, the present volume is composed of three different types of contribution. The first are academic essays on new fairy tales. The second are new fairy tales themselves, both in prose and poetry. The third are process essays that study the craft of writing new fairy stories.

In *New Fairy Tales*, we have worked with both writers and academics, as well as with writers who are academics and academics who are writers. Fiction and critique appear within the same sections rather than separately. We hope the interplay between critical thought and aesthetic practice will inspire even more new fairy tales to come to life. The current table of contents reflects our own biased interests, and hopefully creates an interplay between critical thought and aesthetic practice which will inspire further creation of new fairy tales. The anthology is divided into the following sections thematically: miniatures, shadows and reflections, storytellers, fairy brides, and fairy tale pedagogy. But there is more than one way to read this volume, as several bridges connect the featured pieces and we invite the readers to discover their own paths.

Miniatures: The compact nature of miniatures is both welcoming and paradoxical. Claire Massey, in her story "Glass, Bricks and Dust," follows a boy who builds a city out of scrap materials from a construction site. The danger lurking behind this adventure is that the miniature city begins to mock the real town, casting doubt on the life the boy had previously led. In her process essay, Massey tells us of her fascination with miniature worlds and about how they make dreaming easy through their perfect, miniscule proportions. She also discusses what makes for a good new fairy tale, identifying wonder as one of these primal elements. Jesse Sharpe's essay follows Massey's story, and analyses miniatures through the depiction of the fairy world in Robert Herrick's *Hesperides*. Sharpe argues that the clarity of the miniature fairy world enables Herrick to discuss themes he finds to be of utmost importance: love, nature, divinity, and marriage. Catriona McAra takes us through a visual arts perspective and questions what role taxidermy can play in creating new anti-fairy tales. Through a study of Tessa Farmer's animation work, McAra analyses the flipside to the conventional, playful, innocent fairies. McAra's interviews with Farmer allow readers to eavesdrop on the artist's childhood inspirations from fairy stories. The section concludes with Katherine Langrish's short story "Gnomes." She hints that the little men we have all grown too familiar with through garden decorations may have some secrets of their own.

Storytellers: *New Fairy Tales* takes a non-Western turn with the section on storytellers. Hanna Livnat's contribution is an invaluable contextual essay on the development of Israeli fairy tales. Livnat emphasizes the proximity of Hebrew fairy tales to folk tales and legends and studies stories that are more difficult to classify. Difficulties in classification are also a theme Defne Cizakca investigates in her essay on new Ottoman fairy tales. She focuses on the loss of the Ottoman language and the coffeehouse tales of Istanbul, and charts the ambivalent relationship Turks have formed with their own fairy tale traditions. These place-specific studies are followed by John Patrick Pazdziora's literary study on James Thurber. Pazdziora studies the various guises of the storyteller in Thurber's fiction and distinguishes him from the writer, narrator and heroes of fairy tales, ultimately aligning the storyteller to the Fool of the tarot deck. The section on Storytellers ends with Fiona Thackeray's "Cloud Catching in the Realm of the Drought King." This Brazilian fairy tale follows Rita from Rio de Janeiro to the backlands of the country. Thackeray's fiction focuses on how different places may tell us different stories, and consequently mould us into different people.

Shadows and Reflections: This section opens up with a fairy tale that celebrates communal identity. A strong northern wind, a crooked house, and a tilted girl are the main characters in "A Prevailing Wind" by Elizabeth Reeder. Both the inhabitants of the unnamed town and the readers understand the struggles of the heroine through her body, her shadows and her unspoken words. Reeder's story is followed by an analysis of Oscar Wilde's fairy tales, which were originally labelled unsuitable for children. Colin Cavendish-Jones tries to find out whether this critique is well founded through a discussion of nihilism, beauty and artistic creation in Wilde's fiction. The study of beauty continues in Daniel Gabelman's "Radiant Mysteries". Gabelman goes back to the medieval understanding of clarity and simplicity as the two basic modes of beauty, and discusses how two prominent fairy tale authors – George Macdonald and G.K. Chesterton – viewed their own writing through this Augustinian lens. This section on shadows and reflections ends with a fairy tale by Eric M. Pazdziora that inversely reflects Reeder's story in its playful layers. These are fairy tales within a fairy tale, and each story takes us deeper into magic, longing, and serendipity.

Fairy Brides: This section begins with Mayako Murai's in-depth study of *The Bridegroom was a Dog* by Yōko Tawada. Murai analyses the motif of marriage between different species in Japanese tales and discusses how this theme is subverted and consequently renewed in Tawada's fairy tale. This is followed with an essay by Josh Richards, introducing us to the unexpected inspirations behind his long poem "Dante": the Japanese manga Hayate *the Combat Butler* by Kenjirō Hata. In this passionate article, Richards discusses the metaphysics and unique catharsis of the Gothic backstory in Hata's work. "Dante" itself follows, an eerie tale of love; it is a gothic poem poised between Hata's tale and the poet Dante Alighieri's work.

Fairy Tale Pedagogy: The final section of the collection is on fairy tale Pedagogy. The first essay, by Kate Wolford, is on teaching "The Little Mermaid" to first year literature students and is followed by a joint student essay by Emily Midkiff and Orlando dos Reis which focuses on Barry Deutch's comic "Hereville: How Mirka Got Her Sword." Midkiff and dos Reis focus on the use of images in new fairy tales, and on how they can strengthen the written word through depictions of the unsaid. A Japanese fairy tale by Kirstin Zhang follows suit. Zhang tells us of a strong and gentle empress who forms an unlikely friendship with a little girl – the daughter of the imperial gardener – during a time of war and scarcity. Zhang's story is followed by Travis Prinzi's study on J.K. Rowling's "The Tales of Beedle the Bard." J.K. Rowling presents these stories as the fairy tales of the Wizarding World. Prinzi's essay discusses the ethical codes presented through these tales. The last chapter of *New Fairy Tales* is a fairy tale by Tori Truslow. It talks of deep waters, a bucket that contains a whole world, and a mysterious messenger. It is a new fairy tale about emancipation, the joys of work, and trusting intuitions.

Acknowledgments

It is, of course, impossible to assemble a work of this nature without having very many people to thank. John Granger, owner and publisher of Unlocking Press, has shown unflagging enthusiasm for the project since we first presented it to him. This anthology would not have been possible without the energy, skill, and encouragement provided by him and his team. Claire Massey, editor of the *New Fairy Tales* journal, responded to the idea of the project with similar enthusiasm, letting us build on her ideas and writing a new fairy tale for the volume. She has been our advisor, dialogue partner, inspiration, and a good friend.

Our various colleagues at Glasgow and St Andrews also deserve our appreciation, for putting up with our mad ideas and cheering us through the sloughs of work on this and other projects. We owe a particular and lasting debt of gratitude to Christopher MacLachlan and Elizabeth Reeder, our academic supervisors, who not only supported us in undertaking this project, but graciously added their own contributions to the volume.

Joe Sutliff Sanders of Kansas State University enthusiastically embraced the admittedly peculiar idea of having his graduate class in graphic novels co-author a chapter, and his oversight and keen guidance brought a remarkable academic experiment to life. Zohar Shavit gave us her kind advice during the early stages of the work, and Rabbi Aharon Mendez offered much-needed good humor and encouragement at a key point in the development of the project. Danielle Bett assisted us with her linguistic knowledge and unfailing punctuality, and Gaby Cohn delivered skilled editorial work under immense time pressure with aplomb. Special thanks to Barry Deutsch and Tessa Farmer, who have graciously allowed us to reproduce their artwork. Faye Hanson illustrated and designed the cover, and the resulting image is, in one sense, her own new fairy tale.

In addition, we offer our heartfelt thanks to each of our contributors. Their expertise, creativity and hard work have been a constant source of encouragement throughout the project. We have been honoured to work alongside them, and are proud to present their work in this volume. The strengths and virtues of this anthology are their doing; the blunders and weaknesses are of course our own.

Finally, we are grateful to Kitty and Murat Çizakça, Pedro Germano Leal, Rebecca Pazdziora, and Fern Rose for their unfailing love, support, and patience.

Notes

1   Andrew Lang, preface to *The Lilac Fairy Book* (London and New York: Longmans, Green, & Co., 1910), viii.

2   Dawn C. Chmielewski and Claudia Eller, "Disney Animation is closing the book on fairy tales," *Los Angeles Times*, November 21, 2010, accessed July 18, 2012, http://articles.latimes.com/2010/nov/21/entertainment/la-et-1121-tangled-20101121.

3   Claire Massey, 'Letter from the Editor,' *New Fairy Tales* 1 (October 2008): 2, accessed 6 April 2011, http://www.newfairytales.co.uk/pages/issuet-wo.pdf.

4   Andy Hedgecock, "Letter from an Editor," *New Fairy Tales* 5 (June 2010): 3, accessed 11 June 2012, http://www.newfairytales.co.uk/pages/issue-five.pdf.

5   Claire Massey, 'Letter from the Editor,' *New Fairy Tales* 2 (February 2009): 3, accessed 6 April 2011, http://www.newfairytales.co.uk/pages/is-suetwo.pdf.

6   J.R.R. Tolkien, *Tolkien On Fairy-stories: Expanded Edition, with Commentary and Notes*, edited by Verlyn Flieger and Douglas A. Anderson (London: HarperCollins, 2008), 44-45.

7   Tolkien, *On Fairy-stories*, 46-47.

8   Tolkien, *On Fairy-stories*, 47.

9   J.R.R. Tolkien, "*Beowulf*: The Monsters and the Critics," in *Beowulf—A Verse Translation: Authoritative Text, Contexts, Criticisms*, translated by Seamus Heaney, edited by Daniel Donahue (New York: W.W. Norton, 2002), 123

10 Tolkien, "Monsters," 113, 118.

11 T.S. Eliot, *The Sacred Wood: Essays on Poetry and Criticism* (London: Methuen, 1920), 43.

12 Eliot, *The Sacred Wood*, 44.

13 Tolkien, *On Fairy-stories*, 48.

14 *East Coker* V.15-18.

Chapter 0

Galantha

Josh Richards

Sister Snowdrop died
Before we were born.
She came like a bride
On a snowy morn.

Head bowed and Lilith-pale, a slender
   Girl swayed amid the snow,
   Lending a cold, desolate splendor
   To fields where nothing else could grow.
   Her fairy song softly intruded   5
   The study where I sat secluded;
   Her voice, like winter waves at dawn
   Lapping the wharves of Avalon,
   Shivered amid the heaps of dusty
   Leaves, compelling me to look,   10
   To rise, ignore the holy book,
   Which then had grown desperately musty,
   And throw the window open wide
   To let that haunting song inside.

15   I smiled sadly as I listened;
      Her beauty greened a garden where
      The frost on stone was all that glistened
      In the February air.
      Then, with a pining note, she lifted
20   Up her eyes, and something shifted
      In my heart. I left the sill;
      I left my books; I ran until
      I knelt breathless beside the girl
      And asked if she would stay and sing
25   To me. Her soft response will ring
      Within my mind like the dark curl
      On Beatrice's crimson dress;
      I still can hear the fatal yes.

PART I

Minatures

Chapter 1

Glass, Bricks, Dust

Claire Massey

At the top of the mound he was king. The broken-brick, gravel and glass mountain had stood for over a year in a deserted street not far from the boy's house. When the excavators and bulldozers had come to demolish the old mill, a high metal fence had barricaded the site. But when the men in high-vis vests and hard hats disappeared with their machines, they took the fences with them. They left polystyrene cups balanced on top of the gateposts, where they filled with rainwater. They left the building's ribs—inner walls and doorways without doors. They left lumps of concrete, lengths of pipe, metal girders, and fire exit signs. And they left the mound. As the days passed, rubble and red-brick dust spread onto the pavement and gathered in the gutters of the road.

On summer evenings, he crept around the edge of the mound, toeing shards of glass and empty cider cans. He circled his kingdom, noting newly burnt lumps of wood and scrunched-up cigarette packets, but he never caught sight of the grown-up intruders who'd left them. There were lazy red butterflies on the tangle of flowering weeds that had pushed through the building's remains. Blackbirds gathered on the street's only lamppost before darting off overhead. He clambered up the mound, which looked like an enormous sand dune against the bright blue sky. From up there he could see the whole town: rows of terraced roofs, two church steeples, the town hall clock, and the last mill chimney with its luminous supermarket sign. At his back were the moors and the wind.

One evening, the boy was crouched on the top of the mound making a new town out of a heap of broken glass. He liked this time of day best—after tea, before bed. The air seemed to get grainy as its colour changed from vinegary yellow to candyfloss blue. He could rub it between his fingers like dust and slow time down. At the top of the mound he was in charge and he didn't want to go home to bed. He collected green glass shards and broken brown bottle necks. He tumbled fragments of old window in his hands like shattered marbles. He pushed the glass into the mound, making houses, balancing roofs on them, building towers. The last of the sunlight caught and glinted in the tiny glass walls.

More of the blackbirds than he'd ever seen before rushed overhead and gathered on the lamppost. The orange light hadn't yet switched on but the shadows were growing. He heard nine chimes of the town hall clock. For a moment, the lamppost looked like a tall thin man wearing a large black hat. When the man turned towards him, he looked like a lamppost. The man had a greyish-green coat speckled with rust and a black hat that quivered with beaks and feathers. The man didn't need to climb the mound; he was face to face with the boy with his feet still planted in the pavement.

"What are you making?" asked the man.

The boy didn't answer.

"It would be better to tell me. I could help. Every child is always making something. Cut them open and shake them out and they're full of dust and dreams."

The boy squirmed at the mention of cutting. He stood up, ready to run, but then he remembered that at the top of the mound he was king. He dug his heels into the rubble. "I'm making a new town, better than this one. The sun can shine in through the walls. The buildings look grander. It'll be a great glass city."

"All it needs is people," said the man.

"Yes, it needs people," said the boy. And when he looked down, tiny creatures were scuttling beneath the glass roofs. They looked like ants or spiders, but the sky was darkening and the creatures were moving too fast to be sure. He looked to the man but there was only the lamppost and as its orange light snapped on, the birds launched into the sky.

The boy plunged down the mound and ran, hoping he wouldn't get told off for being late home. Before he reached the end of the street he knew something was wrong. The world was too quiet. Where were the sounds of cars? Of footballs being kicked against walls? Of smokers chatting outside the pub? There were no shouts from parents calling everyone in.

"Mum?" He pushed open their front door. The house was in darkness but the telly was switched on. His mum wasn't in any of the rooms. A half-drunk cup of tea had been left on the arm of the settee.

The boy thundered back along the silent streets. He stood in the orange light beneath the lamppost. "Give them back," he shouted.

Nothing happened, although he could hear the rustle of feathers coming from the darkness above the light.

The boy ran to the top of the mound. "Give them back!"

"But I haven't got them." The man's face glowed. "You have."

In the gloom, it was hard to make out the tiny creatures beneath the glass roofs. They were no longer moving. The boy couldn't be sure what was a particle of rubble and what was a person sleeping in their broken-glass house. "How do I get them back?" he asked.

But the man was a lamppost again.

The boy crouched at the top of the mound and looked out at the night-dark shapes of the town. If he made the town as it really was, an exact replica, maybe that would bring everyone back.

He worked all night, building with bits of old brick. The clouds overhead moved slowly and their bellies were orange. Every time he looked up and caught a glimpse of a star, a bird flew from the lamppost to blot it out.

When the dawn came, it was damp and grey and the boy's fingers were stained red with brick dust. He looked proudly at his miniature town, with its rows of roofs, two steeples and the last mill chimney. He peered into the glass town beside it and saw it was empty.

The boy skidded down the mound and ran home. The streets were still silent, but they would be so early in the morning. In the living room the telly was still on, the cup still on the settee arm. The boy pounded up the stairs, not caring if he woke his mum and got into trouble. But she wasn't there. Her bed was empty.

The boy raced back to the mound. There were an impossible number of birds gathered on top of the lamppost watching him. The light had switched off, ready for a new day. At the top of the mound, he peered into the little broken-brick houses. The gaps he'd left for windows were too small to let in much light; he couldn't separate any tiny people from the darkness. He pressed his fingers into the grit and dust. He had to try again. He gathered small mounds of dust and emptied rainwater from the old polystyrene cups onto them. He moulded houses and steeples and the chimney and the tower for the town hall clock. The buildings were misshapen and muddy.

"Aren't you going to ask me to give you the people back?"

The boy looked up at the lamppost. The creak of its voice had disturbed its hat and wings were thrust out here and there.

"No," said the boy. "I'm going to go and get them." As his words touched the air it thickened with dust and as he rubbed it between his fingers he knew he could make himself small.

The boy was no longer at the top the mound, but standing in the dusty street outside his house. He looked up at the sky, trying to see the edges of the bigger town where there was a mound of rubble on top of which he'd built this town. But the sky was too wide. He walked through the doorway without a door to his house and found his mum, dust collected in the lines round her eyes, sitting in front of the greyish lump of the telly. "Mum."

She didn't look up. "Don't interrupt, love," she said, "this is a good bit." So he took a deep breath, and blew. He blew at the telly and at the walls and at the clouds of dust that surrounded him. He ran out into the street, climbed to the top of a mound of dust and he blew and he blew and he blew the town away.

At the top of the mound he was king. The ruins of the three small towns lay scattered at his feet. He could hear cars and footsteps and voices and the nine chimes of the town hall clock.

When the boy turned away from the mound and the lamppost, he found the streets were coated in dust. Soft greyish-brown snow. He felt the gritty air between his fingers and knew that if he rubbed it he could slow time down. But he didn't want to be in charge again, at least not for a while. He wanted to go home to bed.

Process Essay

Writing New Fairy Tales

Claire Massey

All writers must go from now to once upon a time; *all must go from here to there; all must descend to where the stories are kept; all must take care not to be captured and held immobile by the past. And all must commit acts of larceny, or else reclamation, depending how you look at it.*[1]

I have been exploring the fairy tale form as a writer and editor for several years. A chance encounter with a collection of Grimms' fairy tales in a train station bookshop drew me back into stories half-remembered from childhood. Except these weren't the stories I remembered, they were much darker and much brighter, and I was entranced. From the Grimms, I moved on to Charles Perrault, Hans Christian Andersen, Joseph Jacobs, Oscar Wilde, and George MacDonald. Thanks to the internet, I had instant access to fairy tales from all over the world, but I became particularly intrigued by the stories that had been written as new fairy tales, rather than as literary retellings of oral tales. These stories married the form of the traditional fairy tale with ideas and images from the writers' own imaginations rather than a previous oral or literary source. These stories chimed with my growing desire to write fairy tales, and specifically to write new ones. In late twentieth and early twenty-first century publishing, retellings seemed to be the dominant form of fairy tale. I enjoyed many of the retellings I read, but, perhaps due to innate stubbornness, I wanted to make my own fairy tales.

Writing is a process of discovery, and when writing new fairy tales there are many paths through the forest to choose from, but in this short essay I'd like to discuss three elements I have begun to consider essential to the form.

Drawing on existing tales

the fairy tale has no landlord[2]

If the fairy tale has no landlord, perhaps we are free to do whatever we would like with the form. But new fairy tales can't be written in ignorance of the older tales; they can only be written by those who have immersed themselves in the stories that have come before, by those who have a desire to create new shoots from old branches.

Marina Warner has referred to the store of fairy tales as "that blue chamber where stories lie waiting to be rediscovered" and has said these stories offer "magical metamorphoses to the one who opens the door, who passes on what was found there, and to those who hear what the storyteller brings."[3] But when we visit the store we should heed Margaret Atwood's warning not to be captured by the past.[4] I've felt the temptation to play with the old tales, and to emulate a Mother Goose voice, rather than striving to find my own. It would be too easy to become trapped by these stories. But if we can journey in and out, carrying only what we need, there are many treasures to be pilfered. Atwood compares writers' methods to the ways of a jackdaw: "we steal the shiny bits, and build them into the structures of our own disorderly nests."[5] We should feel free to take from the old tales, but build the material into our new nests with care.

Carol Ann Duffy has retold fairy tales by the Grimms and Perrault. She has also drawn from existing tales to write several new fairy tales. In *The Princess' Blankets* (2008), a beautiful new fairy tale in traditional guise, the blankets of ocean, forest, mountain, and earth recall dresses that resemble the elements, or light from heavenly bodies, in tales such as "Donkeyskin." When Duffy's princess sees the pattern on the ocean blanket, we're told that "many fish swam in it and that dolphins leaped in its borders."[6] Duffy uses the traditional trope of a fantastical fabric in a new and inventive way, giving us blankets rather than garments, yet the line from traditional to new fairy tale is clear.

When drawing on existing tales, we can also subvert what we find. A.S. Byatt retold and translated traditional tales. In "The

Story of the Eldest Princess" (1995) she tells a new tale by subverting the old. The eldest princess is aware of the fairy tales in which the two elder siblings are sent out first and fail at their quest and she wants her story to go differently, realising: "I could just walk out of this inconvenient story and go my own way."[7] Byatt also consciously subverts the fairy tale order by turning the sky green, having acknowledged that "Lüthi makes the point that green, the colour of nature, is almost never specifically mentioned in folk tales."[8]

When writing "Glass, Bricks, Dust," I took inspiration from existing tales in which places are transformed into miniature, such as the Grimms' "The Glass Coffin," whilst consciously subverting several elements of the form. I am interested in finding ways to put a time, date, and place stamp on a form which typically eschews such details, whilst striving to retain the magical feel of the traditional tale. I am very keen on bringing the landscape of contemporary Lancashire into my stories. This is a county of exposed moorland and crumbling old mill towns tucked into valleys. The woods beside the cottage where I grew up became entwined in my mind with fairy tales, as did a tower nearby on the moors. But, for me, there's also a latent magic in the rubbish heaps and abandoned buildings of the postindustrial landscape. With rows of empty shops and boarded-up pubs, the town I live in can feel abandoned by money and politicians, but it doesn't have to be abandoned by story. Lüthi wrote that "The fairy tale portrays an imperishable world."[9] In "Glass, Bricks, Dust" I purposefully wrote about the perishable landscape I see around me.

Playing with wonder

The dimension of wonder creates a huge theatre of possibility in the stories: anything can happen.[10]

Whether a new fairy tale takes traditional or contemporary guise, whether it remains in the realm of "once upon a time" or takes the story into a specific time and place, there is one element that cannot be tampered with if the story is to remain a fairy tale: wonder. Fairy tales present us with the most fantastical of circumstances; without wonder there isn't a fairy tale. Yet, the wonderful events must never be questioned. As Lüthi notes: "The real fairy-tale hero is not astonished by miracles and magic: he accepts them as if they were a matter of course."[11]

So it is possible for the stepmother in Carol Ann Duffy's "The Stolen Childhood" (2003) to cut away her stepdaughter's shadow with scissors and steal it, replacing the girl's shadow with her own "heavy, leathery shadow," and for this exchange of shadows to mean an exchange of old age for youth.[12] As long as the fairy tale author writes with conviction, and the characters accept the elements of the fantastic, the reader will, too.

Lüthi wrote that "Fairy tales are unreal but they are not untrue."[13] I agree with this wholeheartedly, but when writing new fairy tales I try to lessen that sense of unreality, aiming to create what short story critic Ailsa Cox refers to as a "mismatch between the mundane and the fantastic."[14] For me, the presence of the quotidian can amplify the fantastic. By featuring everyday objects and settings the fantastic becomes more unexpected and is heightened. But however far the story strays into reality, maintaining the fairy tale rule that the fantastic should not be questioned is vital to making new fairy tales work. If you allow the question, you draw attention to the artifice and break the spell.

Using lasting images

> *Where do they come from, these images that rain*
> *down into the fantasy?*[15]

There is no doubt that images from fairy tales last. They have often gone on to lead lives outside their tales. Glass slippers, red hoods, glass mountains, iron shoes—whether rooted in oral versions of a tale or literary flourishes added at a later date—all have the power to trap the imagination, pulling us into the state of wonder.

Here I want to concentrate for a moment on the image of a miniature place. This is a motif that appears in tales such as the Grimms' "The Glass Coffin," and Kate Bernheimer continues this tradition in her delightful story *The Girl in the Castle inside the Museum* (2008). In Bernheimer's story, the miniature castle sits inside a glass globe and there are "moats and turrets and bright shining lamps. There are dark winding streets that gleam in the rain."[16]

There is something almost unbearably appealing to my imagination about a miniature place. Not a dollhouse, but an actual place, perfect in its miniscule dimensions, so you feel as a reader you need only shrink down to enter it. Miniaturising the world to a scale at which we can comprehend much more of it can give us an enormous sense of possibility. One of my reasons for writing "Glass, Bricks, Dust", was that I wanted the chance to create miniature towns. Gaston Bachelard wrote, quite rightly, that "miniature causes men to dream."[17]

Making tales

> *[Children] feel irresistibly drawn to the detritus created by building, gardening, housework, tailoring, or carpentry. In waste products they recognize the face that the material world turns to them and them alone. In putting such products to use they do not so much replicate the works of grown-ups as take materials of very different kinds and, through what they make with them in play, place them in new and very surprising relations to one another. In this way children form their own material world, a small one within the large one.*[18]

When I watch my children at play, they seem to have a sense of mastery over the world that we lose as adults. Their sense of story gives them the power to create and destroy. They dismiss impossibility and fall easily into the language of wonder. We first encounter fairy tales as children, yet they're a literature we can draw from throughout our lives. They're also a literature with which we should feel free to play without feeling bound to strict replication. We can take the materials of traditional tales and use them to inspire us in the creation of new tales. As adults, fairy tales give us the ability to reclaim lost wonder; as writers, they allow us to make our own small worlds within the large.

Bibliography

Atwood, Margaret. *Negotiating with the Dead*. London: Virago, 2003.

Bachelard, Gaston. *The Poetics of Space*. Translated by Maria Jolas. Boston: Beacon Press, 1994.

Benjamin, Walter. *One-way Street and Other Writings*. Translated by J.A. Underwood. London: Penguin Books, 2009.

Bernheimer, Kate. *The Girl in the Castle Inside the Museum*. New York: Schwartz and Wade Books, 2008.

Byatt, A.S. *The Djinn in the Nightingale's Eye*. London: Vintage, 1995.

Calvino, Italo. *Six Memos for the Next Millenium*. Translated by Patrick Creagh. London: Vintage, 1996.

Cox, Ailsa. *Writing Short Stories*. Oxon: Routledge, 2005.

Duffy, Carol Ann. *The Princess' Blankets*. London: Templar Publishing, 2008

Lüthi, Max. *Once Upon a Time: On the Nature of Fairy Tales*. Translated by Lee Chadeayne and Paul Gottwald. Bloomington: Indiana University Press, 1976.

Warner, Marina. *From the Beast to the Blonde: On Fairy Tales and their Tellers*. London: Vintage, 1995.

Notes

1 Margaret Atwood, *Negotiating with the Dead* (London: Virago, 2003), 160.

2 Max Lüthi, *Once Upon a Time: On the Nature of Fairy Tales*, translated by Lee Chadeayne and Paul Gottwald (Bloomington: Indiana University Press, 1976), 63.

3 Marina Warner, *From the Beast to the Blonde: On Fairy Tales and their Tellers* (London: Vintage, 1995), 418.

4 Atwood, 160.

5 Atwood, xviii.

6 Carol Ann Duffy, *The Princess' Blankets* (London: Templar Publishing, 2008), 8.

7   A.S. Byatt, *The Djinn in the Nightingale's Eye* (London: Vintage, 1995), 52.

8   A.S. Byatt, "Happy ever after," *The Guardian*, January 3, 2004, accessed January 10, 2012. http://www.guardian.co.uk/books/2004/jan/03/sciencefictionfantasyandhorror.fiction.

9   Lüthi, 45.

10   Warner, xvi.

11   Lüthi, 46.

12   Carol Ann Duffy, *The Stolen Childhood and other Dark Fairy Tales* (London: Puffin Books, 2003), 60.

13   Lüthi, 70.

14   Ailsa Cox, *Writing Short Stories* (Oxon: Routledge, 2005), 83.

15   Italo Calvino, *Six Memos for the Next Millenium*, translated by Patrick Creagh (London: Vintage, 1996), 87.

16   Kate Bernheimer, *The Girl in the Castle Inside the Museum* (New York: Schwartz and Wade Books, 2008), 14.

17   Gaston Bachelard, *The Poetics of Space*, translated by Maria Jolas (Boston: Beacon Press, 1994), 152.

18   Walter Benjamin, *One-way Street and Other Writings*, translated by J.A. Underwood (London: Penguin Books, 2009), 55.

Chapter 2

Robert Herrick's Fairy Epithalamium and Natural Religion

Jesse Sharpe

Robert Herrick's fairies come at the point in which the Renaissance has completely changed the fairy from the Medieval incarnation of a large and imposing supernatural or otherworldly being who needs to be feared, to the small and mischievous being who is enjoyed in a condescending manner due to their now insect-sized stature. Even as recently as Edmund Spenser's *The Faerie Queene*, fairies were portrayed as human-sized beings who lived in a world parallel to, though different than, the world inhabited by humans, but with Shakespeare's miniature fairy court of Oberon and Titania in his play *A Midsummer Night's Dream*, the land of fairy was forever changed. It was no longer a place that existed beside the natural world, instead it was now that fairies lived in our world, but they were so small that they could be easily overlooked, and while they were still magical beings, there was no fear of their stealing babies and replacing them with changelings, nor was there worry of being seduced into their world and made into a slave. By the time that Robert Herrick published his book of poetry, *Hesperides*, in 1648, fairies had basically been domesticated into the English landscape, and they now were figures of amusement rather than dread.

That the fairy poems receive a place of prominence by Herrick can be seen in the opening poem to *Hesperides*. "The Argument of his Book," which acts an introduction to what is to come in the 1,400 poems that follow, gives fairies a rather prominent position in his book, despite the fact that there are only five fairy poems. "The Argument" reads:

> I Sing of *Brooks*, of Blossomes, *Birds*, and Bowers:
>   Of *April, May*, of *June*, and *July*-Flowers.
>   I sing of *May-poles, Hock-carts, Wassails, Wakes*,
>   Of Bride-grooms, Brides, and of their *Bridall-cakes*.
>   I write of Youth, of Love, and have Accesse
>   By these, to sing of cleanly-*Wantonnesse*.
>   I sing of *Dewes*, of *Raines*, and piece by piece
>   Of *Balme*, of *Oyle*, of *Spice*, and *Amber-Greece*.
>   I sing of *Times trans-shifting*; and I write
>   How Roses first came Red, and *Lillies White*.
>   I write of *Groves*, of *Twilights*, and I sing
>   The Court of *Mab*, and of the *Fairie-King*.
>   I write of *Hell*; I sing (and ever shall)
>   Of *Heaven*, and hope to have it after all.[1]

Here Herrick has been able to distil a diverse and large volume of poetry into a simple and elegant fourteen lines of verse. Nature, love, marriage, eating and drinking, and festivals all factor largely in *Hesperides*, and the religious poems mentioned in lines thirteen and fourteen of the sonnet even have their own section, "His Noble Numbers," which contains 272 poems. All of these topics are replete in this book, except for "The Court of *Mab*, and of the *Fairie-King*." It must then be asked why Herrick believed the five fairy poems were important enough to warrant inclusion in "The Argument of his Book." While Herrick, Sir Simeon Steward, and Michael Drayton had all written fairy poems in the 1620s,[2] the publication of *Hesperides* over ten years later hardly indicates that Herrick might be building on the success of an earlier movement. Rather, by describing the miniature world of the fairies, Herrick is allowed to play with the ideas and subjects that interest him the most due to the fact that this small and imaginary world allows him to create by way of whatever he finds to be of most interest. And it is this focus on the miniature and imaginary world that Daniel H. Woodward has used to argue for understanding the fairy poems as a representation of *Hesperides* in miniature.[3]

"The Argument of his Book" informs the reader of what is to come in the volume that follows, but it is in the fairy poems that the reader can see all of Herrick in practice. Of the five fairy poems, three ("The Fairie Temple: or, Oberons Chappell. Dedicated to Master John Merrifield, Counsellor at Law," "Oberons Feast," and "Oberons Palace") form a small narrative, whereas the fourth and fifth poems ("The Fairies" and "The Beggar to Mab, the Fairie Queen") are stand-alone poems. "The Fairies" is a folk poem reminding women to mind their chores lest Queen Mab will pinch their toes, and "The Beggar to Mab" can be read as a reminder to the gentry to fulfill their charitable responsibilities; however, it is "The Fairie Temple," "Oberons Feast," and "Oberons Palace" that tell a fairy tale in which the reader is shown a festival day which moves from church, to feast, and finally to the royal bedroom and the night.

As one begins to consider the relationship between "The Fairie Temple," "Oberons Feast," and "Oberons Palace," it becomes clear that these poems closely follow the pattern of Herrick's epithalamia (or poem commemorating a wedding).[4] From the description of the "Temple" to the "Feast" and ending at the marriage bed in the "Palace," Herrick is moving through his familiar territory of a poem that allows him, in celebrating a marriage ceremony, to sing of nature, festival, feast, and sex in the "cleanly-*Wantonnesse*" of the marriage bed. The epithalamium is one of the poetic modes that he returns to time and again throughout *Hesperides*, with most of the longer poems being epithalamia, and it has been well argued that other poems, such as the much anthologized and praised "Corinna's going a Maying,"[5] are variations on the epithalamium's themes. The appeal of poems celebrating marriage is easy to see when one considers all that Herrick says he will "sing" of in "The Argument of his Book."

In Herrick's paganized Christianity, this priest and poet portrays nature as being inherently sanctified and worshipful.

Flowers and trees and birds all praise through their beauty, and as the participants in the festival, that is the marriage ceremony and celebration, they too sanctify the day by joining in the celebrations. Thus nature and festival and humanity all unite in the divinely-approved celebration that bridges the carnal and the sacred as the poem moves from marriage at church to the consummation of the marriage in the marriage bed. In treating "The Fairie Temple," "Oberons Feast," and "Oberons Palace" as an epithalamium, I wish to argue that the magical world of Herrick's fairies is not only a representation of *Hesperides* in miniature, but a perfect embodiment of the natural religion that permeates the book. Through comparing the natural religion that Herrick espouses in his epithalamia, and particularly in "Corinna's going a Maying," to the sanctified kingdom of Oberon and Mab, the reader sees that it is plants and trees and forest creatures which carry with them an innate spirituality that is transferred to humanity when it participates in festivals such as May Day celebrations or marriage ceremonies. The fairy world, then, completely comprised of natural objects found and re-appropriated for this small and magical race, provides the reader with a complete picture of a church and culture that has perfectly recognized the importance of the natural world and has properly incorporated it into its society.

In addition to "Corinna's going a Maying," the other primary epithalamia are "An Epithalamie to Sir Thomas Southwell and his Ladie" and "A Nuptiall Song, or Epithalamie, on Sir Clipseby Crew and his Lady." Although these three poems may seem scant in view of the 1,400 contained in the volume, they are among the longest poems in the book, and they are the chief marriage poems, but by no means the only ones. Herrick's poems discussing marriage are much too numerous to mention in this chapter, but there are two shorter poems that do nicely lay out the general theme of the rites of the marriage festival and the epithalamium as Robert Herrick sees them. The first, "A Nuptiall Verse to Mistresse Elizabeth Lee, now Lady Tracie," is sixteen lines long and worth quoting in its entirety.

Spring with the Larke, most comely Bride, and meet
    Your eager Bridegroome with *auspitious* feet.
The Morn's farre spent; and the immortall Sunne
    Corrols his cheeke, to see those Rites not done.
Fie, *Lovely maid!* Indeed you are too slow,
    When to the Temple Love sh'd runne, not go.
Dispatch your dressing then; and quickly wed:
    Then feast, and coy't a little; then to bed.
This day is Loves day; and this busie night
    Is yours, in which you challeng'd are to fight
With such an arm'd, but such an easie Foe,
    As will if you yield, lye down conquer'd too.
The field is pitcht; but such must be your warres,
    As that your kisses must out-vie the Starres.
Fall down together vanquisht both, and lye
    Drown'd in the bloud of Rubies there, not die.

The formula of the marriage festival and epithalamium are all here. The poem instructs the bride to rush to church, enjoy a feast, and then off to bed. This formula is also seen quickly summarized by Herrick in his poem "The Entertainment: or, Porch-verse, at the Marriage of Master Henry Northly, and the most witty Mistresse Lettice Yard," when using more pagan imagery he writes

Do all things sweetly, and in comely wise;
    Put on your Garlands first, then Sacrifice:
That done; when both of you have seemly fed,
    We'll call on Night, to bring ye both to Bed (7-10)

While the formula of church, or sacrifice, feast, and bed is established, there is another component—hinted at in "A Nuptiall Verse" when Herrick writes "Dispatch your dressing then; and quickly wed"—in which the religious ceremony is a part of the rites, the magic, of the day, but that the religious rites need be rushed as one moves onto the feast and finally the night. The reasons for rushing through one's religious obligations is well described in "Corinna's going a Maying" when Herrick writes

Get up, get up for shame, The Blooming Morne
   Upon her wings presents the god unshorne.
      See how *Aurora* throwes her faire
      Fresh-quilted colours through the aire:
      Get up, sweet-Slug-a-bed, and see
      The Dew-bespangling Herber and Tree.
   Each Flower has wept, and bow'd toward the East,
   Above an houre since; yet you not drest,
      Nay! not so much out of bed?
      When all the Birds have Mattens seyd,
      And sung their thankfull Hymnes: 'tis sin,
      Nay, profanation to keep in,
   When as a thousand Virgins on this day,
   Spring, sooner then the Lark, to fetch in May.

   Rise; and put on your Foliage, and be seene
   To come forth, like the Spring-time, fresh and greene;
      And sweet as *Flora*. Take no care
      For Jewels for your Gowne, or Haire:
      Feare not; the leaves will strew
      Gemms in abundance upon you:
   Besides, the childhood of the Day has kept,
   Against you come, some *Orient Pearls* unwept:
      Come, and receive them while the light
      Hangs on the Dew-locks of the night:
      and *Titan* on the Eastern hill
      Retires himself, or else stands still
   Till you come forth. Wash, dresse, be briefe in praying:
   Few Beads are best, when once we goe a Maying. (1-28)

The descriptions of a spiritual natural surrounding and the call that "Few Beads are best, when once we goe a Maying" tells the reader that in Herrick's *Hesperides*, the normal modes of devotion are not to keep one from participating in festivals, and that these festivals, which take place out of doors, only take on a divine nature when communing with nature. The importance of the sacred state of the natural world is integral to the understanding of the fairy poems as an epithalamium. Though in "Corinna" Herrick instructs Corinna to "be briefe in praying" because nature has already redeemed the day, he slows the pace of the epithalamium and spends a great deal of time on the "Fairie Temple" because this is not the description of a human needing to catch up with sacred nature but the portrayal of nature being made sacred. The magical, but fully natural, fairy folk are seen in their temple composed of objects that have been tossed aside by people or animals as unimportant or from bits of nature that are easily found lying around the English forest and countryside.

The Marriage Chappel

"The Fairie Temple: or, Oberons Chappell. Dedicated to Master John Merrifield, Counsellor at Law" is where this fairy tale of an epithalamium begins. As can be told by the complete title, this poem is dedicated to a "Counsellor at Law," and indeed, as the poem begins, the reader is greeted by a six line introduction which declares the superiority of this temple over all others that John Merrifield has seen.

> Rare Temples thou hast seen, I know,
>   And rich for in and outward show:
>   Survey this Chappell, built, alone,
>   Without or Lime, or Wood, or Stone:
>   Then say, if one th'ast seene more fine
>   Then this, the Fairies once, now *Thine*.

The description of the temple to follow will not be the normal building of worship that is made great through the hewing and binding of large woods nor through the cutting of rock and the use of cement, instead, the beauty of this "fine" temple is created through the use of the small, castaway, natural. While Roger B. Rollin reads this poem as a satire of the Roman Catholic Church,[6] the poem seems more like Herrick at play than Herrick mocking. The elements of nature that he reads as mocking can just as easily be read as celebrating nature, and so, while there may indeed be a light satiric bent to the poem, the fact the poem is clearly the introduction to a three poem tale, of which Rollin admits that none of the "other fairy poems is satiric in mode,"[7] the fact that the dedicatory poem that introduces "The Fairie Temple" celebrates what will be found, and the fact that Rollin says it could be satirizing "Anglicanism as well as Catholicism and polytheism"[8] argues in favor of "The Fairie Temple" not representing religious satire as much as Herrick's playful imagination.

As Herrick begins his description of "The Fairie Temple," the reader is greeted by a manufactured beauty before being moved into the realm of nature. There is

> A Way enchac't with glasse and beads
>   There is, that to the Chappel leads:
>   Whose structure (for his holy rest)
>   Is here the *Halcion's* curious nest (1-4)[9]

The reader may expect fairyland to have a chapel that would create wonder for the observer through some sort of supernatural, or finely wrought structure made by these magical beings, and there is a sense of that when we read of an entrance that is "enchac't with glass and beads," but just as quickly as this has begun, Herrick changes things, because by the fourth line of the descriptions of the temple, the reader sees that this "structure" is "the *Halcion's* curious nest." The "*Halcion*" being the halcyon or kingfisher, so what the reader finds is that the structure for this chapel is actually not made by the fairies at all; instead, they are more like scavengers than craftsmen when it comes to the building of their holy temple. These magical beings have not created a magical dwelling for their religion, instead they have found a natural object formed by a bird, and in this are sufficient supernatural properties for them. This idea of the magical properties of nature is further supported by the observation made by J. Max Patrick in his annotation to this line when he notes that "The elaborately contrived nest [...] was fabled to charm winds and waves to rest."[10] So a nest, created by an everyday bird, can be more "elaborately contrived" than the "Rare

Temples" that John Merrifield, the poem's dedicatee, has ever seen wrought by human hands. Moreover, these magical creatures recognize the magical properties that already exist in nature, and so they can show their devotion to their gods through simply using natural objects that they would find in their surroundings.

The creation of a sacred place of worship by way of scavenged objects from the English countryside is continued in Herrick's description of this temple.

> First, at entrance of the gate,
>> A little-Puppet-Priest doth wait,
>> Who squeaks to all the commers there,
>> *Favour your tongues, who enter here.*
>> *Pure hands bring hither, without staine.*
>> A second pules, Hence, hence, profane.
>> Hard by, i'th'shell of halfe a nut,
>> The Holy-water there is put:
>> A little brush of Squirrils haires,
>> (Compos'd of odde, not even paires)
>> Stands in the Platter, or close by,
>> To purge the Fairie Family. (38-49)

The "Holy-water" for the fairies and its administration to the practitioners is once again offered by way of found or disregarded objects. The "brush of Squirrils haires" is made through collecting fallen debris, but at the same time, there is an act of deliberate creation, much like that of the kingfisher building its nest of twigs and grasses yet still making a deliberate and well considered structure. The "brush" is "Compos'd of odde, not even paires." The fairies then do not just find random objects and playfully use them in some mock worship; instead there are conscious decisions behind the building of their objects of worship. This is further found in the descriptions of the other objects required for their sacred acts of worship.

As the reader moves through the entrance of the chapel and begins to see the inner dwelling of this sacred space and sees the worship ceremony unfold, the scene is nothing but the appropriation of nature into the devotion of this little race.

The Altar is not here foure-square,
    Nor in a forme Triangular;
    Nor made of glasse, or wood, or stone,
    But of a little Transverce bone;
    Which boyes, and Bruckel'd children call
    (Playing for Points and Pins) *Cockall.*
    Whose Linnen-Drapery is a thin
    Subtile and ductile Codlin's skin;
    Which o're the board is smoothly spred,
    With little Seale-work Damasked.
    The Fringe that circumbinds it too,
    Is Spangle-work of trembling dew,
    Which, gently gleaming, makes a show,
    Like Frost-work glitt'ring on the Snow. (54-67)

The altar, then, is a knuckle bone, over-wrapped with an apple's skin, and has the "Spangle-work of trembling dew." It is a simple and humble affair, but it is also one that cannot be easily created by humans. The tiny details involved and the objects that have, once again, been tossed aside, do give the ordinariness of this decoration a uniqueness that comes through the fact that this could only be a fairy creation. Also, as the description of the altar continues, the reader finds that

Upon an end, the *Fairie-Psalter,*
    Grac't with the Trout-flies curious wings,
    Which serve for watched Ribbands. (70-72)

The inclusion of dew and "Trout-flies" wings helps create a small yet striking image of beauty. Not only would small hands be needed to carefully arrange these details, but it would also require small eyes to be able to fully appreciate the beauty in the small, but multi-faceted parts of this most holy of objects in the temple.

As the fairy parishioners partake in the ceremonies of oblation, sacrament, and offering, the use of the implements of worship continue the theme.

The Bason stands the board upon
　　To take the Free-Oblation:
　　A little Pin-dust; which they hold
　　More precious, then we prize our gold:
　　Which charity they give to many
　　Poore of the Parish, (if there's any)
　　Upon the ends of these neat Railes
　　(Hatcht, with the Silver-light of snails) (86-92)

This listing of the fairies' use of cast aside natural objects reaches
its apex towards the end of the poem when Herrick begins to list
mundane objects and rubbish and loses the ability to align them
with any particular religious practices:

Dry *chips*, old *shooes, rags, grease,* and *bones*;
　　Beside their *Fumigations*,
　　To drive the Devill from the Cod-piece
　　Of the Fryar, (of work an odde-piece.)
　　Many a trifle too, and trinket,
　　And for what use, scarce man wo'd think it. (119-124)

The descriptive narrative is almost lost here. Herrick seems to
have let the descriptions get away from him, and yet, the listing
of various objects also lends verisimilitude to the tale because it
does give the impression that Herrick has indeed seen the chapel,
with all of its accoutrements, and is simply unable to see how
they would fit into a religious ceremony. He regains the tale's
thread as one reads

Next, then, upon the *Chanters* side
　　An *Apples-core* is hung up dry'd,
　　With ratling Kirnils, which is rung
　　To call to Morn, and Even-Song. (125-128)

And as the church ceremony ends, the minister "dons the Silk-
worms shed, / (Like a *Turks Turbant* on his head) / And reverently
departeth." (137-139)

Herrick has written a fairy tale of a church service. In "The Fairy Temple," the reader has been moved both through the actual building and the ceremony of worship that is being held within. In all of this, from the entrance to the exit, and from the altar to the "*Fumigations*" of incense, the reader finds that this whole world is created from the things thrown aside by human and animal. It is a scavenger's temple, yet the rubbish found in the forest is sanctified and redeemed through its use in the religious practices of the miniature, magical creatures that are the fairies. In this, Herrick is aligning the fairies with the form of religious devotion that he prefers for his readers. As was seen in "Corinna's going a Maying," nature is religious in and of itself. The birds singing their everyday songs are their morning matins and prayers. The dew, and the flowers, and the trees, simply through growing, fulfill their religious obligations, and so humanity, in participating in festivals and holy days in natural settings, joins in with the redeemed and holy creation. While Herrick has to goad humans with the reminder that "'tis sin, / Nay, profanation to stay in," the fairies cannot help but worship in nature because their temple, and all of their religious ceremonies, are created from and incorporated with the nature of the everyday. As the poem comes to a close, the final couplet of "The Fairie Temple" points the reader to the next part of this fairy festival

And by the glow-worms light wel guided,
    Goes to the Feast that's now provided. (141-2)

Herrick's promised "wel guided" way to the next section of this fairy tale is not quite as easily followed as Herrick makes out. While the next fairy poem is "Oberons Feast," and while this does indeed continue the narration and gives the reader the feast promised, there are seventy poems in between these two verses. In addition to the passage of many poems, there is also a passage of dedicatees as Herrick has now moved onto another friend, so "Oberons Feast" is not dedicated to John Merrifield, instead this poem, and "Oberons Pallace," is dedicated to Thomas Shapcott, also a man of law.[11]

The Marriage Feast

In keeping with "The Fairie Temple," Herrick provides the reader with a six line introduction to the dedicatee, and once again, the poem and its introduction are written in the same meter. The poem will feel familiar to the reader, despite the distance between the two poems, and it is in the introduction that the reader sees that despite the change in dedicatee, these poems definitely belong together. The introduction reads

> Shapcot! To thee the Fairy State
> I with discretion, dedicate.
> Because thou prizest things that are
> Curious, and un-familiar.
> Take first the feast; these dishes gone;
> Wee'l see the *Fairy-Court* anon.

Here, as in "The Fairie Temple," there is an invitation to the dedicatee to view the extraordinary; however, instead of this being an invitation to witness a structure that can be compared with and found superior to the religious buildings Merrifield had seen before, Shapcott is not asked to compare the feast that will be described to any he has eaten. Now the fairy feast and festival will be "Curious, and un-familiar," but it will not be, as "The Fairie Temple," "more fine" than any he had seen before. This is to be a feast that will entertain the reader, but it will not necessarily make the reader want to join in the celebration. Here the reader will be able to mark a break between the sanctifying nature of the "Fairie Temple" with its scavenged adornments as sacred objects and the grand, but unappetizing, meal presented before a return to the sacred palace and marriage chamber found in "Oberons Palace."

Despite the fact that this poem is not specifically describing the meal in terms of the creation of a sacred place, the feast is a required component of the holy day, and so must take place in order that the divine nature of the ceremony be experienced in its full. The meal then fits in with the part of the festival day in which Herrick, as is his form, moves away from a narration of direct address and begins to describe a feast that will be partaken by those who are joining in the celebrations. In Herrick's epithalamia, the waking and sanctifying of the day are told in the present tense, and there is an immediacy given to the events, one that he does not want the individual addressed to miss. However, once the person is out of bed and dressed for the event, Herrick moves the narrative mode into the future, and from here, all events in the day are portrayed as events that are to be anticipated, and the distance between Herrick and events that have yet to take place gives him greater license, as a priest, to praise events that may not be readily embraced by the Church. In this, he celebrates gluttony, drunkenness, and sex, but is able to portray them as events that have not yet taken place, and so all readers and participants are still pure. In a similar fashion, by moving this fairy tale away from the desire to see and participate in the fairy religious ceremonies, Herrick now no longer offers what will be seen as a rather disgusting meal to his reader, instead, the palette will be pure despite the odd victuals offered.

"Oberons Feast" is less fantastic than "The Fairie Temple," both in length (it is 54 lines versus the 142 of "Temple") and description, but the meal that is presented to the reader, while probably not causing one to salivate, will at least entertain. The "Feast" begins with a pleasant description, but this does not last long, and the reader soon finds that the food being eaten will more closely resemble descriptions in Herrick's "mocking" epigrams[12] rather than the feast in "The Hock-cart, or Harvest home: To the Right Honourable, Midlay, Earle of Westmorland." In "The Hock-cart" the feasters dine on

> Ye shall see first the large and cheefe
>   Foundation of your Feast, Fat Beefe:
> With Upper Stories, Mutton, Veale
> And Bacon, (which makes full the meale)
> With sev'rall dishes standing by,
> As here a Custard, there a Pie,
> And here all tempting Frumentie.
> And for to make the merry cheere,

If smirking Wine be wanting here,
That's that, which drowns all care, stout Beere; (28-37)

This is contrasted with the fairy folk in "Oberons Feast" dining on

His kitling eyes begin to runne
    Quite through the table, where he spies
    The hornes of paperie Butterflies,
    Of which he eates, and tastes a little
    Of that we call the Cuckoes spittle.
    A little Fuz-ball-pudding [...] (24-29)

And then

Of Emits eggs; what wo'd he more?
    But Beards of Mice, a Newt's stew'd thigh,
    A Bloated Earewig, and a Flie;
    With the Red-capt worme, that's shut
    Within the concave of a Nut,
    Browne as his Tooth. A little Moth,
    Late fatned in a piece of cloth:
    With withered cherries; Mandrakes eares;
    Moles eyes; to these, the slain-Stags teares:
    The unctuous dewlaps of a Snaile;
    The broke-heart of a Nightingale
    Ore-come in musicke; (36-47)

And to wash it all down:

        [...] with a wine,
    Ne're ravish from the flattering Vine,
    But gently prest from the soft side
    Of the most sweet and dainty Bride,
    Brought in a dainty daizie, which
    He fully quaffs up to bewitch
    His blood to height; this done, commended
    Grace by his Priest; *The feast is ended.* (47-54)

This feast, which is at times a bit delightful and at others repugnant, is a playful exercise in the imaginary microcosm of the world of the fairies. It is a feast that carries with it the concept of a day of celebration, and as can be seen by the final line of the poem, it is a celebration overseen by a "Priest," and therefore sanctified.

The Marriage Bed

As epithalamia must end in consummation in the bedroom, so too does Herrick bring the reader into the home of Oberon and Mab with the poem "Oberons Palace." Once again there is a brief introductory stanza for the poem, and as in "Oberons Feast," this one is dedicated to Herrick's friend Shapcott. Herrick links this poem with the previous fairy poem, despite the 150 poems that come between them, when he begins his introduction with the lines "After the Feast (my *Shapcot*) see, / The Fairie Court I give to thee." The reader is then reintroduced to Oberon and is told just how well Oberon has held up under the great meal that he has enjoyed:

> Where we'le present our *Oberon* led
>   Halfe tipsie to the Fairie Bed,
>   Where *Mab* he finds; who there doth lie
>   Not without mickle majesty. (3-6)

The stage is then set for this final section of the tale, and in it the reader will be led by a "tipsie" Oberon to the bed of his wife. The description of the palace will come as the reader walks with Oberon through the building, and as will be seen, the description of this royal house is a grotesque mixture of the decorations of the "Temple" and the food from the "Feast."

The reader's guide, Oberon, is described in greater detail as the poem moves from the introductory stanza into the body of the poem. He is full of wine and full of wrath as he desires nothing but his Mab and is upset by anything that would delay him.

Full as a Bee with Thyme, and Red,
   As Cherry harvest, now high fed
   For Lust and action; on he'l go,
   To lye with *Mab*, though all say no.
   Lust ha's no eares; He's sharpe as thorn;
   And fretfull, carries Hay in's horne,
   And lightning in his eyes [...] (9-15)

The poem takes on the tone of the Fairy King, and the reader is then led through the palace. The description of this palace is similar to that of "The Fairie Temple," and, as is found in that poem, the decorations and structure of the building is created from scavenged objects. The poem leads the reader through the palace and to the marriage chamber, and just as "The Fairie Temple" moved through the structure to the holy altar, the most sacred of places in the temple, "Oberons Palace" brings the reader through the halls and into the holy marriage chamber.

Lead by the shine of Snails; a way
   Beat with their num'rous feet, which by
   Many a neat perplexity,
   Many a turn, and man' a crosse-
   Track they redeem a bank of mosse
   Spungie and swelling, and farre more
   Soft then the finest Lemster Ore.
   Mildly disparkling, like those fiers,
   Which break from the Injeweld tyres
   Of curious Brides, or like those mites
   Of Candi'd dew in Moony nights.
   Upon this *Convex*, all the flowers,
   (Nature begets by th'Sun, and showers,)
   Are to a wilde digestion brought,
   As if Loves *Sampler* here was wrought;
   Or *Citherea's Ceston,* which
   All with temptation doth bewitch. (22-38)

Here the language is of pregnancy and life. The bank of moss is "swelling" and "Nature begets" as "All with temptation doth bewitch."

Sweet Aires move here; and more divine
   Made by the breath of great-eyed kine,
   Who as they lowe empearl with milk
   The four-leav'd grasse, or mosse like silk.
   The breath of *Munkies* met to mix
   With *Musk-flies*, are th'*Aromaticks*,
   Which cense this Arch; (39-45)

Now nature's aromas are an incense.

   [...] and here and there,
   And farther off, and every where,
   Throughout that *Brave Mosaick* yard,
   Those Picks or Diamonds in the Card:
   With peeps of Harts, of Club and Spade
   Are here most neatly inter-laid.
   Many a Counter, many a Die,
   Half rotten, and without an eye,
   Lies here abouts; and for to pave
   The excellency of this Cave,
   Squirrils and childrens teeth late shed,
   Are neatly here enchequered
   With brownest *Toadstones*, and the Gum
   That shines upon the blewer Plum.
   The nails faln off by Whit-flawes: Art's
   Wise hand enchasing here those warts, (45-60)

This mosaic is composed of parts from playing cards, bits of die, squirrel and children's teeth all "neatly inter-laid" showing the handiwork and care that has gone into the pathway leading to the royal chamber, and despite the inclusion of the "*Toadstones*" which are often seen as magical object, since Herrick's poems are more concerned with Classical rather than occult imagery, the inclusion of the object probably has more to do with the fact that it is surrounded by dice and cards which are used for gambling and the jewel of the toadstone could be riches to wager with instead of any magical properties that it may hold.

Then as the reader is brought to the entrance, it is named a "holy Entrance."

> The tempting Mole, stoln from the neck
>   Of the shie Virgin, seems to deck
>   The holy Entrance, where within
>   The roome is hung with the blew skin
>   Of shifted Snake: enfreez'd throughout
>   With eyes of Peacocks Trains, and Trout-
>   flies curious wings; and these among
>   Those silver-pence, that cut the tongue
>   Of the red infant, neatly hung.
>   The glow-wormes eyes; the shining scales
>   Of silv'rie fish; wheat-strawes, the snailes
>   Soft Candle-light; the Kittling's eyne;
>   Corrupted wood; serve here for shine.
>   No glaring light of bold-fac't Day,
>   Or other over radiant Ray
>   Ransacks this roome; but what weak beams
>   Can make reflected from these jems,
>   And multiply; Such is the light,
>   But ever doubtful Day, or night.
>   By this quaint Taper-light he winds
>   His Errours up [...] (63-83)

Here Oberon and the reader finally reach their destination—carrying a "Taper-light" which is a common motif in Herrick's epithalamia—and they find that it is a chamber given over to soft light reflected which does not reveal whether it is "Day, or night" allowing the fairy King and Queen to love in peace without worry of the passage from night to day to break their revelry.

While Oberon has staggered his way to the bedroom, the royal chamber of the Fairy monarchy is, surprisingly, not a happy place. The first description of Mab is through the eyes of Oberon, and the description is as such: "and now he finds / His Moon-tann'd *Mab*, as somewhat sick" (83-84). The reader then is ending the epithalamia with a drunken Oberon stumbling his way for a night with his sick bride, a bit of a play on the expected end of Oberon's journey, but Herrick moves the reader's attention to the marriage bed, restoring the magic of the scene. Despite the moods of the two lovers, Oberon and Mab, being less than ready for love, the room is one that is sanctified for marriage and sex through the decorations that surround the King and Queen. Mab lies "Upon six plump *Dandillions*" (86) and these flowers "Whose woolie-bubbles seem'd / Hir *Mab-ship* in obedient Downe." (88-89) She, though feeling ill, is resting upon a bed that soft, welcoming, and "plump." Her sheets are "the Caule / That doth the Infants face enthral, / When it is born." (90-92) The reader now sees that the Queen is already covered in a film of birth with the "Caule" being a remnant of the amniotic sack, and so there is plumpness and pregnancy in her reclining and the marriage bed is with child. The "*Dandillions*" are weeds, often uprooted and cast aside, and the "Caule" is superfluous birth matter, and so, as in "The Fairie Temple" the bed and bedding is made of cast off materials, but this is briefly broken as poem continues, because the reader finds that the bed is also adorned with blankets and hangings made by spiders.

Spiders, or "*Spinners*" as the poem refers to them, have provided further comfort and beauty to the marriage bed of the Fairy king and queen. The sheets of "Caule" are "ore- / Cast of the finest *Gossamore*" (94-95) while

> [...] over-head
> A *Spinners* circle is bespread,
> With Cob-web-curtains: from the roof
> So neatly sunck, as that no proof
> Of any tackling can declare
> What gives it hanging in the Aire. (100-105)

The spiders have taken great care to provide a silk covering that shows the working of excellent skill. Oberon and Mab may be small, and portrayed in a condescending and humorous manner, but they are still royalty, and so in their most intimate of chambers, there is excellent craftsmanship shown in the decorations. However, despite the care and skill shown in the making of these decorations, Herrick is still describing this sacred place with cast aside materials. The poem that comes immediately before "Oberons Palace" is one entitled "To the little Spinners." The "little Spinners" of the poem's title are spiders that are described as "pretty Huswives" (1), thus keeping with the theme of family and home found in the bed chamber of Oberon and Mab, and he promises "that no Broom / Shall now, or ever after come / To wrong a Spinner or her Loome" (13-15). By reading the preceding poem then, the reader is aware that these "*Spinners*" are praised by Herrick, but that their fine work is also constantly in danger of being swept aside by humans who consider it dirt or mess. The fairies recognize the delicate handiwork humans destroy, and the handiwork is so fine as to merit the honor of being the decoration of the king and queen.

After the work of the spiders, the reader is returned to sex and innocence as Herrick completes his creation of this marriage chamber with the cast off relics of the loss of virginity. After the lines of the "*Spinners*" contributions, Herrick continues with

> The Fringe about this, are those *Threds*
>   Broke at the Losse of *Maiden-heads:*
>   And all behung with these pure Pearls,
>   Dropt from the eyes of *ravisht Girles*
>   *Or writhing Brides;* when, (panting) they
>   Give unto Love the straiter way. (106-111)

The use of the "*Threds* / Broke at the Losse of *Maiden-heads*" being broken hymens may be a pun on the name of the god of marriage, Hymen, who is also often referenced in "An Epithalamie" such as with the lines "Then away; come, *Hymen* guide / To the bed, the bashfull Bride."[13] In "A Nuptiall Song, or Epithalamie" Herrick also calls upon Hymen with the line "*Himen, O Himen!* Tread the sacred ground" (31). However, the strongest use of Hymen as a sanctifying force in the marriage celebration can be found in the poem "Julia's Churching, or Purification." This poem which recounts the purification rituals performed after safe and successful childbirth ends with lines that comment on the decorations of this royal bed. "Julia's Churching" ends with these lines:

> Where ceremonious *Hymen* shall for thee
> Provide a second *Epithalamie*.
> *She who keeps chastly to her husbands side*
> *Is not for one, but everynight his Bride:*
> *And stealing still with love, and feare to Bed,*
> *Brings him not one, but many a Maiden-head.* (11-16)

In "Julia's Churching" Herrick provides the commentary for the use of hymens on the bed of Oberon and Mab. As "Julia's Churching" states that an "*Epithalamie*" can be a wife remaining faithful to her husband, this provides a further argument for the reading of "The Fairy Temple," "Oberons Feast," and "Oberons Palace" as an epithalamium. Furthermore, there is also the fact that "Oberons Palace" literalizes the line "*Brings him not one, but many a Maiden-head*" when the reader realizes that Mab has actually brought and adorned the marriage bed with "*many a Maiden-head.*" The decorations then are signs of sexual innocence, a tossed aside waste, and a divinity. Therefore, the bed is surrounded by sacred materials, and these are finished off with tears called "Pearls" also created during the loss of virginity; the use of tears recalling the "dew" used to decorate the altar in the "Temple." And to properly create the mood for love is music, but it is not the music that one may expect. Herrick provides noise that is not what people often associate with songs of love, but for Oberon the reader sees that

> For Musick now; He has the cries
> Of fained-lost-Virginities;
> The which the *Elves* make to excite
> A more unconquer'd appetite. (112-115)

"*Elves,*" a term which Herrick often uses interchangeably with "fairies," are mimicking the sounds of sex as a mode of excitement, and from the poem the reader learns that it does indeed work. Even here, the music is not crafted from instruments and arrangements, but from the sounds thrown out in passion without careful thought as to their composing. And so the description is complete.

The marriage bed is blessed by Hymen and the songs of Virgins as the epithalamia draws to a close. "The Kings undrest," (116) "And now the bed, and *Mab* possest." (118) Herrick ends with the couplet

> We'll nobly think, what's to be done,
>   He'll do no doubt; *This flax is spun.* (120-121)

This three poem cycle of the life of the fairies is complete, and Herrick ends with the couple in bed and the audience led on to other things. The epithalamium is complete at this point, and so all must leave the couple to their own delights and movements.

Herrick has used his fairy epithalamium as a means in which to show his reader the sacredness of the natural world that *Hesperides* so often celebrates. By using this fairy tale as his poetic vision in miniature, he has been able to imagine a small, magical race of beings that are uniquely English, and live and thrive in the English countryside, celebrating Herrick's most revered festival, that of marriage and the wedding night. In returning to "The Argument of his Book," through these poems Herrick has given his readers "*Brooks,* of *Blossomes, Birds,* and *Bowers,*" "*Bride-grooms, Brides,* and of their *Bridall-cakes,*" "*Youth, of Love,*" and he has "Accesse" by these poems "to sing of cleanly-*Wantonnesse.*" He writes "of *Groves,* of *Twilights,* and [he] sing[s] / The Court of *Mab,* and of the *Fairie-King.*" Through using the seventeenth century's vision of fairies as a magical, miniature, and mischevious race, Herrick has found the perfect vehicle through which to dissect and offer up his poetic world in a celebratory microcosm for the reader to enjoy, digest, and enter into.

Bibliography

Coiro, Ann Baynes. *Robert Herrick's* Hesperides *and the Epigram Book Tradition.* London: Johns Hopkins University Press, 1988.

Herrick, Robert. *The Complete Poetry of Robert Herrick.* Edited by J. Max Patrick. New York: New York University Press, 1963.

Rollin, Roger B. *Robert Herrick (Revised Edition).* Oxford: Maxwell Macmillan International, 1992.

Wallingford, Katharine. "'Corinna,' Carlomaria, the *Book of Sports* and the Death of

Epithalamium on the Field of Genre." *George Herbert Journal*. 14.1&2 (1990/91): 97-112.

Woodward, Daniel H. "Herrick's Oberon Poems." *The Journal of English and German Philology*. 64.2 (1965): 270-284.

Notes

1 All quotations from *The Complete Poetry of Robert Herrick*, edited by J. Max Patrick (New York: New York University Press, 1963).

2 Steward 'A Description of the King of Faeries Clothes', Drayton 'Nymphidia'.

3 Norman K. Farmer, Jr., 'Herrick's Oberon Poems' in *The Yearbook of English Studies* 1 (1971): 273-274.

4 Woodward convincingly argues this in his article "Herrick's Oberon Poems."

5 Katharine Wallingford has rightly argued for the understanding of "Corinna" as an epithalamium in her essay "'Corinna,' Carlomaria, the *Book of Sports* and the Death of Epithalamium on the Field of Genre" in *George Herbert Journal* 14.1&2 (1990/91): 97-112.

6 Roger B. Rollin, *Robert Herrick* (Oxford: Maxwell MacMillan International, 1992) 118-120.

7 *Robert Herrick*, 120.

8 *Robert Herrick*, 120.

9 Patrick begins the line numbering sequence again after the dedicatory six line poem.

10 *The Complete Poetry of Robert Herrick*, 131 note 2.

11 *The Complete Poetry of Robert Herrick*, 163 note 2.

12 Coiro, Ann Baynes, *Robert Herrick's* Hesperides *and the Epigram Book Tradition* (London: Johns Hopkins University Press, 1988) 155-173.

13 Is repeated exactly or with slight alterations in lines 9-10, 19-20, 29-30, 39-40, 49-50, and 69-70.

Chapter 3

Anti-Fairy Tale Taxidermy:
The Animations of Tessa Farmer

Catriona McAra

The fairies present the animate human counter-
part to the miniature.
Susan Stewart[1]

Yes, they are kind of anti-fairies, aren't they?
Tessa Farmer[2]

Tessa Farmer and Sean Daniels, *The Den of Iniquity* (still), 2010, stop motion digital animation. Copyright Tessa Farmer and Sean Daniels. Courtesy Danielle Arnaud, London.

More often than not, a fairy tale will turn out to be a hoax. Aside from their obvious status as works of fiction, the term "fairy tales" would lead us to believe that such stories will be primarily about fairies, yet we find there are few actual specimens in the narratives themselves. Scholars and illustrators, such as Katharine Briggs, Brian Froud, Diane Purkiss, and Carole G. Silver have offered rich taxonomic narratives of fairy figures (including wood elves, brownies, sprites, and hobgoblins)[3] but the narrative genre they draw from is unreliable and misleadingly titled, verging on the deceitful. Bruno Bettelheim has noted how inappropriate the English and French terms, "fairy tales" and *contes de fées*, are due to the fact that most key examples contain no obvious fairy figures.[4] Leslie Fiedler similarly claims that "fairy tales ha[ve] nothing to do with the presence or absence of "fairies," for there are no fairies in either 'Red Riding Hood' or 'The Three Bears,' while *A Midsummer Night's Dream* is full of them [...] they are clearly optional."[5] Marina Warner suggests that "more so than the presence of fairies [...] metamorphosis defines the fairy tale," and claims that such "shape-shifting is one of the fairy tale's dominant and characteristic wonders."[6]

Over the last decade or so, a new species of fairy tale has been born. The art of the English sculptor Tessa Farmer (b.1978) tells a Darwinian tale infused with hints of Victorian fairy paintings. Her work harks back to late nineteenth-century pseudo-art formats but offers a distinctly new chapter in the history of contemporary art. Farmer works with taxidermy and found natural materials—tree roots, leaves, moss, dead insects, and such like—in order to conjure her fantastical dioramas, micro-narratives, and skeletal fairies. The fairies that make up these tales are often displayed in the white-cubed realms of contemporary visual art yet they were conceived in the museum, the archive, and the dissection room—the sites of the artist's macabre imagination. Her use of taxidermy enhances the magical atmosphere and believability of these fairy tales, especially the inclusion of woodland creatures such as a swan, a fox, mice, and squirrels, but the struggle between these animals and the fairies lends the work a darker undertone. This paper aims to contextualize Farmer's three animations, and explore how her innovative use of taxidermy might participate in the "anti-fairy tale" genre in order to offer a more solid understanding of taxidermy's place in new fairy tale "texts."

Anti-Fairies

The "anti-fairy tale" is far from a novel concept. It has a long historiography that Wolfgang Mieder has charted back to André Jolles in 1930.[7] Angela Carter's *The Bloody Chamber* collection of fairy tale rewritings (1979) offers useful examples of the anti-fairy tale in practice.[8] More recently, the term has been reintroduced to a broader scholarship by David Calvin's co-edited collection of essays on the topic.[9] It is worth clarifying that the anti-fairy tale is not *against* fairies in any way, but offers a flip-side to the conventional fairy tale narrative. As a critical tool, it comes in at least two forms: on the one hand, it is an intertextual reworking and re-questioning of historical precedents; on the other, it can be conceptualized as a dark and/or subversive, underlying narrative. Both definitions of the term may be used to describe the work of Tessa Farmer.

Farmer's fairies are bred as a kind of "anti-species," the evil twins of the polite and pretty *Flower Fairies* (1922) by Cicely Mary Barker which Farmer read in her childhood during the 1980s. Several articles on Farmer's work have pointed out how her fairies offer the antithesis to the saccharine, popular image of the fairy do-gooder with whom we are overtly familiar courtesy of Disney kitsch. What Farmer gives us instead is the possibility of an "anti- Tinkerbell."[10] These new "anti-fairies" are an entomologically "accurate" looking variety. They are "born" with torturous instincts that at first make them appear malicious and ruthless. However, the artist herself defends their violence in evolutionary terms: "I justify their savagery as a need to survive, in terms of evolution or survival of the fittest which is so inherent in insect behaviour..." This follows her residency at the Natural History Museum in London in 2007, where she studied a species of microscopic wasp called *Mymaridae* or "fairy flies" on account of their minute size. These are a parasitic variety that colonize the bodies of caterpillars in order to lay their eggs.[11] Many of Farmer's fairies have since taken on the elongated form of these minuscule wasps as well as their devious habits: "They were mischievous, now they are just…evil."

To reiterate, the anti-fairy tale is by no means a new critical concept but, in the hands of Farmer, becomes a useful tool for interpreting the evolutionary chapters of her fairy species. Similarly, taxidermy can be marshalled here as an interesting metaphor for the intertextual impossibility of newness. In the wake of those theories that underpin deconstruction and postmodernism, the quest for originality poses a challenge to the cultural practitioner.[12] Farmer's work is deliberately anachronistic and may thus initially appear out of place in a discussion of new fairy tales. In the twenty-first century, the ability to innovate may be compromised but Farmer's labour-intensive practice breeds a potentially infinite series of installations and compositions. Likewise, her taxidermy can be viewed within her anti-fairy tales as refreshed flesh, and road-kill that has been revived. She intends the moth-eaten animals that haunt her works to be "read" as living beings within the visual narratives (that is, until they have been defeated by the anti-fairies and transformed into decorative architecture or edible morsels). As the poet and cultural theorist Susan Stewart reminds us: "narratives that dream the inanimate-made-animate [are] symptomatic of all narrative's desire to invent a realizable world."[13]

Farmer's Borrowings

One might conceptualize Farmer and her fairies' uses of found materials as a series of "borrowings." Indeed, it is curious how both artist and fairy mimic one another. Mary Norton's *The Borrowers* (1952) comes to mind when looking at Farmer's fairies, due to their diminutive scale and their ability to manipulate the miniature world around them for their own purposes. As Stewart tells us: "The miniature has the capacity to make its context remarkable [...] Thistledown becomes mattress; acorn cup becomes cradle..."[14] However, there are some crucial distinctions. Where the borrowers are clothed, English-speaking, proportionally miniature versions of human beings, Farmer's fairy population are skeletal creatures that speak an entirely different language. Her skeletons draw from the human anatomy but as microscopic, fragile, winged creatures, they are surely closer to insects in behaviour and lifecycle. The artist has often emphasized the alien nature of the insect world as a fantastic domain.[15] We are distanced from it in scale and can never achieve full access to it.[16] This new world locks us out while simultaneously inviting us in. While the borrowers lived secretly in the basement of a grand Edwardian house, appropriating spools, crockery and other bits and bobs when it suited them, Farmer's fairies can only ever be semidomesticated. Purkiss makes an astute observation concerning the wildness of fairies within the cultural imagination:

> fairies tend to like areas that are distinguished by being nameless, unmapped, uncharted, and above all unowned. This is why they prefer woods to fields and pastures, and ruins and caverns to houses. Fairies also associate themselves with places linked with the past that is visibly disappearing, and hence they are drawn to ruins...[17]

Ruins are metaphorically significant here too. For Farmer's fairies, taxidermy is a ruin; the animal is conquered then inhabited. Her use of Michael Drayton's seventeenth century poem "Nymphidia" (1627) bears this out. One section in particular is well-worth quoting:

> The walls of spiders' legs are made
> Well mortised and finely laid;
> He was the master of his trade
> It curiously that builded;
> The windows of the eyes of cats,
> And for the roof, instead of slats,
> Is covered with the skins of bats...[18]

In this evocation of a fairy palace, the architecture is constructed out of taxidermy-like remains of various mammals and arachnids. Again it is Purkiss who notes: "Drayton does not try to prevent miniaturization from collapsing into the grotesque."[19] This is true too of Farmer's fairies, which sit on the knife-edge straddling both beauty and disgust. The poem evokes a fairy palace constructed out of bat wings and cat eyes. Like Farmer's practice, we find the innovative use of found natural materials and bits of taxidermy woven into the overall assemblage.

With hindsight, the fairy tales of the Danish writer Hans Christian Andersen also prove to have been important for Farmer's artistic development as a believer in fairy tales. When reading about the genesis of Farmer's fairies in the late 1990s, one is reminded of Andersen's fairy tale "Thumbelina" (1835):

I think [the discovery of my fairies] was 1999 in my mum's garden in Birmingham. It was lying inside a red tulip, like a fetus—quite large, about 7cm long. I showed it to my brother who thought it was real and was quite disgusted by it.[20]

This was confirmed during interview with the artist:

CM: I was wondering about one more potential reference point: Hans Christian Andersen's "Thumbelina"?

TF: Thumbelina! Of course!

CM: Yes because you talk about your own artistic genesis or mythology of finding the first fairy in a flower in your garden and that just seemed like something you had perhaps read and absorbed as a child?

TF: Yes, again I'd forgotten the reference. Yes of course I love "Thumbelina," which has made me feel nostalgic! How could I forget "Thumbelina"? It's because it was overridden the other year by *The Secret Adventures of Tom Thumb* (1993).

Another key visual source for Farmer's belief in fairies is the Cottingley fairy photography of 1917-20. This comparison was first shrewdly noted by Kit Hammonds: "Farmer is the builder of such curiosities, her tiny forms built from roots like a bastard chimera bred from the Cottingley fairies,"[21] swiftly followed by Marie Irving and Alistair Robinson.[22] Farmer herself recently named an exhibition at Viktor Wynd Fine Art (September-October 2011) after Arthur Conan Doyle's notorious study of the Cottingley hoax, *The Coming of the Fairies* (1922). Though they are still images, the photographs offer the possibility of animated fairies captured on camera. Whether fairies or artistic cut-outs, they appear to flicker and dance in the wind. Here they appear in their natural habitat by the leafy beck in Yorkshire, and cavort with the two young cousins who took their photographs: Frances Griffiths and Elsie Wright. Stewart interestingly describes the importance of this case as a cultural phenomenon:

> The Cottingley photographs [...] are significant not only as an example of the linking of the child with the fantastic/natural; they are also emblematic of the developing importance of the image and its potential for exaggeration. Here the Edwardian image is the culmination of the Victorian fantastic as the photograph becomes more believable than the lived experience.[23]

The same could be said of Farmer's practice which is similarly about the presence and possibility of oxymoronic "real fakes."

The Welsh supernatural writer Arthur Machen (1863-1947) has also been of chief importance to Farmer, and it seems a fitting and pleasant surprise to learn that he is her great-grandfather. The work of both contains dark themes and tends towards the unruly with moments of horrific violence. Machen prefigures Farmer's breed of anti-fairies in essays such as "The Little People" (1926) and stories including "Out of the Earth" (1915). Both tell tales from the fringes of art and literature often through the ruse of scientific documentation, and such fairy tale genealogy suggests that Farmer has directly inherited some of her family's magical past.

Farmer's studio in North London is stuffed full of source books and other reference material. Fairy tales are juxtaposed with books on science, anatomy, and museology, intersections which help conjure her work. Books on Barker's light-hearted *Flower Fairies* are to be found in dialogue with Heinrich Hoffmann's anti-nursery rhymes and cautionary tales, *Struwwelpeter* (1846), which in turn mingle with academic studies by Katharine Briggs, Marina Warner, Diane Purkiss, and Carole G. Silver, all of whom Farmer has made reference to during interviews with the author. Indeed, she is no stranger to the scholarship on the topic of fairies and fairy tales: "when I first started making fairies [...] I thought 'I need to know about fairies now.'" Such research enhances her practice and prompts the development of her anti-fairies. The artist is herself a regular contributor to research forums and academic symposia, and one can imagine her returning to scholarship in the future, following her B.A. (2000) and M.A. (2003) degrees at Ruskin School of Drawing and Fine Art at the University of Oxford.

Victorian visual art is also of key importance to Farmer. Richard Dadd's painting *The Fairy Feller's Masterstroke* (1855-64) and Richard Doyle's illustrated book, *In Fairy Land* (1870), serve as further sources for Farmer's practice. She describes visits to view the former painting at Tate Britain as a regular "pilgrimage," while of particular interest in the latter is Doyle's illustration *The Triumphal March of the Elf King by Night*, which depicts a procession of winged beings enslaving a number of unfortunate creatures including rodents and insects in a snake-like formation. This piece no doubt inspired installations as early as *Swarm* (2004), in which the anti-fairies highjack dragonflies and battle with bumblebees. Trials and tribulations against larger creatures is a common narrative thread that we find running throughout Farmer's more recent trio of animations.

This chapter will now explore these animations—a medium which enables a glimpse into the natural habitat of her anti-fairies. All three fairy films use stop-motion, digital animation, and are collaborations between Tessa Farmer and Sean Daniels with sound by Mark Pilkington: a trio of artists pooling their interests in sculpture, sound, and animation. The three animations were recently shown together in Farmer's solo show *Nymphidia* at *Danielle Arnaud* contemporary art, London (May-June 2011), but had previously been shown separately: *An Insidious Intrusion* was made for the exhibition *Little Savages* (October 2007- January 2008) following Farmer's four-month residency at the Natural History Museum, *Nest of Skeletons* for the Tatton Park Biennale, Cheshire (May-September 2008), and finally *Den of Iniquity* was commissioned by Belsay Hall, Northumberland, for her *Extraordinary Measures* show (May-September 2010). In the history of film and animation, precedents might include Ladislaw (*Starewicz*) Starevitch's *The Cameraman's Revenge* (1912), which features a love affair between a beetle and a grasshopper, or Stan Brakhage's avant-garde film *Mothlight* (1963), where wings and other pieces of dead moths were scattered over the film strip after being instinctively drawn to a lantern, captured and collected. The pinning is an ambiguous motif in Farmer's practice. Her obsession with fairies is only a stone's throw from the insect collections of natural history, yet the darker side of the tale is shed by Philipp Blom who observes that in order to collect we have to kill.[24] However, as we will see, Farmer's animations offer a more ethically sound mode of capture.

"An Insidious Intrusion"

Farmer's Natural History Museum residency culminated in an exhibition of her work where her first animation, *An Insidious Intrusion*, was shown alongside a taxidermied fox entitled *Little Savages*, which came from a phrase borrowed from Silver's book *Strange and Secret Peoples:*

> It had long been held that fairies, at their best, were mischievous and capricious, incapable of such human feelings as compassion. Associated with early periods of history and the behaviour of savage or barbarous peoples, they lacked the civilized virtues, behaving like children (the Victorian 'little savages') or like the mob.[25]

Such behaviour seems to have had a hand in *An Insidious Intrusion,* which begins on familiar, "safe" ground inviting us inside the Natural History Museum and "behind-the-scenes" in the drawers and cabinets of the museum collection storage spaces. This framing device seems to directly relate to Farmer's residency at the museum, where the artist herself was granted access to the museum's storage spaces. Here her anti-fairies have escaped the confines of their drawer or curiosity cabinet, transgressed their pinning and flown through a hole in the wall into another world. Analogies between Farmer and Lewis Carroll are perhaps inevitable at this point. The miniature scale of Carroll's heroine Alice and Farmer's own curiosity to know more about entomology could be said to merge here in interesting ways. One might also be reminded of the "Looking-Glass Insects" episode where Alice encounters the Rocking-horse-fly and the Snap-dragon-fly.[26] These offer further Victorian touchstones for Farmer.

Through the hole in the wall, we emerge onto a beach-like scene with a painted backdrop by Lee Young Min. The strange, alien quality of this landscape is enhanced by the ominous thundering sounds: an echoing we might have once heard in the seashells we put to our ears as children, reverberations which effectively capture how everyday noises might sound to something on the scale of an insect. A sea urchin rapidly sprouts and a skeleton fairy prises a bristle which it uses as a weapon against an amorphous caterpillar-like creature and, more climatically, a stag beetle which emerges on a monstrous scale when compared to the anti-fairies. The beetle appears to be a foreboding creature which lurks within dark recesses of the imagination, *i.e.* the sheep-jawbone cave. It is attacked by the anti-fairies who flutter and surround it, spearing its legs with their fairy javelins and sawing its legs off. The intruder hinted at in the title is probably one of the insectoid beasts but the narrative leaves a little room open to suggestion because the fairies are equally, if not more "insidious," devious and strategic in their capture and triumph over the larger creature.

"Nest of Skeletons"

Following the format of *An Insidious Intrusion*, in Farmer's second animation, *Nest of Skeletons,* the jittery camera helps suggest a fairy's point of view and begins panning through the glasshouses before moving out into the kitchen garden populated by a number of scarecrows. The scarecrows serve as a pseudo-art format or faux-taxidermy in their own right, stuffed with straw which crackles like static on a television screen. Tatton Park hosts an annual Scarecrow Festival and these may be the remnants of that exhibition, utilized by Farmer as the ideal residencies for her fairies. Again, Farmer's practice and the concept of a scarecrow conceptually cluster around the idea of the hoax or faked reality. Scarecrows and Farmer's anti-fairies share a particular type of malevolence in the cultural imagination as well as being potentially "Good Neighbours," as a recent symposium at the Last Tuesday Society on Farmer's work and fairy tales suggested. Scarecrows can be found throughout the histories of art and literature, and are often associated with the horror genre, while the crows and ravens they are meant to frighten off point us in the direction of the Gothic, as does the skeletal aspect of Farmer's fairies. The alliance between the scarecrow and the fairies seems to be a mutually beneficial one. In exchange for the use of the scarecrow's straw body as shelter, the fairies maintain the organic and synthetic parts much like bees in a hive. In *Nest of Skeletons*, the fairies are literally infesting or colonizing the scarecrow as their ideal host; the parasitic nature of Farmer's fairies is again a particular point of interest, another idea which she developed during her Natural History Museum residency. Here one witnesses the fairies' birth or pupation. The young, vulnerable, and newly hatched are thrown out of the nest at an early stage like ornithological fledglings in order to learn how to fly. Far from being mollycoddled, like most creatures they have to adapt to fend for themselves. Returning to Drayton's "Nymphidia," there is an architectural aspect to this nest complete with a variety of semi-domestic spaces: a nursery for birthing, an arena for battle, a larder for food. We seem to be shown a-day-in-the-life-of one of Farmer's fairies which might point us in the direction of the nature programme. David Attenborough is the useful reference point for Farmer, and one can easily imagine him presenting a documentary on Farmer's fairy habitats.

Nest of Skeletons includes interesting instrumental sequences. The single wasp and trio of bees which have been harvested in acorn cups are some of the most effective in terms of their scale, as are the snail shells which are beaten with bones creating tribal rhythms which seem to herald dinner time. At this point a bee is selected and quickly devoured. Like ants, the fairies seem to be able to carry more three times their own body weight. There is also a hint of civilization to this species: they are artisans who can make tools out of available resources.

"The Den of Iniquity"

The crafting abilities of Farmer's fairy species seem to be further developed in the third animation *The Den of Iniquity* (2010) where we observe the anti-fairies harvesting a variety of specimens, having evolved to create their own trophies and collection of curiosities as huntsmen displaying their wares and latest kills. Butterflies and moths are pinned, a mole skin is strung up, a blue bird is reanimated, eggs are ensconced in acorn cups, and a mouse's head is mounted. There seems to be a playful self-reference of Farmer's own practice, though, unlike her anti-fairies, Farmer never kills anything.

CM: I was wondering about the tension between animate and inanimate. What does animation do to taxidermy?

TF: I really don't want to say that it brings it back to life because that sounds false [...]

CM: Are the fairies doing a bit of taxidermy? I am thinking about the mole at the end of the third film which you turn round so that we can see that it is a shell. Or has it just been eaten?

TF: Well yes, they have eaten the mole and cleaned out the bones because that animation is interlinked with the piece I made about the squirrels. So the ship they are building in the film was in the static piece *A Darker Shade of Grey*.[27]

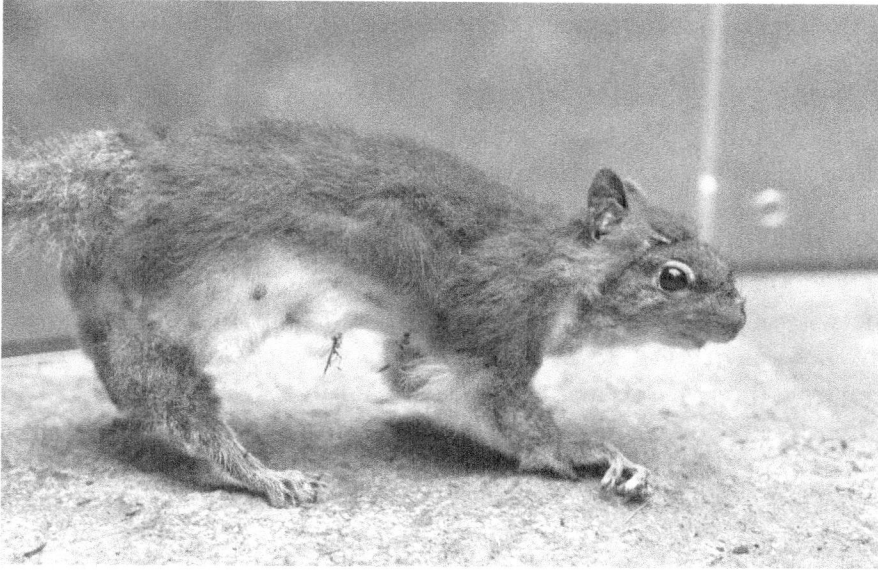

Tessa Farmer, *A Darker Shade of Grey* (detail), 2010, photograph by Clare Kendall. Copyright Tessa Farmer.

Here we learn that Farmer intended there to be narrative continuity between the third animation *The Den of Iniquity* and the installation *A Darker Shade of Grey* (2010) where the fairies join forces with the grey squirrels as the more successful species in order to defeat their weaker and rarer red counterparts. Some of the grey squirrels have cunningly disguised themselves in clumps of red fur like Trojan horses in order to better infiltrate their enemy—surely a strategy suggested by the anti-fairies who often masquerade as wasps and seem capable of fabricating such decoys.

Returning to *The Den of Iniquity*, one is tempted to compare the mole with the magical ambiguity of Dora Maar's surrealist photograph *Père Ubu* (1936) which depicts an armadillo fetus suspended in formaldehyde. Though Farmer is not historically surrealist, her anti-fairies and anti-taxidermy conjure a similar revelatory jolt of surprise. The two creatures by Maar and Farmer are similar in form, weight and in terms of the uncertainty as to whether either creature is yet animate or inanimate. They are temporarily unclassifiable, monstrous beings, presumably the result of abrupt deaths, but are reanimated through their respective modes of art in order to be encountered as curiosities.

In *The Den of Iniquity,* the fairies also appear to be using bones as the building blocks to construct a flying skull ship, one of those recurrent concoctions which appear throughout Farmer's (or her fairies') *œuvre*. The particular model in question has been embellished with butterfly wings that have been manipulated to flutter. Such crafting is temporarily interrupted or put on hold by the wrestle with a dormouse which the anti-fairies maul and take down. As with *An Insidious Intrusion*, we view a battle in motion, much like those that take place in her not-so-still-life tableaux. Here the French word for the genre seems to denote a fuller meaning: *nature morte* (literally, "dead nature"). Like her animations, Farmer's sculptural installations are similarly imbued with narrative; they are not entirely static but narrativized in the space. This was particularly the case at Danielle Arnaud's gallery at her Georgian house on Kennington Road where Farmer's sculptures were able to both play with and interrupt the domestic aspects of the fireplaces, mantelpieces, corners and window ledges. The tension between wildness and domesticity, stillness and motion, life and death is again made manifest.

Musical Notes

The collaborative aspect of Farmer's animations is intrinsic to our interpretation of them. Where Daniels has honed Farmer's skills as an animator, Pilkington contributes an aural dimension that has enhanced our understanding of the fairies' speech as well as how noises sound in their world. Many of the installations themselves are already composed in the space like musical notes, for example older pieces like *Swarm* and newer works like

Battalion (2011). Farmer has also recently collaborated with the electronic musician Amon Tobin on his album *ISAM: Control Over Nature* (2011). According to John Doran: "This synergistic combination of the physical and audio is a mosaic of infinite complexity."[28] While Pilkington's use of foley sound in Farmer's animations differs from Tobin's anthropomorphization of Farmer's sculptures, all three practitioners deploy a found aesthetic which is both synthetic and organic. The sound enchants the visual tactility of the animations. Here a parallel can be drawn between the use of sound and taxidermy in the (re)animation process. Like the fairy tale, they both must unfold through time in the very telling of or listening to. As Susannah Clapp recently wrote of Angela Carter's anti-fairy tales, Farmer allows us to hear "tiny fairy screams."[29]

Conclusion

It seems that Tessa Farmer is no normal taxidermist or animator: she believes in fairies. Rather, it seems more fitting to label her as an enchanted entomologist. Her work presents a curious hybrid forged from many different natural materials and cultural associations. It is a learned, delicate, and time-consuming craft heightened still further when embraced by the electronic and digital technologies of music and animation. The anti-fairy tale emerges as a useful way of classifying a very unruly body of work with all its malevolent titles and violent tableaux. Farmer's anti-fairy tale intertexts are bound up with a longing for childhood, particularly in terms of scale and narrative viewpoint. Her visual narratives are what childhood would wish to make of itself if it possessed the technical ability. The work signals a curious intersection between fairy tale fantasy and the museum cabinet. In doing so, the encounter between animation and taxidermy also becomes apparent: both are modes of preservation. Animation as a medium offers a rare sighting of Farmer's anti-fairies in motion while taxidermy serves as a ripe terrain for new fairy tales to be played out.

Bibliography

Aloi, G. and E. Frank, "In Conversation with Tessa Farmer" in *Antennae: The Journal of Nature in Visual Culture*, 3:1 (2007): 16-24. Accessed January 20, 2012. http://www.antennae.org.uk/ANTENNAE%20ISSUE% 203%20V1.d oc.pdf.

Barthes, Roland. "From Work to Text" in *Image, Music, Text*. Translated by Stephen Heath. 155-164. London: Fontana Press, 1977.

Bettelheim, Bruno. *The Uses of Enchantment: The Meaning and Importance of Fairy Tales*. London: Penguin Books, 1991.

Blom, Philipp. *To Have and To Hold: An Intimate History of Collectors and Collecting*. London: Penguin Books Ltd. 2003.

Briggs, Katharine. *A Dictionary of Fairies: Hobgoblins, Brownies, Bogies and Other Supernatural Creatures*. London: Penguin, 1977.

Calvin, D. and C. McAra (eds.) *Anti-Tales: The Uses of Disenchantment*. Newcastle: Cambridge Scholars Publishing, 2011.

Carroll, Lewis. "Through the Looking Glass" in *The Complete Illustrated Works of Lewis Carroll*. London: Chancellor Press, 1982. 115-233.

Carter, Angela. *The Bloody Chamber*. London: Vintage, 2007.

Clapp, Susannah. *A Card from Angela Carter*. London: Bloomsbury, 2012.

Dornan, John. *ISAM: Control Over Nature: Amon Tobin, Tessa Farmer*. London: Ninja Tune, 2011.

Drayton, Michael. "Nymphidia." In *The Book of Fairy Poetry*. Edited by Dora Owen. New York: Longmans Green and Co. 1920. 146-147.

Ellis, Patricia. "About Tessa." *Tessa Farmer* (2007). Accessed January 19, 2012. http://www.tessafarmer.com/index.html.

Fiedler, Leslie. "Introduction" in *Beyond the Looking Glass: Extraordinary Works of Fairytale and Fantasy, Novels and Stories From the Victorian Era*. Edited by Jonathan Cott. London: Hart-Davis, MacGibbon, 1973. xi-xx.

Froud, Brian. *Good Faeries, Bad Faeries*. Edited by Terri Windling. New York: Simon and Schuster, 1998.

Hammonds, Kit. "Ruins of Nature in the Sculptures of Tessa Farmer" in *The Terror*, exhibition text. Colchester: First Site Papers, 2006.

Irving, M. and A. Robinson, "Entirely Plausible Hybrids of Humans and Insects" in *Antennae: The Journal of Nature in Visual Culture*, 3: 1 (2007): 13-15. Accessed January 20, 2012. http://www.antennae.org.uk/ANTENNAE%20 ISSUE%203%20V1.doc.pdf.

Jolles, André. *Einfache Formen: Legende, Sage, Mythe, Rätsel, Spruch, Kasus, Memorabile, Märchen, Witz*. Tübingen: Niemeyer, 1968.

McAra, Catriona. "Interview with Tessa Farmer," unpublished (19 March 2011).

—. "Tessa Farmer: Nymphidia," exhibition text for Danielle Arnaud contemporary art (May 2011): http://www.daniellearnaud.com/exhibitions/exhibition-nymphidia.html Accessed 31/12/2011

—. "Interview with Tessa Farmer and Mark Pilkington," unpublished (1 October 2011).

—. "Tessa Farmer" in *Jäger und Gejagte: Insekten in der Gegenwartskunst* [*Hunters and the Hunted: Insects in Contemporary Art*], translated by Tanja Diamant. Burgrieden-Rot: Biberacher Verlagsdruckerei, 2012: 10-11, 79-80.

—. "Tessa Farmer: March of the Anti-Fairies." *Preserved!* (2012). Accessed July 2012. http://www.preservedproject.co.uk/tessa-farmer-march-of-the-anti-fairies/.

Mieder, Wolfgang. "Grim Variations From Fairy Tales to Modern Anti-Fairy Tales," in *Germanic Review*. 62:2 (Spring 1987): 90-102.

—. "Anti-Fairy Tale," in *The Greenwood Encyclopedia of Folktales and Fairy Tales*. Edited by Donald Haase. Westport: Greenwood, 2008. 50.

Neal, Jane. "Little Savages," in *Little Savages: Tessa Farmer*. London: Parabola and The Natural History Museum, 2007.

Purkiss, Diane. *Troublesome Things: A History of Fairies and Fairy Stories*. London: Penguin Press, 2000.

Silver, Carol G. *Strange and Secret Peoples: Fairies and Victorian Consciousness*. New York and Oxford: Oxford UP, 1999.

Stewart, Susan. *On Longing: Narratives of the Miniature, the Gigantic, the Souvenir, the Collection*. Durham: Duke UP, 1993.

Warner, Marina. *From the Beast to the Blonde: On Fairy Tales and Their Tellers*. London: Chatto and Windus Ltd. Random House, 1994

Notes

1   Special thanks to Danielle Arnaud and Petra Lange-Berndt for enabling me to explore some of these ideas in exhibition texts and research forums. An earlier version of this chapter was presented at *Good Neighbours: Faeries, Folklore and the Art of Tessa Farmer*, Viktor Wynd Fine Art, London (1 October 2011).

Susan Stewart, *On Longing: Narratives of the Miniature, the Gigantic, the Souvenir, the Collection* (Durham: Duke UP, 1993) 112.

2   Interview with Tessa Farmer (19 March 2011). Unless otherwise stated, all subsequent quotations of Farmer are from this interview.

3   Katharine Briggs, *A Dictionary of Fairies: Hobgoblins, Brownies, Bogies and Other Supernatural Creatures* (London: Penguin, 1977), Brian Froud, Good Faeries, Bad Faeries, Terri Windling (ed.) (New York: Simon and Schuster, 1998), Diane Purkiss, *Troublesome Things: A History of Fairies and Fairy Stories* (London: Penguin Press, 2000), Carol G. Silver, *Strange and Secret Peoples: Fairies and Victorian Consciousness* (New York and Oxford: Oxford UP, 1999).

4   Bruno Bettelheim, *The Uses of Enchantment, The Meaning and Importance of Fairy Tales* (London: Penguin Books, 1991), 26.

5   Leslie Fiedler "Introduction," *Beyond the Looking Glass: Extraordinary Works of Fairytale and Fantasy, Novels and Stories From the Victorian Era*, Jonathan Cott (ed.) (London: Hart-Davis, MacGibbon, 1973), xi.

6   Marina Warner, *From the Beast to the Blonde: On Fairy Tales and Their*

Tellers (London: Chatto and Windus Ltd. Random House, 1994), xv-xvi. The German terms *Kunstmärchen* and *Antimärchen* might be more useful in this respect - the former translating as 'wonder' or 'art' tale, similar to the *Wunderkammer*.

7 *André Jolles, Einfache Formen: Legende, Sage, Mythe, Rätsel, Spruch, Kasus, Memorabile, Märchen, Witz,* (Tübingen: Niemeyer, 1968), Wolfgang Mieder, "Grim Variations From Fairy Tales to Modern Anti-Fairy Tales," *Germanic Review*, 62:2 (Spring 1987), 90-102, and "Anti-Fairy Tale," *The Greenwood Encyclopedia of Folktales and Fairy Tales*, Donald Haase (ed.) (Westport: Greenwood, 2008), 50.

8 Angela Carter, *The Bloody Chamber* (London: Vintage, 2007).

9 David Calvin and Catriona McAra (eds.) *Anti-Tales: The Uses of Disenchantment* (Newcastle upon Tyne: Cambridge Scholars Publishing, 2011).

10 See for example Jane Neal, "Little Savages," *Little Savages: Tessa Farmer* (London: Parabola and The Natural History Museum, 2007), 15, and Patricia Ellis, "About Tessa" (2007): http://www.tessafarmer.com/index.html accessed 19/01/2012

11 For Farmer's intricate drawings of such phenomena, see Neal, "Little Savages," 24.

12 Roland Barthes is the obvious touchstone, see for example "From Work to Text," *Image, Music, Text*, Stephen Heath (trans.) (London: Fontana Press, 1977), 155-164.

13 Stewart, xi-xii.

14 Stewart, 46.

15 John Doran, *ISAM: Control Over Nature: Amon Tobin, Tessa Farmer* (London: Ninja Tune, 2011), 3.

16 Stewart, 70-71.

17 Purkiss, 151.

18 Michael Drayton, "Nymphidia," (1627). See Dora Owen (ed.), *The Book of Fairy Poetry* (New York: Longmans Green and Co. 1920), 146-147,.

19 Purkiss, 181.

20 Tessa Farmer, "In Conversation with Tessa Farmer," *Antennae*, 3: 1 Giovanni Aloi (ed.) (2007), 16 http://www.antennae.org.uk/ANTENNAE%20 ISSUE%203%20V1.d oc.pdf Accessed 20/01/2012

21 Kit Hammonds, "Ruins of Nature in the Sculptures of Tessa Farmer," *The Terror* (Colchester: First Site Papers, 2006), unpaginated leaflet.

22 Marie Irving and Alistair Robinson, "Entirely Plausible Hybrids of Hu-

mans and Insects," *Antennae*, 3: 1 (2007), 13 http://www.antennae.org.uk/ ANTENNAE%20 ISSUE%203%20V1.d oc.pdf Accessed 20/01/ 2012.

23   Stewart, 114.

24   Philipp Blom, *To Have and To Hold: An Intimate History of Collectors and Collecting* (London: Penguin Books Ltd. 2003), 152

25   Silver, 150. Also cited in Neal, *Little Savages*, 27.

26   Lewis Carroll, "Through the Looking Glass," *The Complete Illustrated Works of Lewis Carroll* (London: Chancellor Press, 1982), 151.

27   Interview with Farmer and Mark Pilkington (1 October 2011).

28   Doran, 2.

29   Susannah Clapp, *A Card from Angela Carter* (London: Bloomsbury, 2012), 18.

Chapter 4

Gnomes

Katherine Langrish

"It's disgusting!" said Harold Bennett to his wife. He peered out of the window at the opposite garden and recoiled again.

"That awful man," agreed Evelyn fervently. "He just does it to annoy, I'm sure. Letting down the whole avenue."

"I knew as soon as he moved in he'd do something dreadful."

"It's worse than Blackpool."

"Garish kitsch!"

"Go and talk to him," ordered Evelyn. "Tell him to take them away."

Harold's new neighbour had planted his garden out with gnomes.

Harold stood in his own immaculate front garden and stared across the road. Laburnum Avenue had always been a quiet neighborhood; its unspoken code of conduct was "Good Taste." The houses peeked over symmetrically trimmed hedges of privet or beech. Their front lawns were differentiated by careful single touches: a weeping cherry, a half-moon rose bed, a rockery. Harold's own lawn boasted a corkscrew hazel whose ornamental branches twirled like candy cane: he'd felt rather dashing and different when he'd planted it.

The sight from here was even worse than he'd feared. Gnomes had sprouted everywhere: white-bearded, red-capped, pot-bellied. They were dotted over the rockery, clutching lanterns, shouldering rakes. Beside the front door a couple—male and female—kissed coyly under an improbable scarlet mushroom. There was even one fishing in the pond—no! Harold averted his eyes—not fishing: it had its trousers down and was—

"Admiring my gnomes?" shouted a cheerful voice. Alfred Turnbull lumbered down the drive and beamed at his neighbour. "I've had them in boxes in the garage since we arrived. Time to let them out, I thought. They don't like being cooped up!" He roared with laughter.

Harold pressed a hand to his eyes. He felt a headache coming on. "Not what we usually see in this avenue."

"I've noticed that!" bellowed Alfred. "This'll liven the place up, eh? I've a wishing well and a couple of storks to get out yet. Never thought of having gnomes yourself? I've been collecting them for years. It's my hobby, see?

"Come and meet the little fellows!" he went on, tramping across the lawn with Harold trailing reluctantly in his wake. "This cheeky chap by the pond was the first. Got him when me and the wife was courting. And the two over there, cuddled up under the mushroom—see?—the wife spotted them on our honeymoon. 'Alfred,' she says, 'they'll bring good luck, we have to have 'em.' Then there's the one in the Man-U shirt, over there, see, and these with the musical instruments...all sorts! All different. Terracotta, resin, cement. Wherever we go on holiday, we look around for a new gnome as a souvenir. But the pick of the bunch is this little fellow!"

Alfred tenderly lifted a large gnome from the flower border and held it up. Harold could not repress a shudder. Despite rosy cheeks and a Santa Claus beard, the gnome's small white eyebrows drew together in bad-tempered scowl. Its eyes were hard and cold, and its red mouth was pursed in a mean simper. Its head was too big for its body, and it stood with thick short legs braced aggressively apart. It wore blue dungarees over a yellow shirt, and carried a suitcase.

"This little rascal," said Alfred fondly, "has been round the world! No, listen! One day, the wife tells me, 'Alfred, somebody's thieved our gnome!' I went to look and it were true: he'd gone. We were a bit upset, but you can't go to the police about a gnome!"

"Wouldn't put it past you," Harold muttered.

"But then," Alfred wagged a finger, "we got a postcard from Dublin. Little tiny writing. 'Having a wonderful time in the Land of the Little People—best wishes—Your Little Fella!' And after that—"

"I know, I know," Harold interrupted. "You had postcards from all over the world, all signed by 'Your Little Fella.' And after he'd visited New York, Hong Kong, and Japan, he arrived back in the garden one day with a suitcase covered in tiny luggage stickers."

Alfred looked crestfallen. "How did you know?"

Harold sneered. "Because I've heard it before. It's a practical joke. Someone stole your gnome and got all their friends to send you postcards from their holidays. Surely you didn't believe it?"

Alfred's eyes shifted. "Well no, not believe as such, of course not, no...But we don't know anyone who goes on that sort of holiday."

"I'm sure you don't!" Harold smiled. "If you do put up your, ah, wishing well, could you just make sure it won't be visible from our windows? My wife and I don't care for such things."

That afternoon Alfred Turnbull marched out of his garage cradling a large plastic wishing well in his arms. He planted it firmly in line with the Bennetts' dining room window and stood back, dusting his palms.

It was going to be war.

Within the week, he had added three plastic storks and a birdbath, and Harold and Evelyn were at breaking point. They could no longer enjoy their own pin-striped lawn and tasteful shrubbery.

"I could plant a screen of birches—or a honeysuckle trellis," said Harold desperately.

"No!" A fierce gleam came into Evelyn's eyes. She turned on her husband. "You've heard him telling that story about the travelling gnomes?"

"He's told half the avenue."

"Well then!" said Evelyn triumphantly. "We'll send them all travelling!"

Harold gaped. "You mean—?"

"Steal them!" Evelyn barked. "It'll be a public service. And the best of it is, he won't buy new ones—he'll sit there waiting for the postcards to arrive and expecting them all to come back!"

"But how will we manage the postcards?"

"We'll send some just at first to keep him happy," said Evelyn. "And wear gloves to write them. We mustn't be traced. You steal the gnomes, Harold—that's a man's job. Just two or three to begin with, to get him used to it, and then more. The plaster ones we can smash. But the concrete and plastic ones will have to go to the dump. In dustbin liners."

"Evelyn!" Harold gazed at her in awe. "I never knew you could be so—so dauntless. You're a military genius!"

She blushed.

At two o'clock the next morning, Harold stole into Alfred Turnbull's garden, under the soft light of the pair of carriage lanterns either side of the porch. In the middle of the rockery the pond glistened black. On the lawn, pointy-hatted figures cast pointy-hatted shadows.

Hardly breathing, heart pounding, Harold culled the nearest, dropping them one by one into his black bin-liner. He tiptoed over the rockery and snatched up the objectionable creature which stood peeing into the pool. He crept past the wishing well and grabbed a gnome he'd spotted only that afternoon—mooning, he believed the word was, in the shrubbery. It really was positively obscene. There ought to be a law against it. There probably was.

Into the bag it went.

That was enough for now. In a turmoil of adrenaline-fuelled anxiety, Harold hurried down the drive beside the beech hedge. And low down—low down—a wild little face popped out of the leaves, glaring at him.

A jolt of galvanic terror shot through Harold. He shied away, dropping the bag. Then in shame-faced relief he realised that it was only another gnome. He even recognised it, the large one with the suitcase which Alfred had shown him, the Little Fella. And it hadn't crawled out of the hedge, as for a moment he'd absurdly thought. The wind was waving the beech leaves about—the shadows made it appear to move. He rallied, reached out a hand. Nothing could be easier than to grab this one too.

The gnome's hard little eyes seemed to follow his hand. Its grin suggested a baring of teeth. Harold drew sharply back.

How malevolent the thing looked! How could anyone bear to have it in the garden? And why was it in the hedge? Hadn't it been in the flower border before?

He shook himself. Ridiculous, the things one imagined at night. Alfred had clearly moved it. Well, it could stay here. For tonight, anyway.

He took two steps away, and something rushed after his ankles. He whirled. The beech leaves shook in the breeze. The gnome hadn't moved, of course it hadn't – but its tight, smug little face smirked up at him from the shadows in a way that was hard to take. In the headiness of the moment, Harold spoke to it, threatening it: "You wait, I'll be back." He dashed over the road to his own porch, where Evelyn flung herself into his arms.

A few days later Harold was industriously weeding his drive when Alfred hailed him from across the road.

"It's a miracle! It's wonderful! It's happened again. Look!" He brandished a postcard. "We'd noticed a few of the little chaps had gone missing. The wife wanted me to phone the police." A hard note came into his voice. "It's not just one gone, is it? More like five or six." He waved a hand at his garden. "But I told her we'd wait a while. Now read that!"

He thrust the postcard at Harold, who took it with reluctance. It was from a seaside resort, and not the kind which Harold and Evelyn would normally have frequented. They'd driven down on purpose at the weekend. In miniscule curly writing (in green ballpoint—another touch of genius from Evelyn) the card wished the Turnbulls were there, and concluded, "From Your Loving Gnomes."

"Curious indeed." Harold handed it back quickly. "Not a very exotic destination, though?"

"This is just the beginning," said Alfred. "No knowing where those gnomes will travel next. The wife and I, we can't wait for the next one." He rubbed his hands and chuckled. So did Harold, mentally, although something was bothering him. He craned his neck, trying to see the gnome which had given him such a start on the drive. It was back in the border where it belonged.

On his second expedition, armed with a pencil torch, Harold "lifted" several of the Seven Dwarfs, a maudlin-looking gnome with its arm wound around a fawn's neck, and a cheery chappie wheeling a barrowful of plastic flowers. He had one bad moment crossing the lawn, when the slim beam of light played unexpectedly over the mean little features of the Little Fella. It seemed to screw its eyes up and snarl. What was it doing there? Harold couldn't shake off the stupid thought that it had been *creeping up on him*. It should have been in the border. But of course, with so many gnomes missing, it was only natural that Alfred would rearrange them.

The Turnbulls received postcards from London, Canterbury, and the Isle of Wight. Evelyn and Harold were enjoying one another's company more than they had in years. There were trips to the coast, and trips to the dump, and Harold's lone midnight raids seemed to thrill Evelyn so much that other midnight activities often followed.

"The reward of the soldier," Harold told himself. For after all, it wasn't Evelyn who risked everything night after night, prowling across a garden whose owner must, surely, be more and more on the alert! And Harold didn't care to admit it, but the Little Fella was getting on his nerves. Alfred seemed to be trying it in all sorts of different places. Half buried in a clump of flowers. Hidden behind a tree. Sentinel by the gate, leering at him in the streetlight as he tiptoed past, as if it knew something nasty that he didn't. Sometimes he never saw it at all, but heard thin little shrieks from the hedgerow: cats, he supposed, but still...He never tried to steal it. He didn't ever want to touch it.

On Harold's final expedition, Evelyn sent him out after a set of gnomish musicians, a jazz trio playing sax, keyboard, and drums in a corner of the shrubbery. It was a wet night, full of intimate, pattering sounds. He searched about, creeping through the bushes, while accusatory drops rattled down on his neck and shoulders. When his narrow torch beam picked out the little trio, huddling under the mottled leaves of the laurel, they seemed to cower from his hand. But what nonsense! What morbid, unhealthy fancies! Gritting his teeth, he stuffed the three gnomes into the bag.

On the way back, he almost tripped over the Little Fella, scowling up at him from a spot in the very middle of the gravel drive. It was a ridiculous place to put a gnome, and Harold could have sworn it hadn't been there on the way in. He hurried home, and later that night dreamed of a nasty little creature with grinning mouth and rat-like teeth scurrying around the bedroom. He awoke with a start as it jumped on the pillow. Then he lay taut and sleepless for hours, listening to Evelyn's gentle snores and the patter of the rain outside.

"I've had enough," he told Evelyn next morning.

"But we haven't finished! There's still at least one gnome left. And the wishing well, and the storks."

"We're not taking the storks. And even Alfred Turnbull might find a travelling wishing well hard to credit."

"But it's a shame not to make a clean sweep of the gnomes. It wouldn't be hard to take the last one, wouldn't it? It's very close to the road."

"Is it?" Harold threw a nervous glance out of the window. He shuddered. "No, Evelyn. I feel tired. And I saw the curtain move last night. I think Alfred might have a camera." It wasn't true, but it was easier to lie than to explain. "I don't have to tell you, it would be a disaster if we were caught."

"You're right." Evelyn sighed. "Maybe he is getting suspicious. I saw him snooping around our drive this morning, and he said they hadn't had any postcards for ten days. I told you we ought to have sent at least one more. There was a little bit of coloured plaster lying right by the dustbin, from one of their hats or something. I don't think he saw it, but later on it wasn't there. Yes. Leave that gnome alone."

But a few days later, to Harold's surprise, Alfred Turnbull called out to tell him that the Little Fella was missing too.

"He was there Sunday night and gone on Monday. We feel quite lonely now, the wife and I," he confided. "Abandoned, like. I wonder if the wife wasn't right from the first, and we ought to tell the police."

Harold tried to laugh. "Oh come on—for a gnome?"

"For twenty-four gnomes." There was a mean glint in Alfred's eye that made Harold shiver. "They're not cheap, gnomes. I reckon they was worth two, three hundred pounds, easy. If I thought they'd gone for good, I'd make big trouble for whoever did it. But you know what? I don't have to."

"N-no?" Harold stammered.

"No," said Alfred, and the look he gave Harold was almost pitying. "My last little fellow—he can take care of himself."

Harold went indoors, glad to think that he had never even touched the Little Fella. At least he was innocent in that regard. Evelyn said brightly, "So somebody else has had the same idea as us! Maybe they'll take the wishing well and the storks too."

But they didn't.

On Monday when the post arrived, Harold heard Evelyn cry out. Her voice was shrill with fright. "Harold—Harold, come and look at this!" She held out a crumpled picture postcard of Brighton Pavilion. It was dirty, dog-eared, chewed at the edges, and appeared to be written in—

"Harold," said Evelyn in a trembling voice, "can that be...blood?"

Harold snatched the card. On the back it said in a smeared brown scribble:

> *Bring em back.*
> *Bring em all back.*
> *Or put £100 in the wishing well.*
> *Or else.*
> *The Little Fella*

He dropped the card as if it had bitten him.

"Oh, Harry," breathed Evelyn—she hardly ever called him that—"He knows! Alfred knows. He'll tell the police. Go over there. Give him the money and stop him!"

"This isn't from Alfred," said Harold hoarsely.

"Not from Alfred?" She stared at him. "Who is it from, then?"

Harold thought of that feral little monster. It had vanished from Alfred's garden. It could turn up anywhere now—anywhere. In his own garden. In his house, even. He'd never feel safe again.

Or was that ludicrous? Was blackmail Alfred's style?

"I can't tell you," he said, miserably. "But money won't stop him. And this is only the beginning."

Part II

Storytellers

Chapter 5

Do Fairies Still Exist? Fairy-Tales in Hebrew Nowadays

Hanna Livnat and Gaby Cohn,
translated by Danielle Bett

The Hebrew and Yiddish cultures have always attached importance to the different genres of folk literature, such as
myth, local legend, fairy tale, and fable. These genres of Jewish
and Hebrew folklore flourished throughout the generations, and
in the various communities of the Jewish Diaspora. Certain stories and poems were original literary works, while others were
adaptations of stories and poems from past generations, both local
and universal.

Since there is a wide range of research both on Folktale in general and in children's literature in particular, this chapter derives
largely on sources focusing on Jewish and Hebrew literature, and
on the literature that has been and is being published in Hebrew in
Israel today. Therefore, the literature researched and referred to in
this essay includes Hebrew sources or sources that have been translated into Hebrew.

Professor Eli Yassif describes in detail the history of the Hebrew
and Jewish folk literature in his book *The Hebrew Folktale*, which
was published both in Hebrew and English.[1] Yassif maps the roots,
types, and meaning of Hebrew Folktale, therefore it will suffice to
reference this book here, and focus on fairy tales as a genre of children's and young adult literature in Israel today.

In her book *Just Childhood: Introduction to Poetics of Children's Literature* (in Hebrew),[2] Professor Zohar Shavit argues that at the beginning of the seventeenth century, as in previous centuries, the tradition of listening to stories told by heart, including fairy tales, was widespread. The fairy tales were told in groups among people of all ages and social standings. However, a shift occurred in socio-cultural inclinations in the second half of the seventeenth century: the upper class, which previously openly admitted enjoying these tales, began to see them as part of a lower class culture. As the lower class culture was also identified as children's culture, the folktales crossed to the lower culture. Thus, fairy tales became one of the first literary types to officially name children as its primary audience.

In the beginning of the nineteenth century, fairy tales received a renewed appreciation: they were perceived as a creation representing the authentic national spirit and therefore were collected as part of the search for national culture and identity. Perceiving the folktales as a childhood product of a whole nation led to their view as texts suitable for children. Thus, folktales began to be associated with children's culture, up to the twentieth century, when they were considered by some psychologists as an essential and necessary aspect of child development (Shavit, 1996: 72-73).

The different variations of folk literature throughout history and across cultures suggest that the changes in the texts were neither coincidental nor meaningless. One of the crucial factors in determining the nature of these changes is the varying societal concepts of childhood and the changing social assumptions regarding children's needs and their relationships with adults. Children's literature is closely linked to educational norms as a source of its legitimacy. The social perceptions of children and childhood are what ultimately determine what would unravel on the pages following the book's title. (Shavit, 1996: 121)

According to Dina Stern in her book *Violence in an enchanted world* (in Hebrew),[3] the place of the fairy tales in children's literature is universal (Stern, 1986: 13). Various story and song genres are found in folk literature. Story genres include myths, fairy tales, legends, fables, anecdotes, and pattern stories. Song genres include:

epics, ballads, and certain lyric songs. There are also proverbs, riddles, jokes, and more (Ibid. 14). Despite the variety of definitions, it is agreed that fairy tales are stories that have reached us from past generations, with a supernatural element, and it is emphasised that they do not pretend to be realistic— they are not restricted to the constraints of time, place, and causality (Shavit 1996: 15).

In his essay on the Brothers Grimm's fairy tales in the Introduction to *Brüder Grimm—Kinder- und Hausmärchen* (in Hebrew),[4] Professor Dov Noy argues that the Grimms themselves regarded the disassociation from reality and everyday life as the most typical feature of the fairy tale (Noy, 1994: ז). In our days, the fairy tale is defined as a story with many extraordinary motifs, as well as supernatural motifs which are empirically unverified. The magic fairy tale is a folktale that takes place in an undefined space and time. In the fairy tale there are no geographical or historical indicators, and the anonymity of the characters is derived from this. In comparison, the legend takes place in defined geographical space and historical time. Often listeners are familiar with the names of the characters and their mere mention may lead to geographical and historical associations, even if the listeners are not aware of the specific temporal and spatial frames of the plot (Noy 1994: ז).

Hebrew Legends from Jewish Sources for Children and Young Adults

Hebrew folktales tended to include a definite mention of time and place; most were even rooted in the popular Jewish folk tradition and gave a clear identity to their heroes. Consequently, it seems that the Hebrew folktales tend towards the genre of legend rather than the fairy tale. That is true although supernatural fairy tales have been found in the Jewish folk literature in certain times and places.

Uriel Ofek, one of the first researchers of children's literature in Israel, claims in his study *Give Them Books!* (in Hebrew)[5] that the Jews who gathered in Israel during the twentieth century, clung to the international folklore traditions from their childhood memories in their countries of origin. Therefore it seems that in Israel the existence of previous Jewish legends was almost forgotten. There were some authors that gathered and adapted legends for Israeli children, but this endeavour was not continued until recent years (Ofek, 1983: 92).

Ofek contends that biblical stories and the legends of Chazal (Our Sages of Blessed Memory) have always been loved by the children of Israel. Even in the days of the Second Temple period, children would ask their teachers for biblical stories and legends. Many authors mention in their memoirs the "Melamed" who delighted them with stories or the legends they heard from their mothers and grandmothers during their childhood. For many generations the early collections of *Talmud* legends were among the favourite books of the Hebrew child, who lacked secular books (Ibid. 93).

Many fairy tales and legends were collected over time, among them those relating to biblical heroes or those which tell of Chazal and other exemplary men, as well as fables and tall tales, and the legendary stories of the salvation of Jews and the downfall of Israel's enemies. These legends include most of the international folk literature motifs, such as the triumph of the weak over the strong, miracle tales, and the wisdom of the poor man (Ibid. 99).

Ze'ev Jawitz, perhaps the first Hebrew author to see the old Jewish legend as original folk creation that reflects the nation's spirit and natural birth, composed *Sihot Minni Kedem* (Conversations of Ancient Times), in an attempt to present those legends to children at face value (originally printed in Warsaw in 1888). Yehoshua Hana Ravnitzky, one of Hebrew children's literature nurturers and a devotee of *Talmud* legends, published in Odessa, starting from 1891, a series of thin and elegant booklets named *Pninim MiYam HaTalmud* (Pearls from the sea of *Talmud*). Following his death, a special edition of *Agadot Leyeladim* (Legends for Children), including a dozen of his works, was published in 1952 by Dvir publishing (Ofek, 1983: 99).

Chaim Nachman Bialik, one of the greatest modern day Hebrew poets, known also as "the national poet," published a collection of legends in Hebrew with Ravnitzki. The two began the writing in Odessa, Ukraine in 1903: they collected legends in Aramaic and translated them into Hebrew, arranged them by subject, and integrated similar legends from different sources. Bialik and Ravnitzki published this collection under the name *Sefer HaAggadah* (The Book of Legends). They continued this enterprise in Israel starting in 1930 and even publishing an updated edition, adding many chapters. *Sefer HaAggadah* was published in two volumes of six parts, each with its own central theme: from Creation and the destruction of the Second Temple, through the *Tannaim*,[6] the *Amoras*,[7] and many other topics, such as conjecture and medicine, fables and proverbs. Bialik also published *Vayehi Hayom* (And There Shall Be a Day), sort of a shortened *Sefer HaAggadah* adapted for children (Smit, 2011: 8-10 [in Herew]).[8]

Professor Zvi Scharfstein, writer and researcher of children's literature, was a devout follower of the didactic legend and fairy tale. He published in the United States hundreds of adapted fairy tales and legends in newspapers and magazines. In 1972 his book *Kohavim shel Zahav* (Stars of Gold), a work including 64 of his adapted fairy tales and legends he had collected from old and new sources, was published in Tel Aviv. Two other authors who worked diligently on the adaptation of legends to children were Asher Barash and Zalman Ariel. Also worthy of mention in regard to the collection and adaptation of legends, is the work of Israel Benyamin Levner, Shlomo Skloski, Leib Hazan and Itzhak Avnon, and finally the writing of David Cohen, whose legends originate from the Orthodox folklore (Ofek, 1983: 100-102).

The collection and preservation of Jewish folk stories was given an important momentum by Professor Dov Noy in 1955, when he founded the Israel Folktale Archives (IFA), as part of Haifa's Museum of Ethnology and Folklore. The archives aim to save oral folk narratives passed down over the generations by newly arriving Jewish immigrants, and veteran Israelis alike, from numerous ethnic and cultural backgrounds, by collecting and documenting them. In recent years, the stories are being digitally scanned and the content of the archives is being catalogued into an electronic database in order to preserve the collection and make it accessible to all (Ibid. 102).

Of course, not all collected stories fit the definition of "legend" or "fairy tale," and not all are suitable for children. Still, in recent years there has been a rise in interest in this perspective in Israel, and several collections of Jewish folk stories have been successfully published among the Israeli children. One of these collections, *Ha'Agadot Shelanu, Otzar Ha'Agada Ha'Ivrit Layeled* (Our Legends, A Treasury of Hebrew Legends for Children) by Shoham Smit, is a selection of Jewish legends for children that Smit adapted from Bialik and Ravnitzki's collection.[9] The first part of the book includes adaptations based on biblical stories (such as the story of the flood, the tower of Babel, Abraham, Moses and King Solomon). The second part includes legends of the Sages (such as Hillel the Elder, Hanina Ben Dosa, Honi ha-Ma'agel, Joshua ben Hananiah, and Rabbi Akiva). The third part includes fables about people, foxes and animals. Alongside each adapted tale, Smit added her thoughts and the educational lesson she derived from it.

Chachameinu Leyameinu (Once Upon a Time in Jerusalem), by Uri Orbach[10] is another book recently published in Israel. It is based on stories of Jewish origins and includes dozen of Chazal's (Our sages of blessed memory) legends, adapted for children. The legends aim to spread lessons of helping others, understanding and consideration, as well as the importance of Torah study. Those who act appropriately on these matters will be rewarded; and in the vast majority of these stories the reward is money. Among the legends is "Promises that must be kept," the love story of Rabbi Akiva and Rachel, and stories of Elazar, Rabbi Joshua, Rabbi Zakkai, and others. The novelty of this book lies mainly in Orbach's modern style and humour. The book could be an interesting source for learning the life style and beliefs of Jews in those times, among other things because self-fulfilment manifests in men through Torah study and in women through cooking; this can be understood considering the period in which these legends were written. Orbach has published additional adaptations of Jewish originated legends, such as in his book *Ma Mevarhim Al Glida* (How do you bless over ice cream).[11]

One would assume that works based on Jewish origins have also been published in the Religious and Orthodox sectors, but as this chapter focuses mainly on fairy tales and not on legends, and particularly on texts for the general public, I will not elaborate on this matter.

However, it is important to mention that adaptations of biblical stories for children are also published in Israel, either as independent works or as stories intended for the educational system. One of these adaptations is Meir Shalev's book *Mabul, Nachash, Ushtei Tevot. Sipurei Tanach liYladim* (A Snake, a Flood and Two Arks: Bible Stories for Children), which contains the stories of Adam and Eve and the Snake, Noah's Ark, The Tower of Babel, The Stories of Abraham, Joseph and his Brothers, and Moses).[12] The adaptations of Shalev, one of Israel's leading authors today, are loyal to the source in essence, losing none of its original qualities or its complex perceptions of the world. These adaptations successfully portray for children nowadays stories written originally in a language no longer relevant to them. Rakefet Zohar is also working on a series of Bible stories for children, and three of these adaptions have already been published.[13]

Shlomo Abas, who published many works of folk literature for children, also collected and edited stories from Jewish and Hebrew sources. His book *Hayim VaMavet beyad Halashon—Hasipurim Hahakamim shel Hasafa Ha'ivrit* (Life and Death in the Power of One's Tongue) contains fifteen tales relating to dialects, idioms, and the Hebrew language in general.[14] Abas also published the book *Ta'alulei Juha* (Juha), which includes stories from popular Jewish Diaspora folklore.[15] Juha is the North African equivalent of the Eastern European "Hershele." The book contains forty short stories about the adventures of Juha. Most of these portray his exceptional stupidity, others celebrate his cunning. The stories are humorous; Juha is a source of laughter thanks to his embarrassing actions, which get him into trouble, and the amusing illustrations of Danny Kerman add to their humorous nature.

Author and illustrator Simms Taback published the book *Joseph Had a Little Overcoat*:[16] Joseph has a little overcoat, but it is full of holes, so he turns it into a jacket, and then a sweater, and then a scarf, a tie, and so on. The story is based on a Yiddish children's song, which shows that you can always make something out of anything—or out of nothing. The illustrations in the book are full of imagination and the story itself contains the typical Yiddish humour. The overcoat is a recurring motif in classic and modern Hebrew literature, and even if it does not fit the definition of a fairy tale, it is a Jewish folk story which has been preserved through the generations.

Yannets Levi collected and adapted a selection of legends and fairy tales about nature in Israel, some ancient and some new, published by Zmora-Bitan.[17] At the end of each story there is a page of information about the plant discussed in the legend. In the collection there are an adaptation of "King Solomon Looks for a Crown" based on Ze'ev Vilnay's story; a folktale about the beautiful Hadas (Myrtus), a prince and a cruel dragon; a story about the olive tree and the dove, inspired by the biblical story of Noah and the dove after the flood; a story about the useless oak tree, based on the writings of Chuang Tzu; a story of gossiping canes; the story of a Narcissus who finally fell in love, based on Greek mythology; the story of the Ear of Corn based on the Brothers Grimm, and more. Yannets Levi's book is therefore consisted of adapted legends from the array of early Jewish and Hebrew stories alongside works based on well-known stories of the world. It also contains legends, fairy tales and fables. As such, his book leads to the discussion of today's primary Hebrew folk literature, which is influenced predominantly by the fairy-tales of the world.

Fairy Tales in Hebrew in Modern Israel

Classical Western Literature and its Adaptation for Children

As shown, there has been a revival of children's stories based on Jewish and early Hebrew sources in recent years. However, children and young adult's literature that is based on characteristics of folk literature and published in Israel in Hebrew today, favors the fairy tale genre rather than other genres of the folktale. It is also based mainly on general sources of western literature, rather than on Jewish or early Hebrew sources.

Thus, in recent years there has been a trend of full translations, directly from the language of origin, of a variety of fairy tales—more or less known. Until the 1990's most of the fairy tales known to Israeli children in Hebrew were mere adaptations of the classic versions, most of them adapted to fit the "sheltered" view of the child (in which there is a tendency to soften, refine and moderate the classic sources). The fairy tales of the Brothers Grimm in their various adaptations are especially known In Israel, as are the stories of Hans Christian Andersen, which include artistic legends and fairy tales and short stories. All the Grimm stories and Andersen's 168 stories have been translated in full directly from German[18] and Danish[19] respectively only in the past twenty years. Following these anthologies, collections of fewer stories and even books containing single stories began to be published. This renewal of the full translation of the anthologies was accompanied by contemporary illustrations added to the collections and stories, some added to the editions abroad and some added by illustrators in Israel. These illustrations provide new, fresh and complex perspectives on the original stories.

Andersen's *Samlede Eventyr og Historier* are well known in Israel. First, as aforementioned, in their adaptations for children, and today also in their full translations. The full collection was published by Machbarot Lesifrut and is called *Agadot Andersen*[20] (Anderson's Legends). It was published in five volumes, each containing some of Andersen's stories. Thirteen of Andersen's stories, also translated fully, were published in a new edition printed in 2008, and illustrated by Silke Leffler.[21] This collection includes "The Princess and the Pea," "The Emperor's New Clothes," "The Tinderbox," "The Ugly Duckling" "The Little Match Girl," "The Swineherd," "Thumbelina," "The Steadfast Tin Soldier" and others. The full translation of "The Little Match Girl" was published in individual books as well, by Kinneret, Zmora-Bitan, Dvir and other publishing houses.

The 211 tales of Jacob and Wilhelm Grimm, *Kinder- und Hausmärchen*, also saw new editions over the past twenty years. Poalim Publishing House printed the stories without illustrations, punctuation or spaces and directed it primarily for researchers and other adults interested in the field. The children's edition was published by Machbarot Lesifrut in a series of volumes called "The Legends of the Brothers Grimm." Each volume contains some of their stories, most of which are fairy tales, while a few are short folk stories and fables. At the end of 2011 a collection of stories from this anthology was published, this time with modern illustrations by the young, award winning Israeli illustrator Ofra Amit.[22] Her illustrations allow new and refreshing points of view that do not gloss over the complex stories of the brothers Grimm, but respect the abilities of Hebrew reading children. This collection includes "Sleeping Beauty," "Little Red Cap," "Sweet Porridge," "Snow White," "All-Kinds-of-Fur," "The Shoes that were Danced to Pieces," "The Fisherman and his Wife," and others. The fairy tale "The Elves and the Shoemaker" was published in an independent book in 2008, and again the novelty lies not only in the full translation, but also in the modern, lively and thought provoking illustrations of Jim LaMarche.[23]

Alongside the full translations of well-known fairy tales from the original languages which appeared in the past twenty years, adaptations for children of these fairy tales are widespread. In their tendency to "protect" children, these adaptations have changed the classic texts. Unfortunately, it seems that the aesthetic and literary value of these modern adaptations falls substantially from the quality of Brothers Grimm's and Andersen's versions. This derives from the changes made in language, narrative, characters, events and plot design, and the use of different artistic means. The comparison also reveals that the adaptations tend to be superficial, explicit, dichotomous and stereotypical—especially on issues of gender, morals, social status and ethnic origin, physical appearance and so on. This abundance of adaptations is not peculiar to the Hebrew and Jewish culture, but rather is typical of the phenomenon of adaptations for children in Western culture in general. This is widely discussed in Bettelheim's *The Uses of Enchantment: The Meaning and Importance of Fairy Tales*,[24] and in the research of Professor Zohar Shavit,[25] Professor Rachel Weissbrod,[26] as well as my own.[27] These tendencies are typical of modern adaptations for children of texts originally aimed at various audiences—adults, teenagers and children. It is also typical of texts assuming the fairy tales model and characteristics when adapted to children, even though they were not originally written as such (see the debate on the various adaptations in English, German, French and Hebrew to Jonathan Swift's "Gulliver's Travels").[28] According to Livnat's research (2004), the majority of modern adaptations for children in Israel, as in Western culture in general, prevent the child from experiencing a meaningful reading process, a process involving his or her views of the world and the perceptions of the world around them. The intellectual, emotional and aesthetic experience offered in Brothers Grimm's and Andersen's works is lost in the modern adaptations, turning into a shallow, stereotypical, one-dimensional and pre-dictated presentation, in almost every aspect of the text, aesthetic and normative alike.

In the Brothers Grimm text, as with many classic texts, the description of the characters is complex. For example, in the story of Cinderella, both the main characters and the relationships between them are complex, and as such they change and develop throughout the plot.[29] In the fairy tales, as written by the Brothers Grimm, the reader learns about characters through their actions and words, so he can formulate his opinion on them based on their gradually revealed attributes (Livnat, 2004: 62). At the beginning of the story, the Grimms describe Cinderella as a young girl who endures in silence insults and abuse from her stepsisters and her lack of reaction cries to the heavens. Another attribute revealed in the text, is Cinderella's frugality. For example, when her father travels to the fair, her sisters ask that he brings them beautiful dresses, pearls and precious stones. Cinderella, on the other hand, asks him for the first branch his hat bumps into on his way back home. She plants this branch on her mother's grave. "Her tears fell on the branch and watered it, and it grew into a beautiful tree. Cinderella went to her mother's grave three times a day, cried, and prayed. Each time a small white bird came to the tree, and threw down to Cinderella whatever she wished for" (Grimm, 1993: 133).[30] Cinderella's kind-heartedness and devotion are expressed through these acts and the connection between her acts and the reward she gains, thanks to the bird, is clear to the readers.

Cinderella's sisters demand that she helps them to prepare for the ball, and she, as she has done thus far, did as they said. However, a change in her personality is revealed: Now she cries because she, too, very much wants to go to this ball, and asks her stepmother to allow her to join them. The stepmother denies her request, but this time Cinderella does not accept the verdict, and pleads with her stepmother again and again. When it is clear to Cinderella that her stepmother is not going to keep her promise, Cinderella goes to her mother's grave, and asks the bird in the tree for silver and gold—Cinderella is no longer the girl that she was at the beginning of the story: she is now discovering her own desires and works relentlessly to achieve them, even if it requires persistence and asking for help. The bird grants Cinderella the means necessary to make her wish come true—the dress and the shoes—but the decision of how to use them is left in the hands of Cinderella. In Grimm's version, unlike the adapted versions (and Perrault's version, which was aimed at adults and written as a satire), there is no fairy, carriage, coachmen or the curfew of midnight. Cinderella wears the dress and goes to the ball, and the king's son approaches her, offers his hand, and dances with her. Then, once again, Cinderella's wishes are revealed when she dances until the evening comes, and then wants to go home. It seems, therefore, that the Grimms' Cinderella has a will of her own, and just as she wanted to go to the ball she now wants to return home, despite the humiliation and hard labour that awaits her there, and contrary to the wishes of the king's son.

Cinderella shows initiative and works to get what she desires, and more so—another change takes place within her—she is cunning, agile, and plans ahead. She evades the King's son, sneaks away and returns to her home and to her previous cinder-full attire. This pattern repeats three times. This repetition of rhythmic structure and themes is used by the Brothers Grimm as an artistic mean, illustrating and emphasising processes, within a framework of seemingly apparent stability. The dynamic which takes place shatters the pattern at the third time. On the third evening Cinderella turns to leave the ball, and again the King's son wants to accompany her, but she swiftly escapes from him and vanishes. But now the pattern breaks, because this time the king's son uses trickery and orders that the stairs be covered in wax. The king's son realises that desire alone is not enough to win Cinderella over, and he must also plan and act. And indeed, Cinderella leaves behind her left shoe, stuck in the wax, and with it the King's son ventures to find his bride. At the end of his journey, Cinderella is brought before him. Even though she washes her hands and face before she enters the room and bows in front of the king's son, Cinderella meets him wearing her worn out rags and heavy wooden shoes. The reason for Cinderella's actions is now revealed to the readers: if the king's son does not want her as she is, he cannot have her at all. The Grimms' Cinderella, it seems, does not put marriage to the prince at the top of her priorities. She would rather stay at home, where she suffers, than settle for a prince who wants her solely for her beauty and glamour. He will win her only after he learns to value her as a person. And indeed, the prince does.

The two stepsisters are described in the Grimm version as pretty and fair, but ugly and dark in their heart (Ibid. 132). The Brothers Grimm do not automatically associate wickedness with ugliness and beauty with kindness. The sisters' actions and behaviour towards Cinderella throughout the text gradually gives meaning to their inner ugliness and darkness, and at the end of the story they are punished for their malicious and deceitful ways.

In the current adaptations of this story in Israel, as in other adaptations of stories written originally by Grimm and Andersen, there is an evident tendency to waive indirect characterization and complex and developing characters. The characterisation in the adaptations is often very direct, and the one-dimensional characters remain static throughout the story. In this format, the female characters have two main options: the young passive girl, usually also pretty, obedient, gentle, and kind, and the active and assertive woman, who is mostly characterised as evil, malicious—and ugly. This connection between beauty and positive qualities and between ugliness and negative qualities is prominent in modern adaptations for children and young adults. The male characters in these adaptations also have two main options: the young man, who functions as a *knight in shining armour* through his strength, status or bravery, and the man looking to protect his children and provide for them.

For example, in the adaptations of *Snow White*, the dwarves' house she finds when running from her stepmother is usually portrayed as dirty. She rushes to clean it and even begins to sing. In the Grimms' version, men also know how to clean and upkeep their home; Snow White reaches a clean and tidy house, and does not perceive cleaning the house as her natural and enjoyable role. Only when the dwarves arrive home and find Snow White, they agree to let her take refuge in their house on the condition that she cleans it.

In the adaptations of *Little Red Riding Hood*, the Brother Grimm's ending has often been omitted. The Brothers Grimm have another ending in which Little Red Riding Hood meets another wolf. This time she has already learned her lesson and does not tell him where her Grandmother's house is. When the wolf still arrives at the house, Little Red Riding Hood and her Grandmother deceive him, and thanks to their resourcefulness and intelligence they overcome and kill him. This option is not possible in the adaptations: the hunter, the man, is the only saviour and the women are unable to deal with such threats by themselves. Therefore, in the Grimms' version Little Red Riding Hood is a changing and developing character, but in the adaptations she remains an innocent and naive child who needs a man to save her.

This is also the case in the adaptations of *The Fisherman and his Wife*—generally renamed in Hebrew "The Fisherman and the Golden Fish." While in the adaptations the emphasis is always placed on the supernatural—even in the names given to the stories, in the Grimms' versions the power to change and cope lies in the characters themselves. The adaptations of this story emphasise the "deal" struck between the fish and the fisherman: If the fisherman releases the fish, the fish will grant him three wishes. There is no such deal in the Grimm's story. The fisherman releases the fish simply because he is a good person. In the Brothers Grimm's version, the fish stops fulfilling the fisherman's wife's wishes when she wants to be God-like. This is an essential and fundamental limit on man's aspirations. In the adaptations, however, the fish stops fulfilling the fisherman's wife's wishes when she demands that he becomes her servant. That is an entirely personal limit, rather than a moral-essential one.

As mentioned before, in this the Israeli adaptations are similar to adaptations throughout the Western world.[31] Therefore, I will now only present some examples of popular fairy tales published recently in Hebrew in Israel, which are of specific interest or innovation.

Osnat Yoshpe Gazit published two fairy tales in two different books, one of which is well-known and has been previously published in other Hebrew versions. It is called *Ha'agada al Perach Lev Hazahav*[32] (The Golden Heart Flower), and is actually a fairy tale by most of its characteristics. The fairy tale tells the story of a small boy whose mother has fallen ill, and been told that only the golden-heart flower can cure her. The flower can be found beyond the wide river, and the boy decides to go in search of the flower for his mother. He gets lost in the forest, sobs, and a crow helps him to get through the forest in exchange for his food. He reaches a high wall, cries, and a sheep helps him in exchange for his backpack. He reaches the river, doesn't know how to cross it, cries, and a goose helps him in exchange for his shoes, the only thing he had now. The boy finds the golden-heart flower, runs all the way home, helped again by the animals he had met previously. His mother smells the flower and is cured. The illustrations in this edition place the story in the modern world: The characters and the landscapes seem contemporary. Unlike the wondrous and laboured journey in early versions of this story, here the boy travels for only a day, and although he has a long way to go and needs to give things up, he does not come across serious obstacles. Every time he does meet an obstacle, an animal willing to help him appears. The emphasis is not on the sacrifice; the boy simply learns to conduct himself with the animals he meets along the way. The other story adapted by Yoshpe Gazit is *Ha'agada al Hasi'ach Hakatan*[33] (The Tale of the Little Bush). This is a children's story about a depressed thorn bush that no one wants to look at or touch. The bush asks the forest minister to grow gold leaves instead of thorns, but when his wish is granted, he realizes that it is not easy to be a golden bush, because a robber takes his leaves. The next day, the thorn bush asks the forest minister for crystal leaves, but they prove to be just as problematic, as they break in a storm. The next day the thorn bush grows flowers, but they are picked away by girls. The next day, he asks for green leaves instead of flowers, and a goat eats the leaves he grew. So the thorn bush returns to be a regular thorn bush; he learns to love his thorns.

This story is similar to one of Yannets Levi's aforementioned stories—*Hasirpad Harishon VeHasirpad Ha'acharon* (The first nettle and the last nettle), which is a folk tale. When God distributed qualities to plants, the nettle asked to be the most beautiful, the best smelling, and the most delicious. The nettles quickly discovered they had made a mistake, as thanks to their good taste and smell, they were being eaten and becoming extinct. When only one nettle was left in the world, he went to God and renounced his good qualities, so that he would be left alone.

Rita, the well-known Israeli singer, wrote a folk story she remembered from her childhood, and published it in the book *Halev shel Shiraz*[34] (Shiraz's Wise Heart). Shiraz lives with her step mother and sister, whose behaviour toward her is reminiscent of the behaviour of the step mother and sisters of Cinderella. One day Shiraz's favourite yarn ball falls to the garden of a mysterious old woman. Shiraz asks for her ball back, and the old woman agrees on the condition that she does a few things for her. The old woman asks her to break everything in the dirty kitchen, but Shiraz cleans and tidies it instead. The old woman asks her to destroy the garden, but Shiraz grooms it instead. The old woman asks her to cut off her hair, but Shiraz combs it instead. The old woman gives Shiraz the ball back and sends her to dip in two pools, and when Shiraz returns home she is extraordinarily beautiful. Her step mother and sister are jealous of her, and the mother decides to send the sister to the old woman's house so that she too will be beautiful. The sister, unlike Shiraz, follows the old woman's orders to break and ruin the house. The old woman returns the ball to her and sends her to dip in the pools, where the sister spends longer than necessary. When the sister returns home, she discovers she has become ugly. Shiraz tells that although the old woman told her to wreck everything, she listened to her heart's wishes. As for physical appearance, we find out that the pools do not change it but rather make inner beauty stand out.

Adaptations of classic fairy tales were popular throughout the 20th century, and are still, in the 21st century, being published by almost every publishing house in Israel. It is not often that they are innovative in the spirit of what will be detailed in the following sections. It is important to mention that in Hebrew, fairy tales are often referred to as "legends," as until recent years, the genre distinction between legends and fairy tales was rarely made. Therefore, terms are already changing in research books, but in children's books publishers often continue defining fairy tales as "legends" since the term is widespread among educators, parents and children. Aside from this, the tendencies described in this section and the following sections are similar to those known in Western literature as a whole.

"Politically Correct" Artistic Fairy Tales in Israel

In the 1980's a new trend started in Israel, alongside the common adaptations of classic fairy tales, that reflected the desire and need to "shake" the conservative stereotyping of popular fairy tales. It should be noted that the adaptations of the "politically correct" kind did not usually try to shatter the patterns of the classic fairy tales, which were actually ground breaking in terms of the worldview they expressed, but rather the familiar patterns of the many adaptations for children. In her article "Story Meets Story: Dialogues between Modern Children's Literature and Folk Fairy Tales" (in Hebrew),[35] Osnat Gabayan notes that artistic feminist fairy tales have been published in the United States and England since the 1970's, as part of an attempt to influence behavioural patterns and gender perception. These fairy tales coincided with the feminist demands for social change and gender equality. The goal was to encourage socialization process from early childhood (Gabayan, 2007: 89). Feminist fairy tales appeared in Israel, mainly in the 80s and 90s. Professor Miri Baruch[36] presents two types of

"Feminist fairy tales": first, parodies of classic fairy tales or, to be precise, of their modern adaptations; and second, the genre of the new fairy tale, which uses the traditional component of the fairy tale (e.g., princess, prince and dragons), but these are "freed" from the traditional roles and from the stereotypical views of gender roles (Gabayan, 2007: 90).

Examples of typical books reflecting the parody category published in Israel are, to start, *Agada Hadasha* (New Legend) by Gail Hareven.[37] The main motif in this book is role reversal. The princess refuses to wait by the window for the princes to save her, and she allows herself to fulfil roles which in fairy tales are considered to be "masculine." It should be noted that such role reversal in itself creates stereotyping (Gabayan, 2007: 91). The book is meant for elementary school children and tells the story of a cruel dragon which attacks the people of the kingdom. The king and queen announce that the prince who annihilates the dragon will win the princess. But Princess Rosemarine is not willing to be a prize. She would rather go out and hunt the dragon herself. She dresses up as a man, meets on the way a spoiled prince who is looking for someone to kill the dragon for him, and then meets and befriends a nature-loving prince. Princess Rosemarine, disguised as a man, and the natureloving prince go to kill the dragon: "and so, hand in hand, Princess Rosemarine and Prince Mayoran went out to scatter sweets and ambush the dragon" (Hareven 1986: 47). The cruel dragon turns out to be a nice dragon who is tired of burning fields and people. He hopes that they will be able to tame him, but he does not believe it is possible, because a brave princess is needed for the taming of a dragon. Rosemarine removes her disguise and tames the dragon. Rosemarine and Mayoran return to the castle with the tamed dragon and get married. We have here a brave princess, a nature-loving prince and a friendly dragon, differing from most earlier fairy tales. Still, this new legend ends with the marriage of the princess (to the prince, of course). It seems that some things do not change, even in "new" fairy tales.

Another book of this type is *Nesicha al Sus: Sipurim* (A Princess on a Horse: Fairy Tales),[38] edited by Miri Baruch and published in 1994. The stories collected in this book tell of clever and brave princesses, and kings and princes who love them because they are such. The book includes stories by Eli Rave, Geula Almog, Miri Baruch, Miriam Yalan-Shtekelis and Yael Fishbein. Imitation of the fairy tale as a way of delivering a modern message in children's books can also be found in the stories included in the book *Al Tenashki et Hatzfardea* (Don't Kiss the Frog)[39] from 1998, which includes familiar fairy tales in a new and feminist adaptation and original creations by Israeli authors who imitate fairy tales for the same purpose.

In the story *Hanesicha Yechola Hakol Be'atzmi* ('I-can-do-it-by-myself' Princess) by Yona Tepper,[40] morals are designed in new ways, as the story begins in a realistic manner and takes place during playtime. The various customary morphological roles in fairy tale studies arise through the game. The child heroine can choose which person she wants to be. The modern princess is a princess who can be feminine and adorned and at the same time a great hunter (in her imagination). Her independence does not mar her femininity (Gabayan, 2007: 94-95).

Ami Gedalia's *Nesicha Mechaba Srefot* (The Fire Brigade Princess) from 2005,[41] is another attempt to break the conservative patterns and characteristics of children's fairy tale adaptations through role reversal. Here, again, is an independent and active young girl, and she is even chubby. However, ultimately this story reinforces stereotypization when even this brave young girl needs the help of a young man in order to fulfil her goals. The young man helps her to find the solution to her distress in a patronising and condescending tone, and although she decides that she does not want to get married at a young age, the authoritative figure of the "saviour" and "redeemer" is the young man who leads her to the desired solution.

The "politically correct" stories usually implement three "tricks." The first is the adding of a situation that does not exist in the folktale, through which the resourcefulness of the heroine is expressed. The second is the articulation of the feminist or other modern message clearly through the characters. The third is the design of the young girl or woman as an independent and active character. However, as stated, the role reversal itself in such stories creates stereotypization (Gabayan, 2007: 90-91).

Artistic Fairy Tales in Israel in the 21th Century: Innovations and Surprises

In recent years, original stories in the fairy tale style or original stories which contain fairy tale motifs, whilst presenting fresh combinations and challenging world perceptions, are being written in Israel. These do not accept the formal models and ideas of the classic fairy tales, nor those of their widespread adaptations for children. These creations are thought provoking, they challenge previous fairy tales and break patterns, not in a direct way or by way of reversal.

Ofra Gelbart-Avni's *Sod Hamechashefot* (The Witches' Secret) from 1981[42] is an example of the beginnings of this trend in Israel in the 1980s. This book relies on pre-existing knowledge of familiar fairy tales, such as Snow White, Little Red Riding Hood, and The Princess and the Frog. However, most of the books appearing in these early stages rely on the children's accumulated knowledge of the adaptations and not of the classic fairy tales which, as noted, were fully translated into Hebrew only in recent years.

An example of an original and challenging work, which creates a dialogue both with the adaptations and the classic fairy tales themselves, as well as with classic works from the Hebrew culture, is the book of two central Israeli authors, Shira Geffen and Etgar Keret— *Layla Bli Yare'ah* (A Moonless Night),[43] with illustrations by David Polonsky, one of the best known young illustrators in Israel and the world. These three young Israeli artists created together a story of extraordinary qualities and complex perceptions of the world. The story opens in sophistication with the sentence " והם חיו באושר ועושר עד עצם היום הזה " (and they lived happily ever after until this very day), which is the formulaic ending of fairy tales in Hebrew. It turns out that this is the last sentence that the father read to his daughter Zohar before bedtime. There is not enough space to include all the qualities and innovations of this book here, so I will focus only on the connections to the classic and adapted fairy tale.

The opening sentence, as it seems, already hints to a link with the fairy tale model, even if in reverse, and although immediately afterwards it is revealed that this is a realistic story, so to speak. The girl, Zohar, is in search of light, especially moonlight. She leaves home on a partially imaginary journey at night, a journey similar to that of many children—boys and girls—In fairy tales. On her way she encounters different characters, some indifferent and some threatening, much like the characters in fairy tales. The cat is apathetic to her search for light as he is focused on the basic need of food, whereas the policeman represents adult expectations of order and organisation, of defined forms, and thus is threatening to Zohar. Zohar leaves the city boundaries and takes an unpaved path to the woods, continuing into the unknown, like so many characters in fairy tales (the thick forest, dark castle and so on). In the forest she sees a bright and familiar light, familiar probably from countless fairy tales, such as Goldilocks and the Three Bears, Hansel and Gretel, Little Red Riding Hood, Snow White and many others. Wolves, known as threatening characters, stand and smile amicably at the side of the road. Thus is shattered one of the known fairy tales patterns: while the cat and policeman are indifferent or threatening, the wolves only observe benignly from the sidelines.

A black crooked-beak owl and ancient cypresses await Zohar in the forest, which is only a grove in the eyes of the adults in the story, but their warnings do not stop Zohar's journey. Notice, that Zohar ventures on the journey out of her own free will, in order to 'find herself' and set her own path, after she has received from the adults what they could give her. This stands in contrast to the miserable wanderers in fairy tales, usually cast from their homes, sent with specific orders or lost. Significantly, Zohar is a girl, and nevertheless she bravely chooses to go forward. Farther along the path, she reaches a cabin, knocks three times on the door, and waits. This act is also familiar from fairy tales: the child who knocks on the doors of a world that seems to him as thick as a forest, unsure of what to expect when he ventures through those doors into the world .What is beyond those doors: a witch?

A knight in shining armour? A dragon? Dwarves? A wolf? But in "A Moonless Night" the door opens slightly to reveal a scared looking bald head. Not a prince, not a threatening character, but a frightened bald adult who abruptly shuts the door in her face. Zohar does not give up. She climbs a ladder to the window. The main character—a young girl—is not frightened and compliant, but rather tries and dares. David Polonsky crowned her head from the beginning with the moonlight, foreshadowing the fact that she will find the light she searches for within herself, rather than in a prince or a fairy who will rescue her. But, in this stage of the story, when she judges and reprimands the bald man for stealing the moon, she darkens entirely: she has momentarily lost her childhood innocence, the shine (*Zohar* in Hebrew) which encompassed her in name and nature. When the old man admits his weakness in a shaky voice and eyes shining with tears, explaining that he wanted to play with the moon because he felt lonely, she once again accepts the other, and Polonsky restores her moonlight from within. Unlike the children in the literature of the 1970's in Israel, Zohar is not self-centred. She understands that the moonlight is essential for the ships at sea, for howling jackals, and indeed for her, because without the moonlight, it is difficult for her to sleep... And ever since, when she is sad on dark moonless nights, she remembers that out there, in the middle of the forest, there is one happy man.

Not "and they lived happily ever after" (which is left behind at the beginning of the story), but rather a girl who has undergone a process of maturation, who consolidated her own identity and overcame obstacles by herself. A girl who matured into an independent, strong individual, who uses her strength to help and contain both herself and others, with their weaknesses and desires, and is happy to be all that. With no need for a fairy or a prince, of course.

It is worth mentioning that this book also "corresponds" with the classical book by Fania Bergstein, *VaYehi Erev* (And There Was Evening)[44] which was published in Israel in 1949, and is based on one of Andersen's fairy tales (The fairy tale 'The Second Evening" from a series of fairy tales called "What the Moon Saw"). And here we see a full circle of stories which reflect different writing styles and changing world views in the natural dynamic of culture, both World and Hebrew.

Shira Geffen and Etgar Keret's book also portrays the new wave of stories in Israel, which relate in one way or another to fairy tales. Another book of this nature is Nurit Zarchi's, *Amory Asig Atusa*[45] (Amory Catches Up and Fly), as well as many other works of this notable author. In this book appear a small witch, white horses and a carriage. But these are combined in the story with a school and a final exam, with cockroaches, and with other motifs from the real world of today's readers. Amory Asig Atusa, the little witch, is unable to pass the principal's test. The model she is supposed to force herself to fit in, is capitalist and masculine in essence: she must create something strong, something fast, something buyable, something sellable. She, on the other hand, is only able to create feminine-romantic models. Therefore the principal slams the door to the "world" in her face. She now goes through a complex process where she learns to accept herself and not shy away from who she is, as the principal did in his response to her failure to meet his expectations. At the end of the process, she creates her own independent model, not significantly masculine or feminine, but rather "something wonderful, something exciting, something gallopfull, something loveable"—and this independent take-off is what allows her to fly into the world on her own, to drive the carriage of her life without the need for a prince to carry her or a fairy to help her.

In this regard, one must also mention the book *Leshachrer Et Hafeyot* (Freeing the Fairies), by Yehudit Katzir,[46] a respected adult author in Israel. It tells the story of Noa, a girl who loves fairies more than anything. A circus comes to town, and she goes to see the fairies perform. Rumpus, the Circus manager, is a tall, portly man with a long moustache. Under his lion-tamer-like moustache a gold tooth sparkles. He wears a top hat and holds a whip that looks like a giant black snake. He waves his whip and hits the sand and the fairies appear in the ring. These are real fairies, at whom Rumpus shouts orders as he swings his whip. The fairies fulfil wishes made by the children who have come to the circus, but Noa notices that they are sad. At the end of the show Noa approaches a covered cage and sees the fairies huddled together in the corner of the cage, covering their faces with their small hands. They tell her that Rumpus imprisoned them and forces them to perform at his circus so he can earn a lot of money. The children reading the story realise at this stage that we are dealing with poor fairies and a cruel man. The adults reading the story understand that the book is hinting to the trafficking of women by using motifs from fairy tales. The fairies tell Noa that Rumpus captured them with a butterfly net while they were sleeping in the forest, and he hides their wings so that they cannot escape, returning them only for the performance (as a parallel to taking an ID card or passports). Noa decides to help them, but unlike in fairy tales and other children's stories, she does not rescue them. Instead, she has faith in their own power. The fairies explain that life in captivity weakens them, and what little power they have must be used for performances, rather than escape, because they are threatened by Rumpus. Noa doesn't tell the fairies how to save themselves in ways she already knows. On the contrary, she wants to know how fairies empower themselves—how they hold hands, so that she and her friends can hold hands in the fairies' way and thus help them free themselves. And so it was. Noa empowers the weak and enslaved fairies by having faith in their powers –the fairies feel that the children are holding their hands in the secret method, and that they believe in their powers, and their hearts strengthen. The Fairies are able to break free from their prison using their own resourcefulness. Rumpus is too engrossed in eating his dinner, a fatty steak with chips and a bottle of wine, to notice the escape. It is now clear to the readers, from the illustrations as well, that his gold tooth indicates that he is a meat hunter. Once the fairies retrieve their wings, his teeth fall out one by one, his gold tooth last of all, and he does not know how to eat his steak. The fairies fly into the night sky and their laughter resounds above the city, as clear as bells, and Noa knows that the fairies also made her wish come true—to be a fairy for one night.

There is no doubt that this book is bolder than most in the hidden meanings it presents in a "fairy" tale. It presents critical and complex commentary on the adult world, on weakened groups in society, on abused women and on human (women) trafficking.

Here too, as in *A Moonless Night* and *Amory Catches Up and Fly*, the focus is on one little girl. Noa is able to empower fairies to escape their prisons, just as Zohar in *A Moonless Night* can shine her light and the light of the moon on others, and just as Amory is able to fly out into the world on her own. The three girls succeed on their own strength, not through miracles, but rather through a long and complex self-focused process. They are not intimidated by obstacles, not even by a world that presents them with typical masculine models.

Agada (A Fairy Tale), a book by the well-known Israeli author, Alona Frankel[47] published in 1985, is another attempt to write new and pattern-shattering Israeli fairy tale. The book opens with the words: "Once upon a time in a far away land there was an eternal forest." Fairies of different colours live in the forest, each one in a flower of a different colour and each one falls in love with a prince in her colour. Only the fairy queen of the black flower does not find love, as there is only one black flower. Luckily, her butterfly friends decide to help her and fly in search of a black prince. They find one which has just come out of the thick of the ground, after hundreds of years of trying to do so. He reaches the joyous fairy queen, but it begins to rain, and it turns out that the prince is not actually black. The rain washes him and reveals golden curls, blue eyes, and a white body. However, the queen announces that with the power of love, even ancient customs can be changed, and they get married and all are happy. The ending of the book proves that you can marry a prince of a different colour. However, possibly because this book was published nearly thirty years ago, it is ground-breaking insofar as the princess does not need to marry a prince of her own colour in order to be happy, but she is still expected to marry in order to be happy. The books discussed above break this convention as well, perhaps because they were published in later years. In that, they reflect the process the Israeli society has gone through, at least in terms of subversive worldviews.

These works and others stand out in their literary qualities. They present different models of writing, viewpoints and characters from those seen in fairy tales thus far, both classical and adaptations, yet relate to them in different contexts. They do not display a direct reversal of existing patterns and do not create opposing models, not even parodies, but rather break familiar patterns whatever they are, and create new models of writing and of thinking.

Imagination and Fantasy Books with Fairy Tale Characteristics in Twenty-First Century Israel

Fairy tales offer a platform not only to stories in fairy tale models or stories with fairy tale motifs and characteristics, but also to different types of fantasy Literature. The features which distinguish between myths, legends and fairy tales as folk stories, and different types of fantasy stories, are not always clear-cut qualities. In this section, we will focus on trends in fantasy books written in Israel in recent years which combine characteristics of the fairy tale genres in different ways.

Books in Which the Story Takes Place Entirely in the Fairy Tale and Fantasy World

Roni Ganor's Igniting Yuli[48] integrates models and characteristics from the fantasy genre, changing a dragon from a threatening figure to a friendly one. The book tells the story of a dragon who really wants to eat grapes, but it is winter time, and grapes can only be found in the garden of a cruel witch. He goes out on a journey to reach her and on his way is helped by good friends, including a fairy, a king, an Indian, and a talking duck. He has to fight the witch, who takes away his fire and makes him shrink, but eventually he overcomes her, eats grapes, and even falls in love with a beautiful (female) dragon.

A important author for children and teenagers in Israel, who has written both poetry and fiction, including fantastical literature, is Shlomit Cohen-Asif. For example, her book *Whistle of the Bargools*,[49] where we can find a hunter, a king, a prince, a gardner and a wizard. Her book *The Palace of a Thousand Doors*[50] consists of two parts; the first is called "The Prince of Figs," which tells 'once upon a time' stories about the thousand-door palace in the kingdom of Martilya. In the story there are an evil sorcerer, a little prince, a king, a queen, a good fairy, a forest, a palace, a grandmother and her granddaughter, a cat, flies, a dream adviser, a princess with a spectacular pearl necklace, a lion and birds, a smoking mountain, and a singer-flautist. The second part, "The Monster and the Cage," tells stories about the far away village of Tokada, a village with many miracles, trees, tunnels, witches, and monsters.

Ronen Leshem's *Gorgonzol the Terrible*[51] targets teenagers and takes place entirely in the fantasy world. Thirteen-year-old Arian is the prince of the new kingdom of Sofronia, a kingdom of brave and tough warriors always ready to meet the cruel dragons who had destroyed the old kingdom and forced the Sofronians to migrate to a new area. Arian is not as tough as a Sofronian prince ought to be; he is terrible at fighting and sports, and the children make fun of him. When he sits alone in the palace basement, he discovers a cupboard filled with books, and learns to read and write—skills which the Sofronians had abandoned. When his parents get angry at him, and the pretty girl that he is in love with belittles him, he decides to run away to the most dangerous place in the kingdom: the valley where the terrible dragon, Gorgonzol, is imprisoned. He discovers that Gorgonzol is not a terrible dragon but rather a big friendly turtle, who was imprisoned there for political reasons. Arian befriends the giant turtle, with the help of the pretty and brave girl he is in love with, and together they show the king and the Sofroninans that there is no reason to be afraid. The story suggests that sometimes it is worth getting to know the enemy in order to understand that they are not so terrible, and that there are different types of bravery.

Nava Macmel-Atir, one of the main Israeli writers for teenagers and children, wrote a fantasy for children, called *A Spot for Thought*.[52] In a tiny, picturesque kingdom live cultured and sporty citizens, with beloved king and queen who live in a transparent palace. A daughter is born to the king and queen, but alas: the new princess does not have a beauty mark above her upper lip like the rest of the royal women. How will the princess be a queen without a beauty mark? Different attempts are made in order to grant her a beauty mark, and each day the royal painter arrives and draws a beauty mark at the correct spot in order to hide the shame. When one day the princess leaves the house without the drawn-on beauty mark, the citizens of the kingdom are shocked. Her classmates explain that she cannot be a queen like this, even if she is good, tall, and fair. But who said she wants to be queen? Maybe she'd rather be something else? The book is surprising and amusing: a story about an out-of-the-ordinary princess who shows that there are more important things than outer beauty for a queen, and that there are also more important things for women than being a queen.

Dorit Orgad, one of the most fruitful and central authors for teens and children in Israel, published five short stories for children in the book *The Trial of King Robosta*.[53] In the story about King Robosta, there is a witch named Rodinia, a princess, an old lady, a simple girl who loves nature, and other colourful characters. Orgad also published the book *Watermelons out of season*,[54] in which King Tiran is evil but his wife, Queen Bonita, is kindhearted. She gives birth to identical twin girls, evil Tini and kind-hearted Bini. Tini always mistreats Bini, and poor Bini does not take revenge because she is too kind-hearted. Tini begins to abuse Bini's favourite gardener. She decides to have him executed since he does not grow watermelons as she has demanded, and because he told her about certain mushrooms which cause blindness, but she tried them on him and he failed to become blind. Tini does not know it takes time for the mushrooms to work, and in the end not only does the gardener become blind because of her, but Tini herself and her father the king become blind from eating the mushrooms. Bini finds out that the gardener is going to be executed, and this time she decides to do something. She tries, without success, to speak with her father and sister, and then disguises herself as Tini and releases the gardener from the prison. She cures his blindness using a healing plant, which her sister tries to steal from her, but does not use it correctly and thus dies. After Tini's death and his own blindness, the king rules through the eyes and words of Bini and the queen, and their kind-heartedness influences him to become good.

In the end he can see again, continues to be kind, appoints Bini as the heiress to the thrown and appoints the gardener as the Minister of Gardeners.

Books which have a Realistic World, a Fantasy World, and a Passage Between the Two

Hagar Yanai's *The Whale of Babylon*[55] is the first volume of a trilogy of Israeli fantasy books. The plot begins in Israel and even on a specific date, the first of July, but the year is not mentioned. The protagonists are drawn into another world, the Kingdom of Babel, which is based on elements from mythology. They discover that there is a connection between our world and the kingdom of Babel, and that their parents are also tied to both worlds.

In the series *Winter Blue, Fairy-Child*,[56] Winter Blue is a fairy girl. This means that most of the time she leads a normal life, but occasionally, at night, she is called to a land of magic, where she helps the fairies, the dwarves and other animals in different matters. Her parents were also fairy children in their youth. Winter Blue is independent, brave, clever, adventurous and opinionated, and is the natural leader of her group (which includes boys). The fairies and other creatures in the series are kind creatures, and the world is magical.

The uniqueness of *The Journey to the Kingdom of Oridor: A Fantasy Story* by Michal Aharoni Regev[57] lies in the author's choice of Israeli heroes with Israeli names and the setting in the state of Israel—a rare thing in Israeli fantasy books. However, other than this, the world that she creates is not related to Israel's history. There is a mention of famous places such as the Sambation River or of famous occurrences such as the Maccabean rebellion, but the kingdoms created by the author are not related to real previous kingdoms.

Liat Rotner is a popular author for young adults in Israel, who began publishing at a young age. Her book *Maladar—The Magical Amulet*[58] is a young adult's fantasy, one of the rare fantasy books in Hebrew which partially takes place in Israel. The boarding school described in it is located in a small town in the south of Israel, which suffers from rocket bombardments. In one of these bombardments, the hero and his friends are forced to run away and they find themselves in another dimension, a magical world with strange and intelligent animals, mysterious dwarves, and creatures similar to humans. The latter need them to help win a war against the enemy, which wants to take over not only this other dimension but also the human world. At a certain stage it is revealed that there is a connection between the enemy in the other dimension, and the one in Israel—a dangerous terrorist organisation. The children will have to unite and try to save the world.

Etty Appel published two fantasy books for teenagers. In her book *Different Worlds*[59] an explosion in a mine results in the deaths of most of the miners. A young man and young woman follow the explosion into the "secret world," a world dominated by the green Emerald (Izmargad) queen, a cruel queen who controls her subjects through fear. She is able to read minds and control the souls of humans and other creatures. The noble bear tribe and the dwarves' tribes aren't able to stop her. She dreams of destroying the humans in the upper world, claiming that they take over resources which belong to her. She is dedicated mainly to create the notion of a hidden world ruled by fear and domination of thoughts. In Appel's other book, *The Blue Pearl*,[60] eleven-year-old May runs away to the depths of the woods, where she finds a pearl, a dwarf, and a mysterious girl. May discovers that she has been chosen for unclear reasons to be the bearer of the pearl. She must return the pearl to where it belongs in the lost city, in the world of the dwarf and the mysterious girl. The world that May enters is controlled by a powerful wizard. May has many adventures on her journey with the pearl, discovers that the wizard in power is not necessarily bad, and changes from a spoilt girl to a brave and independent young woman.

Books which Take Place in the Real World and Combine Motifs from the World of Fantasy and Fairy Tales

Eshkar Erblich-Brifman, author of the series *Winter Blue, Fairy-Child*, also wrote *The Darklings*,[61] about a completely normal nine-year-old boy and a normal family, but also a creature named *Darkling*, who resembles a fairy on the one hand, and on the other a sprite and a troll.

The story *Who is the Fairy Queen, or: Do Fairies Have a Queen?* by Aliza Rozen[62] is a short story for children. The narrator describes a normal, average girl who does not excel in anything. One day the girl creates the image of a perfect doll, which is everything that she herself wants to be or to have: very beautiful with long, wavy blond hair, blue eyes and pink skin, and wings. The moment she finishes, a beautiful fairy flies out of her hands. The girl does this every day, and each one of the fairies is as beautiful as the child wishes to be, as clever as she wanted to be, each sings, dances and is kind and delicate. Since then, this girl has been the fairy queen: she creates the fairies, and they come to her when they need to be repaired.

In *Enchanted Mother and the Violet Hat Wizards* by Eti Alboim,[63] the whole plot takes place in Israel. Naama Erez is a married 42-year-old reporter and a mother of three. One day she smells strange flowers and becomes a twelve-year-old girl. Naama discovers that a magical world of wizards exists, and that they turn adults into children every now and then in order to strengthen the bond between parents and their children.

Books which Take Place in the Fantasy World, which Integrate Motifs from the Real World

A well-known children's author in Israel, Ofra Gelbert-Avni, wrote the Series *Troublesome Witch* and *A Witch in Love*.[64] In the first book young Fadicha is a witch from the land of witches. She decides to buy a computer. Following this, the witches' world is caught in a vortex. Fadicha has to talk with Zonda, the leader, and together they cancel the spell. Zonda understands that progress cannot be stopped and promises to allow the witches to use the computer, and Fadicha understands that young people do not know everything and that sometimes changes need to be made gradually. They conclude that computers are good only if they are used correctly, and that everyone needs to be educated so that they know how to use them properly.

In her second book *A Witch in Love*, Fadicha falls in love with a human boy, an unforgivable crime in the eyes of witches who believe that their purpose in life is to abuse humans. The ruling witch tells her: "If we start to like humans, who shall we hate? And if we don't have anyone to hate, what shall we do? What will we have to live for? [...] This hatred gives us power! It unites us!" (pages 45-46). Fadicha does not despair. To her, the boy is one of a kind (page 73). Fadicha gets caught up in adventures and, among other things, turns the boy she loves into a cat and risks being put to death.

Avi Segal wrote a fictional and humorous book, *Human Ghost in Goalbuck*.[65] The book's plot takes place on a star ruled by a cruel king. The ruler's son is actually a kind young man, and he befriends a stray girl whose parents disappeared by order of the ruler. When two "aliens" from earth reach the planet, the boy and girl try to hide them from the ruler, while also trying to save the victims of his rule. Aside from the "nonsense" touch of this book, which includes a lot of humour, the characters are likeable and the ending is surprisingly feministic.

Marit Benisrael's *Daughters of the Dragon*[66] is a fantasy for teens and adults. Next to an ancient city in a far off time, there is a cruel dragon, who demands a new girl between the ages of eight and eleven each year in order to enslave and then eat them. Marta, a ten-yearold girl who lives with a violent father and a wicked stepmother, tries to learn to spit fire and accidentally ruins her father's life's work. In response, he offers her as a sacrifice for the dragon. Marta spends a year in the company of the cruel dragon, but does not give up. After she overpowers the dragon, a girl who is supposed to be his new victim joins her, as well as a girl from Israel who reaches this place through a mysterious book. Marta does not tell the people of the town that she has beaten the dragon, but remains in his place and dreams of building a safe community of refuge for girls.

Works by Uri Orlev, Ahead of Their Time (1979, 1981, 1984)

We end this sample list of writers and literary works with Uri Orlev, the prize-winning children and young adult's author (the only Israeli Hebrew author to win the international Andersen award for children and teen literature). Orlev also wrote books on the basis of the fairy tale and the fantastical, in addition to most of his realistic books (some of which are books on the Holocaust). One of those books is *The Dragon's Crown*,[67] which takes place entirely in a different world. In an imaginary land in that different world there is a kingdom which has only good people. They only do good deeds and do not know what war or swearing is. They do not hit and they do not eat animals. They must smile by law, and anyone who does not behave well enough must go through re-education in the House of Good Measures. In the same country lives a cruel prince from a different country. He lives in a palace he is not allowed to leave, as part of his agreement with the kingdom. He enjoys hitting, abusing, killing and eating animals and he dreams of taking over the kingdom. Meanwhile, the daughter of the kind-hearted king is kidnapped by bad people from another, evil land where everyone is dangerous and violent. In order to save her, some officials from the good kingdom must go on a dangerous journey, encountering dragons and bad people. But how will they survive such a journey when they do not know how to fight and hunt animals? The evil prince offers to help them, as he has his own motives for the success of this journey. Meanwhile, it turns out that the kind-hearted princess has a good influence on the people of the evil kingdom, and that the evil prince has a bad (or good?) influence on the minister and teacher who have gone on the journey with him. It is one of the darker and more complex fantasy books written in Israel. It brings up hard questions about good and bad, moral issues of eating animals, wars, and more. Not only are the ideas complex, the plot itself is complex and not easy to understand.

Orlev's *It's hard to be a Lion*[68] was written for children and young adults. The world in this book is a realistic world, combined with elements of fantasy. The narrator has always dreamed of being a lion. He is a single man who lives with his mother and their dog, a dog which was once a wizard and is still able to talk and perform some magic. The dog suddenly decides to make the narrator's dream come true, and turns him into a lion without giving him prior notice. The narrator now needs to survive like a lion, and it seems that it is hard to be a lion. After many adventures the narrator is found by a lion researcher, turns back into a human being, and marries the researcher. His mother is delighted: he is now married and she will have grandchildren. The book does not have the regular characteristics of fantasy books, such as a magical world or a fight between good and evil. Rather, it is a detailed description of the difficulties of a man who becomes a lion.

In another book, *Granny Knits*,[69] the relationships between imagination and reality are complex. The beginning of the book is in the real, but the conflict begins when reality clashes with fantasy. Orlev tells the story of a knitting grandmother who arrives to a small town. She knits herself a carpet, a house, furniture and dishes, and then knits two grandchildren. The grandmother takes the knitted grandchildren to school, but the school is not willing to accept the knitted children. She protests actively this exclusion in many ways, but everyone rejects her grandchildren made of strings. In the meanwhile many tourists come to the town in order to see this wonder, but the grandmother unravels everything that she has knitted, including her grandchildren. She leaves the city and migrates to a different city where she will knit everything all over again, including her grandchildren, hoping they will be accepted. The book describes the grandmother in a subversive manner, the idea of knitted children being unravelled is unsettling, and through the text Orlev is evidently pointing, among other things, to the story of Jews in the Holocaust.

As is evident, in the last twenty years in Israel there has been a trend of full translations of the classic fairy tales to Hebrew. These are translated directly from the language of origin, and thus they revive the classic fairy tales alongside their widespread adaptations. In addition, there is a rise in the writing of artistic fairy tales in Hebrew by prominent authors and artists. Among these are the "Politically Correct" and other innovative fairy tales, which break literature models and thinking patterns. Fantasy books in Hebrew have also been published in Israel with the expansion of the fairy tale genre, as they are based, among other things, on the characteristics and patterns of fairy tales. All these appear in last years in a variety of books: books which take place in the fairy tale and fantasy world; books which take place in a realistic world and create passageways between the real word and the fantastic world; books which take place in a realistic world but combine motifs from the world of fantasy and fairy tales; and books which take place in the fantasy world, but integrate realistic motifs.

Notes

1   יסיף, עלי, 1994. סיפור העם העברי. תולדותיו, סוגיו ומשמעותו. ירושלים: מוסד ביאליק והוצאת הספרים של אוניברסיטת בן גוריון בנגב.

2   שביט, זהר, 1996. מעשה ילדות. מבוא לפואטיקה של ספרות ילדים. תל-אביב: האוניברסיטה הפתוחה, מהדורת עם עובד.

3   שטרן, דינה, 1986. אלמות בעולם קסום: מחקר באופיה האלים של המעשייה הנשית לילדים. רמת גן: אוניברסיטת בר-אילן.

4   נוי, דב, 1994. "מבוא: מסה על אסופת המעשיות של האחים גרים." בתוך: האחים גרים. מעשיות: האוסף המלא. עמ' א-טז. תל-אביב: ספרית פועלים.

5   אופק, אוריאל, 1983. תנו להם ספרים: פרקי ספרות ילדים. תל-אביב: ספרית פועלים, הוצאת הקיבוץ הארצי השומר הצעיר.

6   Translator's Note: The *Tannaim* were the Rabbinic sages whose views are recorded in the Mishnah, from approximately 10-220 CE.

7   Translator's Note: *Amoras* means "those who say/those who speak over the people," viz., scholars who repeat and expand on the oral law, teaching gathered in the Gemara.

8   סמיט, שהם, 2011. "על האגדות שלנו." בתוך: האגדות שלנו: אוצר האגדה העברית לילדים. אור יהודה: דביר, עמ' 8-10

9   סמיט, שהם, 2010. האגדות שלנו: אוצר האגדה העברית לילדים. ולי מינצי (איור). אור יהודה: דביר.
Smit, Shoham, 2011. *A Treasury of Hebrew Legends for Children.* Or Yehuda: Kinneret, Zmora-Bitan, Dvir—Publishing House Ltd (in Hebrew).

10 אורבך, אורי, 2010. חכמינו לימינו. ירושלים: ספרי מגיד. הוצאת קורן.
Orbach Uri, 2010. *Once Upon a Time in Jerusalem.* Jerusalem: Maggid (in Hebrew).

11 אורבך, אורי, 2010. מה מברכים על גלידה. יערה בוכמן (איור). תל אביב: אחוזת בית
Orbach, Uri, 2010. *What Blessing do We Make on Ice Cream? : Jewish Con-*

cepts for Children and for Parents. Illustrated by Yaara Buchman. Tel-Aviv: Achuzat Bayit Books (in Hebrew).

12 .שלו, מאיר, 1994. מבול, נחש ושתי תבות. סיפורי תנ"ך לילדים. עמנואל לוצאטי (איור). ירושלים: כתר.
Shalev, Meir, 1994. *A Snake, a Flood and Two Arks.* Illustrated by Emanuel Luzzati. Jerusalem: Keter (in Hebrew).

13 זהר, רקפת, 2011. אברהם המאמין הראשון. גרישה בלוגר (איור). תל-אביב: דניאלה די-נור.
Zohar, Rakefet, 2011. *Tales of the Bible: The Patriarch Abraham—The First Believer.* Illustrated by Grisha Bloger. Tel-Aviv: Daniella De-Nur publisher Ltd (in Hebrew).

זהר, רקפת, 2011. אמהות ואבות. תמר מסר (איור). תל-אביב: דניאלה די-נור.
Zohar, Rakefet, 2011. *Tales of the bible: Mothers and Fathers.* Illustrated by Tamar Messer. Tel-Aviv: Daniella De-Nur publisher Ltd (in Hebrew).

זהר, רקפת, 2011. בראשית. אלסנדרו סאנה (איור). תל-אביב: דניאלה די-נור.
Zohar, Rakefet, 2011. *Tales of the bible: Genesis.* Illustrated by Allesandro Sanna. Tel-Aviv: Daniella De-Nur publisher Ltd (in Hebrew).

14 אבס, שלמה, 2011. חיים ומוות ביד הלשון—הסיפורים החכמים של השפה העברית. דני קרמן (איור). הוד השרון: עגור.
Abas, Shlomo, 2011. *Life and Death in the Power of One's Tongue.* Illustrated by Dany Kerman. Hod Hasharon: Agur publishing house (in Hebrew).

15 אבס, שלמה, 2004. תעלולי ג'וחא. דני קרמן (איור). הוד השרון: עגור.
Abas, Shlomo, 2004. *Juha. 40 Tales.* Illustrated by Dany Kerman. Hod Hasharon: Agur publishing house (in Hebrew).

16 טבק, סימס, 2001. המעיל המופלא של יוסף. אור יהודה: כנרת.
Simms Taback, 1999. *Josef had a Little Overcoat.* New York: Viking Press.

17 לוי, ינץ, 2010. ספורי איש היער. ליאורה גרוסמן (איור) אור יהודה: זמורה ביתן.
Levi Yannets, 2010. *Tales of the Forest Man.* Or Yehuda: Kinneret, Zmora-Bitan, Dvir—Publishing House Ltd (in Hebrew).

18 Published by Sifriat Poalim and by Machbarot Lesifrut.

19 Published by Machbarot Lesifrut.

20 אגדות אנדרסן.

21 אנדרסן, ה.כ., 2008. ספר האגדות של אנדרסן. זילכה לפלר (איור). אור יהודה: כנרת זמורה ביתן, דביר.
Andersen, H.C. 2008. *Das Andersen Märchenbuch.* Illustrated by Silke Leffler. Or Yehuda: Kinneret, Zmora-Bitan, Dvir—Publishing House Ltd (in Hebrew).

22 גרים, האחים, 2011. זאב, נסיכה ושבעה גמדים. תריסר מעשיות קלסיות. עפרה עמית (איור).

Do Fairies Still Exist? Fairy-Tales in Hebrew Nowadays

.אור יהודה: כנרת, זמורה ביתן, דביר

Grimm, Wilhelm und Jakob, 2011. *Kinder- und Hausmärchen*. Illustrated by Ofra Amit. Or Yehuda: Kinneret, Zmora-Bitan, Dvir—Publishing House Ltd (in Hebrew).

23 למרש, ג'ים, 2008. הסנדלר והגמדים. אגדה מאת האחים גרים. אור יהודה: כנרת, זמורה-ביתן, דביר.

Lamarche, Jim, 2003. *The Elves and the Shoemaker*. San Francisco: Chronicle Books.

24 בטלהיים, ברונו, 1987. קסמן של אגדות ותרומתן להתפתחותו הנפשית של הילד. תל-אביב: רשפים.

25 שביט, זהר, 1996. מעשה ילדות. מבוא לפואטיקה של ספרות ילדים. תל-אביב: האוניברסיטה הפתוחה, מהדורת עם עובד.

26 ויסברוד, רחל, 2004. "סרטי 'דיסני' ומקורותיהם הספרותיים." בתוך: עולם קטן, כתב עת לחקר ספרות ילדים ונוער 2, עמ' 39-55. בית ברל: מרכז ימימה לספרות ילדים ונוער; אור יהודה: כנרת, זמורה-ביתן, דביר.

Weissbrod, Rachel, 2004. "Disney Films and their Literary Source" in *Small World* (Olam Katan) 2, Pp 39-55 (in Hebrew).

27 לבנת, חנה, 2004. "אופיה האמיתי של לכלוכית: מגמות במעבר ממעשיות בנוסחי פרו וגרים לעיבודים המודרניים לילדים." בתוך: עולם קטן, כתב עת לחקר ספרות ילדים ונוער 2, עמ' 79-56. בית ברל: מרכז ימימה לספרות ילדים ונוער; כנרת, זמורה-ביתן, דביר.

Livnat, Hanna, 2004. "The Real Nature of Cinderella: The Aims in the Transition of Fairy Tales from Perrault and Grimm Terms to Modern Editions for Children" in *Small World* (Olam Katan) 2, Pp 56-79 (in Hebrew).

28 לבנת, חנה, 1985. תרגום מודלים ספרותיים מספרות מבוגרים לספרות ילדים. עבודת גמר לתואר מוסמך, תל-אביב: אוניברסיטת תל-אביב; שביט, 1996: 339-364.

Livnat, Hanna, 1985. *Translating Literary Models from Adult Literature to Children's Literature* (in Hebrew); Shavit, 1996: 339-364 (in Hebrew).

29 As described in Livnat, "The Real Nature of Cinderella: The Aims in the Transition of Fairy Tales from Perrault and Grimm Terms to Modern Editions for Children" in *Small World* (Olam Katan) 2, 2004 (in Hebrew).

30 גרים, האחים, 1993. הענק והחיט ועוד 33 אגדות אחרות. יעל ליאור (איור). ישראל: מחברות לספרות, זמורה.

Grimm, Wilhelm Und Jakob, 1993. *Kinder- und Hausmärchen*. Israel: Machbarot Lesifrut, Zmora Ltd (in Hebrew).

31 See also Bettelheim 1987; Weissbrod 2004 (in Hebrew); Livnat 2004 (in Hebrew).

32 י. ישפה, גזית, אסנת, 2010. האגדה על פרח לב הזהב. אור יהודה: זמורה ביתן.
Yoshpe Gazit, Osnat, 2010. *The Golden Heart Flower*. Or Yehuda: Kinneret, Zmora-Bitan, Dvir—Publishing House Ltd.(in Hebrew).

33 ישפה, אסנת, 1997. האגדה על השיח הקטן. תל-אביב: זמורה-ביתן.
Yoshpe, Anita Osnat, 1997. *The Tale of the Little Bush*. Tel-Aviv: Zmora-Bitan, Publishers (in Hebrew).

34 ריטה, 2010. הלב של שירז. ולי מינצי (איור). אור-יהודה: כנרת זמורה-ביתן.
Yahan-Fouruz, Rita. *Shiraz's Wise Heart*. Illustrated by Vali Mintzi. Or Yehuda: Kinneret, Zmora-Bitan, Dvir—Publishing House Ltd (in Hebrew).

35 גביאן, אסנת. 2007 "סיפור פוגש סיפור: על דיאלוגים בין ספרות ילדים מודרנית למעשיות עממיות" בתוך עולם קטן 3 (עמ' 107-83).
Gabayan, Osnat, 2007. In: *Small World* (Olam Ktan) 3, pp.83-107 (in Hebrew).

36 ברוך, מירי, 1994. "ספרות ילדים פמיניסטית." בתוך: ספרות ילדים ונוער כ', (ג-ד), עמ' 64-59.
Baruch, Miri, 1994. "Feminist children's literature" in: *Literature for Children and Teenagers*, 1994. 20 [3-4], Pp 59-64 (in Hebrew).

37 הראובן, גיל, 1986. אגדה חדשה. איציק רנרט (איור) תל-אביב: עם עובד.
Hareven, Gail, 1986. *New Legend*. Tel Aviv: Am Over Publishers Ltd (in Hebrew).

38 ברוך, מירי (עורכת), 1994. נסיכה על סוס: ספורים. אלונה פרנקל (איור). תל-אביב: עם עובד.
Baruch, Miri (editor), 1994. *A Princess on a Horse: Fairy Tales*. Tel Aviv: Am Oved Publishers Ltd (in Hebrew).

39 ברוך, מירי (עורכת), 1998. אל תנשקי את הצפרדע. מישל קישקה (איור). תל-אביב: ידיעות אחרונות וספרי חמד.
Baruch, Miri (editor), 1998. *Don't Kiss The Frog*. Tel Aviv: Yedioth Ahronoth Books and Chemed Books (in Hebrew).

40 טפר, יונה, 1996. הנסיכה יכולה הכול בעצמי. גיל-לי אלון קוריאל (איור). חמ"ד: ספרות עכשיו. גבעתיים: מסדה.
Tepper, Yona, 1996. "*I-can-do-it-by-myself*" Princess. Illustrated by Gil-ly Alon Curiel. Giva'ataim: Masada (in Hebrew).

41 גדליה, עמי, 2005. נסיכה מכבה שרפות. תמר נהיר-ינאי (איור). תל-אביב: הקיבוץ המאוחד.
Gedalia Ami, 2005. *The Fire Brigade Princess*. Israel: Hakibbutz Hameuchad (in Hebrew).

42 גלברט-אבני, עפרה, 1981. סוד המכשפות. מושיק לין (איור). תל-אביב: הקיבוץ המאוחד.
Gelbart-Avni, Ofra, 1981. *The Witches' Secret*. Illustrated by Moshik Lin. Tel Aviv: Hakibbutz Hameuchad Publishing House Ltd (in Hebrew).

43 .גפן, שירה; קרת, אתגר, 2005. לילה בלי ירח. דוד פולונסקי (איור). תל-אביב: עם עובד
Geffen Shira and Etgar Keret, 2005. *A Moonless Night*. Tel Aviv: Am Oved
(in H   ebrew).

44 .ברגשטין, פניה, 1949. ויהי ערב. חיים האוזמן (איור). תל-אביב: הקיבוץ המאוחד
Bergstein, Fania, 1949. And There Was Evening. Illustrated by Haim Haus-
mann. Tel Aviv: Hakibbutz Hameuchad Publishing House Ltd (in
Hebrew).

45 .זרחי, נורית, 1992. אמורי אשיג אטוסה. הלה חבקין (איור). תל-אביב: ספרית פועלים
Zarchi, Nurit, 1992. *Amory Catches Up and Fly*. Tel-Aviv: Sifriat Poalim
Publishing House (in Hebrew).

46 קציר, יהודית, 2006. לשחרר את הפיות. טלי מנשס (איור). בני-ברק: ספרית פועלים–הקיבוץ
המאוחד.
Kazir, Yehudit, 2006. *Freeing the Fairies*. Illustrated by Tali Menashes. Sifriat Poalim—Hakibbutz Hameuchad Ltd (in Hebrew).

47 .פרנקל, אלונה, 1985. אגדה. תל-אביב: זמורה, ביתן
Frankel, Alona, 1985. *A Fairy Tale*. Tel Aviv: Zmora-Bitan (in Hebrew).

48 .גנור, רוני, 1999. להדליק את יולי. נתן הלפרן (איור). תל אביב: הקיבוץ המאוחד
Ganor, Roni. 1999. *Igniting Yuli*. Illustrated by Nathn Halpern. Tel Aviv:
Hakibbutz Hameuchad Publishing House Ltd (in Hebrew).

49 .כהן-אסיף, שלומית, 2009. שריקת הברגולים. נהיר-ינאי תמר. תל-אביב: ספרית פועלים
Cohen-Assif, Shlomit, 2009. *Whistle of the Bargools*. Illustrated by Tamar
Nahir-Yanai. Bnei-Brak: Sifriat Poalim—Hakibbutz Hameuchad Ltd (in
Hebrew).

50 כהן-אסיף, שלומית, 2003. ארמון אלף הדלתות. תמר צינמון (איור). בני-ברק: ספרית פועלים/
הקיבוץ המאוחד.
Cohen-Assif, Shlomit, 2003. *The Palace of a Thousand Doors*. Illustrared by
Tammy Zinamon. Bnei-Brak: Sifriat Poalim—Hakibbutz Hameuchad Ltd
(in Hebrew).

51 .לשם, רונן, 1999. גורגונזול האיום. נעם נדב (איור). תל-אביב: ספריית פועלים
Leshem, Ronen, 1999. *Gorgonzol the Terrible*. Illustrated by Noam Nadav.
Tel Aviv: Sifriat Poalim Publishing House Ltd (in Hebrew).

52 מקמל-עתיר, נאוה, 2011. נקודה למחשבה וסוד הארמון השקוף. הילית שפר (איור). תל-אביב:
ידיעות ספרים.
Macmel-Atir, Nava, 2011. *A Spot for Thought*. Illustrated by Hilit Shefer.
Tel-Aviv: Miskal—Yedioth Ahronoth Books and Chemed Books (in
Hebrew).

53 אורגד, דורית, 1995. משפטו של המלך רובוסטה. ליאורה גרוסמן (איור). אור-יהודה:

ספרית מעריב.

Orgad, Dorit, 1995. *The Trial of King Robosta*. Illustrated by Liora Gross-man. Or Yehuda: Sifriat Maariv (in Hebrew).

54 אורגד, דורית, 1990. אבטיחים שלא בעונה. מרגלית שלי (איור). תל-אביב: ספרית מעריב.

Orgad, Dorit, 1990. *Water-melons out of season*. Tel-Aviv: Maariv (in Hebrew).

55 ינאי, הגר, 2006. הלווייתן מבבל. ירושלים: כתר.

Yanai, Hagar, 2006. The whale of Babylon. Jerusalem: Keter (in Hebrew).

56 ארבליך-בריפמן, אשכר, 2005. וינטר בלו, ילדת-פיות. תל-אביב: ידיעות ספרים.

Erblich-Brifman, Eshkar, 2005. *Winter Blue, Fairy-Child*. Tel-Aviv: Miskal—Yedioth Ahronoth Books and Chemed Books (in Hebrew).

57 אהרוני רגב, מיכל, 2009. המסע אל ממלכת אורידור. וולף בולבה (איור). תל אביב: אריה ניר.

Aharoni Regev, Michal, 2009. *The Journey to the Kingdom of Oridor: A Fantasy Story*. Illustrated by Volf Bulba. Tel-Aviv: Aryeh Nir (in Hebrew).

58 רוטנר, ליאת, 2010. מאלאדר, קסם הקמע. תל-אביב: ידיעות ספרים.

Rotner, Liat, 2010. *Maladar—The Magical Amulet*. Tel-Aviv: Miskal—Yedioth Ahronoth Books and Chemed Books (in Hebrew).

59 אפל, אתי, 2007. שני עולמות. תל-אביב: ידיעות אחרונות.

Appel, Etty, 2007. *Different Worlds*. Tel-Aviv: Yedioth Ahronoth Books (in Hebrew).

60 אפל, אתי, 2010. הפנינה הכחולה. ישראל: הוצאת רימונים.

Appel, Etty, 2007. *The Blue Pearl*. Israel: Rimonim Publishing (in Hebrew).

61 ארבליך-בריפמן, אשכר, 2009. האפלוליות. גיל טרויצה (איור). תל-אביב: ידיעות ספרים.

Erblich-Brifman, Eshkar, 2009. *The Darklings*.Illustrations by Gil Troiza. Tel-Aviv: Miskal—Yedioth Ahronoth Books and Chemed Books (in Hebrew).

62 רוזן, עליזה, 2009. מי היא מלכת הפיות, או: האם לפיות יש·מלכה. ולי מינצי (איור). רעננה: אבן חושן.

Rozen, Aliza,2009. *Who is the Fairy Queen, or: Do Fairies Have a Queen?* Illustrated by Vali Mintzi. Ra'anana: Even Hoshen Publishers Ltd (in Hebrew).

63 אלבוים, אתי, 2011. אמא קסומה, וקוסמי המצנפת הקסומה. תל-אביב: ידיעות ספרים.

Elboim, Eti, 2011. *Enchanted Mother and the Violet Hat Wizards*. Tel-Aviv: Miskal—Yedioth Ahronoth Books and Chemed Books (in Hebrew).

64 גלברט-אבני, עפרה, 1996. מכשפה מקולקלת. מושיק לין (איור). תל-אביב: הקיבוץ המאוחד.

Gelbart-Avni, Ofra, 1996. *Troublesome Witch*. Illustrated by Moshik Lin.

Tel Aviv: Hakibbutz Hameuchad Publishing House Ltd (in Hebrew).

גלברט-אבני, עפרה, 1996. מכשפה מתאהבת. מושיק לין (איור) בני ברק: הקיבוץ המאוחד

Gelbart-Avni, Ofra. A Witch in Love. Illustrated by Moshik Lin. Bnei-Brak: Hakibbutz Hameuchad Publishing House Ltd (in Hebrew).

65 סגל, אבי, 2001. רוח אנושית בכוכב. גלעד סליקטר (איור). תל-אביב: ידיעות ספרים

Segal, Avi, 2001. *Human Ghost in Goalbuck*. Illustrated by Gilad Seliktar. Tel-Aviv: Yedioth Ahronoth Books (in Hebrew).

66 בן ישראל, מרית, 2007. בנות הדרקון. בני-ברק: הקיבוץ המאוחד.

Benisrael Marit, 2007. *Daughters of the Dragon*. Bnei-Brak: Hakibbutz Hameuchad Publishing House Ltd (in Hebrew).

67 אורלב, אורי. 1984. כתר הדרקון. אבנר כץ (איור). ירושלים: כתר.

Orlev, Uri, 1984. *The Dragon's Crown*. Illustrated by Avner Katz. Jerusalem: Keter (in Hebrew).

68 אורלב, אורי, 1979 . קשה להיות אריה. יוסי אבולעפיה (איור). תל-אביב: עם עובד

Orlev, Uri,1979. *It's Hard to be a Lion*. Illustrated by Yossi Abulafia. Tel Aviv: Am Oved (in Hebrew).

69 אורלב, אורי, 1981. סבתא סורגת. אורה איתן (איור). ראשון לציון: מסדה

Orlev, Uri, 1981. *Granny Knits*. Illustrated by Ora Eitan. Rishon LeZion: Massada (in Hebrew).

Chapter 6

Deciphering the Ottoman Fairy Tale: *Tayyarzade* Throughout the Centuries

Defne Çizakça

The original is unfaithful to the translation.
Jorge Luis Borges

It is perhaps unusual to study new fairy tales, when the term "fairy tale" brings to mind generally old things: well-worn stories, firesides, memories of grandmothers. Searching newness in history presents a similar reversal in logic. The researcher has to position herself in the presence of the past, and decipher what would have been considered fresh in a time gone by. The present essay tries to combine these two tasks by studying a new fairy tale from the Ottoman past. Clarifications of terminology and methodology are essential before venturing into this relatively unknown field. What are new fairy tales, and what is an Ottoman tale?

Claire Massey's *New Fairy Tales* (2008) was the first journal to feature and discuss new fairy stories exclusively. In her first editorial Massey noted: "We don't believe the fairy tale canon is complete or that we should only retell old stories. We believe that there are many new fairy tales out there waiting to be written, read and, loved".[1] The journal published six issues, each of them filled with previously untold stories that incorporated and played with elements from traditional fairy tales. John Patrick Pazdziora has built on Massey's work and defined new fairy tales as tales whose first telling could be situated in a particular time, and whose teller could be determined. Pazdziora's definition enables new fairy tales to acquire a historical scope; if its telling can be situated and its author identified, a new fairy tale may appear in any old century. The aim of this paper is to incorporate one such tale from sixteenth century Istanbul within the new fairy tale canon.

An Ottoman tale, on the other hand, is any tale created by an Ottoman citizen, and as such it can belong to a myriad of nationalities and may span a vast period of time. The Ottoman Empire lasted from 27 January 1299 to 29 October 1923 and was succeeded by the Turkish Republic, which is now heir to the Ottoman literary archives.

There are two ways to search for a new Ottoman fairy tale. The first requires the mastery of the Ottoman language, direct access to the maze of Ottoman archives scattered throughout contemporary Turkey, and the patience to decipher the baroque curves of Ottoman handwriting. The second method does not presuppose the above expertise but is no less complicated; it requires a search for the Ottoman new fairy tale from within Turkish sources. The present essay opts for this second route since its author lacks the required language skills and also because the aim of this investigation is twofold: to embark on a cultural *and* a literary study. The goal is not solely to discover a new Ottoman fairy tale but also to study its reception in modern Turkey; to chart the manners in which a contemporary culture (Turkish) understands its own literary past (Ottoman). Consequently this article delves into collective memory and also, inevitably, into collective forgetfulness.

The Difficulties in Searching for New Ottoman Fairy Tales

Searching for the new Ottoman fairy tale through the medium of the Turkish language is not a straightforward task. First, the language used in the Ottoman Empire was loosely termed the Ottoman language (*Lisân-ı Osmânî*). It was written in the Arabic alphabet, its content was largely Turkish with a strong influence from the grammar and vocabulary of Persian and Arabic primarily, and the local languages of the empire secondarily. The Ottoman language went throughout many transformations within the 600 years of the Empire. These periods can broadly be marked as the Old Ottoman Turkish (from the thirteenth till the sixteenth century), the Middle Ottoman Turkish (from the sixteenth till the nineteenth century) and lastly, the New Ottoman Turkish (from the nineteenth till the end of the empire in 1923). One must note that many languages apart from Ottoman were used in the empire as well; there was no centralization of language outside of state administration.

When the Ottoman Empire came to an end and was succeeded by the Turkish Republic, the newly formed nation went through a language reform conducted by its new president, Mustafa Kemal Ataturk. This language reform had two constituents; the adoption of the Latin alphabet, and the purification of the language from its Persian, Arabic—in other words Ottoman—lineage. The reforms were applied widely and with precision. One result of this transformation was the increased literacy rate throughout the nation; while the Arabic alphabet took children a long time to learn, the Latin alphabet was mastered in about three months.

Another consequence of the language reforms came to light with the second generation of Turkish nationals: the ability to read Ottoman Turkish was lost. This resulted in an inevitable disengagement from the Ottoman past. Teaching the Arabic alphabet was discouraged in the first years of the republic. These cautious measures suggest that the eradication of the Ottoman language was deemed necessary for the creation of a new and independent Turkish identity, freed from the Ottoman legacy. In contemporary Turkey, nearly ninety years after the transition from the empire to the republic, the Ottoman language continues not to be a part of school curriculums. As a result, the ordinary Turkish citizen is not equipped to read written sources from before 1923. Only a very small number of the population, historians and scholars of Ottoman literature, can read and understand primary Ottoman sources. This language shift puts Ottoman fairy tales out of the ordinary citizen's reach, making their access only possible only through secondary sources.

Second, even for the rare reader who has mastered Ottoman the available fairy tales are few and far in between. One reason for this is the medium in which most Ottoman fairy tales were told: the largest portion of this genre was narrated orally rather than written down. Traditionally, Ottoman fairy tales were passed down from one storyteller to the next, making them dependant on either good memory or handwritten notes, most of which have been lost in time.

Third, even in cases where Ottoman fairy stories have been written down, published, and shared, their translation into modern Turkish has been scarce. Most translations have shortened and summarized the Ottoman texts in question, as shall be discussed in the following sections. Furthermore, no study has so far focused on the Ottoman fairy tale heritage exclusively. This omission forces the fairy tale enthusiast to search unsystematically, with hopes that a tale may be found in unexpected places.

An Unexpected Sourcebook: *Turkce'de Roman*

Mustafa Nihat Ozon's *Turkce'de Roman* (The Novel in Turkish) is one such place and constitutes the locus of our research. The primary reason I have chosen to focus on Ozon's book is its popularity. *Turkce'de Roman* was published in 1936, and was the first book which studied the Ottoman heritage of the Turkish novel; it was required reading at many universities. No other book took the Ottoman genealogy as theme again till 1978 [2].

In the introduction to the first edition Ozon states that the chapters of his book might be seen as too weighty or numerous but that he must be excused for three reasons. Firstly, all the texts he investigates are written in the Arabic alphabet secondly they are written in a language and style that is now (in 1936) difficult to understand, and thirdly the acquisition of most of these books was by sheer chance.[3] Ozon's third reason, the element of chance, shows how undervalued these pieces of old literature were, and in fact still are, in the Turkish Republic.

The following sections of our paper will focus on a fairy tale Ozon translated from Ottoman and then summarized in *Turkce'de*

Roman: it is called *Tayyarzade*. Along with the other fairy tales Ozon summarizes in his work, *Tayyarzade* would have been the first Ottoman tale Turkish readers who had forgotten Ottoman would have read.

Tayyarzade: An Ottoman Fairy Tale

The story of Tayyarzade, goes as follows[4]:

Huseyin Efendi was a retired accountant. Once upon a time his seaside house in Yenikapi was filled with guests, but nowadays it was empty and Huseyin Efendi was sitting in it moaning and groaning from loneliness, complaining about the state of the world.

One of Huseyin Efendi's aquaintances, a dervish by the name of Mahmut, brought a boy called Tayyarzade to Huseyin Efendi. This boy was very polite and he soothed the heart, there was no one that could outdo him in elegance or eloquence. He knew Persian and Arabic, he knew music, his voice was beautiful and he played the tambur. He was perhaps eighteen, not a day older than twenty. Huseyin Efendi liked the boy and considered him no different than his son. He did not bid Tayyarzade leave his side day or night.

Even though their relationship progressed flawlessly for a while, a misunderstanding eventually arose that muddied the waters. Huseyin Efendi had prepared a gift package for Tayyarzade on occasion of the feast, but it got mixed up with the package of another servant. Tayyarzade was greatly saddened by this turn of events and swore never to set foot in Huseyin Efendi's house again.

Huseyin Efendi sent word that Tayyarzade return, but to no avail. Upon his failure, he changed his clothes and ventured to find Tayyarzade himself. He did not come back home for a long while. But a man that brought back papers with Huseyin Efendi's signature came. With each signature he withdrew a thousand lira from Huseyin

119

Efendi's caretaker. His caretaker let the women of the harem know of this conundrum. All the women thought Tayyarzade to be guilty of the misdeed.

Huseyin Efendi's wife and five other women of his harem hid sticks underneath their skirts and went to Tayyarzade's house to question him about the money. Upon arrival to his house they learned that Tayyarzade had not seen the Efendi since he had left his house, in fact he was now getting worried and made prompt to go and seek his master himself.

Tayyarzade began to follow the man, who again came and asked for a thousand lira with the signature of Huseyin Efendi. The man entered the palace of Fazli Pasa in the district of Sultanahmet. Tayyarzade sat in front of the palace and began to think; suddenly, out of the palace came eight handmaidens and a beautiful girl. The beautiful girl began to talk to Tayyarzade and welcomed him to the palace.

When the gates of the palace opened, Tayyarzade saw two times twenty Hungarian slaves on either side of the door. The girl, the eight handmaidens, and Tayyarzade gave their bahsis to the slaves, and the slaves opened another door behind which there was a courtyard through which they walked towards another gate which opened and revealed two times twenty Bosnian and Albanian slaves. They too were given their bahsis. Behind a third gate they found thirty eunuchs. Once they passed the eunuchs, on the stone stairs at the end of a marble courtyard, there were twelve Hungarian concubines and upon seeing Tayyarzade, they said to the beautiful girl that welcomed Tayyarzade to the palace: "Our dear Kalfa, this prey of yours leaves us speechless indeed!" and they began to clap their hands. Tayyarzade was taken to a room where he was served drinks and food and from there to another room where Gevherli Hanim was to be found.

Gevherli Hanim was a spinster who had rings and earrings and necklaces and anklets and nose rings, and then more of each of these things. Much later the beautiful girl told Tayyarzade that Gevherli Hanim was the daughter of the Pasa who owned this palace and that she had married three younger Pasas herself, one after another, and after they had each died she went ahead and turned her father's palace into a prison.

The old palace, new prison, had forty rooms, and each room had one odabasi and four concubines. Every day, one concubine went out into the streets to hunt for a man that was dressed well and looked pleasing to the eye. The concubines would take him and entertain him and eat away his money until the man was penniless. Then they would give him a conical hat and a cloak, and lock him into the prisons. They would take his signature and begin to rob his house, just like they had done with poor Huseyin Efendi. When Gevherli Hanim understood that the man's house was robbed penniless too, she would order her slaves to kill her prisoner.

The beautiful girl told all this to Tayyarzade, but also reassured him that no harm would ever come his way since she herself would stand between him and harm's way.

The next day Tayyarzade was taken to Gevherli Hanim's court but by one excuse or another managed to ask for four free hours in the outside world and was granted his wish by Gevherli Hanim. When he left the palace Tayyarzade happened to pass by Sultan Murat IV who was walking in the vicinity with his storyteller, Tifli. Tayyarzade told these two companions his story. The two broke into the palace grounds, ordered that Gevherli Hanim be killed, and saved all those poor men from their prisons.

The Tifli Canon

Tayyarzade is a story that belongs to the canon of the storyteller Tifli. The information we have about Tifli the storyteller is scattered and fragmented. We know, for instance, that Tifli was born in the city of Trabzon on the Black Sea coast of Anatolia in the sixteenth century, but we do not know in which year he was born. We also do not know in which year he moved to Istanbul. Tifli's real name was Ahmed Tifli Celebi and his father was Abdulaziz Efendi. He is said to have recited poetry from an early age but is best known as a storyteller who became a personal *meddah*[5] to Sultan Murat IV (1623-1640). Tifli was a Sufi, a follower of Sheikh Idris-i Muhtefi of the Melami order of dervishes. Evliya Celebi, a famous Ottoman travel writer, mentions that Tifli was also known as "Tifli the Stork" due to his exceptional height. It is known that Tifli's poetry continued appearing in 18th and 19th century Ottoman journals, long after his death. His fame also lived on in oral narrations where he was mentioned side by side with Sultan Murat IV.[6]

It is difficult to fit the tale of *Tayyarzade* into one clear literary category. The reception of *Tayyarzade* in particular, and the canon of Tifli stories in general, has been complex and still affords no consensus. Some scholars have viewed the Tifli canon as a part of the anonymous pool of *meddah* stories. Yet others have classified the Tifli canon as a part of the folk tale tradition, and some have viewed the stories as part of the literary (written) Ottoman lineage.[7] This confusion is not so much the result of muddled criteria as it is the result of the richness within the canon at hand. The Tifli stories carry elements of various disparate traditions within themselves; their eclecticism constitutes a particularly difficult case for literary differentiation. Some Tifli stories contain components of written language, such as catalogues and indexes, while others do not. Some Tifli stories are made up of several connected tales, while others contain many side stories, yet others are episodic and some are only made up of two episodes that are based on simple plot lines, similarly, the length of the stories varies greatly. While some Tifli stories have been embellished with pictures and decorations, others are plain. While some of them make use of causal logic, others move forward by coincidences or miraculous events. While some tales of the canon are realistic, others delight in exaggeration and turn into fairy tales.[8]

Even though there is no clear categorization of the Tifli stories, most scholars believe them to have been either told by Tifli himself, or to have been written down by him. Ozdemir Nutku refers to the Tifli stories as the creations of Tifli, while Metin And refers to these tales as Tifli's personal canon in his article on the *meddah*. Pakize Atac suggests that the stories were written down by Tifli himself, while Pertev Naili Boratav suggests that the stories were narrated by Tifli and possibly passed down to us by anonymous scribes.[9] Whether they were written down by him, or narrated by him, the stories of Tifli are unanimously traced back to the persona of Ahmet Tifli Celebi. His presence enables *Tayyarzade* to fit the first criteria of a new fairy tale; that its author be identifiable and be situated in a particular time, seventeeth Century Istanbul during the reign of Sultan Murat IV (1623-1640).

While we have established Tayyarzade's maker as Tifli, it is less straightforward to categorize it as a fairy tale. Tayyarzade has not typically been considered a fairy tale in Ottoman studies, with the exception of two notable scholars, Ozdemir Nutku and Robert P. Finn. Finn has classified all of Tifli's canon as fairy tales, *masal*, while Nutku has noted that Tifli's canon contains many elements that can be found in traditional fairy tales such as the appearance of helper figures who try to unite separated lovers.[10] The main reason scholars of Ottoman have not considered *Tayyarzade* and other Tifli stories to be fairy tales is the following: Turkish literary studies perceive fairy tales, masal, to be anonymous stories, having no identifiable tellers.[11] We have already established that new fairy tales are those tales that can be traced back to their creator, and in this sense Tifli's *Tayyarzade* can indeed be considered a fairy tale, even though this definition is not commonly adhered to in Turkish literary studies.

Another reason forwarded for excluding *Tayyarzade* from the fairy tale canon has been its realistic components. Sukru Elcin has noted these attributes as the following: "The names of the main characters are traditional Muslim names while the names of places and the architecture is one we are familiar with throughout Istanbul. The heroes and heroines of the stories are ordinary folk that have ordinary lives and jobs. Almost all of them live within the scope of reason, whether they are ethical or not."

Elcin's arguments are interesting to keep in mind while studying Tayyarzade, but it must be noted that the employment of real locations, architecture, common names and ordinary people are not characteristics that would lead one to exclude the possibility of *Tayyarzade* being a fairy tale. Fairy tales can have many realistic components and still remain true to the fairy tale genre by highlighting the element of wonder. *Tayyarzade* forms just such an example by utilizing the wonderful and the unlikely through various cultural codes.

The Significance of Forty

Within the Eastern fairy tale canon, particularly in the *1001 Nights* and Ottoman fairy tales, there is a devoted repetition of particular numbers. These numbers are one, three, seven, and forty. Of these, the number forty is probably the most beloved. *Tayyarzade* makes use of these ciphers frequently.

Turkologist Mehmet Yardimci considers forty to be one of the holiest numbers within Turkish folklore, as it is repeatedly used both in the Qur'an and the Alevite legends of Anatolia to suggest divinity. Important days of mourning and days of celebration last forty days and forty nights within Islamic settings. The number forty is also significant within the shamanistic past of the Turkic people prior to their arrival in Asia Minor. Hence in the Oğuz Kağan ve Satuk Buğra Han legends of Central Asian Turks, the hero Oğuz begins to walk in forty days of infancy, signaling his unusual strength. In the legend of Manas the number forty is repeated one hundred and twenty seven times and is used in reference to forty brave men, forty soldiers, forty brides etc. Repetition of numbers is imbued with magical, mythological, and religious connotations within Turkic fairy tales. The effect such repetition has in written texts is one of allusion: the numbers suggest the presence of the supernatural.[12]

Even though our analysis of *Tayyarzade* is based on the summary of its translation which is only 864 words, it contains fourteen numbers within it. These numbers in appearing order are: 18, 20, 1000, 5, 1000, 8, 40, 30, 12, 40, 3, 1, 4, 4, 2. Forty has a special importance in this sequence since through it the gates of the secret palace, that is later turned into a prison, open. Through the number forty, *Tayyarzade* distances itself from the ordinary and opens up a world that no longer operates with common logic.

Daytime Wonder

Turkish/Ottoman fairy tales in general, and the canon of Tifli in particular, are unique in that they employ what could be termed a day time wonder. Kunos, a collector of Turkish fairy tales has noted this specificity as the following:

> Turkish fairy tales are as crystal; reflecting the sun's rays in a thousand dazzling colours; clear as a cloudless sky and transparent like the dew upon a budding rose. In short, Turkish fairy tales are not the stories of the Thousand and One Nights, but of the Thousand and One Days.

This statement is nowhere clearer than in the Tifli canon, where it is mostly the daytime which houses the unusual, the uncanny, the repetitive and the wonderful.

The character of Gevherli Hatun, a female bluebeard, appears in daytime. Strangers enter her palace at daylight. The slaves and the maids hunt for newcomers in sunshine. This violent order could surely have been portrayed at night, and had this story been a part of the Arabian Nights, it probably would have been. But Tifli has placed all these unusual elements in the middle of a well-known city, amongst the ordinary happenings of the day. Rather than interpreting the daily feel of the tale as suggestive of realism, as Elcin has done, it is more reasonable to interpret these elements in the line of Kunos's analysis as constituting day time fairy tales.

Sultan Murat IV as Savior

Ottoman Sultans were revered and feared within the Ottoman Empire. There were not many instances in which they were visible to the public. The involvement of Murat IV in the daily dealings of a storyteller and palace entertainer would have been unlikely. Yet in all the stories within the Tifli canon, the Sultan and Tifli appear to be the best of companions. They travel in the city on a regular basis, they appear to save the distressed citizens just at the right moments and together they are invincible; solving the plethora of problems that is Istanbul. It is not too far-fetched to understand this pair as typical fairy tale helpers, guarantors of a happy ending.[13]

The Missing Aspects of *Tayyarzade*

To the listener used to the traditional fairy tale narrated in private homes or coffeehouses or to the reader used to reading the fairy tale from stylistically arranged written sources, *Tayyarzade* seems to be missing several elements of the Ottoman fairy tale.

Ottoman fairy tales, just like the tales of Romania and Ireland amongst others, typically start with a run. Runs are employed to start or end the tale, signal topic shifts and mark episode boundaries.[14] The following three examples are commonly used Turkish/Ottoman runs and their translations.

1. *Ben ben iken, deve tellal, kopek hamal iken, leylek muhtar, kedi berber iken, kurbaga tuccar, yilan urgan, hirka yorgan iken, babam bes yasinda, ben on besimde iken, ben babamin besigini tingir mingir sallar iken, kediler koyunlari kirpar, sivrisinek saz calarken, ben su icer, develer elekten gecer iken, tilki hakli ile haksizi secer, ben de o sirada arpa bicer iken, esek mihmandar tavsan ile kaz hukumdar iken bir varmis bir yokmus.*[15]

(When I was me, and the camel a town crier, and the dog a porter, and the stork a muktar, and the cat a barber, and the frog a merchant, and the snake a hawser, and the cardigan a duvet, and my father in his fifth year, I in my fifteenth, softly rocking his cradle, and when the goats sheared the sheep, and the mosquito played the lute, and I drank water, and the camels passed through the sieve, and the fox distinguished just from unjust, and while I at that time reaped barley, and the donkey was a guide, and the rabbit and the goose were a ruler, once here once nowhere.)

2. *Onlar ermis muradina, biz de cikalim kerevetine.*[16]
(They have reached their desire, I heard, may we go up to its wooden bed.)

3. *Gokten uc elma dusmus. Biri bana, biri masal anlatana, biri deSidika Hanima. Copu, kabuklari da dinleyenlere.*[17]
(Three apples fell from the sky, I heard. Let one be for me, one for the storyteller, and one for Sidika Hanim. Let the stalk and the peel be for the listeners.)

Tayyarzade is devoid of runs. In other words, the beginning, end, and transition points of the story are missing. The tale begins from a late, arbitrary start: our hero is already in old age, and steeped in sadness. The story ends suddenly as well, without giving us details as to how all its problems were solved. It seems highly probable that Tifli the storyteller began his tale with a set of runs that formed a smoother introduction to both the storyline and the hero and that he embellished his tale with more runs of transition and finality. These runs are likely to have either been lost in time or omitted during transcription.

Nuances of Characterization

Tayyarzade was probably narrated in a coffeehouse, or directly to the Sultan in the Ottoman palace. It must either have been transcribed immediately by other listeners, or written down by Tifli himself after or before the occasion of narration. There is no historical evidence to support either theory. In both cases, there is an essential part of storytelling that cannot be transferred to the medium of writing however, and that is the art of acting out different character types, their facial expressions and accents.

Ozdemir Nutku goes so far as to say that the main plot of a *meddah* story is merely an excuse for the storyteller to bring his acting talents to the fore. Nutku points out that the main story of the *meddah* would always be accompanied by unplanned jokes, poems, anecdotes, songs, sayings, legends and local gossip. (p.105) The *meddah* had acquired fame due to their ability at—*taklit*—copying. The meddah were not only apt at copying the behaviour and accents of the many ethnic groups that comprised the Ottoman Empire but they also mimicked the sounds of nature such as trees in the wind, animals, rivers and even earthquakes. These fundamental pieces of oral culture are lost in the transcribed Tifli canon, even though they might have been the core reason behind Tifli's fame.

Detail

Tayyarzade is a layered tale. Doors open onto courtyards, which then open on to more rooms, which are opened by many slaves who are guarded by many women who then all lead to and serve a mysterious female bluebeard figure, Gevherli Hanim. Yet as layered as the tale is, there is not much emphasis on detail in *Tayyarzade*. How do these doors look, for example? Are they made out of brass or iron? How does the handsome youth look, or the lonely old man? The lack of detail is noticeable not only when it comes to physical attributes, but also to the details of the plot line. The time Tayyarzade spends with Gevherli Hanim is not elaborated: what do the two talk about? What are their impressions of one another? How are their bodies situated within the bigger room? And why would Gevherli Hanim—a cruel, disciplined and intelligent woman with a mind for deceit—allow Tayyarzade four hours of freedom? Equally important and missing from the tale is the manner in which Tifli and Sultan Murat get rid of Gevherli Hanim and her servants. Tifli leaves us guessing as to why a Sultan would get involved in such mundane matters anyway.

It is likely that all these details were told during long story nights, also likely is the possibility that these details morphed and changed with each telling, affording Tifli and his audience new pleasures every evening. The medium of writing is devoid of these playful components. If the story is indeed in the details, it becomes increasingly difficult to determine just how much of *Tayyarzade* has been lost.

From the New Fairy Tale to the Inevitable Rewrites

The missing elements of *Tayyarzade* suggest a complex history of cultural and literary transmission. The journey of new Ottoman fairy tales follows an interesting trajectory which makes the incomplete nature of *Tayyarzade* necessary rather than accidental. Four important stages must be differentiated and discussed when it comes to the reception of *Tayyarzade* in contemporary Turkey: narration, transcription, translation ans summarization.

Pertev Naili Boratav believes the Tifli Canon to have been made up of *meddah* stories. The *meddah* stories were tales narrated in coffeehouses of the city. Boratav notes that the Tifli canon incorporates the styles (*uslub*), themes (*mevzuu*), and flair (*eda*) of the *meddah* stories. Boratav goes so far as to suggest that the Tifli canon might indeed be the first transcribed versions of the presently available *meddah* stories. According to Boratav these transcriptions would have then inspired more stories, and would have been used as study material by practising storytellers, *meddah*. Hence, in the case of the Tifli canon a continuous interplay between writing and performance is the norm.[18] The first form *Tayyarzade* took would have been performative storytelling rather than written text.

Transcription

It is unknown whether *Tayyarzade* was noted down immediately by one of the listeners present during the occasion of storytelling or by Tifli himself either prior to the occasion or afterwards. It is also possible that *Tayyarzade* was transcribed after many such evenings of storytelling, perhaps even by several writers.

These uncertain speculations create space for several versions of *Tay-yarzade*. Indeed, though they all ascribe *Tayyarzade* to Tifli the storyteller, several differing transcriptions of the tale have been discovered. It is possible that many more versions exist in the archives of Istanbul. So far, five distinct versions of *Tayyarzade* have been identified.

According to chronological order these versions are from the year 1872-3, 1875, 1917-8, 1924-5, and 1957. The four first editions are in Ottoman, while the one from 1957 is in the Latin alphabet in modern Turkish, but at the time of this writing, has been out of print for several years.

The first edition is titled "Hikaye-i Tayyarzade" (Tayyarzade's Story), and has been printed by the *hurufat* technique. Though the name of the scribe is unknown, it is noted that the printing took place in *Camli Han*. The second version of Tayyarzade is from the year 1875 and is an edition titled "Tifli Efendi Hikayesi" (The Story of Master Tifli). This second edition has been printed by the lithography technique in the printing house *Litografya Destgahi*. The third edition of the story is titled "Tayyarzade Yahud Binbir Direk Va'kasi" (Tayyarzade or the Happening on the Thousand and One Poles), it has been printed in *Bab-i Ali Caddesi'nde Cihan Matba'asi'nda* (Cihan Printing House on the Street of Bab'i Ali), using the hurufat technique. The fourth edition of the text is titled "Tayyarzade Bin Bir Direk Batakhanesi" (Tayyarzade the Thousand and One Pole Batakhane), has been printed in the hurufat technique, two different publishing houses are mentioned on its cover page: *Sems Matba'asi* and *El-Abdl Matba'asi*. The fifth edition has been printed in the new alphabet by *Hadise Basim* in hurufat technique. The scribes are unknown for all five editions. A sixth later version of Tayyarzade has been written by a famous Istanbulite author, Resad Ekrem Kocu. This edition must be considered a re-write since Kocu takes ownership of the story.

Hence, at the level of transcriptions there are two possible ways in which *Tayyarzade* has changed. The first stage is constituted by the differences between oral storytelling and the written word. Inevitably, the writing loses important elements of the performance: the mimicry of the storyteller, his body language, acting abilities, and expressions are untranslatable.

On a second level, when we begin discovering different transcriptions of *Tayyarzade* throughout the centuries, the singularity of the story is lost. We can no longer trace back words, idioms, and expressions to Tifli the storyteller. Even though *Tayyarzade*'s plot has not changed through its different transcriptions, the language must surely be affected by the individual scribes of each edition. The different transcriptions of the story make it difficult to separate Tifli from the literary talents of its anonymous scribes. A study of these nuances requires fluency in Ottoman, which, as has been noted above, is lacking in contemporary Turkey.

Translation

For the sake of accuracy, those who study *Tayyarzade* must go back to its earlier print editions. These editions are in the Arabic alphabet and in the Ottoman language. Some scholars have translated *Tayyarzade* from its Ottoman versions into modern Turkish but the accuracy of their translations is again difficult to confirm. What can be confirmed is the difficulty of undertaking the translation of Ottoman texts in general. Even for the scholars of the Ottoman language, translation is not without its enigmas, mostly due to the absence of vowels in the Arabic script. The following account charts the difficulties in transcribing Ottoman texts:

> One consequence of this situation [the language reform] is that the "authoritative" text of Ottoman documents and especially literary works has grown increasingly distant from the original, Ottoman manuscripts. Because the Arabic/Ottoman [A/O] script does not indicate some vowels, because Turkish vowels written as "long" Arabic vowels are transcribed as "short," and because several A/O script vowels and consonants have multiple possible readings, there is no way to create a readable (letter for letter) transliteration of an Ottoman text. Every Ottoman text transcribed into a Latin alphabet contains major interpretive interventions by the transcriber. There is no

possibility of reading back from any current form of transcription to the original text.[19]

Summary

Unfortunately, the scope of literary loss does not end with the stage of translation. *Tayyarzade*, along with many other Ottoman fairy tales, has reached contemporary Turkish readers only through summarization. Most students of fairy tales are familiar with *Tayyarzade* through *Turkce'de Roman* as has been noted previously. *Turkce'de Roman* studies many primary examples of Ottoman fairy tales, but none of these tales are presented in their entirety. Ozon has summarized each translation in order to cover as much material as possible in his canonical work. Ozon bases his translation on the original first prints of *Tayyarzade*, he also includes pictures of these editions in his text. But despite Ozon's loyalty to first editions, a summary in translation moves even further away from *Tayyarzade* as Tifli would have told it.

The New Fairy Tale as the Inevitable Retelling

Ottoman new fairy tales are paradoxes in transmission and translation. The sentiments, the locations, the *lebenswelt* of the Ottoman fairy tale are all familiar to the Turkish reader, but access to them has been severed, language bridges have been burnt. *Tayyarzade*, along with other Ottoman fairy tales, is readable only through a long list of omissions.

We have charted the difficulties in discovering new Ottoman fairy tales. Without the knowledge of a lost language, that of Ottoman, the search for the literary past comes up against too many obstacles. The incorporation of Ottoman as a second language into school curricula would eradicate all these problems, but in the near future another language shift appears unlikely. What options remain then for the enthusiast of Ottoman fairy tales?

The remoteness of the Turkish reader from the original Ottoman texts need not only present a problem; this position can also open up new and exciting possibilities. Reading the Ottoman past, unintentionally but inevitably, becomes a game of deconstruction. The reader has to stay aware of the omissions within the available texts and try to reconstruct what an original tale could have said and meant, how it would have felt on the tongue, in the coffee-houses of the city and in the imagination. Guessing what has been passed over silently, deciphering the untranslated or even mistranslated, understanding the exact meaning of terms, places, relations no longer in use; in short, learning the language of ghosts, comes with the territory of the Ottoman tale.

Derrida suggests that every text is *undecidable*, in that it conceals conflicts within it between different authorial voices. This conflict is very tangible in the transmission of the Ottoman tale and its various scribes. The *undecidability* of language is fundamental to the nature of language for Derrida. It is not a problem of particular texts, but of writing sui generis. The problems it presents can only be solved through more language, which in its turn needs to be deconstructed through even more language ad infinitum. A stable, singular meaning can never be reached. The novelty of deconstruction is that this lack of certitude is not presented as a loss but as a gain, not as a problem, but as an ongoing solution. Stability of language and certainty of meaning are not necessarily desirable since they freeze the process of understanding.

As with all deconstruction, deciphering the Ottoman fairy tale becomes an activity of re-writing. In the attempt to understand, new interpretations are added to the tale. So much has been excluded from its summary that filling in the gaps constitutes the act of reading. Consequently, the search for understanding includes an inevitable re-writing of the fragmented fairy tale at hand. Reading becomes an active seeking that incorporates guesswork, language and cultural translation, mistranslation, omission, and interpretation. Reading the Ottoman fairy tale requires agency.

Ironically, the act of reading the Ottoman tale in Turkey resembles the liminal form of the Ottoman fairy tale itself. From its very beginnings, the Ottoman fairy tale is both narrated and written; it belongs to both an oral and a scribal tradition. In its reception within the Turkish setting, the Ottoman fairy tale stays true to its original, amorphous form. And just like those old evenings in coffeehouses; every story invites a new telling, every telling invites a new writing, every writing is met with several readings and each reading turns into a myriad of new narratives.

Bibliography

Andrews, Walter G., Murat Inan, Sevim Kebeli, and Stacy Waters. "Rethinking the Transcription of Ottoman Texts: The Case of Reversible Transcription." Accessed January 5, 2012. http://courses.washington.edu/otap/reverse/reverse/o_Reverse_trans_article728.html.

Cinar, Bekir. "Tifli Ahmet Celebi: Hayati, Edebi Kisiligi, Eserleri ve Divani'nin Tenkitli Metni." Ph.D. diss., Firat University, 2000.

Eggar, Ben. "Critical Theory, Poststructuralism, Postmodernism: Their Sociological Relevance." *Annual Review of Sociology,* 17 (1991): 105-31.

E.J Brill's First Encyclopedia of Islam 1913-1936, s.v "Ahmet Celebi Tifli".

Ekici, Metin. "Turk Sozlu Geleneginde Anlaticilar ve Anlatmalar Arasindaki Iliskiye Art Zamanli (Diyokronik) Ve Es Zamanli (Senkronik) Bir Bakis" *Fikret Turkmen Armagani.* Izmir: Kanyilmaz Matbaasi, 2005.

Kunos, Ignacz. *40-4 Turkish Tales.* Accessed November 1, 2010. http://www.scribd.com/doc/4190498/Kunos-Forty-Four-Turkish-Fairy-Tales.

Massey, Claire. "Letter from the Editor." *New Fairy Tales* 1 (October 2008): 2. Accessed December 3, 2011. http://www.newfairytales.co.uk/pages/issueone.pdf

Ozon, Mustafa Nihat. *Turkcede Roman.* Istanbul: Remzi Kitabevi, 1936.

Ozturkmen, Arzu, "Folklore on Trial: Pertev Naili Boratav and the Denationalization of Turkish Folklore." *Journal of Folklore Research* 42 (2005): 185-216.

Sayers, Selim David. "Tifli Hikayelerinin Tursel Gelisimi." PhD. dissertation, Bilkent University, 2005.

Yardimci, Mehmet. "Geleneksel Kulturumuzde ve Asiklarin Dilinde Sayilar." Accessed January 20, 2012. http://turkoloji.cu.edu.tr/CUKUROVA/sempozyum/semp_3/yardimci.pdf

Zengin, Dursun, "Tekerlemelerin Cevirisi." *A.U. Tomer Dil Dergisi* 125 (2004): 44.

Zeyrek, Deniz. "Runs in Folktales and the Dynamics of Turkish Runs: A Case Study." Accessed January 20, 2012. http://nirc.nanzan-u.ac.jp/publications/afs/pdf/a948.pdf.

Notes

1   Claire Massey, "Letter from the Editor," *New Fairy Tales* 1 (October 2008): 2, accessed December 3, 2011, http://www.newfairytales.co.uk/pages/archive.html.

2   Guzin Dino's *Turk Romaninin Dogusu* was published in 1978 (Istanbul), O. Evin's *Origins and Development of the Turkish Novel* in 1983 (Minneapolis), Robert P. Finn's Turk Romani 1872-1900 in 1984 (Ankara).

3   Mustafa Nihat Ozon, *Turkce'de Roman* (Istanbul: Remzi Kitabevi: 1936), 9-11.

4   The translation is mine.

5   The term *meddah* means storyteller in Turkish.

6   Cinar, Bekir, "Tifli Ahmet Celebi: Hayati, Edebi Kisiligi, Eserleri ve Divani'nin Tenkitli Metni" (Ph.D. diss., Firat University, 2000), 11.

7   Sayers, David Selim, "Tifli Hikayelerinin Tursel Gelisimi" (Ph.D. diss., Bilkent University, 2005), 4.

8   Sayers, 186.

9   Sayers, 32.

10 Sayers, 42.

11 Ekici, Metin, "Turk Sozlu Geleneginde Anlaticilar ve Anlatmalar Arasindaki Iliskiye Art Zamanli (Diyokronik) Ve Es Zamanli (Senkronik) Bir Bakis," *Fikret Turkmen Armagani* (Izmir: Kanyilmaz Matbaasi, 2005), 226.

12 Mehmet Yardimci, "Geleneksel Kulturumuzde ve Asiklarin Dilinde Sayilar," 646, http://turkoloji.cu.edu.tr/CUKUROVA/sempozyum/semp_3/yardimci.pdf

13 While the present paper judges *Tayyarzade* as a new fairy tale, this category is not the only one within which Tayyarzade can be placed. Kavruk notes the following: Whatever classification system is used, it is not possible to fit a classic story strictly into just one category. Stories generally have aspects of several different categories even if they can mostly be judged as an exemplar of a single type. Sayers, 14.

14 Deniz Zeyrek, "Runs in Folktales and the Dynamics of Turkish Runs: A Case Study," 163, http://nirc.nanzan-u.ac.jp/publications/afs/pdf/a948.pdf.

15 Kunos Ignazc, *Turk Masallari* (Istanbul: Sosyal Yayinlari), 277, cited in Zeyrek, 164.

16 Naili P. Boratav, *Az Gittik Uz Gittik* (Ankara: Bilgi Yayinevi), 155 cited in Zeyrek, 164.

17 Boratav, 175 cited in Zeyrek, 164.

18 Sayers, 36.

19 Walter G. Andrews, Murat Inan, Sevim Kebeli, Stacy Waters. "Rethinking the Transcription of Ottoman Texts: The Case of Reversible Transcription," http://courses.washington.edu/otap/reverse/reverse/o_Reverse_trans_article728.html.

Chapter 7

Cloud Catching in the Realm of the Drought King

Fiona Thackeray

When she was growing up, her mother would take her to the *Jardim Botânico* to lie among the ferns and the reeds and feel lizards scuttle over their bare legs. Or they'd go to the *Parque Público* and sit in the darkest corner, far from the old men propped on canes and kids spinning candyfloss from plastic pouches. Mother would tell her stories of the backlands, stories of the creatures that watched over you and of the ones that would eat you alive at night. "That's the countryside, child, there are friends and foes, but you know exactly who they are. You don't have to be afraid."

Rita remembered those tales when, all grown up, she led agronomy students on field trips. Lying once again among ferns, her skin traversed by dry-tongued creatures, she chanted, "Don't be afraid," easy for her mother to say but Rita was a child of the city. The backlands never loosened up its grip on her mother, not in all those years of snaking through the city's right angles and cement-lined arteries. The velvet certainty of the backlands night was a thing of memory now, long since replaced by the peachy sodium nimbus at her bedroom window.

From the street, Rita looked fondly in the window of the Brás Cubas café, its caramel walls painted with ants and scraps of the famous story and hung with abacuses, the counter a-glow under bright pendant globes. Now that her new apartment was just piled up boxes and bare floorboards, this place, more than ever, was home. She took her seat. Pedrosa made her usual espresso, in a cup stencilled with the monocole and moustache of the great Machado de Assis.

"I'll make you a hot cheese sandwich, sweetie."

"No thanks, just coffee."

"Ahh, *minha Princesa....*".

"I'll eat at the university."

He slid the sugar jar along the counter. She picked it up, then put it back.

"Don't tell me you're dieting?"

"No...it's, um, for Lent."

She looked around for her *Diário*, but every copy was taken. One old man held the newspaper captive under leathery elbows, pontificating on the day's news to whoever was listening. She turned to her phone for the headlines, but there was no signal. Pedrosa leaned over, "Sorry, the line burned in yesterday's storm—we're waiting for the engineer."

Rita sighed and went to a window seat. Pedrosa's was the best espresso in Rio—she knew, she'd tried them all, or nearly. But without sugar, coffee scoured her mouth, hot and bitter. No one deserves that, her mother would say. She imagined adding a spoonful—the mellow sweetness on her tongue—but it summoned Fernando's barbed remarks at the beach. His attempts to rephrase the casually spoken cruelty were lame—Rita covered up her bikini with a roomy tee-shirt, and that evening rigorously edited the contents of the fridge. When they first met, he'd seemed charmed by her bookish ways, but in time he revealed himself to be concerned mainly with the surface of things.

The café staff waltzed around each other, frothing milk, spinning plates along to customers. The crush of office workers, joggers, and locals grew. Rita, teeth and tongue smarting from the coffee, noticed a poster on the wall and went to take a closer look. *Projeto Rondon*: seeking volunteers to help communities in the Northeast. Her father's tales of working with the Project as a young engineer had been her favourite bedtime stories: trying to pipe water to drought stricken towns, the elusive underground lake, the weeks spent craning through a theodolite, earning a burnt neck and a reputation as a *louco*, and of course, the day he met her mother. She paused, imagining those remote places, with no water, never mind decent coffee or broadband.

"Sweetie?" Rita jumped, lost in her thoughts. Pedrosa leaned over the counter looking worried, "Don't look now, but the Underwear King just came in. He has company."

Rita couldn't speak. Trembling, she grabbed her laptop bag and phone. She thought, "I am not going to look." But her eyes disobeyed and searched for Fernando. He was there, sure enough, with some skinny blonde, with high-end clothes and measurements from a galaxy far beyond Rita's. Entwined, flushed, they had a feline air of brazen langour. Rita pushed through the door, bumping into a delivery guy laden with chocolate eggs. The traffic lights changed, two lanes of cars slid past her, spicing the air with the cinder-toffee scent of combusted alcohol. She burst back into the cafe, headed to the wall, hardly breathing. The poster tore away easily.

Her father gave his blessing—how could he refuse? He remembered his own months on the Project, and the day he met her mother. Barefoot, hair like spilled ink, she came bringing eggs to Izuela's Guesthouse. Marcelo watched, forgetting to breathe, coffee pouring from his cup onto his boots. He didn't rest until he found her again, and when he did, he finally found water too, for Rita's mother's small, dusty feet stood exactly on the spot where, a few spade depths down, the source of life bubbled up.

Her mother was a different matter. Rita wanted to explain that she was leaving town for a while though without saying where she was headed, so close to the place her mother wrenched herself away from years ago.

Sometimes her mother told it as if she was brought to the city against her will, a wild thing driven south bundled in tarpaulin and ropes. And though for years she rode the number 77 bus around the city, she stayed on its surface like a tick on the hide of a tapir, never absorbed into the metropolitan organism.

Rita's mother was nowhere to be found. She searched in the Parque Público and the Botanic Garden, saying goodbye to her favourite trees and avenues as she walked. She checked at Doctor Alencar's place, where her mother worked occasionally, cataloguing botanical specimens and reading for the old man whose eyesight was failing.The phone at her apartment rang and rang—well, she never was home, until the sun was quite gone from the sky and there was nothing else for her to do but go indoors and sleep.

She waited, next day, on the roof of her mother's building round sunset. It was her habit to feed two parrots up there. They flew in each afternoon and perched on the lift-shaft housing. But neither she, nor the parrots, appeared.

Rita left Rio and tried not to be afraid.

The bus driver took his time over the potholes, cursing softly. A rosary dangling from the mirror beat the windscreen in a syncopated commentary on the road's cavities. Rita's bones ached after 46 hours in a chair with a faulty reclining mechanism. The brakes squealed, the door lunged open. She staggered down the gangway and out into the hot dust of Nova Angola.

From the wide shade of a jackfruit tree, a small crowd watched her alight. Some stood, smoking, toeing the dust between tree roots. Others lolled on upturned crates. Old women rested bundles of firewood on the ground to take a better look.

Rita could see a couple of market stalls along the road with stacks of plastic basins and pumpkins. The road itself was a patchwork of asphalt islands adrift in a sea of red earth.

So this was famine country.

The people were coated in red dust. Their knees and elbows were bulbous knots, their limbs twigs. Small children clung to their mothers' legs, huge shy eyes turned towards Rita, stomachs ballooning beneath ragged shirts.

The bus roared out of sight on its journey north. Rita stood amid the staring backlands people, as if she and they did not speak the same language. The Project people had said someone would be there to meet her, but no one stepped forward. This was to be her home for three months; this place where people waited under a tree for buses to arrive and greeted strangers with stares, where the hub of life was a stall selling plastic basins.

She tapped her phone. No signal.

"Dona Rita?" She jumped. "Moreira. Sorry to be late." Behind her stood a man clasping a Stetson to his faded shirt. He extended a callused palm. Rita grasped it with disproportionate gratitude. He shouldered the luggage and led the way towards a cart hitched to a skeletal horse. Rita realised that in her rush to escape the city, and Fernando, she hadn't prepared for this place—centuries, not just decades behind. But Moreira walked past the horse and cart and slung her bags into the back of battered pick up. They drove over the islands of asphalt. The people looked a little less daunting now that she had a connection, a guide. Sweat crept down her temples; her stomach relaxed a little. Every part of the truck rattled. She studied Moreira's reflection in the windscreen—weathered face shrunk tight against his skull, shirt buttons glittering over his sunken belly. They stopped by a wooden house on stilts at the edge of some fields. It had been mint green once, but the paint had blistered and peeled. Moreira gave her the key, showed her the well and water filter. There was a bed, a table and chairs, a lamp, fridge and stove, and, through a curtain, a shower and latrine.

Rita dined with Moreira and his wife at his insistence—broken rice, some old, tough-skinned beans, no meat: a modest plateful, more perhaps than she'd eaten in one sitting for weeks.

The moon hung fat and yellow in the sky that first night. Rita looked out of her glassless window, marvelling at the depth of darkness. The scrubland was still, but a whole cast of creatures animated the air with their sounds. Owl calls shredded the sky's black silk; bats clicked and whistled. Among the stones and dry leaves, unseen beings rustled and stirred. The crude sawn edge of the window prickled her elbows and she suddenly felt a wrenching ache for all her loss.

When she lay down to sleep, she missed the reassuring hum of traffic and the tangerine street light. The backlands night fell heavy and thick and the chorus of unseen creatures made her jumpy. She longed for her air-conditioned flat, at the least a fan. Despite several soakings in the rusty shower, she couldn't cool her skin.

By dawn she hadn't slept, she was a rag. The sun was climbing in the sky, creeping towards her across the boards. Finally she gave up on sleep and reached for her clothes. Everything she owned was red with dust.

Moreira drove her around local farms. She walked with him in the collapsing furrows. The soil rose in small puffs at the slightest disturbance. Last season's hopeful sowings leaned at crooked angles, baked to straw.

Moreira kicked over a corn stalk, its brittle roots pointing skywards. "One month dry, it grows; two months, still holding out. But three months dry..." He shrugged, lips pressed together. "When bad luck comes, she comes to stay."

Rita watched his neat features against the cloudless blue. She felt a surging admiration for this farmer who worked the spiteful soil of the kingdom of drought, undeterred.

The two fields by her house were ploughed. Rita got to work sowing trial plots of drought-tolerant beans. Often, the locals watched her work—bit by bit they lost their timidity and came closer, offering advice. And though their farming methods differed, they all spoke of one man: Hipólito, who had a gift for finding water. Across the district, people had lost faith in everything but still believed in Hipólito. In the interior, rain hadn't fallen for decades, yet shrivelled farmers told the same story with a twinkling eye: Hipólito would save them. His name sounded like raindrops.

Weeks passed. Rita tried to keep busy but couldn't block out the gnawing ache for her urban pleasures, her computer, the newspaper. Making her rounds of the scrubland farms, she inspected fields, dispensed advice, diagnosed dry-rots and mites. At every farmstead she noticed some talisman, hot peppers on a fencepost, herbs in certain combinations by a threshold, offerings at crossroads and corners: cachaça tots, tobacco bundles, candles.

Each night, she recorded sowing dates and weather conditions in a notebook: she was an engineer's daughter. Each night, her heart ached to hear the earth gasping with thirst: she was the daughter of a barefoot backlands woman. One evening she noticed small bumps in the bean rows. Next day, shiny green shoots peeped through. Rita felt full of hope.

Afternoons were spent weeding and staking. When she paused, she sometimes saw a solitary figure, pacing out the horizon. Perhaps this was the famous Hipólito, in a quest for water. She invited locals to walk with her between the furrows, to learn about the tiny hairs and channels on the beanstalks that would draw water from the morning air. It must sound like an exotic brand of city magic, she knew. In return they told their stories of this land of dead trees and dust.

Most nights Rita ate with the Moreiras. Every meal was a spell cast by Senhora Moreira on her cooking pot, conjuring ingredients from her bare cupboards. They told her about the years when the farm seemed to have potential, proud seasons of digging their own cassava crop, and the hunger and despair that followed: relatives migrating to southern cities, never seen again.

The Rio they heard about from family was a place of smothered dreams and violence, so she told them about the things she loved: the parks of flowers and shady trees; the friendly ways of the Cariocas. She told them of her father's work here on the irrigation project. Then, to avoid mentioning her mother, she told them about Fernando. Senhora Moreira stirred her pot and said she thought things would turn out OK. For the first time since leaving Rio, Rita slept soundly.

The bean plants that looked so strong began to wither. Rita ran down to inspect them in the dawn light, shaking. She knelt to examine the young plants. The growing tips drooped; patches of brown blemished every stem. Rita sank to her knees, the hems of her nightshirt trailing in the dirt. She clenched handfuls of soil, thrust her fists hard against her chest till her ribs hurt and from her mouth she let rise a terrible, animal howl. She slumped forwards, tears dousing the parched earth.

Climbing the stairs, she roared to the empty farmland, "It's impossible!" She kicked the next step, "No one can farm this...dustbowl. Who was I kidding?" She sat on the top step, "I was just running away! From that lowlife. That weevil, that...sap-sucker Fernando! I'm a dumb city girl..." she wailed to the shimmering air, "...clueless about the countryside." She came to help grow fat red beans to strengthen their bones, but—she slumped on the bed—she couldn't even feed herself.

A deep gurgling sound came through the window. Rita rolled over, squashing the pillow over her head. The gurgling noise began again. Now a heavy tread on the steps, boots against wood. Rita stood and moved cautiously towards the door.

The mudman on the threshold looked like an archaeological find from *National Geographic*—a piece of history unearthed. Surprising lines of skin appeared when his face moved out of its habitual creases. Rita didn't need to ask his name. Hipólito spoke gruffly. He'd seen the wilting beans and thought he could help. She wondered what he might propose—a raindance, a pilgrimage to the shrine of a wild-haired god? Today she was ready to try anything.

Before she'd found a clean shirt, he was among the furrows, pacing, frowning. When she reached him, Hipólito was watering methodically, tugging behind him a hose hooked up to a mud-covered tank on wheels. As he walked back up the field, Rita's eyes fixed on the bean rows. The plants were straightening up as if a puppetmaster was pulling on their strings. Hipólito's eyes shone like sun on puddles, the soil glistened like blood. They breathed in the scent of wet earth.

"Where did you get water?" she asked.

He nodded towards the horizon. "There are places. I'll show you."

Rita and Hipólito walked out across the scrub in the midday sun, she sweating under her father's wide-brim hat, he protected in his mud cocoon. The land ahead quivered. A little beyond the last houses of Nova Angola, the plain began to rise—this was the Hill of Fish. Rita noticed tiny diamonds of Hipólito's skin appearing—his mudsuit beginning to flake away.

They climbed in silence in towering heat. Near the hilltop, they came upon a strange wooden structure: mesh stretched on a frame over a stone channel. Hipólito explained: this was a Cloud Catcher. Even now, in the driest hour, beautiful beads of water formed on the clever green mesh.

After an hour or two, they entered a thicket of stunted thorn trees. In the middle of the grove was a huge excavation. Rita lay on her belly and peered inside—the source of Hipólito's armour of mud. No mirror surface of water winked back at her. She reached an arm inside the well, the damp earth cooled her blood. Rita, too, was beginning to take on a skin of mud. She dropped a pebble into the shaft. There was no splash, no noise. "A well without water?"

He shrugged. "There was water here before. Now I need to find somewhere new." Hipólito was piebald now, his mudskin falling away in clods. He moved into the thicket's scrappy shade.

She walked around the well in awe of the brutal exertion, the courage and determination it must have required. Rita felt her phone buzz in her pocket. She pulled it out, eager, but the screen showed the taunting, familiar message, *no signal*. Just then, her nose filled with her mother's bay leaf scent. And she thought she heard her voice, faintly, as if through a wall. "There you are, *querida*!" Rita thought she saw her mother, wavering like a heat haze, irradiated by late afternoon light. Rio's skyline was behind her, two green parrots feeding from her outstretched palm, "Don't be afraid, *filha*. Don't be afraid."

Rita felt an itch on the soles of her feet. The ground here seemed too quiet, too solid. From the corner of her eye, she saw two green parrots flying ahead. She called Hipólito. "Come on."

They walked a long, winding way through canyons and across rocky plains, the birds leading, the two mud people behind. Soon they came upon an area scattered with thorn trees. Rita felt the ground change here, no longer solid. The parrots flew ahead, alighting now and then on an outcrop. Rita walked stealthily, listening, sensing the earth change beneath her feet. She saw Hipólito a little way behind, growing weaker as he lost his layers of mud. The parrots squawked from a thorn tree and began grooming each other. A strong pulse beat from the soil, Rita's whole body tingled. Hipólito stood beside her, pointed at the ground under her feet. The roar of water beneath the earth filled her ears.

Rita fell to her knees and started to dig.

Chapter 8

"On Fairy-stories" and Tolkien's Elvish Tales

Christopher MacLachlan

J.R.R. Tolkien's essay "On Fairy-stories," coming from a writer who himself has made massive contributions to the corpus of fantasy writing, has become a landmark publication in the history of the genre it discusses. It is natural to wonder how "On Fairy-stories" applies to Tolkien's own fairy-tales and the obvious stories to consider are clear examples such as "Smith of Wootton Major" (1967), in which the hero travels to Fairy-land and meets the king and queen of the fairies. This essay will however look instead at tales by Tolkien that do not at first sight appear to be fairy-stories and have not usually been regarded as such, stories published in *The Silmarillion* in 1977 as "Of Beren and Lúthien," "Of Túrin Turambar" and "Of Tuor and the Fall of Gondolin" (Chapters XIX, XXI and XXIII of the "Quenta Silmarillion"), although the brevity of this third tale in *The Silmarillion* makes full discussion awkward, since it reduces the story to little more than an outline. This raises the question of how textual issues in relation to all three tales have a bearing on interpreting them.

The text of *The Silmarillion*

Tolkien's elvish tales exist in versions written over many years, stretching back to his earliest work on the literature of Middle-earth. Although there are gaps, enough of this material survives to show how he repeatedly returned to his stories, revising, rewriting, and sometimes entirely recasting them. The story of Beren and Lúthien, for example, appears in *The Book of Lost Tales* (published under this title by Christopher Tolkien as the first two volumes of *The History of Middle-earth* in 1983-4), a collection probably begun during the First World War. Christopher Tolkien states that the tale itself was written in 1917. In 1925 Tolkien began a retelling of the story in verse but abandoned this in 1931, after writing over four thousand lines. In 1926, however, he also began a prose sketch of his mythology, including the tale of Beren and Lúthien, that would eventually grow into the mass of materials that Christopher Tolkien drew upon for the published *Silmarillion* of 1977. The story of Túrin Turambar underwent much the same process, as did the third tale, on the Fall of Gondolin.

The Silmarillion itself was published in 1977, after the death of J.R.R. Tolkien in 1973, by his son Christopher. Douglas Charles Kane, in his book *Arda Reconstructed: The Creation of the Published Silmarillion* (2009), has examined the origins of each section of *The Silmarillion* chapter by chapter, tabulating the links between each paragraph of The Silmarillion text and the texts of the earlier versions and of the source materials published by Christopher Tolkien in the twelve volumes of *The History of Middle-earth*. Kane is able to show how the texts of the elvish tales in *The Silmarillion* are based on several earlier versions by Tolkien and often contain examples of what Kane terms editorial additions, that is, passages added by Christopher Tolkien.

Perhaps all this would not matter if the details of each story remained constant from version to version, but they do not. Names are changed, episodes are added, expanded or omitted, and significant details appear in some versions but not others. Many of these alterations are quite crucial to the meaning of the tales. For example, in some versions Beren is an elf, like Lúthien, but in others he is a human, so that the objection of her father Thingol to his request to marry her becomes more than a matter of Beren's lack of status, and the eventual marriage becomes a unique bonding of the two leading races of Middle-earth, elves and humans.

There are perhaps no differences between versions of the tale of Túrin that are so momentous but the multitude of smaller alterations and the inclusion in the story of new episodes do affect the central questions about the hero and the reader's judgments on him. In short, while it would be restrictive to confine discussion solely to the versions of these tales that appear in *The Silmarillion*, especially in so far as these have been shaped by Christopher Tolkien, allowing reference to the earlier versions presents the question of what it means to say there is a tale of Beren and Lúthien and there is a tale of Túrin Turambar. To what do we think we are referring when we discuss them?

The situation is not however impossible, or even unusual, except insofar as we are dealing with the writings of one modern author, since the question of the identity of the text is here much the same as with classic fairy-stories that exist in several versions, though they are all in some sense the same story. Tolkien, as with other aspects of his mythology, or legendarium as it is often called, has reproduced in his own work a parallel with a feature of real legends and genuine folk tales, whereby a range of different versions of a tale are accepted as variants and nobody objects to talk of the story of, say, Cinderella or Snow White, though in fact there may be no single, definitive, and fixed text of either. Tolkien's stories take on one of the distinguishing features of myths or fairy-tales and become, unlike modern printed books, the alterable sum of several parts. In his now famous letter of (probably) 1951 to Milton Waldman, where Tolkien writes of his aim to create "a body of more or less connected legend...dedicated to...England" (*Letters*, 144), he anticipates this:

> I would draw some of the great tales in fullness, and leave many only placed in the scheme, and sketched. The cycles should be linked to a majestic whole, and yet leave scope for other minds and hands, wielding paint and music and drama.

This implies a process of growth and development beyond the outlines "sketched" by Tolkien himself. In practice, this has hardly happened, given the ferocity with which the Tolkien copyrights have been asserted, but in the end Tolkien himself, and his son Christopher, have virtually created a shifting body of myth and legend that mimics what might be termed "natural" myth and legend. But the upshot is that, in discussing the tales, one cannot directly refer to one version as sufficient. This essay will therefore look beyond the versions in *The Silmarillion* and take the liberty of using the titles "Beren and Lúthien," "Túrin Turambar," and "The Fall of Gondolin" to refer to each tale as such and not to any particular version of it, which will, when mentioned, be given its published title.

The elvish tales as Fairy-stories

What justification is there for regarding the three elvish tales as fairy-stories? The simplest answer is that they are all about fairies, although this is obscured for readers of *The Silmarillion* by the fact that the word "fairy" and its cognates is never used there. A glance at the indices of the volumes of *The History of Middle-earth*[1] in which earlier versions appear, however, reveals that "fairy," in singular and plural, is used several times in *The Book of Lost Tales* (although not in "The Fall of Gondolin"). In the verse "Beren and Lúthien" and "Túrin Turambar" in *The Lays of Beleriand* there are also many uses of the related forms "faery" and "faerie," no less than eleven times in the poem about Túrin. In the *Lost Tales* version of "Beren and Lúthien" the heroine, who is there called Tinúviel, is twice referred to as "Princess of Fairies" (on pages 26 and 28) and when at the end of the second canto of the poetic version Beren comes to the land where she lives he is said to reach "the borders of the faëry land" (168).

Tolkien, in short, was not at first embarrassed to refer to his elves as fairies and their land as faëry land, though he became so later. As Dimitra Fimi has pointed out in her book *Tolkien, Race and Cultural History* (2010), the origins of Tolkien's work lie in the Victorian cult of fairies, but, as she also shows, Tolkien came to realise that the change in fashion that led to the rejection of Victorian fairy art and literature as sentimental and unreal, the worst sort of fantasy; this meant that he tried to repudiate what had been dear to him in his youth, renouncing some of his early verses, such as one of his first published works, the poem "Goblin Feet," written as late as 1915. Fimi quotes a remark by Tolkien about this poem recorded by his son in the first volume of *The Book of Lost Tales*, "I wish the unhappy little thing, representing all that I came (so soon after) to fervently dislike, could be buried for ever" (32), but she points out that he was still planning to republish "Goblin Feet" into the 1930s, and "the fairies did not disappear from his writings 'soon after' 1915" (Fimi, 195). Indeed, it is arguable that they never did. All that happened was that Tolkien ceased to refer to them as such, using instead the more English word "elf."

At the same time he began suppressing the word "gnome" as the name of his fairies or elves, and instead used a word ("noldo") from his own elvish language, and he also began the replacement of "goblin" with the more idiosyncratic "orc." This in turn led to his repudiation of the influence of George MacDonald's fairy-stories containing goblins, and of MacDonald as a writer, to the point where Tolkien would announce that he detested MacDonald's work.[2] In "On Fairy-stories" itself the process of the renaming of the fairies goes on. Although Tolkien, having committed himself to the title "On Fairy-stories" when he agreed to give the Andrew Lang lecture at the University of St Andrews in 1939, uses that term and refers to fairies repeatedly at the beginning of his text, he later begins to parallel it with the word "elves" and, in a manner that might be taken as only stylistic variation, increasingly substitutes "elves" for "fairies." He justifies this on etymological grounds, writing that "[f]airy, as a noun more or less equivalent to elf, is a relatively modern word, hardly used until the Tudor period" (12), but there is more to this than linguistic history. We shall return to the matter of the subtext of "On Fairy-stories" later.

The second reason for treating the three tales as fairy-stories is that they contain so many fairy-tale elements, too many indeed to enumerate here, where illustrative examples must suffice. In "Beren and Lúthien," for instance, Lúthien's father Thingol, to prevent her running off after Beren, has a tree-house built for her, with a guard below it. To escape, Lúthien casts a spell on her own hair so that overnight it grows immensely long. She cuts it off and weaves it into a cloak of invisibility, with enough left over to make a rope by which she climbs down from the tree-house. Slipping unseen past the guards, she runs off to join her beloved. He meanwhile has been captured by the minions of the evil Morgoth. In the earliest versions of the story Beren is imprisoned in the dungeons of a castle full of cats, whose lord is Tevildo Prince of Cats. Lúthien goes to Tevildo's castle and, with the aid of Huan, a gigantic talking dog, overpowers the Prince of Cats and forces him to reveal the spell that holds the stones of his castle together, knowledge that allows Lúthien to destroy the castle and release Beren. Tolkien however changed his mind about the cats and in later versions it is Sauron who catches and imprisons Beren. There is still an animalistic element present, however, as Sauron is akin to a werewolf, and when Lúthien defeats him he turns into a bat and flies off, Dracula-like, in a "vampire shape with pinions vast," as the versified version puts it (*The Lays of Beleriand*, 254).

In "Túrin Turambar" there are also talking beasts, notably the dragon Glaurung. Tolkien of course was familiar with the dragon Fafnir slain by Sigurd in the Old Norse saga of the Volsungs, but he must have known of other talking dragons, like the firedrake in Andrew Lang's fairy-tale *Prince Prigio* (1885), a story Tolkien refers to in "On Fairystories." Tolkien makes Glaurung cold and deceiving, with the power not only of words but also of mind-control. He deprives Túrin's sister of her memory so that when he, who left home when she was no more than a baby, meets her as a grown woman they fall in love and marry. Only when Túrin slays Glaurung and the dragon's spells are broken does Níniel recover her memory and, appalled at the realization that she is now with child by her own brother, throws herself into a lake in remorse. The element of incest here also relates to the Norse saga, since Sigurd's parents, Sigmund and Siglinde, were, like Túrin and Níniel, brother and sister, although in the saga this is not a matter for horrified self-destruction. The story of Túrin is in many ways a re-imagining of that of Sigurd the dragonslayer (the slaying of Glaurung is done in a way similar to Sigurd's slaughter of Fafnir), but with some even darker touches.[3] Túrin is always doomed to disaster. Everywhere he goes, and to everyone he meets, he causes death and destruction, usually after a period of success and popularity because of his prowess as a warrior. The cursed aspect of his life is related to another source, the Finnish *Kalevala*, and the character in it called Kullervo, whose violence and rage lead him to commit numerous crimes, including incest with a sister who then commits suicide. Like Túrin, Kullervo kills himself with his sword, which is able to talk and answers when asked if it will take his life.

There are fewer fairy-story elements in "The Fall of Gondolin" and, because of the fragmentary state of its later versions, some details are not very fully worked out. An example is that of the shield, sword, and armor Tuor finds in a ruined palace early in the story (see *Unfinished Tales*, 27). These were left there by Turgon, the king of Gondolin, at the inspiration of one of the god-like Valar, in order that a future messenger should find them and so be identifiable as divinely-guided when he comes to Gondolin. Tuor is led to discover the weapons by supernatural guidance. He takes them, saying "By this token I will take these arms unto myself, and upon myself whatsoever doom they bear" (*Unfinished Tales*, 27). Another element repeated in all three stories is the finding of a hidden entrance into a secret realm. The chief instance of this is the entry to the secret kingdom of Gondolin itself, a task made difficult by the spells cast on the entrance but which Tuor accomplishes with the aid of an elf called Voronwë. His meeting with this elf is as fated as his discovery of the elven weapons.

Tuor's breaking into the secret kingdom of Gondolin parallels Beren's entry into the forbidden lands of Lúthien's father Thingol, lands that are protected against strangers by spells cast by Melian, Thingol's queen. The fact that Beren circumvents this magic marks him out as fated, like Tuor. In the tale of Túrin Turambar the motif is not so clear-cut. The young Túrin is sent by his mother to Thingol for his safety and upbringing after the capture of his father by the evil Morgoth. Túrin reaches the secret kingdom under the guidance of elves. Later, after he exiles himself from Thingol's court, having killed an elf in a fit of rage, Túrin enters another secret elvish kingdom, Nargothrond, whose inhabitants have tried to hide their existence from Morgoth. Túrin, however, by his exploits in attacking Morgoth's orcs, draws the attention of the enemy to Nargothrond, leading to its destruction.

There is another parallel here with the other stories. Beren, intruding into Thingol's land in quest of his daughter and set a task to win her, in so doing rouses the wrath of Morgoth and so eventually leads to the invasion of the kingdom and its destruction. Tuor comes to Gondolin, hidden behind its circling mountains, but he falls in love with and marries the king's daughter, rousing the jealousy of Maeglin, who betrays the kingdom to Morgoth. All three stories, then, have the same basic theme of the intrusion of a man (if we discount the version of "Beren and Lúthien" in which he is an elf as a false step) into an elvish kingdom that has remained hidden from its enemy. As a consequence, that security is ended and the kingdom falls. The progressive elimination of the elvish enclaves contributes to the main theme of *The Silmarillion*, the decline and fall of the Middle-earth of the elves and their fading away, to be replaced by men as the dominant race, a process that is shown nearing completion in *The Lord of the Rings*. The stories therefore present particular examples of the general pattern of *The Silmarillion*, and indeed of all Tolkien's work, the fading of the elves before the rise of men.

Encounters between men and elvish or fairy kingdoms are however not purely Tolkienian. Near the beginning of "On Fairy-stories," when Tolkien is attempting to define them, he writes:

> fairy-stories are not in normal English usage stories about fairies or elves, but stories about *Fairy*, that is Faërie, the realm or state in which fairies have their being....
>
> Stories that are actually concerned primarily with "fairies," that is with creatures that might also in modern English be called "elves [,]" are relatively rare, and as a rule not very interesting. Most good "fairy-stories" are about the aventures of men in the Perilous Realm or upon its shadowy marches....
>
> The definition of a fairy-story—what it is, or what it should be—does not, then, depend on any definition or historical account of elf or fairy, but upon the nature of *Faërie*: the Perilous Realm itself, and the air that blows in that country. (14)

Many classic fairy-stories do indeed tell of the encounters of human beings, male or female, with fairies. Examples range from ballads like "Tam Lin" to mediaeval works like *Sir Gawain and the Green Knight* and Chaucer's "Wife of Bath's Tale" (both well known to Tolkien), and more modern works that Tolkien tended to disparage, Milton's *Comus* and Shakespeare's *A Midsummer Night's Dream*, and later George MacDonald's *Phantastes*.

The point to make here, however, is that this definition of a fairy-story fits "Beren and Lúthien" and "The Fall of Gondolin" very closely, and is not unsuited to "Túrin Turambar." They are all three essentially stories about "the *aventures* of men in the Perilous Realm or upon its shadowy marches," to quote Tolkien himself. The French word "*aventures*" looks like the English word "adventures," and that is the modern meaning, but Tolkien probably has also in mind the mediaeval meaning, which is closer to "an accident or chance," or even "a mischance," something, to go back to the Latin roots, that arrives or comes to pass unexpectedly. In the glossary to Tolkien's edition of *Sir Gawain and the Green Knight* the meanings given for "aventure" are "adventure, marvellous event," and "auenturus" is defined as meaning "perilous" (163: there is no separate entry for "adventure"). Tolkien's use of "aventures" suggests, then, what his use of "perilous" does, that the contacts between humans and elves are risky and liable to end in unforeseen consequences, which is very much the case with Beren, Túrin, and Tuor. Their stories are all about the way men's actions, sometimes with the best of intentions, or with intentions that seem quite specific and directed, lead to outcomes that nobody could foresee, although with hindsight the causes and connections are obvious. In that sense even *The Hobbit* and *The Lord of the Rings* might be classed as fairy-stories.

The double meaning of "On Fairy-stories"

"On Fairy-stories" appeared at a pivotal moment in Tolkien's career. Tolkien critics and biographers are agreed in finding the timing of the lecture significant for Tolkien's own writing.[4] In a letter of 22 November 1961 to Jane Neave, Tolkien himself says

that thinking about fairy-stories for the lecture "was entirely beneficial to *The Lord of the Rings*, which was a practical demonstration
of the views that I expressed" (*Letters*, 310). This is too glib, of
course, and endowed with hindsight, but it makes the point that
the lecture came while Tolkien was struggling with the early stages
of the sequel to *The Hobbit* and so his attempt to define fantasy and
its purposes is related to the beginnings of *The Lord of the Rings*
project. "On Fairy-stories" comes after the gap between *The Hobbit* and *The Lord of the Rings*. As such it looks forward to the latter
but it also looks back to *The Hobbit*, and further back to the mass
of Middle-earth writing before *The Hobbit*, the already large collection of poems and stories of the proto-*Silmarillion*. In writing
"On Fairy-stories" Tolkien is not only explaining to himself what
he is trying to do with his new book, *The Lord of the Rings*, but
also trying to justify his previous book, *The Hobbit*, and the many
unpublished works that have accumulated in the previous twenty
years and more.

In this way "On Fairy-stories" is a text with a double purpose
and a double meaning. Its public face, as the eleventh Andrew Lang
lecture, is that of an academic discussion of the meaning and use
of fairy-stories, related to Lang's own interest in them; in a private
sense, however, "On Fairy-stories" is part of Tolkien's debate with
himself about his own non-academic writings and their justification. Clearly he must have been anxious about the seriousness of
works of fiction that he knew his academic colleagues would regard as distractions from his real work. The question of what was
worth doing must have been sharpened by the political situation of
1939, with the growing prospect of another European war. If we
consider the public and the private aspects of his situation, in both
spheres he was under pressure to justify a commitment to writing
fairy-stories.

Tom Shippey, in the second chapter of his first book on
Tolkien, *The Road to Middle-earth*, provocatively says that "On
Fairy-stories" is "Tolkien's least successful if most discussed piece
of argumentative prose" (56). Shippey's explanation for what he
calls the "comparative failure" of "On Fairy-stories" is that it
lacks "a philological core or kernel" (56). He proceeds to try to

supply the defect, but he also makes the interesting comment that beneath the surface of the essay "it is just about possible to make out the bones of an argument, or rather a conviction." He goes on:

> The conviction is that fantasy is not entirely made up. Tolkien was not prepared to say this in so many words to other people, to sceptics, maybe not to himself. That is why he continually equivocates with words like "invention" and "no idle fancy," and also why a good deal of "On Fairy-stories" is a plea for the power of literary art; this is dignified with the form "Sub-Creation". (56f)

Shippey describes Tolkien's "hovering around some central point on which he dared not or could not land," (57) but actually it is quite clear what point Tolkien wants to make: that it was fine for him, an Oxford professor approaching his fifties without having produced a major book, to dedicate what he realized was going to be considerable time and effort to writing a lengthy fairy-story or fantasy work, *The Lord of the Rings*, at a time of national crisis. Behind this point lies a wider justification of the whole of the legendarium, including the tales of the elves.

This is why "On Fairy-stories" has such a long section denying that they are only fit for children. Tolkien had already written enough of the sequel to *The Hobbit* to know it was not going to be a book for children any more than his tales and histories of the elves were. There can hardly be any doubt that Tolkien himself reads, and writes, fairy-stories. His attack on the idea that they are naturally meant for children is in turn a defense of his own serious interest in and use of the form. Some of the other things Tolkien says about fairy-stories therefore should apply to the tales of the elves, too. "On Fairy-stories," after the section asserting fairy-stories are not for children only, goes on to make four specific claims about the defining features of the form, under the headings "Fantasy" and "Recovery, Escape and Consolation." How far can these be applied to "Beren and Lúthien," "Túrin Turambar," and "The Fall of Gondolin"?

Fantasy, recovery and escape, and the elvish tales

Tolkien begins the section headed "Fantasy" by discussing the terms "imagination" and "fancy," echoing what Coleridge says in *Biographia Literaria*, although, as Ann Swinfen says in the first chapter of her book *In Defence of Fantasy* (1984), "[t]o all intents and purposes, Tolkien reverses the terminology" (8). Coleridge describes the fancy as "no other than a mode of memory emancipated from the order of time and space" (Chapter 13), and thinks of it as, in Swinfen's words, "a mechanical process" (7) that puts together selected bits of experience into simple constructions, whereas the imagination is "essentially *vital*" and "dissolves, diffuses, dissipates, in order to re-create...it struggles to idealize and to unify." Tolkien in contrast writes:

> The faculty of conceiving the images is (or was) naturally called Imagination. But in recent times, in technical not normal language, Imagination has often been held to be something higher than the mere image-making, ascribed to the operations of Fancy (a reduced and depreciatory form of the older word Fantasy); an attempt is thus made to restrict, I should say misapply, Imagination to "the power of giving to ideal creations the inner consistency of reality"... The mental power of image-making is one thing, or aspect; and it should appropriately be called Imagination. (44f)

For Tolkien, the simpler faculty that combines images is not Coleridge's fancy but the imagination, and the more advanced creation of something that, as he says in a footnote, "commands or induces Secondary Belief" (45) belongs to fancy, or as he prefers to say, fantasy. Fantasy is the highest and purest art *because* it does not slavishly depend on being realistic but conceives of worlds other than the one we know, a task that Tolkien implies is self-evidently more difficult than mirroring the known world. He says a work of true fantasy that makes a secondary world credible is "a rare achievement of Art" and "story-making in its primary and most potent mode" (45). It is hard to believe he does not have in mind his own tales of Middle-earth here, his legendarium. The debate in "On Fairy-stories" on the meaning of "sub-creation" and the author as creator of a secondary world, though it is a defense of fantasy in a general sense, is also a justification of his own fantasy writing in a private and particular sense, too. In these passages Tolkien is writing about himself, and talking to himself, as much as he is addressing his public audience on a public topic.

It hardly needs explaining to today's readers that Tolkien created a secondary world. It would have been more difficult to convince an audience of this in 1939, or even in 1947, when the lecture "On Fairy-stories" was published, that is, before the publication of *The Lord of the Rings*, with its rich depiction of Middle-earth, and its more than a hundred pages of appendices, and its maps. When versions of the elvish tales at last appeared in print in *The Silmarillion* nobody was surprised that they too were set in a fully named and described geography, with characters belonging to full genealogies. This is not fantasy in the sense of something gratuitously incoherent or irresponsible but very much an alternative and yet believable version of the world that is. Such has been the success of *The Lord of the Rings* that this has almost become the definition of fantasy. Its origins, however, lie not in that work or even in its prequel *The Hobbit* but in the earlier material about elves, including the tales of Beren, Túrin, and Tuor.

The secondary world created by fantasy is nevertheless somewhat paradoxical as it continues to depend on the primary world. Tolkien writes that "creative Fantasy is founded upon the hard recognition that things are so in the world as it appears under the sun; on a recognition of fact, but not a slavery to it" (51). This in turn is related to the second aspect of fairy-stories Tolkien identifies, recovery, which has two aspects. One is a refreshing vision of the world, that rids our perceptions of tired assumptions. Tolkien says that we "need...to clean our windows; so that the things seen clearly may be freed from the drab blur of triteness or familiarity" (53). "Fantasy," he continues, "is made out of the Primary World" (54). If in defining the imagination Tolkien contradicted Coleridge, here he seems to be a follower of Coleridge's friend Wordsworth in advocating a poetic art based on a cleansed perception, without what Wordsworth calls in the preface to *Lyrical Ballads* "the gaudiness and inane phraseology of many modern writers" (20). Wordsworth opposes to "frantic novels, sickly and stupid German tragedies, and deluges of idle and extravagant stories in verse" his own concern with "certain inherent and indestructible qualities of the human mind, and likewise...certain powers in the great and permanent objects that act upon it which are equally inherent and indestructible" (25). The second aspect of Tolkien's concept of recovery has also to do with objects. He says that "fairy-stories deal largely, or (the better ones) mainly, with simple or fundamental things, untouched by Fantasy" and adds that "[i]t was in fairy-stories that I first divined the potency of the words, and the wonder of the things, such as stone, and wood and iron; tree and grass; house and fire; bread and wine" (55).

As the final pair here suggests, there is more to these things than meets the eye, but setting aside Tolkien's religious purposes, what these images indicate is a world that is simple in the sense of being pre-modern. He is justifying the setting of his stories in the quasimediaeval world of Middle-earth, a time and place mostly free of modern technology and progress. One is not supposed to ask where all the weapons and armor are mass-produced to equip the enormous armies of elves; the orcs get theirs from the workshops of Morgoth, whose evil nature is only confirmed by his connection with mines and forges. Outside his hellish, underground realm, the peoples of Tolkien's stories live in forest dwellings, subsisting on a little hunting and gathering and some sort of peasant agriculture. Their material culture is somewhat sparse, apart from a taste for fine jewelry and metal-work. The males wear, one assumes, clothing practical for war or travel; the females tend to be arrayed in fine, flowing garments that inspire imagery from flowers or birds. There is wealth but no money, and riding but no horse-trading.[5] This is surely recognizable as the traditional world of fairy-tales, a world the reader cannot enter without a taste, if only an assumed one, for the rather mythical simple life that haunts so much of English literature, a vision of Merry England. Again, because of the precedence of its publication, and the reputation of *The Lord of the Rings* as the portrait of a Tolkienian universe, the stories of *The Sil-*

marillion are seen as fitting into that environment and their link with the world of traditional tales has been missed.

It is into this world that Tolkien clearly escaped from the modern world. His discussion of escapism in fantasy confirms this, being at first taken up with diatribes against street-lamps, motor-cars, and railways. The evidently personal irritation here undermines his appealing argument that escape is justifiable if one is trying to get out of a prison, since the metaphor becomes trivialized by the grousing about "the Robot Age" (56) and the "rawness and ugliness of modern European life" (58). For a moment in the lecture Tolkien shows the sentimental side of his mythological project, its escapist side in the common sense, as an alternative to a real world he found increasingly uncongenial. The essay recovers, however, by returning to an earlier thought, that fantasy is a literature of desire, probably a more powerful idea than the more famous concept of secondary worlds. Tolkien, saying "fairystories offer...old ambitions and desires...to which they offer a kind of satisfaction or consolation" (60), writes movingly about the human desire to visit the deep sea, or to fly like a bird, or "to converse with other living things" (60), and lastly about the desire to escape from death. At this point the essay comes extremely close to Middle-earth. In his talk of how fairy-stories told by humans are about the escape from death while the "Human-stories of the elves are doubtless full of the Escape from Deathlessness...the burden of that kind of immortality, or rather endless serial living" (61f), Tolkien touches on the state of his elves.[6]

The deep subject of Tolkien's stories and legends is the contrast between the long-lived elves and the short-lived mortal humans and how their respective immortality and mortality determine their ethics and their politics. The catastrophic effects of the intrusions of Beren, Túrin, and Tuor into the elvish kingdoms in their stories is a manifestation of the impatience and intemperance of mortals in contrast with the passivity and resistance to risk and change of those who have centuries behind and before them. The elves, who have seen everything and forgotten nothing in their long lives, cannot foresee how the short-lived men will force the pace of events in their attempts to give their brief existences meaning.

The paradox Tolkien's work explores is that those who have most to lose because of their mortality are those who take most risks in trying to make the years of their lives memorable. So Beren takes up the impossible challenge of retrieving a silmaril from Morgoth's crown, a task Lúthien's father regards as so self-evidently impossible that nobody would attempt it single-handed; Túrin leads the elves of Nargothrond in increasingly open warfare against Morgoth, making a reputation for himself as a great warrior, but bringing upon them all the full might of their enemy; and Tuor forces his way into the forbidden kingdom of Gondolin and sets in train the events that lead to its downfall. Each man hurries the pace of events and makes history, knowing that, unlike the elves, time is against him.

There is a personal background to this in the form of Tolkien's self-imposed task of completing the work of creating a new mythology for England that he and his school-friends had planned before the intervention of the First World War broke their fellowship. Only Tolkien kept up the work, both during and after the war, but he must have had moments of despair, especially when his publisher, Stanley Unwin, rejected some of the stories and legends as a publication to follow up the success of *The Hobbit*. Tolkien then turned to the new *Hobbit, The Lord of the Rings*, a story centered on the determination of a mere mortal to carry out a task that elves decline. For Tolkien himself the task of writing *The Lord of the Rings* was both a fulfillment of his vow to make his legends known and also a bid to justify the time and energy he had already spent on them and that he knew in 1939 he would have to spend to complete what was forming in his mind.

Ending the story

So we come to the climax of Tolkien's discussion of the fairy-story and his last concept, what he terms "the Consolation of the Happy Ending" (62). "Almost I would venture to assert that all complete fairy-stories must have it" he writes, but he cannot have forgotten that few of the examples he himself had written end happily.

There is a sort of happy ending to "Beren and Lúthien." After Beren's death Lúthien petitions the Valar and they offer to revive him provided she accepts human mortality. They then live together quietly for a few years before peacefully dying together. Tuor also has a relatively good ending as he escapes the fall of Gondolin with his wife and son, like Aeneas from the fall of Troy. Túrin, on the other hand, ends by killing himself in disgust at learning that once again he has brought about a vile disaster, this time by unwitting marriage with his own sister. In the paragraph in which Tolkien says fairy-stories must have happy endings he introduces his own coinage for such endings, "eucatastrophe," a word that has become widely used and whose attribution to Tolkien is well-known, and yet his own work contains very little eucatastrophe, the somber endings of *The Hobbit* and *The Lord of the Rings* not excluded. It has to be conceded that if a happy ending is something a fairy-story "must have" then "Túrin Turambar" and "The Fall of Gondolin" may not be fairy-stories, and "Beren and Lúthien" is only just within the definition.

This is, however, to argue on Tolkien's own terms and to accept him as a disinterested observer, which this essay has already suggested he is not. Perhaps we should follow this up by asking what Tolkien himself might have sought to gain from his definition of the fairy-story, and from the qualities of recovery, escape, and consolation he asserts they must have. At the end of his discussion of Tolkien and "On Fairy-stories" in his book *Breaking the Magic Spell* (1979), Jack Zipes effectively reverses Tolkien's climactic move, in which he claims the Christian Gospel is the greatest fairy-story, by pointing out that, if the modern reader seeks recovery, escape, and consolation, it is to be found as much in fantasy of the kind Tolkien has fashioned as in scripture. Zipes accuses Tolkien of "the secularization of religion" (146):

Fantasy as it takes form in the fairy tale serves as a redeemer of humankind. It sets free the wants and wishes of human beings and declares that the pursuit of their fulfillment is valid and can provide validation of the self. (144)

Zipes points out that the response to Tolkien's fantasies has been based on the consolation Tolkien claims fantasy offers, a consolation that does not involve the faith and theology found in orthodox religion. Zipes writes:

> The powerful interest expressed by people in the Western world in Tolkien's fantasy world is indicative of a need for a new eschatology of religion...The religious imagination responds to the genuine utopian thrust in his works, and, whether one considers his fairy tales low or high art, serious fantasy or mere commercial entertainment, it must be recognized that he uncovers a social need of the religious imagination and points to the widening gap between a technologically constraining society and its alienated individuals in search of authentic community. Orthodox though Tolkien as a Catholic may be, he is a radical as a sub-creator of Utopia. (158f)

Ironically, Zipes's inversion of Tolkien's argument for taking fairy-stories seriously because they resemble the Gospels bestows on them a new seriousness as secular replacements for religion in the modern world. Consolation comes not through fantasy but in it; not by moving beyond the secondary world but by escaping into it. Tolkien's Middle-earth becomes a mythology not just for England, but for all humanity.

What this implies is a dislike of the primary world and a desire to avoid it, a desire that Tolkien often implies and expresses in his letters and in "On Fairy-stories." He was however quite able to see that such an escape from reality is impossible for the sane. Perhaps this explains the overall gloominess of his fairy-tales and the theme of the fading of the elves in all his work. The gradual encroachment of men on the elvish lands in Middle-earth dooms them to a future of ordinariness that becomes our present. The three elvish tales discussed here show this process. Lúthien actually becomes human in order to live out her days with Beren in quiet domesticity. Tuor's story ends more colorfully but also in a movement into family life. Túrin in contrast dies because he is unfit for the domestic, his incestuous marriage a perversion of normality, like all his attempts to conform to social customs, and so he points the moral of his tale in the same direction as the other two. It would be far-fetched to claim this shows Tolkien was fundamentally a realist, teaching that fantasy must always give way to the real world. His regret for the fading of the fairies is too evident. In the end he is, as suggested above, like Wordsworth, a man lamenting the loss of "the visionary gleam," or like Keats's forlorn knight, "alone and palely loitering...on the cold hill's side."

Bibliography

Anderson, Douglas A. *The Annotated Hobbit*. London: HarperCollins Publishers, 2003.

Carpenter, Humphrey. *J.R.R. Tolkien: A Biography*. London: George Allen & Unwin, 1977.

Fimi, Dimitra. Tolkien, *Race and Cultural History*. Basingstoke and New York: Palgrave Macmillan, 2010.

Hart, Rachel. "Tolkien, St. Andrews and Dragons," in *Tree of Tales*, edited by Trevor Hart and Ivan Khovacs. Waco, Texas: Baylor University Press, 2007), pages 1-11.

Kane, Douglas Charles. *Arda Reconstructed: The Creation of the Published Silmarillion*. Bethlehem, PA: LeHigh University Press, 2009.

Lang, Andrew. *Prince Prigio*. London: J W Arrowsmith, 1889.

MacLachlan, Christopher. *Tolkien and Wagner: the Ring and "Der Ring"*. Zurich and Jena: Walking Tree, 2012.

Scull, Christina and Wayne G. Hammond. *The J.R.R. Tolkien Companion and Guide*. 2 vols. Boston and New York: Houghton Mifflin, 2006.

Shippey, Thomas A. *The Road to Middle-earth*. London: George Allen & Unwin, 1982; revised edition, London: HarperCollins Publishers, 2005.

Swinfen, Ann. *In Defence of Fantasy*. London: Routledge and Kegan Paul, 1984.

Tolkien, J.R.R. "On Fairy-stories," in *Tree and Leaf*. London: George Allen & Unwin, 1964; second edition, 1988): see also *Tolkien on Fairy-stories*, edited by Verlyn Flieger and Douglas A. Anderson. London: HarperCollinsPublishers, 2008.

—. *The History of Middle-earth*, edited by Christopher Tolkien. London, George Allen & Unwin and HarperCollinsPublishers, 12 volumes, 1983-96.

—. *The Hobbit*. London, George Allen & Unwin, 1937.

—. *The Letters of J.R.R. Tolkien*, edited by Humphrey Carpenter, with Christopher Tolkien. London: George Allen & Unwin, 1981.

—. *The Lord of the Rings*. London: George Allen & Unwin, 1954-55; fiftieth anniversary edition, London: HarperCollinsPublishers, 2005.

—. *The Monsters and the Critics and Other Essays*, edited by Christopher Tolkien. London: George Allen & Unwin, 1983.

—. *The Silmarillion,* edited by Christopher Tolkien. London: George Allen & Unwin, 1977.

—. *Unfinished Tales of Númenor and Middle-earth*, edited by Christopher Tolkien. London, George Allen & Unwin, 1980.

Tolkien, J.R.R., E.V. Gordon, and Norman Davis (eds). *Sir Gawain and the Green Knight.* Oxford: Oxford University Press, 1967.

Wordsworth, William. "Preface," in *William Wordsworth and Samuel Taylor Coleridge: Lyrical Ballads,* edited by Derek Roper. 18-48. London and Glasgow: Collins, 1968.

Zipes, Jack. *Breaking the Magic Spell.* London: Heinemann, 1979.

Notes

1   That is, Volume 2, *The Book of Lost Tales Part II* (1984), and Volume 3, *The Lays of Beleriand* (1985).

2   See Christina Scull and Wayne G. Hammond, *The J.R.R. Tolkien Companion and Guide: Reader's Guide*, pages 570f.

3   Andrew Lang included the story of Sigurd in his second collection of fairy-stories, *The Red Fairy Book* (1890), where Tolkien probably found it as a boy.

4   See page 3 of Rachel Hart's chapter "Tolkien, St. Andrews and Dragons" in *Tree of Tales*, edited by Trevor Hart and Ivan Khovacs (Waco, Texas: Baylor University Press, 2007), pages 1-11.

5   There is of course some horse-trading in *The Lord of the Rings*, when the hobbits acquire a pony before they leave Bree. This kind of development, mostly associated with hobbits, is part of the shift from fable to novel in the writing of *The Lord of the Rings*.

6   See the third chapter of my book *Tolkien and Wagner: the Ring and "Der Ring"* (Zurich and Jena: Walking Tree, 2012).

Chapter 9

"Oh, You Wicked Storytellers!"

John Patrick Pazdziora

Once upon a time, stories were told by storytellers.
At first glance, this seems self-evident. In fact, it is the root of a literary puzzle. Even though the storyteller belongs to an oral tale tradition, and even though that oral culture has largely vanished from the West, authors of written, literary tales still place themselves in an uneasy relationship with their predecessors. It has never been entirely clear—and perhaps it never will be—precisely how literary and oral tales interrelate. The storyteller in literary fairy tales is a numinous, evasive figure. In new fairy tales, most of which never had a direct oral original, the storyteller becomes even more puzzling. He becomes, in fact, a character in his own right. So it should be no surprise that this complex character of the storyteller appears in the works of two twentieth-century masters of the new fairy tale.

"A Happy Madman": Neil Gaiman and James Thurber

In late 2001, several months after launching his online journal, Neil Gaiman wrote a baffled, passionate blog post about James Thurber's indescribable novella *The 13 Clocks* (1950).[1] Gaiman had been reading his youngest daughter the battered duplex edition he acquired when he was "about eight," the same copy he read aloud to his little sister. But when he decided to buy a new edition, he discovered it was out of print:

> Which leaves me perfectly gobsmacked. I mean, it's one of the great kids' books of the last century. It may be the best thing Thurber ever wrote. It's certainly the most fun that anybody can have reading anything aloud [...]. If I ever wrote something half as good I'd be over the moon. And it's out of print.

He concluded his post with an appeal to publishers: "I'll happily write an introduction to the book if you can bring it back into print."

It took around six years, but his appeal was heard. The New York Review of Books arranged to reprint the volume for their Children's Collection, and in February 2008 Gaiman could announce that his promised introduction was "finished and delivered."[2] By the end of that year, Gaiman happily reported that *The 13 Clocks* "is riding high in the Amazon.com top 100. (#33 as I type this.)" and noted that "my burbling about [it] in this very blog helped bring [it] back into print."[3]

It seems to have been an act of literary homage, or perhaps more correctly the payment of a literary debt, for Gaiman to write the introduction. He begins by declaring: "This book, the one you are holding, *The 13 Clocks* by James Thurber, is probably the best book in the world."[4] Nor does he relent from this claim, beyond a modest concession to critical tentativeness. His introduction, indeed, seems calculated both to tempt and intimidate interested critics, almost in the manner of a genteel sideshow barker. Though cautioning that it may be "likely to dissolve if examined too long or too closely,"[5] he offers his own style of examination:

> *The 13 Clocks* isn't really a fairy tale, just as it isn't really a ghost story. But it feels like a fairy tale, and it takes place in

a fairy tale world. It is short—not too short, just perfectly short. Short enough. [...] I watch Thurber wrap his story tightly in words, while at the same time juggling fabulous words that glitter and gleam, tossing them out like a happy madman, all the time explaining and revealing and baffling with words. It is a miracle. I think you could learn everything you need to know about telling stories from this book.[6]

This image of Thurber as "a happy madman" juggling well-balanced words like torches is striking, and significant for a reading both of Thurber's fairy tales and Gaiman's own. The verbal shadow-play in this section seems careful and deliberate: *The 13 Clocks* both is and is not a fairy tale. Gaiman in fact coyly concludes his introduction with a list of forms and genres which, he says, *The 13 Clocks* is not.

Gaiman even goes so far as to declare that: "It doesn't need an introduction. It doesn't need me."[7] The gesture could, perhaps, be read as confidence—absent in his blogs on the matter—that the book would have returned to print without his help. Yet this would miss the significance of the gesture. *The 13 Clocks* stands admirably on its own merits, true. But it is worth considering that Thurber wrote a laconic foreword to the work, which is dutifully placed alongside Gaiman's introduction. For whatever reason, Thurber himself seemed to consider it the sort of story that needed an introduction. In light of Gaiman's outspoken admiration for Thurber's ability as a literary craftsman, it seems strange to suggest he is hinting Thurber should not have written the foreword. With his gesture at the end of the introduction declaring the introduction unneeded, Gaiman seems to be turning aside authorial responsibility for his analysis, and for his involvement in the project. He appears to will himself to vanish precisely at the moment his influence is most felt, creating the illusion that the reader is encountering the book without his mediation. It is perhaps no coincidence that Gaiman employed this device to introduce Thurber. Occlusion of the narrative voice, authorial contradiction, and the self-subversion of narrative are all modes of storytelling both Thurber and Gaiman play with.

In much of Thurber's best prose, his narrative voice sounds as helpless and confused as his hapless anti-heroes. This is exemplified by "The Secret Life of Walter Mitty" (1939), perhaps his best known work. The narrative interlaces a henpecked husband's mundane afternoon shopping for puppy biscuits with his oscillating, self-aggrandising daydreams. Walter Mitty has a furtive, frustrating life and imagines himself the hero of various pulp thrillers. Biographical readings of this story have proved irresistible to critics, to such extent that a recent biography of Thurber was titled *The Man Who Was Walter Mitty*.[8] Yet to unequivocally claim that an author should be directly equated with a character imagining himself to be other characters seems too convoluted, and too neat. Gaiman's own view on narrative seems closer to the mark:

> Stories are, in one way or another, mirrors. We use them to explain to ourselves how the world works or how it doesn't work. Like mirrors, stories prepare us for the day to come. They distract us from the things in the darkness.
>
> Fantasy—and all fiction is fantasy of one kind or another—is a mirror. A distorting mirror, to be sure, and a concealing mirror, set at forty-five degrees to reality, but it's a mirror nonetheless, which we can use to tell ourselves things we might not otherwise see.[9]

In this understanding, story is *apophasis*: revelation by occlusion. Mirrors, Gaiman says, "appear to tell the truth, to reflect life back out at us; but set a mirror correctly and it will lie so convincingly you'll believe that something has vanished into thin air, that a box filled with doves and flags and spiders is actually empty, that people hidden in the wings are floating ghosts upon the stage."[10] A story, and in particular a fantasy, distorts and re-interprets life and experience; contemplating a story, or modifying it to put oneself as a character can be seen as a sort of catharsis. Seen from this perspective, "The Secret Life of Walter Mitty" seems to say less about its author than about its readers, and perhaps reading in general. It creates a dedoublement where the reader is simultaneously observing

Walter Mitty escape to imagined worlds, while engaging in nearly the same activity themselves by reading the story.

The author, then, is not the figure reflected in the mirrors; the author is behind them, moving the screens and angling the panes, creating the distorting, transforming effect. The narrator, or narrative voice, is thus potentially a character within the story. As Gaiman does directly in his introduction to *The 13 Clocks*, this allows the author to sidestep authorial responsibility; the author remains in the shadows, manipulating the mirrors of story but unobserved, and seemingly uninvolved.

Narrators and storytellers are not to be entirely trusted; they are shape-shifters and shadow players, continually unravelling and complicating the thread of their own narratives. Jack Zipes has argued that a storyteller held an almost cabbalistic "authority and power" within an oral culture; a "magic tale" referred not only to the miraculous transformations within the story, "but also the magical play of words by the teller as performer":

> Storytelling is fluid, alive, and unpredictable, and can be altered to fit any setting. The taleteller changes in the telling of the story and shifts his or her identity like the remarkable trickster of the folk-tale tradition. Telling a magic folk tale was and is not unlike performing a magic trick, and depending on the art of the storyteller, listeners are placed under a spell. They are in awe, and to be in awe is to be in a special place, linked with the teller and other members of the group, transcending reality for a brief moment, to be transported to extraordinary regions of experience.[11]

The literary fairy tale was simultaneously a preservation and transformation of the oral narrative. From the sixteenth to the eighteenth centuries, written tales became more reflective of the sociological complexities facing the increasingly urbane, educated readership; the nineteenth century saw fairy tales become a pedagogical, civilising tool to expound the values of the new bourgeois classes.[12] Thus, Zipes says, "the identifiable voice of the storyteller who was part of a community had shifted to the literary voice, with a narrator who is no longer present and is not clearly identifiable" and which often "assumed a paternal role."[13]

Zipes traces this development into the twentieth century specifically through the medium of fairy tale film, but it influenced the literary world as well. Writers became fascinated by function of the narrator's voice within a written tale. It was not necessarily their own voice, but it performed a somewhat different role from the storyteller. Author, narrator, and storyteller emerged as separate figures. It was not clear that they were all the same person; the author could successfully hide behind his characters in a way that the storyteller, physically present in the room with his hearers, could not. The author wrote the story, and the narrator was the central presence and voice of the tale. Where, then, was the storyteller in the written text? How could the fluid magic of oral storytelling be preserved in a literary, printed tale? What was the role of a storyteller in the new, literary fairy tales?

"They Must All Be Right"

Thurber approached his new fairy tales with delight; there is an unmistakeable playfulness running throughout the stories, as he juggles the verbal and structural forms of the tales. Nor is his storytelling complexity limited to *The 13 Clocks*. His fascination with the storyteller figure runs through all his fairy tales, appearing with particular clarity in his first children's story, *Many Moons* (1943). This may in part be due to the unique circumstances surrounding its composition. In the summer of 1941, Thurber was suffering the devastating initial stages of his blindness, having already undergone five eye operations.[14] His stories from this period, notably "The Whip-poor-will" and "The Cane in the Corridor," are dark and troubling, morbid black comedies depicting histrionic levels of paranoia and violence.[15] In the midst of his physical pain and psychological turmoil, Thurber wrote a cheerful story which he thought "might make a good Christmas book."[16] Almost immediately afterward, he suffered a complete nervous breakdown, experiencing severe panic attacks, hallucinating, and drinking heavily in an attempt to calm himself.[17] Although he regained his mind quickly, full recovery was slow and coincided with near-complete loss of vision.[18] In the midst of this upheaval, he seems to have forgotten that he wrote *Many Moons*.[19] The manuscript was rediscovered in 1943—fortuitously, both for Thurber and for children's literature—and published later that year with illustrations by Louis Slobodkin, promptly winning the Caldecott Medal for 1944.

Given the turmoil surrounding its composition, the story's sprightly delicacy is all the more remarkable. Princess Lenore, "ten years old, going on eleven," falls ill from "a surfeit of raspberry tarts" and takes to her bed.[20] When the King her father anxiously offers to give her anything her heart desires, she declares that she only wants one thing: "I want the moon. If I can have the moon, I will be well again." In quick succession, the king summons his wise men: the Lord High Chamberlain, the Royal Wizard, and the Royal Mathematician. Each wise man shows more inclination for reading the King long lists of their distinguished services than for helping Princess Lenore. Jessica Tiffin correctly observes that "[t]he assertions of each apparently wise man are alike in that they insist on the impossibility of the quest, while simultaneously attempting to aggrandize the speaker, his authoritative knowledge, and his particular skills."[21] And they are all agreed that getting the moon is impossible, though they disagree about precisely how difficult it would be. At last the King sends for the Court Jester.

The Jester came bounding into the throne room in his motley and his cap and bells, and sat at the foot of the throne.

"What can I do for you, your Majesty?" asked the Court Jester.

"Nobody can do anything for me," said the King mournfully. "The Princess Lenore wants the moon, and she cannot get well till she gets it, but nobody can get it for her. Every time I ask anybody for the moon, it gets larger and farther away. There is nothing you can do for me except play on your lute. Something sad."

The King has put himself in the ludicrous position of asking a Court Jester to sing "[s]omething sad." In other words, owing to his own despondency, he wants the Jester to perform the exact opposite of his role. The Court Jester is not deterred. He coaxes the whole story out of the king, and considers:

> The Court Jester strummed on his lute for a little while. "They are all wise men," he said, "and so they must all be right. If they are all right, then the moon must be just as large and as far away as each person thinks it is. The thing to do is find out how big the Princess Lenore thinks it is, and how far away."

Princess Lenore, it turns out, insists that the moon is no bigger than her thumbnail, and that "it gets caught in the top branches" of "the big tree outside my window." The Court Jester is able to acquire this moon easily enough—or at least a cunning representation of it—and the Princess is well again, for a while.

Many Moons is the only one of Thurber's fairy tales to be composed before the shift in his writing style that followed his blindness. In contrast to the sonorous lyricism of his later work, *Many Moons* retains the minimalist precision of prose that marked his contributions to *The New Yorker* in the 1920s and 1930s.[22] It is also his only fairy tale to antedate World War II. As such, it seems to be his most personal fairy tale; the political cataclysms and nefarious villains of the later works are markedly absent. *The Great Quillow* (1944) sees a toymaker facing down a village-devouring giant; in *The White Deer*, King Clode is beset with fear about his kingdom and his dynasty, declaring "I blow my horn in waste land, so to speak." The whimsy in *The 13 Clocks* seems to be directed against the inhuman cruelty of the Cold Duke, all too believable after the Second World War. *The Wonderful O* (1957), written during the decline of McCarthyism, sees a boatload of pirates invading a peaceful island to steal their treasure and remove all occurrences of the letter O, including "hope" and "freedom." Thurber's last and least-known fairy tale, "The Last Clock: A Fable for the Time, Such As It Is, of Man" (1959), reflects the bleak collapse of society through obsessive governance by an ogre who eats clocks, and an incompetent populace who cannot function without them. In other words, there is a political, societal element to these tales, outside invaders and paranoid politicians leading kingdoms to ruin.

Many Moons, by contrast, is domestic. The story is set entirely within the palace; there is no foreign invasion, no political repression, or anything more inherently complicated than a tummy-ache. It could be objected that the king's wise men serve as political satire. Richard Tobias suggests that the Lord High Chamberlain "represents the prodigious success of commerce and distribution," the Wizard embodies "a failure of technical society to ease human need," and the Royal Mathematician "brings to our minds the modern physicists and linguistic philosophers who probe so deeply into our universe."[23] But this is too ponderous, and not entirely convincing. Jessica Tiffin strikes closer to the mark when she notes that "[i]n their endless lists and provision of absurd solutions to the princess's illness, the ministers take on the mantle of the ill-mannered and arrogant elder sons of fairy tale"; their function in the narrative is domestic, not socio-political. It is, after all, the Lord Chamberlain—the overseer of the royal household—whom the king summons first. The lists the wise men read are items only of personal importance to the king; in the case of the Lord Chamberlain and the royal wizard, they actually double as grocery lists. The political currents which Thurber would address later are hardly in evidence here; the role of the storyteller within the palace, for shaping and nurturing an individual imagination, is the primary concern of this story.

Many Moons is a many-layered, polyvalent tale in which several stories compete against each other for legitimacy. The Court Jester seems to accept the impossible assertion that the contradictory accounts of the moon's size and location can all be true. Empirically, of course, this is impossible.Princess Lenore does not have the actual moon. But it is *her* moon. The Jester's cleverness lies not in eliding empirical fact, but in acknowledging the power of stories; by admitting the various stories of the wise men as all equally true, he recognises that a cure can be effect simply by finding the right story.

Biographers and critics have tended to see Thurber's likeness in the Court Jester.[24] Yet if a biographical reading were attempted, there seems to be more textual evidence for seeing Thurber in the Princess Lenore—not Thurber as he actually was, but as he may have seen himself shortly before his breakdown. A dream child, perhaps, yet on inspection it seems a troubling, even alarming self-portrait. Lenore is innocent, privileged, with other people making decisions for her; she has had nothing worse to face in life than a tummy-ache. But she has been crying for the moon, and cannot get it. To conceal this fact from her, the wise men suggest dark glasses, heavy curtains round the palace, and perpetual fireworks displays. Each remedy explicitly involves obscuration, narrowing of vision, incapacitation, and blindness. Dark glasses cut Lenore off from sight. Blackout curtains keep her in the confines of her home, unable to see beyond familiar settings. And perhaps most tellingly of all, seeing incessant showers of brilliant light is a serious symptom of the retinal and ocular trauma that Thurber experienced. All these treatments, as the king points out, offer only one solution: "she would be ill again." It would not be difficult to see this passage reflecting Thurber's own mounting fear of his disability, that, as a writer and illustrator he would be cut off from his creativity and his livelihood; more ominously, it suggests a fear that his entire creative project has been a delusion, that he can never attain his dreams and any success he'd had was another one of his jokes. The Court Jester again turns to Lenore for her own story to explain the moon's reappearance. In 1941, however, Thurber could not have known for certain that he would find such a story to tell.

Thurber did keep writing stories; in 1941 some of his greatest works were still before him. His next new fairy tale seems to reflect his determination to maintain the viability of his art. In *The Great Quillow* (1943), Quillow the Toymaker saves his village by convincing the giant Hunder to believe a patently ludicrous story. More than just telling the story—and there are nonsense stories within nonsense stories in this tale—Quillow holds a clandestine meeting at a merry-go-round and convinces the villagers to enact the story, to make it come true. Quillow's silly story becomes a catalyst for collective action against the monstrous reality of the giant. The proportions are greater, but Quillow seems to face the same conundrum as the Court Jester: the conflict between child and adult, between a world of imagination and a world of fact. The storyteller is presented as a whimsical aggressor, facing down and vanquishing even a grown-up giant.

Biographical considerations, of course, are not needed to recognise the thematic simplicity and poignancy *Many Moons*: telling stories defies the reality of a bleak world. The King and his advisors, without the resources of a child's imagination, are either overblown with their successes or in perpetual crisis and despair. Lenore retains the ability to make silly stories that explain a distressing world, and bring her comfort. The Jester allows Princess Lenore to tell her own story; he allies himself on the side of the child and her stories against the hostile and fact-obsessed world of the adults. It is correct that "the person who eventually solves the fairy-tale dilemma of the princess's illness is the princess herself."[25] But the Court Jester, as a performer and storyteller, allows the princess's story to be told. His silent tale creates a space sympathetic to her tale where her voice can be heard, and listened to. To borrow Gaiman's image, the Court Jester is the storyteller angling the mirror in such a way that a child's fancy becomes true.

"The Crocodile was Alive"

Tellingly, in *The Tragical Comedy or Comical Tragedy of Mr. Punch* (1994), Gaiman has his nameless narrator say of his childhood: "I lived in a land of giants in those days. All children do."[26] Gaiman has described *Mr. Punch* as part of a "sequence of unreliable autobiographies," the ostensible sequel to *Violent Cases* (1987), his first collaboration with Dave McKean.[27] In *Mr. Punch*, Gaiman places the conflict between the child and the adult at the heart of the story. The narrative relates a small boy's attempt to understand the adult turmoil of his Jewish family as his grandparents are ageing; his own fears about growing-up and identity are given exaggerated force as he watches his paternal grandfather age into decrepitude and mental instability; the first-person narrator is clearly meant to be the little boy as an adult. The narrative is thus inherently unreliable, as the adult narrator cannot be trusted to tell the child's truth. The narrator seems self-conscious of this dichotomy, when, for instance, he tries to explain his experience of half-delight, half-terror when his grandfather is threatening to throw him into an indoor swimming-pool:

> Adults are threatening creatures. Shall I throw you into the water? I'll put you into the rubbish-bin. I'll eat you all up. That's what they say. And no matter how much you tell yourself that they're lying, or teasing, there's always a chance. Maybe they are telling the truth. [...] Adults lie. But not always. ([24-25])

The adults' playfulness progresses from a harmless ducking in a swimming pool to cannibalism. Aside from resonances with fairy tales such as "Hansel and Gretel" and "The Juniper Tree," it seems likely that Gaiman is alluding to Maurice Sendak's classic picture book *Where the Wild Things Are* (1963); Sendak seems to have had a significant influence on Gaiman's work.[28] Sendak depicts the uncertainty of children around adults; he has said that the wild things themselves originated in part from childhood fear of his adult relatives, and a real alarm that they wanted to eat him.[29] In *Where the Wild Things Are*, the little boy Max gets to wear a wolf suit and say "I'll eat you up!" to his mother. He is allowed to escape into a fantasy world of his own creation, where he is "king of all wild things"; it is a child-world, in which adults are preyed upon and monsters can be easily cowed. Sendak's story re-imagines childhood imagination and escapes from boredom or loneliness. Gaiman's placement of the allusion is quite different; the child is in the know that the adult is joking, but at the same time is not able to easily escape into imagination. The child's imagination is what leaves him helpless and uncertain.

Significantly, Sendak's wild things have the large eyes and small features of cartoon children; in a way, they are reassuring monsters. McKean surrounds the boy with fractured pictures of the adults themselves, and unnerving composites of devil puppets.

During the sequence of frames quoted above, McKean depicts the boy as a small, wire marionette, set on a shadowed stage of printed type. The text is sideways and backwards, inscrutable; the child must act out his role against a script he cannot understand. Even when, with the realization that "[a]dults lie," he loses his strings and gains his autonomy, his shadow vanishes from the frame and he himself slips out of focus. Stories, told of necessity by adults, are unreliable, and inscrutable.

In this context, the storyteller becomes an even more important ally for the child. He is a childlike adult, or a grown-up child; his realm is liminality, the unstable, in-between places. When Professor Swatchell, the Punch-and-Judy man, befriends the little boy, he gives him a way of understanding the complex and intimidating adult world. He is the only adult in the book to speak to the little boy as an equal, and he frankly acknowledges the boy's bewilderment and fear: "[P]eople, eh? Mystery plays the lot of them" ([32]). And he shows the boy his puppets, the cast of "the greatest, oldest, wisest play there is, the comical tragedy, the tragical comedy, of Mister Punch" ([35]). Swatchell himself claims to be an original member of the cast: "I used to be the crocodile, you know" ([38], emphasis in original). When the boy is skeptical, Swatchell protests: "The tale of Mister Punch isn't only a puppet show, y'see. [...] I was following him around back in the dawn days, in the winter's time. He'd play his little pranks, then as now, he'd best the Devil and fight the dragon. That was me, at his side" ([39]). Then he lets the little boy put on the crocodile puppet. The narrator recalls:

I slid the puppet onto my left hand; and it came to life.

I'm not talking about anything fantastical here. You can try it yourself—find a hand puppet, slide it on your hand, move your fingers. And somehow, in the cold space between one moment and the next, the puppet becomes alive.

And the crocodile was alive.

I didn't ever want to give it back. I wanted it to sit on my arm forever, brave where I was fearful, impetuous where I held back. I would have taken it to school and scared my teachers, taken it home and made me eat my sister... ([40]).

The narrator's claim that he isn't "talking about anything fantastical" is undercut by McKean's illustration. The crocodile arcs across the page in a burst of fire, the boy lit vibrantly in the red-gold glow; the dragon has become a part of him. The illustration displays fantastic metamorphosis while the narrator feebly protests it was only a trick of the light. Professor Swatchell has taught the boy how to find his identity among the characters of a story; the boy begins gradually identifying the adults around him with the other puppets in the play. In the denouement of the story, when he begins to fully understand both his grandfather and how the adults in his life correspond to the characters in the play, he becomes a puppet himself. The boy, in fact, has realised what story he is in; *Mr. Punch* presents almost a full Punch-and-Judy show, interlaced with the narrator's memories. It is in fact never entirely clear whether the show frames the narration or the narration frames the show. The discrimination between story and reality, between one narrative and another, is elided, and blurred.

For all his identification with the crocodile, in this story Professor Swatchell is Mister Punch himself. McKean draws him to resemble Mr Punch: large craggy features, domed forehead, beaked nose, sharp chin, and bright playful eyes. He dominates the left side of the frame, or stage-right, where Mister Punch, as a right-hand puppet, appears continually throughout the show. When he shows the boy the cast, he appears beside them as though he's on stage, drawn just head-and-shoulders like a monstrous puppet. When the boy sees Swatchell in a distorting mirror, he sees "[a] huge head: beady wooden eyes" ([62]). Swatchell is at once the puppet and the puppeteer, part of the story and the storyteller. Like the Court Jester, Swatchell and his Punch-and-Judy show offer a means of letting children discover their own stories.

Gaiman similarly plays with this idea in "Harlequin Valentine" (2000).[30] The narrator, a demigod Harlequin, flits through the world identifying the other people in his pantomime, particularly looking for girls to be Columbine. Harlequin transforms the mundane life of Missy, an office girl, into transcendence and love. He soliloquizes:

Oh Missy, I saw you yesterday in the street, and followed you into Al's Super-Value Foods and More, elation and joy rising within me. In you, I recognised someone who could transport me, take me from myself. In you I recognised my Valentine, my Columbine.[31]

Harlequin brings her into his world; by giving her his heart, he gives her his own creative vision. From being his Columbine, the object of affection, Missy becomes the adventurous Harlequin herself, saying: "That's the joy of a harlequinade, after all, isn't it? We change our costumes. We change our roles." [32] The result of hearing the storyteller is transformed vision, and transformed role; it opens the possibility of telling one's own stories.

But, like Lenore's stories in *Many Moons*, the stories themselves prove to be no more trustworthy than the adults. The thematic centre of *Mr. Punch* seems to be when the little boy goes into the Hall of Mirrors, a fixture at his grandfather's decrepit amusement arcade: "To get in, you had to walk through a maze constructed of mirrors and sheets of transparent glass, which went from floor to ceiling. You had to find your way through" ([61]). He loses himself several times, but eventually finds his way:

Finally, I made it through the labyrinth and walked into Looking-Glass Hall.

It was a dusty room, empty but for the mirrors.

Each mirror was attached to the wall, and was the height of a tall man. There were mirrors that made me look small, or bent, or thin, or fat. One of them gave you a giant head; another split you into two people. I raised my hand and two of me waved our hands in return.

For the first time I understood that mirrors could lie. ([62])

Gaiman appears to be invoking Lewis Carroll's *Through the Looking Glass, and What Alice Found There* (1871). More wistful and nostalgic than its predecessor, *Through the Looking Glass* sees Alice struggling to understand her place as a pawn in a giant chess game in Looking-Glass World. Carroll was well aware of Coleridge's use of the mirror as a symbol for story and imagination; in a reversed dream-world Alice can ponder the complexities of adulthood while remaining forever a child. The little boy in *Mr. Punch* is similarly facing a transformation of vision, but what he sees in the mirrors are versions of his adult self. The labyrinth of deceptive mirrors, itself an image of sexual maturation, opens to reveal not a single looking-glass to crawl through, but a plethora of choice; the little boy gets to choose where he will go, which reflection he will become. He has begun by framing his life in a story, and now realises that stories are no more trustworthy than adults. At this crucial place between worlds and lives, Swatchell—the storyteller, Mister Punch—appears, and finally begins explaining the boy's family history, revealing the knowledge which had been hidden from him before. For the first time, Swatchell is drawn on the right side of the frame, the place of a left-hand puppet; the boy appears on the right. By giving him a family history, Swatchell gives the boy his own story to tell.

The ability of a child to choose an identity through story is, again, a theme Gaiman revisits in other works. In "One Life, Furnished in Early Moorcock" (1994), a story directly contemporary with *Mr. Punch*, twelve-year-old Richard Grey, also an autobiographical character,[33] has a dream experience in which he meets his literary hero: Michael Moorcock's series protagonist Elric of Melniboné. Elric leads the way into a ruined temple, where Richard finds himself on a surreal quest:

Inside the temple, Richard found a life waiting for him, all ready to be worn and lived, and inside that life, another. Each life he tried on, he slipped into, and it pulled him further in, further away from the world he came from; one by one, existence following existence, rivers of dreams and fields of stars, a hawk with a sparrow clutched in its talons flies low above the grass, and here are tiny intricate people waiting for him to fill their heads with life, and thousands of years pass and he is engaged in strange work of great importance and sharp

beauty, and he is loved, and he is honoured, and then a
pull, a sharp tug and it's...

...it was like coming up from the bottom of the deep end
of a swimming pool. Stars appeared above him and dropped
away and dissolved into blues and greens, and it was with a
deep sense of disappointment that he became Richard Grey,
and came to himself once more [...].[34]

Like the boy in *Mr. Punch*, Richard can choose among several possible lives, and what sort of grown-up he wants to be. And significantly, again like *Mr. Punch*, it is a story, and a storyteller, that leads
him to the place where choice is possible. The other lives he tries on
suggest the sort of paperback fantasy Richard loves; as with Walter
Mitty's secret lives, this passage seems to be as much about reading as growing up. It hardly seems accidental that Richard chooses
to fill the heads of "tiny intricate people" with life, and to under-
take "strange work of great importance and sharp beauty"—in other
words, to be a storyteller. It is not a choice that real-life Richard is
quite ready to make—"[t]here were other things to be"—and instead
he decides he wants to be a good werewolf. He is still finding his
identity in stories, and even beginning to try storytelling.

"Not a Mere Device"

In Thurber and Gaiman's works alike, the storyteller appears
to guide the child through the liminal border of adulthood—not
taking responsibility for what happens along the way, but en-
couraging the events to take a certain shape. It is this role, the
storyteller as guide, that seems exemplified in *The 13 Clocks*,
which Gaiman so deeply admires. Here the storyteller/jester figure is the whimsical, indescribable figure of the Golux. "Every
tale needs a Golux," Gaiman declares. "Luckily for all of us, this
book has one."[35]

The Golux is undoubtedly one of Thurber's finest and most
perplexing creations. He is a "little man" man who appears to
help the Prince Zorn of Zorna on an impossible quest: "He wore

an indescribable hat, his eyes were wide and astonished, as if everything were happening for the first time, and he had a dark, describable beard."[36] He introduces himself as "the only Golux in the world, and not a mere Device" (32). He is a rhymester, a jokester, and a trickster; a school-based education convinces people that he doesn't exist (37). It's in his nature to be in the middle of danger, to help those in need or at least cause them some perplexity: "I must always be on hand when people are in peril" (32). What's more, he's a storyteller. Prince Zorn is confronting the sadistic Cold Duke of Coffin castle; when the prince is in danger of being fed to the Duke's geese, the Golux's response is "We must invent a tale to stay his hand" (35). Then, after devising a tale, the Golux exclaims with satisfaction: "The tale sounds true, [...] I'm certain he will stay his hand, I think" (35-36). Later, as the prince sets off to complete his task, the Golux announces, "I will tell you the tale of Hagga" (66). The ridiculous story that follows burlesques the fairy tale mode ("she came upon the good King Gwain of Yarrow with his foot caught in a wolf trap") but in fact contains crucial elements of the overarching narrative (66ff). He concludes: "'I hope,' the Golux said, 'that this is true. I make things up, you know.'" (70)

This continual deflection of certainty is typical of him; he refuses both the power of the oral storyteller and the auctorial responsibility for written narrative. When he appears beside the prince in a locked dungeon, the prince understandably asks, "How came you here? [...] And can you leave?" (42). The Golux replies: "I never know" (43). On the few occasions when he claims certainty, he is wrong; the narrator hints the reason is senility, or perhaps wilful ignorance: "The Golux had missed her age by fifty years, as old men often do" (78). Yet while absolving himself from a narrator's responsibility or knowledge, and sending up a smokescreen of riddles and puns, he manages to manoeuvre the characters and the events of the story as thoroughly as an author:

"I can do a score of things that can't be done," the Golux said. "I can find a thing I cannot see and see a thing I cannot find. The first is time, the second is a spot before my eyes.

I can feel a thing I cannot touch, and touch a thing I cannot feel. The first is sad and sorry, the second is your heart. What would you do without me? Say 'nothing.'"

"Nothing," said the Prince.

"Good. Then you're helpless and I'll help you." (65)

This attitude, the storyteller as helping the helpless, characterises the Golux's approach to narrative. His goal throughout the story seems simply to help two young people be happy, summed up in his parting dictum: "Remember laughter. You'll need it even in the blessed isles of Ever After" (120).

The Golux, like the Court Jester and Mister Punch, is once again allied with children against the adult world. In a scene evoking *Richard III*, the Duke recalls with malicious pleasure "the children locked up in my tower" for sleeping in the camellias—children who are now ghosts, after an unspecified incident which makes even the Duke's chief spy squeamish (92). While the Duke is gloating, however, "[a] purple ball with gold stars on it came slowly bouncing down the iron stairs and winked and twinkled, like a naked child saluting priests" (95). The Duke is appalled, and the chief spy remarks that it looks "very like a ball the Golux and the children used to play with"—an observation that convinces the Duke the ghosts are on the Golux's side (96). It would be more correct to say the Golux is on theirs. By taking the side of children, lovers, and ghosts, the Golux creates a space where they can tell their stories and be heard. "I make mistakes," the Golux declares, "but I am on the side of Good, [...] by accident and happenchance" (34). Though he adds, somewhat wistfully, "I had high hopes of being Evil when I was two" (34).

The Storyteller as The Fool

The question remains as to what interpretation this reading may suggest. Jessica Tiffin follows earlier critics in seeing the Court Jester *Many Moons* as Thurber's projection of himself, with "the persona of the humorist, the classic archetype of the Wise Fool."[37] It is not

necessary to identify the author with a single character for the broader point to stand: the motley Jester and Mister Punch are both Wise
Fools. It hardly seems coincidence that Thurber and Gaiman employ
the same symbol when putting the storyteller into stories: the
storyteller is the esoteric Fool, the Zero card in the Tarot deck, standing at once at the beginning and the end of the soul's journey.

Gaiman employs Tarot symbolism throughout his work: his
series of flash fiction, "Fifteen Painted Cards from the Vampire
Tarot" springs readily to mind. So, too, do the characters of Cain
and Abel in the *Sandman* series (1989-1996), who are also evoca-
tions of Punch and Judy. And Dream himself, the great storyteller,
is critically connected to the symbol of The Fool. Discussion of the
Sandman world is, unfortunately, beyond the scope of this study.
Most significantly for our purposes, the image of The Fool forms
a dominant visual motif of *Mr Punch*. Waite, in his classic study of
esotericism in the Tarot, calls The Fool "the most speaking of all
the symbols"[38]; he gives this description of the card:

> With a light step, as if earth and its trammels had little to
> restrain him, a young man in gorgeous vestments pauses
> at the brink of a precipice among the great heights of the
> world; he surveys the blue distance before him—its expanse
> of sky rather than the prospect below. His act of eager
> walking is still indicated, though he is stationary at the giv-
> en moment; his dog is still bounding. [...] He is a prince of
> the other world on his travels through this one—all amidst
> the morning glory, in the keen air. The sun which shines
> behind him knows whence he came, whither he is going,
> and how he will return by another path after many days.
> He is the spirit in search of experience.[39]

Elsewhere, Waite explains that the Fool "is looking over his
shoulder and does not know that he is on the brink of a precipice;
but a dog or some other animal [...] is attacking him from behind,
and he is hurried to destruction unawares."[40] The Fool appears as
Zero, "an unnumbered card"; by having no fixed position within
the Tarot deck, the Fool may occur at any place within the esoteric

journey, standing simultaneously at the beginning and the ending. Waite explains that "[h]e signifies the journey outward, the state of the first emanation, the graces and passivity of the spirit."[41]

Mister Punch's jester-like cap and motley most obviously suggest The Fool. Perhaps more significantly, Swatchell is accompanied by a small, bounding dog. After showing the boy the puppets, Swatchell is shown from behind, walking way. He stands in mid-step, arms spread crucifix-like, as if he is preparing to jump or dive. The dog is leaping beside him, in the sketch suspended in mid-air ([41]). As Waite writes of The Fool, "[h]is act of eager walking is still indicated, though he is stationary at the given moment; his dog is still bounding."[42] There is no realistic background to the frame, and no border; Swatchell hangs over blank paper, in front of blurred cuttings from a historical book on Punch-and-Judy. As The Fool, he is poised blissfully on the edge of the precipice, though whether of transcendence or of destruction is not clear. Mister Punch, indeed, stands perpetually unawares on the precipice; he lives, and jokes, and dances, on the edge of the long fall from the stage to the ground.

Thurber, as far as I am aware, had little or no interest in esotericism or Tarot. So it is all the more curious that he turned to the symbol of The Fool for his storyteller characters. Waite notes that The Fool can also be depicted "in the form of a court jester, with cap, bells and motley garb."[43] This is precisely the description Thurber chose to use for the court jester in *Many Moons*; even if Thurber arrived at these images independently, he clearly found the underlying symbolism useful. And his presentation of the whimsical storytellers fits with the liminal vision of the Fool. His storytellers career through their stories with aplomb, their faces and laughter raised to the "blue distance" before them.

The storyteller, then, stands both within and without the story. Within the tale, he contains the potential of all the characters, the impetus toward adventure and experience. Yet unlike the narrator, or the adult voices in the tale, he does not try to control; his movement is one of levity and grace. By aligning with the symbol of The Fool, the storyteller can be said to represent both a fixed point in the narrative—the moments when he appears in the text—

and the whole development of the character. His presence is one of promise—that there will be danger, yes, and dragons, but that there will be the leap into adventure, the journey of the child into adulthood, the soul into transcendence. The storyteller dwells thus at a point that is both end and journey, a still fluidity of movement, "a prince of the other world on his travels through this one."[44] He both points the way of adventure and acts as the guide; he is an adventurer himself. It is, after all, his story.

Conclusion

When Prince Zorn first meets the Golux, he too quickly accepts him as a magical helper:

> "I place my faith in you [said the prince], and where you lead, I follow."
> "Not so fast," the Golux said. "Half the places I have been to, never were. I make things up. Half the things I say are there cannot be found. When I was young I told a tale of buried gold, and men from leagues around dug in the woods. I dug myself."
> "But why?"
> "I thought the tale of treasure might be true."
> "You said you made it up."
> "I know I did, but then I didn't know I had. I forget things too." (33-34)

The storyteller may, like the esoteric Fool, contain all the potentialities, the introduction and the conclusion, of the whole story. But it is a knowledge he wears lightly. Thurber's storytellers are busied with solving crises, and making things up; Gaiman's storytellers are shadowy, ambivalent figures, often threatening and not entirely to be trusted. Yet they both share this in common: a refusal to accept responsibility for the stories they tell. It almost seems as if the oral storyteller is revelling in the freedom of being a character in a story without bothering to listen to the narrator. The Court

Jester, the Golux, Swatchell, and Mister Punch all destabilize the stories they enter; they create riotous mayhem, acting outside the restrictions of narrative and the authorial voice of the adult. They are the Zero Card within the tale, unbound to any order or system, a part and not a part of the stories. They embody "the journey outward,"[45] away from the confines of the wise men with their well-tabulated list of accomplishments. They take the side of the child-reader, not only to convey the story at hand but to help the children find their own stories.

When, during the show, the children begin to talk back, telling Judy that the Baby's been killed, Mister Punch shrieks "Oh, you wicked storytellers!" (18). The word's double meaning—both crafters of tales, and liars—suggests no one more than Mister Punch himself. And it seems possible that his shriek of indignation is also one of delight, recognising that he is leading the children into his own anarchic world of story, liminality, and wonder.

Bibliography

Fensch, Thomas. *The Man Who Was Walter Mitty: The Life and Work of James Thurber.* The Woodlands, TX: New Century Books, 2000.

Gaiman, Neil. *Fragile Things: Short Fictions and Wonders.* New York: Headline Review, 2006.

—. Introduction to *The 13 Clocks*, by James Thurber, 7-10. New York: New York Review, 2008.

—. "My hero: Maurice Sendak." *The Guardian.* May 11, 2012. Accessed July 18, 2012. http://www.guardian.co.uk/books/2012/may/11/maurice-sendak-my-hero-neil-gaiman.

—. "Neil Gaiman on Dave McKean." Neil Gaiman. Accessed July 19, 2011. http://www.neilgaiman.com/p/Cool_Stuff/Essays/Essays_By_Neil/Neil_Gaiman_on_Dave_McKean.

—. *Neil Gaiman's Journal.* http://journal.neilgaiman.com.

—. "One Life, Furnished in Early Moorcock." 1994. Heliotrope 1.5 (2009). Accessed 6 August 2012. http://www.heliotropemag.com/04/one-life-furnished-in-early-moorcock-by-neil-gaiman/.

—. *Smoke and Mirrors: Short Fictions and Illusions.* London: Headline, 1999.

Gaiman, Neil (w), and Dave McKean (a). *The Tragical Comedy or Comical Tragedy of Mr. Punch: A Romance.* London: VG Graphics, 1994.

Grauer, Neil A. *Remember Laughter: A Life of James Thurber.* Lincoln: University of Nebraska Press, 1994.

Holmes, Charles S. *The Clocks of Columbus: The Literary Career of James Thurber.* New York: Atheneum, 1972.

Long, Robert Emmet. *James Thurber.* New York: Continuum Publishing, 1988.

Thurber, James. *Many Moons*. 1943. New York: Harcourt Brace & Company, 1970.
—. *The 13 Clocks*. 1950. New York: New York Review, 2008.
—. *The Great Quillow*. 1944. New York: Harcourt Brace Jovanovich, 1994.
—. "The Last Clock: A Fable for the Time, such as it is, of Man." *The New Yorker*, February 21, 1959: 28-31.
—. *The White Deer*. 1948. New York: Harcourt Brace Jovanovich, 1984.
Tiffin, Jessica. *Marvellous Geometry: Narrative and Metafiction in Modern Fairy Tale*. Detroit: Wayne State University Press, 2009.
Tobias, Richard C. *The Art of James Thurber*. Athens, OH: Ohio University Press, 1969.
Waite, Arthur Edward. *The Key to the Tarot: Being Fragments of a Secret Tradition under the Veil of Divination*. New Edition. London: Rider & Co., [n.d.].
Zipes, Jack. *Happily Ever After: Fairy Tale, Children, and the Culture Industry*. New York and London: Routledge, 1997.

Notes

1   Neil Gaiman, introduction to *The 13 Clocks*, by James Thurber, 1950 (New York: New York Review, 2008), 8; *Neil Gaiman's Journal*, November 13, 2001, http://journal.neilgaiman.com/2001/11/so-im-reading-james-thurbers-13-clocks.asp. Gaiman has recommended Thurber as an author of short stories, which seems to suggest his familiarity extends beyond just *The 13 Clocks*, but there is to my knowledge no formal documentation on this point (cf. *Neil Gaiman's Journal*, December 23, 2001, http://journal.neilgaiman.com/2001/12/i-really-do-plan-to-put-up-page-of.asp).

2   *Neil Gaiman's Journal*, February 16, 2008, http://journal.neilgaiman.com/2008/02/alan-moore-knows-score-as-of-half-time.html.

3   *Neil Gaiman's Journal*, December 20, 2008, http://journal.neilgaiman.com/2008/12/trees.html.

4   Gaiman, Introduction, 7.

5   Gaiman, Introduction, 10.

6   Gaiman, Introduction, 9.

7   Gaiman, Introduction, 10

8   Thomas Fensch, *The Man Who Was Walter Mitty: The Life and Work of James Thurber* (The Woodlands, TX: New Century Books, 2000)

9   Neil Gaiman, *Smoke and Mirrors: Short Fictions and Illusions* (London: Headline, 1999), 3. Gaiman, of course, seems here to be deliberately positioning himself in the Romantic literary tradition, Coleridge as filtered through George MacDonald and the various Inklings, [cp. John Granger,

The Deathly Hallows Lectures (Allenton, PA: Zossima, 2008), ch. 5, for a popular introduction to this complex subject] . A full study of mirror imagery in Gaiman's writing, and its likely debt to Coleridge and his legacy, to my knowledge has not been done at the time of this writing. It is, however, regrettably beyond the scope of this study.

10 Gaiman, *Smoke and Mirrors*, 2-3.

11 Jack Zipes, *Happily Ever After: Fairy Tale, Children, and the Culture Industry* (New York and London: Routledge, 1997), 63.

12 Zipes, *Ever After*, 64-65.

13 Zipes, *Ever After*, 66.

14 Charles S. Holmes, *The Clocks of Columbus: The Literary Career of James Thurber* (New York: Atheneum, 1972), 222-224.

15 Cp. Neil A. Grauer, *Remember Laughter: A Life of James Thurber* (Lincoln: University of Nebraska Press, 1994), 86-87.

16 Holmes, 224.

17 Grauer, 87; Holmes, 225.

18 Grauer, 88; Holmes, 227.

19 Grauer, 92; Robert Emmet Long, *James Thurber* (New York: Continuum Publishing, 1988), 167.

20 James Thurber, *Many Moons*, 1943 (New York: Harcourt Brace & Company, 1970), n.p. All references to the text are to this edition; there are, however, no page numbers given in this or other standard editions of the work, and no attempt has been made to add them.

21 Jessica Tiffin, *Marvellous Geometry: Narrative and Metafiction in Modern Fairy Tale* (Detroit: Wayne State University Press, 2009), 46.

22 Cf. Holmes, 236-238.

23 Richard C. Tobias, *The Art of James Thurber* (Athens, OH: Ohio University Press, 1969), 125-126.

24 Tiffin, 44; cf. Holmes, 231. Mark Simont, an artist friend of the Thurbers, caricatured Thurber as the Jester in the illustrations for Harcourt's 1990 reissue of *Many Moons*.

25 Tiffin, 47.

26 Neil Gaiman (w) and Dave McKean (a), *The Tragical Comedy or Comical Tragedy of Mr. Punch: A Romance* (London: VG Graphics, 1994), [13]. Further citations will be given in the text.

27 Neil Gaiman, "Neil Gaiman on Dave McKean," Neil Gaiman, accessed July 19, 2011, http://www.neilgaiman.com/p/Cool_Stuff/Essays/Es-

says_By_Neil/Neil_Gaiman_on_Dave_McKean.

28 Neil Gaiman, "My hero: Maurice Sendak," *The Guardian*, May 11, 2012, accessed July 18, 2012, http://www.guardian.co.uk/books/2012/may/11/maurice-sendak-my-hero-neil-gaiman.

29 Ramin Stoodeh and Andrew Romano, "'Where the Wild Things Are,'" *Newsweek Magazine*, October 8, 2009, accessed July 19, 2012, http://www.thedailybeast.com/newsweek/2008/10/08/where-the-wild-things-are.html; Emma Brockes, "Maurice Sendak: 'I refuse to lie to children,'" *The Guardian*, October 2, 2011, accessed July 19, 2012, http://www.guardian.co.uk/books/2011/oct/02/maurice-sendak-interview.

30 Neil Gaiman, *Fragile Things: Short Fictions and Wonders* (New York: Headline Review, 2006).

31 Gaiman, *Fragile*, 171

32 Gaiman, *Fragile*, 176.

33 See, for instance, his Tumblr post on April 6, 2012 (http://neil-gaiman.tumblr.com/post/20632410128/of-all-the-fictional-characters-youve-written-which), where he also asserts that the little boy in Mr. Punch and Violent Cases is also "completely me." Curiously, on another Tumblr post a few days later, April 9, 2012, Gaiman remarked that "Richard Grey" was one of his early early pen-names.

34 Neil Gaiman, "One Life, Furnished in Early Moorcock," 1994, *Heliotrope* 1.5 (2009), accessed 6 August 2012, http://www.heliotropemag.com/04/one-life-furnished-in-early-moorcock-by-neil-gaiman/.

35 Gaiman, Introduction, 10.

36 James Thurber, *The 13 Clocks*, 1950 (New York: New York Review, 2008), 31. Further citations will be given in the text.

37 Tiffin, 44; cf. Holmes, 231: "In short, the man of imagination and love is the only true savior." Marc Simont, an artist friend of the Thurbers, caricatured Thurber as the Jester in the illustrations for Harcourt's 1990 reissue of *Many Moons*.

38 Arthur Edward Waite, *The Key to the Tarot: Being Fragments of a Secret Tradition under the Veil of Divination*, New Edition (London: Rider & Co., [n.d.]), 130.

39 Waite, 125-126.

40 Waite, 37.

41 Waite, 130.

42   Waite, 125.
43   Waite, 37.
44   Waite, 125.
45   Waite, 130.

PART III
Shadows and Reflections

Chapter 10

A Prevailing Wind

Elizabeth Reeder

The wind blew from the south, manifesting out of thin air just beyond the village limits and blowing itself into a body with wide capable hands that pushed at the first house in the village, a tiny little brick house that wasn't very old, a few decades at most, and not very much loved. Day and night the wind forced itself upon the small ugly house that resisted because it had to, and beyond its sad form the wind broke into more whimsical currents as it moved further into the pretty little town.

In this plain little red brick house with its three steps up to the front door, the girl waited for her father to leave for work. He was a short man who walked straight and true each morning, his black tie knotted tightly against his neck. Each night he'd arrive home under the cover of dark, avoiding each streetlight and the illuminating circle it cast, and no one could witness his gait then, except his daughter standing at the window, listening as the wind picked up. When he was close she saw him lean distinctly against its gusts, gripping the railing to pull himself up the stairs. He'd eventually get his hand on the doorhandle and nudge the door open with his low stooping shoulder. All night that wind howled.

Each morning when the girl stepped out into the weak autumn sunlight, the wind encouraged her along, almost lifting her off the ground with each step until not far beyond the house it took a fancy to back gardens and wove itself like a ribbon between fence posts. She carried a single book and her thin legs were short and appeared uneven with one side thinner and more beaten than the other, and she resembled a tree struggling to grow in the direct line of the prevailing wind. This unevenness was noticed by those who watched her and took note of those days when her cough was bad and her breath was quick and shallow. This lean could perhaps be considered a defeat, and a few of the people of the town pondered this, when they saw her.

The girl herself did not know how she appeared and these villagers who watched her walk to school never discussed her with each other and so it was an observation without a home, so common, so seamlessly a part of life, that it had become an everyday essential activity like breathing or pausing at a traffic light or the onset of a sudden rage that might arrive while waiting in a longer-than-usual-queue at the butcher's counter.

This town sat on a globe that was a fast spinning top and on this autumn Tuesday strange new birds arrived with the whitest wings edged by the blackest black and each had a thin red crescent over one eye. Everyone looked at these birds as they swept high up in flight, in arcs, as if they were the thin metal spheres of a gyroscope turning turning tilting. Swoon. Swoon. And so swift, these passage migrants filled the sky and people looked up and paid more attention to the ground beneath their feet, because there is sky and earth and the living walk between.

The villagers, young and old, turned their attention from the birds to the girl as she passed. Some people shoulder-shoved her as they passed on the street or jostled her as she waited to cross the road. But one boy offered to carry her book and held the school door open for her, a girl gave up her seat in class, another brought her a tray of food at lunch, and the teachers never called on her until they knew she had enough strength to answer.

On most days she'd straightened a bit by lunch, breathing more easily, finding words—although she was always, still, economical with those. At school, in her hand, a pencil was a tool but she did not know what could be done with it. What could she do? A fact might be of some use or perhaps a number could come in handy, but even as she thought it she knew these absolutes were so often contested, these facts often lacked conviction. What is true, true, true? She is sixteen, seconds and minutes are found on both clocks and maps, and her dad, her dad.

She could be a good singer, Charlie Barton the choir master supposed, a troublesome alto with perfect pitch but problematic rhythm, and a lean to her like a lilt but downward: a tilt. A bit like a stumble, he thought. Charlie Barton, the music teacher, saw potential in her but did not know well enough how to get the most out of her, to help her sing with that cough she had, on some days, which cleared by midday, on some days. There was simply a thinness to the air she freed from her lungs and he couldn't decide how to help her, not really. She was the opposite of a little thing, more flat perhaps, like a cut out drawing, sure, her voice was flat too, a little hollow like an echo, and she wasn't able to refine it. It was improper, he knew, to look, but he looked at her flat chest, and saw it hollow, even as it expanded; not enough air there, not enough difference between taking air in and letting it out, but he moved his eyes quickly, because even though it was his job, he knew it wasn't proper to stare at the girl's chest.

The girl didn't like choir and on the even days, Tuesdays and Thursdays, she wore jeans and a t-shirt and a sweater. She curled her toes in the middle row, where he placed her near the end, and she balled and unballed her hands; she kept her nails neatly trimmed so there were no scratches or crescents, and she sang. She'd never remember the notes or the songs she'd sung or who stood next to her but she remembered that when she sang she did not feel the scrapes on her shins and elbows or the dull pain up under her ribs, her heart, she supposed, if she got that far into this thought, which she didn't.

Her skin was young, but she did not think that; she thought about how her skin held her together and she was hands and feet and the length of her arms and legs and she had edges and her skin kept her together. Beneath her clothes, she had miles of blood vessels, stretched and contracted muscles, and a cage of ribs with her skin holding it all together. There's something at the edge, perhaps just beyond the edge of her, something new and necessary, that protected her. She imagined it there, again and again it was there when she needed it, and the world couldn't always see her, or it, and sometimes she walked and was seen only by a fluke, or a trick of light, and her voice was both sweet and hollow and she was full of a talent that couldn't be named but it could be seen and heard, if you paid attention.

Twice a week, on Tuesday and Friday, the girl waited in the queue at the butcher's. She thought about his knives and saws, and the metal tables where blood gathered briefly and then dripped onto the floor where a gutter wove its way, like rivers or roads on a map, towards the copious drain beneath the curled hose hanging on the wall, which they used twice a day to wash it all down. In the queue she saw the dirt under Mrs Fellows nails and yet knew she had neither window-boxes or a garden and wondered where she'd been digging; and she saw the cut on Rab Billies' lip and above, his eye, a shiner too, and his hands shook when he took his ribeye and his kidneys for his lunch, which he ate every day, along with two oranges and an apple and a bar of chocolate with almonds, if they had it on the shelves of the corner shop, or even if he had to ask Sally, the shop owner's new young wife, to go into the back to bring it out for him.

In the corner shop, young Sally Turner had just been shagged against the wall of the stock room by her new husband Eric, and the flush of her cheeks and the ostentatious way she displayed her newlywed ringed finger as she placed Myg Trammer's newspaper into her bag and said, "Lucky dip today?" gave it away. Young Sally had been a delightful seamstress, but she'd chosen the shop-keeper and hadn't been sewing for months now. It seemed that she'd forgotten how and had misplaced all her needles and thread.

Myg settled the bag in the crook of her arm thinking that with that flush she must be pregnant and doesn't know it yet. Soon her belly will connect her to the earth and in a year's time she will have a happy fat baby, dark circles beneath her eyes, and an inconstant husband who'll touch any woman who buys almost anything with cash; he'll place a warm finger in their palms when he gives them change. Myg, old enough to be his older sister, won't fall for it but some of the younger ones may be fool enough to believe in it. She nodded to Sally with a small smile and exited through the door that Rab held open, touching his arm and saying thank you.

The butcher, Sam Lanlow, gave the girl a thick slice of ham placed between two slices of his wife's home-baked *pain au levain,* a sandwich he'd made for his own lunch, and he handed it to her in neat little wrap of brown paper, and he also gave her the pork hock she and her dad had on standing order. She asked each Tuesday, in her clear stern quiet voice, if he could he put it on their bill and she'd settle it on Friday. The girl had a strong firm grip and she'd make a good butcher, a bold one, and he thought he could teach her to do what he did because, although his son Torque had cool hands and a skill for making the steak and ale pies, he certainly wasn't a butcher. Sam had known that since his son was a boy. The girl's eyes were careful and noticed the details of each cut, watched everything. She complimented him, thanked him each time she did her errands, and he saw she'd be able to tell the difference between fillet and sirloin, and with the intensity of her gaze there'd be no thieving when she was around. He will ask her if she needed a job for the summer, next time she came when there weren't so many people, and he'd find a way to do it so he didn't seem like a perv.

In the village square pigeons blustered about, some of them one-legged, and they squabbled and mated and lifted as a messy mixed cluster. They flew out and up chaotically, out and up and back to nearly the same spot they'd alighted from. In front of the inn on the square, tables lay in wait for sun and heat, but it was the end of October and Myg Trammer, the owner, ever the optimist, walking across the square on her way back from the corner shop was nonetheless considering bringing them in for the season.

Myg's inn had nine rooms, nine fine rooms, and now her son Jonny was the chef and a good one and he seemed to enjoy it although how long he'd be around, she couldn't guess. He had a way in this world that might not suit this small town; she'd seen that since he was a boy and later. He had grown into himself almost daily from the time he turned seven, an amazing transformation, more and more himself and less and less likely to stay. She never said why or how or what she knew, for it would be a cliché of course, how she'd come to realize it. So one day when he was just fourteen, she said to him "Oh that Simon Smith, he's a nice boy, those abs," she said, "right through his t-shirt, see those abs?" Jonny blushed and nodded and that was that. She wondered if they had similar tastes in men.

The boy's father had been a talker, what a talker, and her ears were red and sore and nearly worn out after just a year. Only sixteen, she'd been charmed at first, the whole town had been. Myg remembered when her first house, her young husband's house, had been filled with people, full of his friends and her friends and friends of friends and musicians, painters, builders, climbers and cobblers and how all their beds and floors and shelves were filled with people and the silence couples made, just a bit of creaking, some caught breaths, and she became a couple too, sometimes with her young husband, sometimes with this silent painter or this un-talking carpenter. And the town stopped its labour earlier and earlier each day to party and drink and gossip. There were a few happenings, Myg remembered, an incomer robbed and beaten up, his book defaced; a woman who said one thing, a man another, about an encounter. Things strange to this town.

Myg started to think that perhaps they'd not been charmed, but rather overpowered by his talk, talk, his talk. She laughed at the old adage that women rattled on and on, clattered on about this and that and did not know how to cease to talk, and she knew this was another tall tale, so many abounding, so many meant to keep this or that person in place, and she laughed. Her young husband had blah blah blah blah'd, twisted and beguiled, and she was deaf in one ear by the time she was twenty. Her son was only a toddler and she worried for his hearing too so she started to shoo folk out of the house in the morning and refuse to open her doors again until evening. Her husband complained and complained that she had no sense of how to have fun and she was glad when he found some reason, this or that, he must have told her, to find someplace else to talk talk talk or stick his stick and she was left with her son, who cried, but only when he wanted something.

Within a week of her young husband's departure, this sweet welcoming inn, out of the blue, had fallen into her hands. It had appeared almost overnight as if the earth had given birth to it, but really it had been constructed by a pair of rovers (one giant and impossibly strong, one tall and lean and supple) who arrived at sunset, worked nearly without stop for three days and, without being beckoned or refused, this magnificent building then existed as if it had always been there. The skinny one left the front door keys on her bedside table as he left. He'd hesitated at her bedroom door to take his coat off the hook, turned on his heel, came back, had another romp and it was evening before he and his giant friend left town and they'd not been seen since. Her inn was now the center of the village, the center having migrated over the years to meet her here, and she'd noticed a few other recent shifts: Rab's shiners, the girl's tilt, and that house ready to fall right off the town.

The girl walked directly, this afternoon, towards the butcher's. Myg went inside to the kitchen and made herself a nuisance as she moved around her son making the girl a plain old hot chocolate, thick and satisfying. She carried it out to the girl in a cream-colored sturdy ceramic cup and saucer, met her just as she moved to cross the square to go directly home, with three square flat parcels in her hands.

"Here, child," Myg said. And the girl placed the meat under her arm, a quick light clamp of the meat to her ribs, and Myg laid the cup and saucer in her open palm.

"Thank you, Mrs Trammer."

"It's Ms," she replied, "Actually, call me Myg."

The girl lifted the cup and the thinnest narrowest package fell to the ground.

Myg picked it up, turned it over in her hands. "What did you get from the butcher today?"

"The usual. And he lent me a knife, in case I need it."

Myg looked past the girl, to Sam's place, shook her head. The girl drank quickly because she was smart and knew that thick chocolate did not keep its heat long and both the girl and the woman looked up to the wild daring birds and the wind picking up and the cold it carried on its streams and the girl drank quickly and said, "Thank you Myg,' as she handed the cup and saucer back and continued on her way. Only now she didn't head exactly in the direction of the house where she lived, but not exactly away from it either, but rather she headed towards the edge of town, in a direction that did not surprise Myg one bit.

She started to collapse the tables and stack the chairs and she called out, "Jonny, will you help me bring the tables in." And he came out in his short sleeves at first, and grabbed a sweater when he returned for the second and third trips. Six months later, four days before the solstice, they will carry the tables and chairs back out; she'll unfold the tables and unstick the chairs and she'll weight them down on that day out on the square, facing the spring sun.

The tiny ugly weary brick house was in the center of nothing, at the edge of everything. Old and tired, it butted up against the house next door—pressing so close to the one nearer town you couldn't even stick your head out of the side windows. The windows opened in winter when the wood shrunk back and so on the coldest days the girl might catch a bit fresh new air when her father was not at home. On the other side, a perpetual gale struck the house and sometimes the girl felt as if she should lean against that wall to hold it up against the wind. She did not lean and it managed to stay righted. Outside, on the side facing the wind, there was a troublesome brick that kept half popping out, about waist height, and it'd angle itself out about once a week; her father did not notice it and the girl would take the rubber mallet and tap tap tap it back into place and the house bolstered itself up against the wind once more, having been scuppered in its attempt to simply give in. The earth pushed its foundations up, the wind pressed it sideways, and the whole time the house had to remain calm and unassailable even though it was weary and very much assaulted. The father pushed against the girl too, her against the earth, against the pressure of his wind and rain and low pressure systems and she remained calm and unassailable all through the winter.

In this sad little mean exhausted brick house, her dad was thin and short and by morning he stood straight as he walked to his tiny dark office at the factory where he was some middleman. By noon he was just himself, a mast buckled by the wind, bent over at the middle, perhaps with a curved back, like he had osteoporosis.

At night he stared at his daughter, who had become so upright and graceful during the day.

Between them the dinner table stretched as far as it could until it was touching the walls and they couldn't walk around and he was on one side, his daughter on the other. Her dead mother could do nothing and he climbed over the table to grab his daughter by her skinny little arm and he was his own storm system. Sometimes he'd drag her to the window, this window here with a view of the bright little town with all its aspirations and kindness and blindness. He grunted as people strolled along the road, down the hill and turned onto the winding graveled path through a small woods. He was hidden from the outside world, at these times, by the thick quilted curtains, and she was visible through the fine muslin of the slip curtain, and people saw her standing alone, so young and graceful and possible. He gripped her arm and left a ringed bruise there as she fought to stay longer by the window. And people raised a hand in greeting to her, this girl, and she lifted her free hand, in a small gesture and smiled. Hoped they saw her smile.

The father grew tired and she held him up; her ears grew weary and dark circles blossomed beneath her eyes, and no matter how much he grunted, the villagers waved to her and they did not stop living their lives exactly as they wanted. She stood and instead of shutting off her ears or closing her eyes as some might do, she opened them wider. She thought about atoms and the bottom of the ocean and moons around planets. Foundations needed to go deep and walls needed to be bolstered and air currents are important as the earth in holding things together. And space, everything needed space.

Circles too, she learned that they were possibilities in clocks and compasses and bicycle wheels and nearly everyday she stood by the window waiting for the satisfying circling of the bicycle tyres, turning turning turning. Little Missy Channelbock would weave down the street, her wheels circling and whizz by the house, no handed, and down the gentle slope of the hill that started just outside the door. The girl watched Missy's face, bright and open, and she leaned forward so she could watch Missy's open arms, her spread-wide hands, and hear, just barely above her dad's tirade, the other girl's shouts of glee.

Near the winter solstice her dad shot a deer and it had rolled down the hill. Fetch it, eviscerate it, he said. With the short strong knife from the butcher, she closed her eyes against this task, leaving the gralloch for any animal that might need help making it through the winter, and then she was pulling pulling pulling it up the hill. He'd left her to skin it, to cure it, to hang it. She didn't know what to do and she made it up. She cut some of it into strips, which she salted and hung over a fire, and they cured tough and salty. She stored these and her father said they did not need to visit the butcher all winter. Her father started to keep her from school too. When he was at the factory she worked through the pages of her textbooks, understanding, she thought, as best she could, the information they expected her to learn.

She turned seventeen that winter and worked with her hands, doing this and that, and holding on to whatever she could as her dad grabbed at her and the cold and wind and low pressure pushed against everything in that small sad exhausted house. She kept the knife but did not use it and she pushed that brick back into place each week, sometimes twice a week if it needed it, and in the spring the windows still opened on some days but only just barely and one morning when the sun hit the front room just this way, just this way with a light that finally held some heat, she opened them all; she opened all the windows and the doors and the house shook and shook and it all rattled and it rattled and sighed and she shook herself free, her one arm hanging so low, her hand brushing her knee with each swing of her stride, which had never been long, but it was shorter now and determined, and she walked with her body facing forward towards school, but she did not walk there directly.

Heading east with the sun on her face, low and spring-like and definitely holding a faint new warmth, she walked out through the fields past the small farmhouses that stood at the edges of the village land and she walked around each one, like the town was the face of a clock, each house a number or the seconds and spaces between the numbers. She walked for hours, past nightfall, circling the town, counterclockwise, unwinding time.

She slept in a field and bright-eyed Jackie Stalt protected her with the heavy woolen blanket. Bright-eyed Jackie Stalt, a farmer held in the highest regard until her eighth child had been born and her husband lost two seasons to a stubborn bout of pneumonia and had never quite regained his full strength, and she and everyone else was waiting for her children, the baker's dozen of them, to leave the house or put their minds to helping her. Here before spring truly arrived, she kept a child warm. The next day the girl folded Jackie's blanket and lay it over her fence, went to school where she wrote down a few facts and numbers, and she sang, although by the end of the day she did not remember the songs or the notes she'd sung.

The girl visited the butcher and held out the knife to him, by holding the blade wrapped in brown paper and offering him the handle. He said she could keep the knife but she shook her head and he accepted it back with a shrug. She looked so winter-beaten, he asked her to be his apprentice and she said yes.

Myg was putting out her tables and the girl waved and Myg waved back and the girl didn't see the worry Myg felt as she watched the girl still leaning with such a pronounced tilt, defeated so late in the day, with her winter weight filling her out and if Myg had seen her earlier in the day or yesterday she'd have been even more worried, how low she'd been bent, how stooped, how old she'd looked. Now she was more herself, both weighted into the earth but also existing beyond it and above it. The girl had skinny little legs beneath her dead mother's old dress and she carried a single parcel from the butcher and Myg did not know it yet, but he'd given the meat to her for free.

In March her knees were purple, a cold sort of exposed purple when she walked by in that sad sagging floral dress. Myg ran out with a pile of sweaters and a couple pairs of jeans and a belt of Jonny's (he was skinny, skinny as a rake, and it would fit the girl just fine) and she knew in the days and weeks that followed that her knees were still purple and possibly swollen but now they were hidden beneath her old jeans. And she thought about Sally Turner at the shop and how her face was blotchy and red because of her autumn and winter miscarriages.

Jonny had big feet in broad flat shoes and he ran marathons and he ran well and his feet were just his own and in proportion to everything and if not perfect, functionable. His own bed was long enough, but often his feet stuck out of the beds of others, and if he sprawled and let his feet dangle sometimes he felt greedy and he'd curled himself in but that felt mean too, like he was hiding part of himself. He often did not spend the night, and he didn't ever bring anyone home to his mother, and in the early morning he didn't understand how celebrity chefs could also be raffish and keep those hours—his mom's small enterprise suffered on the days he walked home at dawn. Here in the late spring, with her worn chairs sitting on the sagging square, all the customers who frequented the place knew it wasn't modern or in the least bit contemporary but this place had something, they all knew it had something.

And that girl had been stopping by, nearly every day. By stopping he meant she'd walk by and his mom would make her a drink, often hot chocolate, sometimes lemonade or simply water, and he started to make her a sandwich or fancy wrap, chips to go, sprinkled with sea-salt and rosemary (no, not rosemary, his mother had said, that could be dangerous to her, in her condition). And, finally, he noticed her condition.

The girl did not stop, she merely paused, and always thanked his mother, and him too, sometimes.

In the back of the butcher shop the girl proved to be a disaster. A voice like an angel, she sang as she worked out front and that disappointed the butcher but pleased his son Torque, and she never made a noise when she worked the short sharp knife and made a mistake or even when she mastered a fiddly task like the butterfly joint or the guard of honour. However, it soon become clear that even if she had some skill in her, she was not suited to butchering, he saw that now. Her hands and arms were full of earnestness and humor and a lightness until she entered the back room. She had such a droop on that one side and on too many days she never straightened while in the shop. Only once she left and he watched her accept a cup from Myg had he seen her hips even out in the mis-sized jeans held together by a big belt. By the time the heat arrived, she only came into the shop once a week, and then only for a few hours, her belly now firm and rounded, and she worked the till and he was grateful for that but he still had to have "the talk" with her, which he did. He told her he had to let her go and she kissed him on the cheek and said, "Finally," and "Thank you." And his son Torque gave her two parcels, one for herself, and one for Myg and that boy of hers, and the butcher was disappointed and ashamed and so relieved.

She'd floundered at the butcher's and he fired her; she was uncoordinated and getting bigger and she walked in large spiraling circles, one edge connected to the other by the wind. She often slept in this field or that or in barns people left open with freshly forked hay and a wooden tray with a pitcher of cold milk, a tall cool glass, and sandwiches carefully covered to protect them from flies. She'd return the tray with the pitcher and glass and plate, running a finger around the edge, touching the door handle, and if they were quick, they'd receive a kiss on each cheek, a hug, her belly pressing out, and in the heat of the summer, she'd press her cool cheeks against their hot ones and although everyone wanted to invite her in, they did not, because people could see now, after many weeks, that she was walking in slightly widening circles, and the town was within her protection.

Each day she'd pause at the north of the town, listening more than looking; noticeable not so much in herself but by how the world moved when she was present. She made a path around the town. Her face grew younger again and her father's house shook visibly, but the walking did nothing to stop her belly from growing, although no one talked about it.

In the early summer Jonny will whisper something in his mother's good ear, about a local boy with long legs and cool hands (he'll be a genius with pastry) and she'll move out of the big bedroom and into the small, smooth room at the top of the house, with windows on all sides but no room even for a chest of drawers, only a bed and a floor lamp and all she'll do in this room is sleep, unless the right man happened by, in the night.

Kids went back to school just before the leaves started to turn, but the girl did not join them. Instead she started to dig, in the north, out in a field that belonged to Farmer Smith and he let her, for he was no fool. She dug by herself until the butcher helped after he closed his shop, early, sometimes, and his son Torque with his cool hands and long legs, who now dug side by side with Jonny. It was a deep wide rectangular hole they dug and two strangers arrived, one big and all muscle, one thinner and graceful; both so young and so beautiful and they seemed to know this town and the tall skinny man waved at Myg and knew he had a bed for the night. These two men arrived, one with a cement truck and the other with a lorry full of stones and wood piled high on the back.

The girl was large by this time and it was Hollie Smith who, a few weeks back, had handed her the overalls she now wore. Straight-hipped Hollie Smith, who had such talent with the adze, such skill with felled trees, and then she'd had four children, one of them a regular firestarter. She'd have dealt with that, but she also had a senile mother, an unemployed father, a competent husband, and debt, such debt. It was Hollie who gave her the overalls and looked to this girl and her tilt with such hope because, just because.

So the girl's belly stretched the overalls full out but she moved lightly, so lightly, and with such strength she wasn't a girl, but simply strong and good with her hands and all of them worked together, day and night for three days and by the morning of the fourth she had a house, a pretty little house, and a baby girl. And a trade. Her hands were calloused and she now stood over six feet tall, with a wide stance and a tool belt firmly buckled tight around her waist, the handles of the hammer and the grips of the pliers jangling as she walked.

She put the baby in a sling held close to her beating heart and it beat beat beat so strongly and the people of the town stopped for they heard it too. The wind had stopped. The villagers looked up and saw birds, those strange birds from last autumn, with the whitest wings edged by the blackest black and each with a thin red crescent over one eye. And they watched these birds at play in the sky, spiraling and diving, flying with ease. The edges of the town were alive with light and these birds held the light on their wings, so white and dark and witnessed everything with their curious eyes. And the town was centre and all the world was shaking and alive around and through it.

The creaking of the tired ugly broken house grew louder. The girl's father had been trapped in the house for weeks and weeks by the rallying, rigorous wind, and gusts, such gusts. He'd been calling out to his daughter and he'd called and called and called. He had been calling for weeks and months but no one had heard him because of the wind. He wouldn't have recognized the girl now, even if she was to come, because now she was a woman and any fool could see it was her walking across the square to the newsagents to get a paper and a pint of milk, like it was any normal day. The father continued to call and call and call and the people of the town could hear the beating of the witnessing birds' wings, the air through them, and this weak man's calling, calling and the thunderous sound of the house, finally released from the wind, creaking and cracking and breaking apart and the father was shushed as if his call became like that of a baby bird from deep within the steepest nest, deep within the hollow tree, far in the shadows. And the collapsed house sank lower and lower until the earth filled in and grass grew and trees appeared—a rowan and two birch and a small cluster of wild roses.

Myg was the first to hear the silence in one ear—that was nothing new—but then, her other ear filled with silence and it was as if the sound had evaporated. What house, thought the villagers? What man? There had never been sad little brick house built too close to its neighbor; there had never been a man there.

The girl-woman arrived at the corner shop and loosened the sling. The baby, a strange little thing, waved its newly freed arms and she wondered where it had come from and she walked through the door and over to Sally Turner, with her empty arms and blotched red face, and the girl-woman placed the baby in Sally's arms. The baby gave a long deep cry and Sally shushed her against her heart and her cheeks grew smooth and full and flushed, her lips grew bright. The tips of her fingers tingled when she saw the tiny gold needle glided across the fabric of the sling and she could feel the muffled rattle of spools of thread within its folds, dozens by the feel of it.

The tall woman nodded to the seamstress and walked a broad generous circle around the village, waving to folk, sometimes saying thank you, and often offering to lend a hand. As evening fell, the beautiful birds held the last of the light on the their wings and the woman walked through the freshly harvested field and back to a sturdy little house made of stone and wood.

Process Essay
On Leaning Into

Elizabeth Reeder

*On some hills, where rocks balance on inclines,
there is a point geologists call the angle of no
strain. Rocks repose despite steepness because all
conditions allow for rest. I sleep lying down, pace
upright, and when I lean I need a wall or a chair
or a person to lean against.*[1]

I have a stolen hour, a pencil, and my notebook. There's no pre-
amble. At the top of the page I write the date, 25.11.11, and the
following sentence arrives, unbidden: "Her thin legs were short
and uneven, like a branch growing in the direct line of the prevailing wind."

A girl appears walking in one direction and I watch her walk
with that lean of hers and then look past her, down a street
that leads to the edge. I am close to her, like I'm watching her
from the porch of a house, and I am also her, walking. When
I see the edge of the town (of the story), it is the edge as it is
for her and for me, standing on the porch or passing her on the
street. This girl brings with her these long sentences—rambling
and visceral like thoughts moving from one thing to another.
The image of her and her language arrive at the same time, but
I still need to take time to figure out exactly what they are in
the story. These sentences feel Steinian in their insistent repetition and with their clustered, varied adjectives. This girl also
brings a fluid point of view, both panoptic and intimate, and
not owned by her or anyone in particular, but belonging, I
start to realize as I write, to the people of a town. Each shift in
perspective has a distinct personality and I come to understand
that each shift belongs to a particular character, like the music
teacher or Myg.

The girl walks straight through the story and beyond the line of her walking curves an edge that seems to circle the town above and below ground, and the space becomes a sphere. Within (and just beyond) this circle lives the story. Imagine the circle start to spin and within its space a world appears. As she walks, she expands the circle and the world of the town, of the story, becomes bigger.

Despite all I know about how I write and edit, how a story arrives remains a mystery, and I prefer it that way. So it's the 25th November, and after an hour I have five handwritten pages on which exist the girl, the wind (although it starts out as a simile), the butcher, school, choirmaster, innkeeper and her son, and the girl's purple knees (although I move these to later in the story). This place, which I come to know as a specific village, is very much peopled.

When I think of a fictional place—a town, a house, a landscape—it is rarely static. The places I imagine are "made" by how people move through that space and how their movements alter the qualities and meanings of these places. This was a small town, old-fashioned, or perhaps poor so not kept up well, perhaps even with some dirt roads, especially out to the farms and this town had magic in it, that was clear, with her lean and how it was more pronounced or more resolved depending on emotion. The kindness of the people in the town, that's an emotion and therefore also active, and it's a town where people are aware of each other. As a writer this makes the free indirect narration possible, characters are made more real by each other and what they see, how they'll tell the story. It is also, I suppose, about the metaphorical potentiality of a space or a landscape, and the metaphor's potential to magnify or call into question the human, emotional, and occasionally fraught happenings of the story. A useful definition of metaphor is one offered by Epsom in his *Seven Types of Ambiguity* as he quotes Read: metaphor as "complex ideas made sudden by an objective relation."[2]

This reminds me of Lyn Hejinian's complicated discussion about the aliveness of language, about how "even words in storage, in the dictionary, seem frenetic with activity, as each individual entry attracts to itself other words as definition, example, amplification"[3] Writing and reading are often about the potential connections within the language itself and how we as writers and readers can make these "maximally excited"[4] by drawing connections to other words, structures, images and ideas within a text and outside it as well. Hejinian talks about this type of language as being "productive of activity."[5]

For me, a story almost always starts with a sentence like the one I started with for this story: a concrete sentence that gives specific, fertile details but also doesn't give too much of itself away. As I write I try to travel through this place and make real the potential held in that first line. Rebecca Solnit suggests that, "To write is to carve a new path through the terrain of the imagination, or to point out new features on a familiar route."[6] So by attempting to tell the story, I begin a narrative map of this fictional sentence, this place, and I attempt to give it form, following the same theory of building details, of making the place and the story more concrete and developed but not giving too much away. This attempt at storytelling, at mapping, paradoxically, makes this place limitless. And this is as it should be, for a story should never have a singular meaning or reading. It becomes a map for the reader and "to read is to travel through that terrain with the author as guide."[7]

I see my creative cartography as being analogous to those early maps of places that contain necessary terra firma, terrifying terra incognita, and imaginings of beasts and monsters, wild burgeoning plant and wildlife. What cannot yet be seen cannot be mapped, but still exists: it becomes possibility and can be imagined into existence.

witnessing

The girl walked right to the center of the story and she was being watched. Her initial path from the old mean house to the school was direct through the town, right up its center, no diversions. It's a complex relationship initiated here: as the town (and by implication, the villagers) becomes defined by her, so the villagers witness the girl and her tilt and become crucial to our understanding of her.

The girl too is complicated, because the wind, and her father, act upon her but as she moves through the town, she rouses people to thoughts, storytelling or action, and she influences this world a bit like a wind: most noticeable in how it moves objects in its path.

We sleep lying down, pace upright, and when we lean we need a wall or the wind or a person to lean against.[8] In no way can this girl exist without this community. She is dependent on witnesses like the girl in Angela Carter's *The Bloody Chamber* (1995). Carter's girl is defined by the "connoisseur" she marries and how he dresses her in the "sinuous shift of white muslin tied with a silk string under the breasts,"[9] and how he defines her throat with the choker of rubies. Carter's girl narrates her own tale and readers understand how aware she is, has been, of how other characters see her: "The night at the opera comes back to me even now... the white dress; the frail child within it; and the flashing crimson jewels around her throat, bright as arterial blood."[10]

My girl shares this essential nature of being witnessed: the nature of her *self*, as well as what she means to the village, is defined by what the villagers see in her. In this case it is not necessarily her "potentiality for corruption"[11] as in Carter's tale, but her potential to inspire hope. She's somehow crucial to the shape and future of the town and individuals see her potential in different ways, because she's not yet aware of what she wants, of what she's capable of.

panoptic

For thirty-two days I did no more writing on this story. Then on the 28th of December, I sat down to write the novel I'm working on. After noting the date at the top of the page and writing a few lists to clear my mental decks, this girl arrived, again unbidden, at the butcher's. Two more written pages and then I paused, assessed, named it: this is a story, this is the fairytale. When I felt I have a critical mass of writing and a shape has started to emerge, I move from notebook to screen. And this is what I did, typing up the story as I had it so far. Then I went back to an old notebook to make sure I'd not missed any notes or ideas. Flipping through pages, these sentences jumped out at me: "The house was in the center of the neighborhood, old and brick and small. Each room could hold no more than five people." A bit further down on that page there was a short paragraph on a pregnancy. They both belong to my novel, *Fremont*. They *belonged* to my novel, for on this day I pilfered both thinking, they belong to this story, too.

The next day the seasons of the story guided the writing. Winter arrived, sudden with the death of the deer, and the unremitting pressure of storms. Then spring. What had been implied became obvious. Spring arrives and the innkeeper puts out the tables on the square and the girl opens all the windows and doors of the house. Winter disallows; Spring encourages.

Anything can be mapped and we often map-make what we don't understand or know, in order to attain a better grasp of it. The process of mapping, like the process of writing an essay or a story, often starts with questions and curiosities. As Hejinian writes, "Language is one of the principal forms our curiosity takes. It makes us restless."[12] Many of us don't want all the answers, but rather images or ideas made sudden that we can take out of the world of the story and test in other places against other texts, ideas and emotions. For me this links to multiple sources and influences and many of these were present as I continued to write and edit. People like Stein and Carter were embedded in the very start of the story, while others are linked more tangentially to threads of thought or research I was involved with at the time.

The map of this story, "a prevailing wind," is circular, like seasons or a clock. It is also an object that helps orientation and navigation, like a compass or a gyroscope. Its story-map functions on multiple levels, both concretely physical and metaphorical. One way this can manifest is the immanent style of the writing, where different perspectives of a place both panoptic and intimate are revealed by who tells the story and how they tell it. Different characters definitely alter the lines of the story map, the direction of the story, and the actions other characters take; they all live in this same place, but their memories, motivations and needs impact how they view the town and what's possible within it. The free indirect narration of this story can reflect the omniscient or panoptic view of the wind or the birds or the ground, and also the intimate perceptions of individual villagers and its language connects the different perspectives.

It's possible that fairy tales are *terra incognita* landscapes—unknowable, familiar, existing at the edges of what we hope for and fear. By placing real (specific, physical details) beside the fantastical or emotional, the stories function like metaphors and we extrapolate knowledge in the same way.

wonder

John D'Agata, in one of his lyrical essays on the essay form itself, draws attention to Barry Lopez and his commitment to fable, drama, wonder and quotes Lopez: "I know I can derive something useful from this world if I can get a reader to say, "I am an adult, I have a family, I pay bills, I live in a world of chicanery and subterfuge and atomic weaponry and in humanity and round-heeled politicians and garrulous, insipid television personalities, but still I have wonder."[13]

So a story can be a map of wonder, which may sometimes look like horror and hope kneaded together like a round of bread put in a dead hot oven, fit to burst in the alchemy of heat. We map the solar system and beyond, we map the deepest oceans, and these are both places we are unable to travel to, unable to confirm by walking their floors, flying through their dark matter. So too with fairy tales. To explore these places, the reader only has this text —what is imagined—and rereading can be considered an attempt to create familiarity with the story's terra incognita. The pieces I most enjoy hold up to this re-reading as their worlds remain exciting, always new, but also remain unfamiliar and ultimately unknowable, full of risk. I'm thinking of Stein's word play; Carson's active and constant resistance to singularity; the irreducible nature of Carter's heroines. And I think of Nan Shepherd, a hill walker and writer, who wrote about the Cairngorms, a range of Scottish mountains connected by a moody, unpredictable plateau, in this way: "However often I walk on them, these hills hold astonishment for me. There is no getting accustomed to them."[14]

It's January, and the story and the essay are due. They're both close to being finished. Writing them at the same time has complicated the process with a back and forth of creative and critical imagination and realization that cannot be untangled by reflection or mapping. There's a palimpsest in both that holds the outline of the other, the edits erasing the most obvious signs of impact, but the embossment of influence is clear. For example, I'm still working on movement in the story and this morning reading Lyn Hejinian on form both complicates and roots my thoughts: "Writing's forms are not merely shapes but forces; formal questions are about dynamics—they ask how, where, and why the writing moves, what are the types, direction, numbers and velocities of a work's motion."[15]

As a writer, certain themes or questions often cross over and back between different projects I'm working on and the fairy tale and essays are shaped, in part, by my ongoing considerations of cartography and modals of navigation and identity, which are strong undercurrents in *Fremont*, the novel I'm editing. In particular, questions of how we navigate when we are in movement have surrounded one of the novel's characters, Utah, and I have long conceived of her as functioning as an emotional compass within the book. Through my work on the fairy tale and essay, it's clear now that she understands the world as a gyroscope moves, within a sphere, but fluid and multi-directional. I don't know why I didn't realize this before now.

For the story and the essay, I am still grappling with how this idea of mapping, circles and hope work together. This is, perhaps, an example where making and critiquing both diverge and overlap: lines, transects, and circles are all in movement, and each piece of writing influences the substance of the others.

For me, I imagine the story, the world of the story, and my novel's character Utah, each as an earth spinning, and as DaVinci's Vitruvian Man, an atom, a three dimensional compass. The feeling or image that guides the writing and my editorial decisions is a fast spinning top that turns into a gyroscope, a globe shaped aid to navigation, full of space and movement, made up of many circular parts and capable of maintaining balance amidst tilting and spinning and dramatic shifts of direction.

Bibliography

Carter, Angela. *The Bloody Chamber*. London: Vintage, 1995.

D'Agata, John, ed. *The Next American Essay*. Saint Paul, MN: Graywolf Press, 2003.

Epsom, William. *Seven Types of Ambiguity*. 1961. London: Penguin, 1973.

Hejinian, Lyn. *The Rejection of Closure*. Berkely: University of California Press, 2000.

Reeder, Elizabeth. "angle of repose" In *direction is the moment you choose*. Unpublished manuscript, 2012.

Shepherd, Nan. *The Living Mountain*. 1997. Edinburgh: Canongate Books, 2008.

Solnit, Rebecca. Wanderlust: *A History of Walking*. London: Verso, 2002

Notes

1 Reeder, "angle of repose", 2012

2 Epson, 1973, 2

3 Hejinian, 2000 51.

4 Hejinian, 2000, 43

5 Hejinian, 2000, 51

6 Solnit, 2002, 72

7 Ibid.

8 Reeder, edited for essay

9 Carter, 1995, 11

10 Ibid.

11 Ibid.

12 Hejinian, 2000, 49

13 D'Agata, 2003, 22

14 Shepherd, 2008,1

15 Hejinian, 2000, 42

Chapter 11

Not for Children: The Development of Nihilism in the Fairy Tales of Oscar Wilde

Colin Cavendish-Jones

> *And out of the bronze of the image of* The
> Sorrow that endureth for Ever *he fashioned
> an image of* The Pleasure that abideth for a
> Moment.

On 20 October 1888, an unsigned review of Wilde's first book of fairy stories, *The Happy Prince and Other Tales,* appeared in the *Saturday Review*.[1] Its author, Alexander Galt Ross, was appreciative, though scarcely encomiastic, of Wilde's "delicate humour" and "artistic literary manner" but firmly of the opinion that these stories were too "bitter" to be suitable for children. "No child will sympathize at all with Mr. Wilde's *Happy Prince* when he is melted down by order of the Mayor and Corporation," Ross insisted. "Children do not care for satire." Wilde took exception to this notice, describing the *Saturday Review* as a "wicked and Philistine paper,"[2] but seems to have experienced some difficulty in deciding whether he agreed with the reviewer that his tales were not for children and, if not, why not. Sending William Ewart Gladstone a copy of *The Happy Prince* in June 1888, he wrote: "It is only a collection of short stories, and is really meant for children,"[3] but within a few days he was telling the poet and painter George Kersley that his audience had expanded along with his ambitions:

> They are studies in prose, put for Romance's sake into a fanciful form: meant partly for children, and partly for those who have kept the childlike faculties of wonder and joy, and who find in simplicity a subtle strangeness.[4]

By the beginning of 1889, Wilde's notion of his public had narrowed again, this time to exclude children altogether. In a letter to the American writer Amelie Rives Chanler, he claimed that his fairy tales were "not for children, but for childlike people from eighteen to eighty!"[5]

In fact, Wilde's initial audience for *The Happy Prince* consisted of a group of Cambridge undergraduates, all over the age of eighteen, who called themselves "the cicadas." Consequently, as Jarlath Killeen observes, many critics "have found the biographical impulse almost irresistible when looking at this tale."[6] In these readings, the relationship "of an older, taller lover with a younger, smaller beloved"[7] prefigures Wilde's attachments to Robert Ross, John Gray and Lord Alfred Douglas. In the Swallow's initial courtship of the Reed, however, it is Wilde who becomes the Swallow, with his wife Constance represented as the slender-waisted Reed, who curtseys gracefully but has no conversation.[8]

Whatever the sexual subtext of *The Happy Prince*, it is so thoroughly sublimated that it is unlikely to be the reason why Wilde or his critics felt the tale to be unsuitable for children. Wilde himself regarded it as a piece of social and political commentary, writing in a letter to Leonard Smithers:

> The story is an attempt to treat a tragic modern problem in a form that aims at delicacy and imaginative treatment: it is a reaction against the purely imitative character of modern art—and now that literature has taken to blowing loud trumpets I cannot but be pleased that some ear has cared to listen to the low music of a little reed.[9]

It is difficult to see what Wilde means by "a tragic modern problem" here. The principal problems in *The Happy Prince* would seem to be poverty and injustice, neither of which is at all modern. The rest of the statement is clear enough. Wilde's social criticism will be veiled with fantasy, unlike the stark and unsubtle realism of the writers who are "blowing loud trumpets." Children might therefore read it, but fail to appreciate the political and social commentary, much as they might read the Bowdlerised versions of *Gulliver's Travels* that were such a feature of Victorian nurseries. This, however, would scarcely justify Wilde's "Certificate Eighteen" rating for the stories in his letter to Mrs. Chanler. The tragic modern problem to which Wilde refers, and which is far more pervasive in his fairy tales than poverty, is the realisation of humanity's contingent position in a cosmos without purpose or justice; in other words, that of Cosmic Nihilism.

In *The Specter of the Absurd,* the most influential of the recent academic texts on Nihilism, Donald A. Crosby defines Cosmic Nihilism as that which "disavows intelligibility or value in nature, seeing it as indifferent or hostile to fundamental human concerns."[10] It is therefore the *fons et origo* of every other type of Nihilism (Crosby specifically mentions Political, Moral, Epistemological and Existential Nihilism, though these categories are clearly not exhaustive), each of which is an application of this general meaninglessness to the various areas of life with which we are concerned. The problem of Cosmic Nihilism becomes more acute and insistent as the fairy tales progress, but it is there in all of them. Certainly by the time he had finished *The Devoted Friend*, it must have been clear to Wilde that the bitterness in these stories was usually far more evident than any "joy and wonder," and was more appropriate for those whose age had allowed them to experience some of the world's disappointments and arrive at a considered view of the universe and their place in it than it was for children.

It is the stupidity of adults in authority that is the first target for satire in *The Happy Prince*. The Town Councillor "who wished to gain a reputation for having artistic tastes"[11] can think of nothing more beautiful than a weathercock as a standard of comparison for the statue, then qualifies his aesthetic appreciation by observing that weathercocks are more useful than statues, "fearing lest people should think him unpractical." The sensible[12] mother who tells her child that "The Happy Prince never dreams of crying for anything" is to be proved spectacularly wrong on the next page, when the Swallow is drenched with the statue's tears. The Mathematical Master, who does not approve of children dreaming, is the stock unimaginative adult of the fairy story, refusing to believe in anything he has not seen, the very antithesis of the type of tale in which he finds himself.

All this is certainly written *for* children in the sense of being enthusiastically pro-child. The adult society of the City is continually represented as corrupt, self-serving and pretentious. When the Professor of Ornithology writes to the local newspaper about the Swallow, everyone quotes his letter because "it was full of so many words that they could not understand," (273) as though incomprehensibility were the gold-standard of learning. The Mayor and Town Councillors finish the story locked in an argument of pure egotism. The beautiful lady in waiting, whose life seems to consist entirely of parties, reproaches her toiling seamstress with idleness. The victims of their callousness are almost all young: the Charity Children in their red cloaks, the boy dying of a fever, the little match-girl,[13] the two little boys sleeping under the bridge. This order, the oppression of the young and sensitive by the old and stupid, is never subverted, a lack of progress which has perturbed such critics as Jack Zipes[14] and Rodney Shewan,[15] who argue that the Prince's sacrifice is ultimately futile. The ruby from the Prince's sword-hilt goes unnoticed in the seamstress's garret, and the greatest service the Swallow can perform for the sick child is to fan him with his wings. The little match-girl does not go to heaven, like Andersen's match-girl, but merely escapes being beaten for a single night. The satire against the rich and powerful in the city is compounded by the fact that even the recipients of the Prince's charity are strangely obtuse. It does not occur to the young playwright, for instance, to wonder how a sapphire has appeared on his desk. He merely decides it is an anonymous gift "from some great admirer" (274). A miracle is happening in the city and no one notices.

Wilde must have felt that it would be too bitter for these stolid citizens to constitute the Prince's only audience, for the story ends with an awkward *deus ex machina*. God, who has never been in evidence before, abruptly affirms his angel's valuation of the Prince's broken heart and the Swallow's dead body as "the two most precious things in the city" (277) and apparently grants eternal life to the two protagonists (albeit a conventional and unimaginative one, consisting entirely of praising and singing). What God does not do, however, is to overturn the structure of his earthly city. He does not release the Charity Children from the tyranny of the Mathematical Master, stop the match-girl's father from beating her, or wrest power away from the squabbling Mayor and Councillors. Nor is there any hint of a hereafter in which these wrongs will be righted.

God appears to be as powerless to subvert the tyranny of the strong and the stupid as the Prince was when he lived behind the palace walls at Sans-Souci. In the city, the narrow-minded urban bourgeoisie are in control, equally impervious to attack from God and King. God's role in this story is not that of an omnipotent deity, but of a sympathetic reader, affirming the symbolic value of the sacrifice made by the Prince and the Swallow. *The Happy Prince* fails to deliver a happy ending, and this is by no means the only expectation the story subverts. Its eponymous hero does not set out on a quest, for he is utterly immobile. When he embarks on his career of philanthropy, he encounters no active antagonists: no dragons, devils, bandits, witches or wicked stepmothers.[16] Indeed, no one tries to stop him from sacrificing his wealth and beauty, and the only enemy he encounters is the obtuseness of both the recipients of his gifts and those in authority who judge solely by appearances

Andersen's fairy tales, closer to Wilde's in time and spirit than Perrault's or the Brothers Grimm's, often have happy, rather sentimental endings, which rely on the progress and development of the protagonist (as in, for instance *The Ugly Duckling, The Snow Queen or Thumbelina*). Yet even when the story concludes in a rather melancholy fashion, as with *The Little Mermaid or The Little Match-Girl*, it does so in a universe of order and purpose utterly removed from the meaningless, contingent world of *The Happy Prince*. The difference between Wilde and Andersen is nothing less than Nihilism. It is this cosmic meaninglessness that makes Wilde's tone seem so bitter. Dickens, for instance, is far rougher in his satire of such analogous characters as Bounderby, Casby, and Pecksniff than Wilde is with his Mayor and Town Council, but the Mayor and Town Councillors, unlike the shallow hypocrites in Dickens, are never exposed or punished. The good does not end happily and the bad unhappily: that is what Nihilism means. It is this cosmic meaninglessness, this lack of a moral order, which made both Ross and, ultimately, Wilde himself, wary of recommending *The Happy Prince* as suitable for children.

If the sudden appearance of an almost impotent God provides an uneasy conclusion to *The Happy Prince*, the dominance of Cosmic Nihilism in *The Nightingale and the Rose* is even more complete. The Prince and the Swallow could talk to and, indeed, love one another. It is one of the conventions of fairy tales and fantasy literature that men and beasts can understand each other's language, a convention that makes the world seem at once more integrated and more explicable than the one we live in. The Student and the Nightingale cannot communicate at all, so that each one drastically misunderstands the other. The Nightingale thinks the Student is "the true lover" (278) and decides he is worth dying for, while the Student, with bitter irony, describes the Nightingale as selfish and unfeeling (280). A correspondent of Wilde's, who later dedicated a book of poems to him,[17] wrote enthusiastically of the Student as the archetype of the true lover. Wilde replied very graciously to this thoroughly unintelligent comment:

> I am afraid that I don't think as much of the young Student as you do. He seems to me a rather shallow young man, and almost as bad as the girl he thinks he loves. The nightingale is the true lover, if there is one. She, at least, is Romance, and the student and the girl are, like most of us, unworthy of Romance.[18]

Every subsequent critic has condemned the Student, as we are evidently intended to. His callousness and lack of sensibility mirrors that of the human characters in *The Happy Prince*. Like the Town Councillor, he believes that "in this age to be practical is everything" (282).[19] Like the Mathematical Master he rejects romance in favour of logic, and like the little match-girl, he has no idea of the value of what he has found. What we are supposed to think of the Nightingale is less clear. Philip Cohen argues that "Wilde exposes her beliefs as mere delusion"[20], Jarlath Killeen proposes a reading in which "the Nightingale—and by implication, Christ—has so radically misunderstood her audience that her sacrifice is useless"[21] and Rodney Shewan insists: "We are left with two alternative inferences: that self-sacrifice for altruistic motives is futile and wasteful, or that self-sacrifice in pursuit of a personal vision...is as egotistical as any other form of self-realisation."[22]

If the Nightingale is deluded and her sacrifice useless, then it is difficult to find any locus of value to combat the story's Nihilism. The Nightingale, however, is the heroine of the story, not only because she is romantic, but because she is an artist. In the rose, she creates an artefact of perfect beauty, which is disdained by the Professor's daughter, thrown away by the Student, and crushed beneath a cartwheel in the gutter. This, clearly, is not the fate she envisioned for her creation. Yet, presumably, if she had thought about the matter at all, she would have known that neither the rose nor the Student was destined to last forever. The point is the rose itself, not what happens to it or how long it lasts. In creating the rose, the Nightingale also creates another work of art, which is outlasted even by the rose: her song. For this, she has a more appreciative audience:

The white Moon heard it, and she forgot the dawn, and lingered on in the sky. The red rose heard it, and it trembled all over with ecstasy, and opened its petals to the cold morning air. Echo bore it to her purple cavern in the hills, and woke the sleeping shepherds from their dreams. It floated through the reeds of the river, and they carried its message to the sea. (281)

The last two sentences contain obvious echoes of *Lycidas* and it can scarcely be an accident that the shepherds provide the only sympathetic human audience for the Nightingale's song, for the shepherds were not only Christ's first worshippers but also Milton's artists, who "strictly meditate the thankless Muse"[23] and may be wakened by the echo of the Nightingale's sacrifice to song of their own.

Even if they are not, even if no one had heard the song or seen the flower, "Beauty is its own excuse for being."[24] The poem ends in a petulant denial of love and life, with the bookful blockhead grinding away at his Metaphysics. One must not expect things to end happily; not lives, not love affairs and not even fairy tales. This is the Nihilist backdrop to the story. But against the darkness, Wilde's Nightingale, like Hardy's Darkling Thrush, chooses to fling her soul upon the growing gloom. The fact that this gesture appears futile in practical terms is an indictment of practicality, not of the gesture. As Wilde was to demonstrate ever more compellingly in his fairy tales, it is not in the nature of endings to be happy, but then the end is not what matters.

The absence of traditional fairy tale villains—ogres, dragons, witches and the like—from Wilde's stories has already been noted, but the next story in *The Happy Prince* does at least contain a giant. *The Selfish Giant* may be the best-known of all Wilde's fairy tales, but has received relatively little critical attention, perhaps because its brevity and simplicity make it appear self-explanatory.[25] Its most significant oddity, given the genre within which it operates, is the remarkable tameness of the giant. When he returns home to find the children playing in his garden, the giant does not threaten to kill them or to grind their bones to make his bread. He merely enquires "in a very gruff voice" (283) what they are doing there. When he has chased them away, he builds a high wall and puts up a noticeboard, announcing that trespassers will be prosecuted. The threat is not one of death or physical harm, but of litigation, and the giant's behaviour is not that of a monster in a fairy tale, but of the sort of irascible old gentleman any child might encounter on his way home from school.

Nonetheless, the giant's perfectly ordinary selfishness causes real harm to the children, to himself, and to the world, which has lost a thing of beauty in the garden and gained an act of

petty cruelty in the giant's refusal to share it. When the Christ-
child kisses the giant, the other children see that the giant is not
"wicked" any longer and return to the garden. "Wicked" does not,
in the context, seem an inappropriate adjective to apply to the
giant's behaviour and accords with the views Wilde expressed a
decade later about the treatment of children in prison:

> People nowadays do not understand what cruelty is. They
> regard it as a sort of terrible mediaeval passion, and connect
> it with the race of men like Eccelin da Romano, and others,
> to whom the deliberate infliction of pain gave a real madness
> of pleasure. But men of the stamp of Eccelin are merely ab-
> normal types of perverted individualism. Ordinary cruelty is
> simply stupidity. It is the entire want of imagination.[26]

The giant does not enjoy hurting the children. When he sees the
change in his garden after they have crept back in, he repents immediately, but until then he was too stupid and unimaginative to
see the harm he was doing. Both Wilde's early plays contain villains of the perverted individualist type: Prince Paul Maraloffski
in *Vera* and the Duke of Padua[27] in *The Duchess of Padua*. Each
of them is the most interesting and charismatic character in the
play and takes all the best lines. It did not take Wilde long to
realise that these "types of perverted individualism" were not his
true target, both because they were intelligent and colourful and
because, however badly they behaved, they were responsible for
very little of the world's misery. This aspect of Wilde's fairy tales is
profoundly realist. It is axiomatically very rare to encounter some
embodiment of evil, who has determined to devote himself heart
and soul to your extermination. Almost all the frustration and un-
happiness in life comes from people like the Mathematical Master
and the Town Councillors, the Student and the Professor's daughter, or the Selfish Giant, whom we meet every day. They do not
threaten to eat us or burn us alive; perhaps they would be less
tiresome if they did. Instead they suffocate their victims with in-
flexible stupidity. The litigious old curmudgeon is, for Wilde, a
greater menace than the flesh-eating monster, and this was presci-

ent of him, for it was the former type of giant who was to bedevil his own existence.

The giant is the last character in any of Wilde's fairy tales who is assured of a place in Paradise. The story is too brief to provide much description of the world outside his garden wall, but since the children had nowhere else to play except the road, which was "very dusty and full of hard stones" (283), it seems clear that the giant's garden, like Paradise, is a refuge from the harshness of the outside world. The world outside the garden, like the giant himself before his epiphany, is not particularly dangerous. There are no witches or fire-breathing dragons, not even a wicked nobleman who crushes children beneath his chariot wheels, merely dust and stones. The children are unhappy there because they are cut off from beauty and pleasure. If the giant is selfish and uncaring, the world outside his garden is equally so. Once again, Cosmic Nihilism is endemic in the story, the indifference of the cosmos mirrors the stupid cruelty of those in authority over the world, suggesting that nothing anyone can do will make any difference to the order of things. Such minor, localised acts of rebellion as the Prince's or the Nightingale's are of value precisely because they go against the grain of a universe whose direction no one can hope to permanently reverse. The giant who turns his garden into a playground is doing the same type of small, good thing as Candide when he makes his garden grow.

Little Hans in *The Devoted Friend* is also a gardener. His story opens with a litany of the flowers in his superlative and perfectly-ordered garden:

Sweet-Williams grew there, and Gilly-flowers, and Shepherds'-purses, and Fair-maids of France. There were damask Roses, and yellow Roses, lilac Crocuses and gold, purple Violets and white. Columbine and Ladysmock, Marjoram and Wild Basil, the Cowslip and the Flower-de-luce, the Daffodil and the Clove-Pink bloomed or blossomed in their proper order as the months went by, one flower taking another flower's place, so that there were always beautiful things to look at, and pleasant odours to smell. (287)

This fusion of art and nature is plundered by the rich and practical Miller, who owns a great many useful things (cows, sheep, sacks of flour, casks of wine and ale) but nothing as beautiful as Hans's garden. The satire in this story is, as Ross pointed out, even more bitter than in any of the others ("at once the cleverest and least agreeable in the volume"[28]) and seems to be directed against Hans as well as the Miller. Killeen calls Hans "bizarrely compliant and almost masochistic"[29], while Cohen remarks that: "The nightingale's wasted gesture excites pity, but stupid Hans seems thoroughly deserving of his fate."[30] The comparison with the Nightingale is a telling one. The Nightingale may be sacrificing herself for a false ideal of love, as Hans does for a false ideal of friendship, but in doing so she uses her art as a singer to create something of perfect beauty. Wilde's description of Hans's garden makes it clear that he is also a creator of beauty, but his sacrifice spoils his garden by allowing the Miller to plunder it and, ultimately, by leaving it untended after his death. When the Miller says that true friendship should be "quite free from selfishness of any kind" (290), the most obvious irony lies in the disparity between this lofty sentiment and his own extremely selfish behaviour. Yet Wilde does not approve of the Miller's lofty sentiments any more than his base actions. The artist may choose to sacrifice himself to his art, as the Nightingale does. To sacrifice himself and his art for the convenience of an oaf like the Miller is a frantic blasphemy against the religion of beauty.

Personal relationships could, of course, be used as a counterforce to Nihilism, but after the first ardent attachment of the Prince and the Swallow, Wilde's protagonists in these stories are very conspicuously alone. In his work at least, Wilde always puts Art before personal relations. "One half-hour with Art was always more to me than a cycle with you," he wrote to Lord Alfred Douglas in *De Profundis*:

Nothing really at any period of my life was ever of the smallest importance to me compared with Art. But in the case of an artist, weakness is nothing less than a crime, when it is a weakness that paralyses the imagination. (983)

This type of weakness is the subject of both *The Devoted Friend* and *The Remarkable Rocket*, the concluding story in this volume. The motif of shining against the darkness has appeared before in the Swallow's nocturnal philanthropy and the Nightingale's moonlight song, but never so literally as in this story, where the principal characters are fireworks, each of which has the opportunity for a single brief moment of brightness before disappearing, like Bede's sparrow, into the dark again. The Rocket bursts into tears after imagining a fate closely resembling that of Little Hans for the royal couple's putative son:

> Why, perhaps the Prince and Princess may go to live in a country where there is a deep river, and perhaps they may have one only son, a little fair-haired boy with violet eyes like the Prince himself; and perhaps some day he may go out to walk with his nurse; and perhaps the nurse may go to sleep under a great elder-tree; and perhaps the little boy may fall into the deep river and be drowned. What a terrible misfortune! Poor people, to lose their only son! It is really too dreadful! I shall never get over it. (297)

The Roman Candle and the Fire-balloon warn the Rocket that he had better keep his powder dry, but he insists on soaking himself with tears and fizzles out, while even his poor relations shoot into the sky "like wonderful golden flowers with blossoms of fire" (298). The Rocket, like Hans, wastes his talent through sentimentality, though it is significant that in his case the subject of the sentiment is an imaginary future. Walter Pater, who wrote to Wilde that *The Happy Prince* had consoled him during an attack of gout, singled out "the wise wit" of this particular tale for praise[31] and its philosophy is clearly influenced by *The Renaissance*. It is the beautiful moment that matters, not the hereafter, for the tale of the rocket after he is thrown into the ditch by a workman would presumably have been much the same if he had gone off in a blaze of glory. In his prose poem, *The Artist*, Wilde writes of a sculptor who cannot find any bronze to fashion his image of *The Pleasure that abideth for a Moment*. In the end, he melts down another sculpture,

The Sorrow that endureth Forever, and uses the bronze for his new work (900). This, for both Wilde and Pater, is the essential business of the artist. He must not lose himself in contemplation of limitless sorrow, but use it as raw material for the creation of beauty, however ephemeral.

The Rocket is obviously satirised, but in this story, as in *The Devoted Friend*, no one escapes unscathed. The other fireworks are naïve and parochial. When a little Squib congratulates himself for having travelled as far as the end of the garden, the Roman Candle admonishes him:

> The King's garden is not the world, you foolish Squib...the world is an enormous place and it would take you three days to see it thoroughly. (295)

The Frog who thinks croaking "the most musical sound in the world" (299) and the Duck, "considered a great beauty on account of her waddle" (300), who prefers practical skills such as ploughing fields and pulling carts to the creation of ephemeral beauty, are as deficient in artistic taste as the fireworks are in worldly sophistication. The Rocket's pomposity and self-delusion (recalling Whistler, whose 1875 painting *Nocturne in Black and Gold—the Falling Rocket* provided the occasion for Ruskin's scornful dismissal of his work in *Fors Clavigera*[32]) is perhaps pardonable in the face of such ignorance and indifference. If he were not so self-regarding, it seems no one else would regard him, or take the slightest notice of him. His unpardonable sin is to waste his ability, to deprive himself and the world of that shower of golden rain with which he was capable of illuminating the night sky. In giving way to despair (and specifically to despair about the future) the Rocket has allowed Nihilism to triumph.

Wilde's essential project in *The Happy Prince* is, like Nietzsche's in *The Birth of Tragedy*, to interpret the world in aesthetic rather than moral terms. This provides a counterforce to Cosmic Nihilism because the cosmos, which has no morality, clearly contains an abundance of beauty. Since morality is a human construction, inapplicable to animals and objects, Wilde continually shifts human beings away from the centre of the action to present a more aesthetically balanced picture of the cosmos. Only one of the five stories, *The Devoted Friend*, features a human protagonist, and this tale is presented as a reversal of the beast fable which has been a traditional way of illustrating a moral from Aesop to *Animal Farm*. *The Devoted Friend* subverts the conventions of the beast fable by making a bird tell a story about humans to some other animals, then failing to reveal the moral because the Water-rat will not listen to it (so that the ostensible moral of the story is that it is dangerous to tell stories with morals). In all the other stories, the human characters are marginal and either unsympathetic (*The Happy Prince, The Nightingale and the Rose*) or merely trivial, as in *The Remarkable Rocket*.

The reviewers of Wilde's second volume of fairy tales, *A House of Pomegranates*, which appeared in November of 1891, continued to harp on the theme of whether these were children's stories or not. "Is *A House of Pomegranates* intended for a child's book?" enquired the anonymous reviewer in the *Pall Mall Gazette*. "We confess that we do not exactly know."[33] The critic went on to object to the "ultra-aestheticism" of the pictures and the "fleshly" style of the writing, which he said had a tendency to "wander off too often into something between a 'Sinburnian' ecstasy and the catalogue of a high art furniture dealer."[34]

This time Wilde responded directly and decisively. In a letter to the editor he wrote:

> Now in building this *House of Pomegranates* I had about as much intention of pleasing the British child as I had of pleasing the British public... No artist recognises any standard of beauty but that which is suggested by his own temperament. The artist seeks to realise in a certain material his immaterial idea of beauty, and thus to transform an idea into an ideal. That is the way an artist makes things. That is why an artist makes things. The artist has no other object in making things.[35]

However disingenuous Wilde's assertions that he wrote to please himself, without taking account of public taste, *A House of Pomegranates*, issued in a limited *edition de luxe*, was clearly aimed at a rarefied audience. Although the initial tale, *The Young King*, was first published in the same year as *The Happy Prince*, and may not have been composed very much later, the atmosphere is already darker and more luxuriant, closer to Huysmans or Baudelaire than to Hans Andersen. Wilde's description of all the magnificent objects in the palace of Joyeuse recalls the gilded opulence of Des Esseintes's chateau at Fontenay and the King's "strange passion for beauty" (214), which leads him to worship Venetian painting or a silver image of Endymion, is a purer, youthful version of that idolatry which eventually draws Des Esseintes to the cosmic pessimism of Schopenhauer.

The first reviewers of *The Young King* described the tale as Socialist[36] and more recent critics have tended to agree with this reading. George Woodcock calls it "a parable on the capitalist system of exploitation as severe as anything in William Morris"[37] and Jack Zipes praises the King for his "rejection of private property, ornamentation, and unjust power."[38] The King's first dream opens with a scene which, as Philip Cohen remarks, "could be integrated more smoothly into a novel by Zola than into the average fairy tale"[39]:

He thought that he was standing in a long, low attic, amidst the whir and clatter of many looms. The meagre daylight peered in through the grated windows and showed him the gaunt figures of the weavers bending over their cases. Pale, sickly-looking children were crouched on the huge cross-beams. As the shuttles dashed through the warp they lifted up the heavy battens, and when the shuttles stopped they let the battens fall and pressed the threads together. Their faces were pinched with famine, and their thin hands shook and trembled. Some haggard women were seated at a table sewing. A horrible odour filled the place. The air was foul and heavy, and the walls dripped and streamed with damp. (215)

When the King points out to the weaver that he is not a slave; no one is forcing him to work in such loathsome conditions, the weaver replies with Ruskinian eloquence:

> In war...the strong make slaves of the weak, and in peace the rich make slaves of the poor. We must work to live, and they give us such mean wages that we die. We toil for them all day long, and they heap up gold in their coffers, and our children fade away before their time, and the faces of those we love become hard and evil. We tread out the grapes, and another drinks the wine. We sow the corn, and our own board is empty. We have chains, though no eye beholds them; and we are slaves, though men call us free. (216)

This is a powerful condemnation of the system over which the King presides and which he seems never to have considered before now, though he has spent most of his life as a peasant. For Wilde, the difference between a peasant and a proletarian is greater than the gap between a peasant and a king. The King's former life, "bare-limbed and pipe in hand" (213) following the flock of a poor goatherd, does not appear to have been particularly harsh and the horror of urban poverty comes as a frightening revelation to him.

The Young King's story has obvious parallels with *The Happy Prince*, but the structure is even closer to *A Christmas Carol* (1843). The King, like Scrooge, has three visions in the course of a single night, which cause him, on waking, radically to alter his *modus vivendi*. Scrooge and the Happy Prince both choose to redistribute their wealth in acts of practical philanthropy. In *The Young King*, more Socialist than either in its rhetoric, no such redistribution occurs. Critics such as Rodney Shewan have complained that the King's response to his dreams confers no benefit upon his suffering people,[40] but Wilde forestalls these criticisms by including them in his text. One of the crowd harangues the King with a swingeing critique of both renunciation and Socialism:

> Sir, knowest thou not that out of the luxury of the rich cometh the life of the poor? By your pomp we are nurtured, and your

vices give us bread. To toil for a master is bitter, but to have no master to toil for is more bitter still. Thinkest thou that the ravens will feed us? And what cure hast thou for these things? Wilt thou say to the buyer, "Thou shalt buy for so much," and to the seller, "Thou shalt sell at this price"? I trow not. Therefore go back to the Palace and put on thy purple and fine linen. What hast thou to do with us, and what we suffer? (220)

The man's position is Nihilist because there is apparently nothing one can do to make things better. The Socialist solution of a planned economy is the very one he singles out for ridicule. In *The Soul of Man under Socialism*, Wilde explicitly rejects the notion of this type of Socialism "What is needed is Individualism," he writes:

If the Socialism is Authoritarian; if there are Governments armed with economic power as they are now with political power; if, in a word, we are to have Industrial Tyrannies, then the last state of man will be worse than the first. (1175)

In an earlier essay on the Chinese philosopher Zhuangzi,[41] Wilde agreed with his subject in condemning all forms of government *per se:*

In an evil moment the Philanthropist made his appearance, and brought with him the mischievous idea of Government. "There is such a thing," says Chuang Tzu, "as leaving mankind alone: there has never been such a thing as governing mankind." All modes of government are wrong. They are unscientific, because they seek to alter the natural environment of man; they are immoral because, by interfering with the individual, they produce the most aggressive forms of egotism; they are ignorant, because they try to spread education; they are self-destructive, because they engender anarchy.[42]

This sounds like a right-wing plea for small government, but neither Wilde nor Zhuangzi will accept laissez-faire capitalism either. Later in the same essay, Wilde declares:

The accumulation of wealth is to him the origin of evil. It makes the strong violent, and the weak dishonest. It creates the petty thief, and puts him in a bamboo cage. It creates the big thief, and sets him on a throne of white jade. It is the father of competition, and competition is the waste, as well as the destruction, of energy. The order of nature is rest, repetition, and peace. Weariness and war are the results of an artificial society based upon capital; and the richer this society gets, the more thoroughly bankrupt it really is, for it has neither sufficient rewards for the good nor sufficient punishments for the wicked. There is also this to be remembered--that the prizes of the world degrade a man as much as the world's punishments. The age is rotten with its worship of success.[43]

The age for Wilde clearly does not mean the fourth century before Christ. It means all ages, including his own and the Young King's (whenever that is, the historical background to all the stories is deliberately vague). The problem of government is perennial and this story prefigures *The Soul of Man* in showing that Wilde, like Zhuangzi, is a Political Nihilist who believes that no realisable form of government will ever make things better. Wilde explicitly identifies the Nihilist element in Zhuangzi's thought:

Chuang Tzu spent his life in preaching the great creed of Inaction, and in pointing out the uselessness of all useful things...Like the obscure philosopher of early Greek speculation, he believed in the identity of contraries; like Plato, he was an idealist, and had all the idealist's contempt for utilitarian systems...and in his worship of Nothing he may be said to have in some measure anticipated those strange dreamers of mediaeval days who, like Tauler and Master Eckhart, adored the *purum nihil* and the Abyss.[44]

This shows an important development in Wilde's thought between the composition of *The Happy Prince* and *The Young King*. The Happy Prince would presumably have responded to the King's three dreams as he did to the scenes of misery he saw from his tall column, high above the city, with practical philanthropy. He would have introduced a mandatory minimum wage for the weavers and a new foreign trade policy to promote ethical practices in pearl-diving and ruby-mining. At the very least he would have capered around like Scrooge, handing out money and turkeys. The Young King, in sharp contradistinction, does nothing practical, nothing that requires political power or wealth. His gesture is purely personal and symbolic. It is also ephemeral. The story ends with his angelic face. A miracle has just occurred, but it is not a practical miracle, like the feeding of the five thousand or the Happy Prince's wealth-sharing scheme, which would suggest that the King is going to return to the palace and start governing the kingdom more equitably. It is a miracle of beauty, a divine coronation after which the King cannot rule at all, cannot do anything, cannot exist. He cannot do any of these things because he is suspended in an eternal moment, frozen in the last lines of the tale so that, in sharp contrast to Dorian Gray, he retains his beautiful face forever.

Wilde is not quite saying that there is no counterforce to Political Nihilism. He is saying that the counterforce to Political Nihilism is not political but individual: even the King can only escape from Nihilism by escaping from government. In *The Birthday of the Infanta,* the melancholy King of Spain wants to give up his throne and retire to a Trappist monastery (a denial of life as absolute as suicide by Wildean standards). He maintains a feeble grasp on power only because his successor, if he were to abdicate, would be his brother, Don Pedro of Aragon, whom he hates and fears and "whose cruelty, even in Spain, was notorious" (224). The King, like the old Czar in Vera, is motivated entirely by misery, fear and hatred. Even his love for his daughter emerges only in negative terms; he is afraid that Don Pedro will harm her, but cannot summon enough positive affection to smile at her or speak to her, even on her birthday.

The cruelty and artificiality of the Spanish Court, "always noted for its cultivated passion for the horrible" (228) is continually emphasised. Royal weddings are celebrated by burning heretics like hecatombs; poisoned wafers and gloves dispatch princes and princesses, even the flowers in the royal garden are formal and affected. The Infanta is as lonely as her father: "On ordinary days she was only allowed to play with children of her own rank, so she had always to play alone" (223). Into this nightmarish atmosphere comes the Dwarf, who until the day before had been running wild in the forest. The Dwarf, like the Infanta, has had a loveless childhood. His father was "well pleased to get rid of so ugly and useless a child" (228). Yet he is happy, high-spirited and natural. He is also an artist,[45] whose art, the dance, is the perfect expression of *The Pleasure that abideth for a Moment*, as ephemeral as the fireworks' rain of fire or the Nightingale's song—indeed, he is explicitly compared with the nightingale, who is also "not much to look at" (229). The birds and the lizards, the only things in the King's garden which can leave whenever they want to, are alone in liking and valuing the Dwarf. Even the children who are delighted by his dance are constrained by a rigid system of etiquette only to enjoy themselves at such special occasions, and then not too much. The first quality Wilde attributes to them is "a stately grace" (223) not a phrase often used to describe children at play, who are more usually depicted as behaving with the carefree abandon of the dancing Dwarf. These children of the Spanish nobility are imitation adults, already schooled in the perverse refinements of cruelty and snobbery; only the Dwarf is a true child.

The Court is grotesque and evil, but it cannot be held responsible for the Dwarf's death, except insofar as it is the first place he has visited to be equipped with mirrors. It is the truth that breaks his heart. The harshness of the universe, which has sent him before his time into this breathing world scarce half made-up, is reflected in the Spanish Court and also in the Dwarf's own soul, since his first response to the monster he sees in the mirror is one of mocking amusement. The Dwarf could only have survived by remaining true to his artistic nature and providing himself with a mask. We can none of us bear very much reality: "The nineteenth century dislike of Realism is the rage of Caliban seeing his own face in a glass."[46]

While *The Birthday of the Infanta,* probably written shortly before *The Picture of Dorian Gray,* prefigures one of that novel's major themes, *The Fisherman and his Soul* subverts its central plot device.[47] Far from making a Faustian pact to sacrifice his Soul, the Fisherman cannot even give it away. The irony of this is not lost on him. "How strange a thing this is!" he exclaims. "The Priest telleth me that the Soul is worth all the gold in the world, and the merchants say that it is not worth a clipped piece of silver" (239). The nature and value of the Fisherman's Soul is perhaps the greatest conundrum in this, the most complex and obscure of Wilde's fairy tales. Satan does not seem at all anxious to get it and the Fisherman is quite happy without it for three years. When he is reunited with his Soul, he does not even seem to notice what is happening and after the reunion the Soul, whose experience of solitary travel has turned it into a sort of evil Daemon, is still excluded from the Fisherman's heart, which it enters only at the moment of his death. The Soul tries to tempt the Fisherman unsuccessfully with wisdom and riches, then successfully with pleasure in the shape of dancing girls. Later, when the Fisherman is again partially joined to his Soul and is pining for the Mermaid, it tries vice and philanthropy. It is curiously omnivorous.

Evidently, there is no simple dualist dichotomy of soul and body, the deathless spirit fastened to the dying animal, in this tale. It is the Soul which seems to have the baser appetites and Wilde, who uses the masculine pronoun to refer to the Fisherman, calls the Soul "it" like an animal or an object. "Those who see any difference between soul and body have neither" (1244) he wrote in *Phrases and Philosophies for the Use of the Young,* a collection of epigrams published in December 1894, in a periodical with the very Wildean name of the *Chameleon.* His assertion sounds suspiciously like nonsense (one might accuse some philistine acquaintance of having no soul, but what sort of sense does it make to tell him, or anyone else, that he has no body?), unless the operative word is "have." The Fisherman, like all of us, has a heart and a mind, a body and a soul. He is none of these things, but a mysterious and monstrous entity which possesses all of them. To become overly emotional, cerebral, physical, or soulful is to identify oneself with one of these aspects of one's personality: to become a heart or mind, body or soul and lose the indefinable essence of selfhood which once kept these constituents in balance. It might, therefore, be possible to tell a lover obsessed with his inamorata that he no longer *has* a heart, but merely is a heart, or to inform some flannelled fool at the wicket or muddied oaf at the goal that his body is not his, but he is his body's.

Even if this is true, it does not give us anything like a conventional fairy tale with a neat moral. Wilde is not telling us what to do, and in this sense *A House of Pomegranates* is far removed from the didacticism of *The Happy Prince,* where it was obvious what Hans or the Rocket, for instance, ought to have done. As, in *The Birthday of the Infanta,* the world's harshness was mirrored both in the Spanish Court and the individuals who peopled it, so *The Fisherman and his Soul* reflects the world's randomness and unreliability. The microcosm of the Spanish Court might have persuaded us that the universe, if not kindly, is at least orderly. *The Fisherman and his Soul,* which ranges more widely in time and place than any of the stories which precede it, shows us that it is not even that. The universe is as chaotic as the Witches' Sabbath and this lack of design is reflected on the level of the individual by the arbitrary, unpredictable behaviour of the Soul. "I did a strange thing, but what I did matters not," says the Fisherman's Soul (though by this point in the story, he cannot call his Soul his own) and it doesn't seem to matter very much what the Fisherman does either (247, 251). In this respect, the story plumbs new depths of Nihilism. The Soul is evidently a Moral Nihilist, not even attempting to justify or explain the random crimes he prompts the Fisherman to commit, but merely murmuring "Be at peace, be at peace" (253-254). Some of the Soul's actions, such as smiting the child who was standing by the water-jar, do not benefit the Fisherman in any way and are merely random acts of spite, as arbitrary as the rules concerning the disposal and resumption of souls or any other principle by which the universe fails to be governed.

The story's ending is as contradictory and chaotic as the rest of it. The Priest, who has been the harsh voice of unalterable law throughout the text, is reformed by the scent of the flowers from the Fisherman's unmarked grave, recants his curse, and blesses the sea "and all the wild things that are in it" (258-259). One might see this as a marriage of land and sea, which have been divided throughout the narrative, symbolising all the other divisions in the chaotic universe of Wilde's tale, including the division between the Fisherman and his Soul, since it is the Soul that sunders him from the Sea-folk (the irony being that the Soul, supposedly the profoundest part of one's nature, is what keeps him on the surface, preventing him from plumbing the depths with his beloved Mermaid). The people on land seem to feel this, and are filled with joy and wonder. But the Sea-folk do not appear to feel any such connection and the story ends with them moving to another part of the sea. The end is as arbitrary as everything else. There is no unification, healing or understanding. Nothing is explained.

The Star-Child, which concludes *A House of Pomegranates,* is Wilde's harshest and bleakest tale. When the Woodcutters escape death in the forest, they are so overjoyed at their escape that "the Earth seemed to them like a flower of silver, and the Moon like a flower of gold" (261). Yet they quickly return to their former gloom, agreeing that "Injustice has parcelled out the world, nor is there equal division of aught save sorrow." There is plenty of sorrow in *The Star-Child,* but compared with the stories that precede it, there is a good deal of justice as well. The Star-Child is punished for his cruelty and rewarded for his kindness as punctiliously as in the strictest morality tale. When he seeks help from the animals he has harmed, it is precisely because of the injuries inflicted by him that they are unable (and presumably also unwilling) to assist him. The type of punishment inflicted on the Star-Child exactly suits his crime and at the end of the story, redeemed by suffering and compassion, he metes out justice in exactly the way the Young King doesn't, rewarding the kindly Woodcutter and banishing the evil Magician, clothing the naked and feeding the hungry. It would be the most conventional of happy ever afters, but for the final brief paragraph, concluding both the book and this section of Wilde's *oeuvre*:

> Yet ruled he not long, so great had been his suffering, and so bitter the fire of his testing, for after the space of three years he died. And he who came after him ruled evilly. (270)

The re-imposition of order after the chaotic universe of *The Fisherman and his Soul* is subverted in two brief sentences, a reverse which reaffirms Wilde's Cosmic Nihilism. The isolated appearance of moments of moral order in the Cosmos only emphasise its essentially chaotic nature. Indeed, they increase it, since complex and orderly units in disorder appear more chaotic (and uglier) than simple lack of order (compare a wilderness or a void, for instance, with a car crash or a rubbish dump). If there were literally *no* justice, if no one in history had ever received his or her due, then we might be able to make some deduction from this about the nature of justice and its place in the universe. It is the fact that justice is sometimes done, but often isn't, that emphasises the randomness of the world.

The trajectory of Wilde's thought over the period of the fairy tales' composition (perhaps about five years), is very clear. He begins by seeking solutions to the monumental indifference of the universe in philanthropy, Christian love, and a sympathetic, if unconvincing, deity. None of these is satisfactory and only artistic creation provides, in the words of Robert Frost, "a momentary stay against confusion." In *A House of Pomegranates*, he abandons all such solutions. Here, Cosmic Nihilism is taken as read. Chaos and cruelty are the prevailing themes of the cosmic drama and counterforces, even of the most ephemeral variety, become increasingly hard to find (though this is at least partly because the protagonists of the last two stories are not artists, even in the limited senses that the Young King and the Dwarf are). It is this Nihilistic note in the later fairy tales which pervades all Wilde's writing in the period immediately before the composition of the social comedies, and which harmonises so exactly with "the note of Doom that like a purple thread runs through the gold cloth of *Dorian Gray*" (1026). It is this that finally led Wilde to pronounce the fairy tales unsuitable for children.

Bibliography

Works by Oscar Wilde

Wilde, Oscar. *Complete Letters* (London: Henry Holt, 2000)
Wilde, Oscar. *Complete Works* (London: HarperCollins, 2003)

Works by Others

Beckson, Karl (ed.). *Oscar Wilde: The Critical Heritage* (London: Routledge, 1974)
Cohen, Philip K. *The Moral Vision of Oscar Wilde* (Cranbery, NJ: Dickinson University Press, 1978)
Crosby, Donald A. *The Specter of the Absurd* (Albany: State University of New York, 1988)
Edwards, Owen Dudley. *The Fireworks of Oscar Wilde* (London: Barrie & Jenkins, 1989)
Ellmann, Richard. *Oscar Wilde* (London: Hamish Hamilton, 1987)
Killeen, Jarlath. *The Fairy Tales of Oscar Wilde* (Aldershot: Ashgate, 2007)
Schmidgall, Gary. *The Stranger Wilde* (London: Abacus, 1994)
Shewan, Rodney. *Oscar Wilde: Art and Egotism* (London: Macmillan, 1977)
Weller, Shane. *Modernism and Nihilism* (Basingstoke: Palgrave Macmillan, 2011)
Woodcock, George. *The Paradox of Oscar Wilde* (London: Boardman, 1949)
Zipes, Jack. *Fairy Tales and the Art of Subversion* (New York: Routledge, 2006)

Notes

1 *Saturday Review*, 20 October 1888, lxvi, 472.
2 Wilde, Oscar (Ed. Holland & Hart-Davis), *Complete Letters* (London, 2000), 366. Wilde made this comment in a letter to Ross himself, though he gave no indication that he knew who was responsible for the notice.
3 Wilde, *Complete Letters*, 350.
4 Wilde, *Complete Letters*, 352. The letter is dated 15 June. Holland and Hart-Davis place it after the letter to Gladstone, which was simply dated 'June 1888' by the recipient.
5 Wilde, *Complete Letters*, 388. Merlin Holland takes this last view as definitive and claims that Wilde "hated the idea" that the tales were written for children (Wilde, *Complete Works* 907).
6 Killeen, Jarlath. *The Fairy Tales of Oscar Wilde* (Aldershot, 2007), 21.
7 Ellmann, Richard, *Oscar Wilde* (London, 1987), 253.

8   A point made by Gary Schmidgall (*The Stranger Wilde* (London, 1994) among others.

9   Wilde, *Complete Letters*, 355.

10   Crosby, Donald A., *The Specter of the Absurd: Sources and Criticism of Modern Nihilism* (New York, 1988).

11   Wilde, *Complete Works*, 271. Further citation given in the text.

12   'Sensible', like 'practical' is always a term of disapprobation in Wilde's writing.

13   This is one of Wilde's more obvious borrowings from Hans Christian Andersen, to whose stories Wilde's were often compared. The first instance in print is probably that of an anonymous review in the Athenaeum (1st September 1888, 286). Ross, in his *Saturday Review* article, also draws the comparison, though he points out that Wilde's "bitter satire" differs widely from Andersen's manner.

14   Zipes, Jack, *Fairy Tales and the Art of Subversion* (New York, 2006), 116.

15   Shewan, Rodney, *Oscar Wilde: Art and Egotism* (London, 1977), 41.

16   These are the specific antagonists suggested by Vladimir Propp in *The Morphology of the Folktale*.

17   The poet's name was Thomas Hutchinson (1856-1938) and the book he dedicated to Wilde was called *Jolts and Jingles: a Book of Poems for Young People* (1889). The volume is, unsurprisingly, out of print, but its title does not give rise to any great hopes that Hutchinson's poetry was much more accomplished than his literary criticism.

18   Wilde, *Complete Letters*, 354.

19   The irony is compounded in the Student's case by the fact that he decides to study Metaphysics, not a subject with any immediate practical application, but 'practical' is always a damning word in Wilde's lexicon.

20   Cohen, Philip K., *The Moral Vision of Oscar Wilde* (Cranbery, N.J., 1978), 90.

21   Killeen, 49.

22   Shewan, 47.

23   Milton, *Lycidas*, line 66.

24   Emerson, *The Rhodora*, line 12.

25   Philip Cohen, for instance, remarks that he has excluded it from his discussion of the fairy tales because it "hardly needs explication" (Cohen, 81).

26   Letter to the Editor of the *Daily Chronicle* [Published 28th May 1897]. Wilde, *Complete Works*, 1060.

27   Ezzelino da Romano (1194-1259), identified as the archetype of Mediaeval cruelty in the letter quoted above, was in fact Duke of Padua, as well as Ver-

ona and Vicenza. He clearly provides one of the models for Wilde's Duke. Ezzelino also appears in the pageant of those "whom Vice and Blood and Weariness had made monstrous or mad" (Wilde, *Complete Works*, 109) in *The Picture of Dorian Gray*.

28 *Saturday Review*, 20 October 1888, lxvi, 472.

29 Killeen, 81.

30 Cohen, 92.

31 Letter from Pater to Wilde, dated 12th June 1888. Quoted in Beckson, Karl, *Oscar Wilde: The Critical Heritage* (London, 1974), 59.

32 Both Ellmann (279) and Dudley Edwards (Edwards, Owen Dudley, *The Fireworks of Oscar Wilde* (London, 1998), 11-12, discuss Whistler's relation to the Rocket in this story, regarding it as a satire on Whistler's vanity. While this reading is persuasive, the ignorance and incomprehension with which the Rocket is surrounded suggest some sympathy for Wilde's former friend. Cohen (93) suggests that the Rocket represents Wilde himself, in which case the same point would apply.

33 *Pall Mall Gazette*, 30 November 1891, 3.

34 The *Athenaeum* (6 February 1892, 177) echoes this complaint, remarking that Wilde's inventory of the contents of the Young King's chamber "reads for all the world like an extract from a catalogue at Christie's."

35 Wilde, *Complete Letters*, 503.

36 For instance in the *Pall Mall Gazette* (see note 53) and the *Saturday Review* (6 February 1892, LXXIII, page 160).

37 Woodcock, George, *The Paradox of Oscar Wilde* (London, 1949), 148.

38 Zipes, 124.

39 Cohen, 82.

40 Shewan, 54.

41 This is the pinyin transliteration of his name; Wilde, using the Wade-Giles system, called the philosopher Chuang Tzu "whose name must carefully be pronounced as it is not written."

42 *The Speaker*, 8th February 1890.

43 *The Speaker*, 8th February 1890.

44 *The Speaker*, 8th February 1890.

45 Although there is no indication that the Dwarf is a proficient dancer, to paraphrase Chesterton, just as a bad man is still a man, so a bad artist is still an artist.

46 Wilde, *Complete Works*, 17. Preface to *The Picture of Dorian Gray*.

47 *The Star-Child* is also obviously thematically linked to *Dorian Gray*, with its themes of spiritual and physical beauty, and its protagonist whose greatest delight when young is gazing at his reflection in a pool. These two stories may well be exactly contemporary with the novel.

Chapter 12

Radiant Mysteries: George MacDonald, G.K. Chesterton, and the *Claritas* of Fairy Tales

Daniel Gabelman

airy tales are sometimes accused of being too clear and simple. The boy always gets the girl, and the stepmother is always foiled. The characters lack psychological depth and nuance—they are flat and predictable. Fairy tales, this argument goes, are primarily for children because the adult mind is bored by simplicity. As people mature, they learn to like the rich complexity of novels, which, since they are messy, more accurately reflect reality as we experience it.

Rather than arguing that the fairy tale genre is actually extremely complex[1], I am going to embrace the assertion that fairy tales are clear and simple. Instead, what I believe needs recovery is an understanding and appreciation of clarity and simplicity and the ways in which these characteristics function within fairy tales. In the Middle Ages, *claritas* was the crowning achievement of beauty and one of the traits of saints in heaven. Amongst creators of new fairy tales, two writers in particular noted the significance of clarity and potently used it in their own stories, George MacDonald and G.K. Chesterton. These authors demonstrate that far from making things boring, clarity and simplicity transform tales into "radiant mysteries," causing them to generate ever fresh and vibrant meanings.[2]

Drinking the Clarity of Being: A Pre-Modern View of Beauty

Midway through "The Fantastic Imagination" (1893), an essay in which MacDonald describes and defends the fairy tale genre, an imagined interlocutor asks: "You write as if a fairy tale were a thing of importance: must it have a meaning?" To this he responds:

> It cannot help having some meaning; if it have proportion and harmony it has vitality, and vitality is truth. The beauty may be plainer in it than the truth, but without the truth the beauty could not be, and the fairy tale would give no delight. Everyone, however, who feels the story, will read its meaning after his own nature and development: one man will read one meaning in it, another will read another.[3]

It is commonly assumed that MacDonald's concept of beauty is taken wholesale from the Romantics. The echo of Keats's famous line, "beauty is truth, truth beauty," in the above passage is obvious whilst Coleridge's view that beauty is "multitude in unity" seems implicit in MacDonald's idea of "harmony."[4] Interestingly though, MacDonald's understanding of beauty also seems to have resonances with Aquinas' aesthetic theory.[5]

According to Aquinas, beauty includes three conditions: integrity, proportion and clarity.[6] By "integrity" (*integretas*) he means wholeness or completion for "those things which are impaired are by the very fact ugly." A human, for example, is supposed to have two legs and two arms; if one appendage is missing this is a lessening of the ideal and therefore less beautiful. Aquinas also calls this condition "perfection"—how close does a thing come to being complete in itself, to fulfilling the idea that informs it. The closer it comes to perfection the more fully it participates in the divine being and thus the more reality or vital life that it has. Relating this to Christ (Aquinas' main concern in the text where he discusses these ideas most fully), he says that Jesus "as Son has in Himself truly and perfectly the nature of the Father." The second member of the trinity is beautiful, therefore, because he lacks nothing of divinity. He has within himself the full and supreme life of the Father—"in him the fullness of God was pleased to dwell" (Colossians 1.19).

At first glance, the second condition "proportion" (*proportio*) is difficult to distinguish from integrity. Describing how Christ displays proportion. Aquinas says "He is the express image of the Father" (I.39.8). In the words of St Paul, Christ "is the image of the invisible God" (Colossians 1.15). This sounds very close to having "in Himself truly and perfectly the nature of the Father," but instead of the emphasis being upon whether or not a thing is complete in itself, it is on how well something relates to other things. This condition is also called "harmony" for it has to do with the proper interaction of a thing with both its environment and that which informs it. Thus Aquinas says that "an image is said to be beautiful if it perfectly represents even an ugly thing." The image relates faithfully both to what it represents and to its viewers, creating a harmonious exchange. Proportion for Aquinas is therefore not merely mechanical or mathematical but is fundamentally relational. Umberto Eco points out that "proportion is not form" (in the classical and medieval sense of "form") "but rather the disposition of matter to receive a form."[7] What this means is that one cannot create a mathematical system whereby one can predict and declare something to be beautiful. Instead, to quote Eco, "proportion is a transcendental matrix which can realize itself in ever new and unsuspected ways."[8] Beauty is not static and fixed; it is dynamic and full of vitality, much like the *perichoresis* or divine dance within the Trinity.

But the final condition of beauty is perhaps the most intriguing. Aquinas associates clarity (*claritas*) with colour and brightness, saying "things are called beautiful which have a bright colour" (I.39.8). The current English usage of "clarity," meaning translucent, is here slightly misleading for in the older usage "clarity" meant primarily brilliancy or splendour.[9] Bright colours, therefore, display greater clarity because they seem to give off more light than dull or dark colours.[10] Elsewhere Aquinas talks about how "beautiful things are those which please when seen" and how as opposed to goodness which "has the aspect of an end," beauty "relates to the cognitive faculty" (I.5.4). In other words, beauty necessarily has to do with transmission and communication. An object that has full integrity and proportion is still not beautiful (though it is good) until it conveys those harmonious attributes to a receptive subject. Umberto Eco helpfully summarizes: "clarity is the fundamental communicability of form, which is made actual in relation to someone's looking at or seeing of the object."[11]

This explains why Aquinas says that Christ displays clarity "as the Word, which is the light and splendour of the intellect" (I.39.8). In Christian understanding, Christ is the fullest expression of divinity—he is God made perfectly communicable to the receiving subjects, humanity. He is "the true light, which enlightens everyone" (John 1.9). Though parts of God could be discerned elsewhere with greater effort and difficulty (in creation or scripture), Aquinas says that in Jesus God's perfect and harmonious beauty manifests itself in a way that can be immediately and easily received. Clarity thus also creates a light and joyous effect in the perceiving subject, as Jacques Maritain argues:

> The mind then, absolved from all effort at abstraction, enjoys without labour and without discursion. It is dispensed from its ordinary toil, it has not to disentangle the intelligible from the material in which it is buried, in order to go, step by step, over its different attributes; as the stag at the well-spring it has nothing to do but drink; it drinks the clarity of Being.[12]

The clarity of beauty lightens the burden of the subject's search for truth and goodness in the external world by manifesting these attributes in a pleasing and readily received manner.

Returning to the MacDonald passage that began this section, we can now clearly see how closely his position aligns with Aquinas. For MacDonald, whatever has "proportion and harmony" has "vitality, and vitality is truth."[13] As with Aquinas, it is wholeness in itself and harmony with its environment that shows that something has "vitality"—that is, a connection with the ultimate source of life—and it is because of this connection that it is true.[14] MacDonald then says that "the beauty may be plainer in it than the truth, but without the truth the beauty could not be, and the fairy tale would give no delight." Beauty in this context sounds very similar to Aquinas' use of "clarity" in that it has to do not with the "proportion and harmony" that comprise truth but with the swift and "plain" communication of those attributes to the subject and the giving of delight.[15] This beauty requires that the reader "feel the story," or, as MacDonald says later, not spoil it "by intellectual greed."[16] To use Maritain's phrasing, readers of fairy tales must "drink the clarity of being" rather than strenuously exercise their analytical faculties. Yet if they do "feel the story," meanings mysteriously multiply for everyone; each will read its meaning after his own nature and development." This lack of hermeneutical fixity is not a defect of beauty, but one of the necessary and good consequences of drinking the clarity of being. For MacDonald fairy tales are particularly good at creating this effect.

Seeing Halos from the Hidden Sun: Fairy Tales and Mystics

What is it about fairy tales that makes them so full of clarity? One reader of MacDonald's fairy tales who reflected most on this question was G.K. Chesterton. About MacDonald's *The Princess and the Goblin* (1871), Chesterton claims that it "made a difference to my whole existence," whilst about fairy tales in general he says, "the things I believed most then, the things I believe most now, are the things called fairy tales."[17] In the chapter of his *Autobiography* (1937) entitled "The Man with the Golden Key" Chesterton explains how an atmosphere of clarity in his childhood affected his lifelong conception of reality:

> Of this positive quality, the most general attribute was clearness. [...] Mine is a memory of a sort of white light on everything, cutting things out very clearly, and rather emphasizing their solidity. The point is that the white light had a sort of wonder in it, as if the world were as new as myself; but not that the world was anything but a real world.[18]

Chesterton's "white light" "cutting things out very clearly, and rather emphasizing their solidity" sounds almost identical to Aquinas' *claritas*. This light manifests the wonder of things just being themselves such that Chesterton "had a sort of confident astonishment in contemplating the apple-tree as an apple-tree."[19] Contrary to popular opinion, it is not the child who lives in a hazy dream world: "it is only the grown man who lives a life of makebelieve and pretending; and it is he who has his head in a cloud."[20] The clarity of the child, on the other hand, connects them to the real vitality of life. They are able to see and delight in the beauty that actually surrounds them (not some remote abstraction) and in so doing come closer to the source of truth and reality. Moreover, it was fairy tales that "created" in Chesterton this "certain way of looking at life."[21]

Fairy tales did this first of all by exemplifying a kind of wondering and peaceful sanity. "The beginning of all sane art criticism," says Chesterton in talking about the fairy elements of pantomime, is "wonder combined with the complete serenity of the conscience in the acceptance of wonders."[22] Chesterton suggests that fairy tales, though they inspire wonder or even tell of terrible deeds, never deceive people into believing that they literally happened in everyday life (or at least, they never deceived him). "I know I knew the scenery and costume were 'artificial,'" he says, "because I deeply rejoiced that they were artificial."[23] There is serenity in contemplating an imaginary world that has no possibility of existing—dragons are wonderful as long as they don't visit your house—but there is also sanity because one can see clearly what is fictional and what is not. By being closer to the everyday world, "realistic" fiction or poetry is actually more deceptive because a person can easily slip into thinking that what it describes is "true to life." On this point C.S. Lewis observes that "the more completely a man's reading is a form of egoistic castle-building, the more he will demand a certain superficial realism, and the less he will like the fantastic."[24]

In his own fairy tales, Chesterton emphasized the artificiality of the story even more than most writers in the genre. For example, in "Prince Wild-Fire" (one of many unfinished stories from

Chesterton's youthful notebooks) the narrator comments in the opening sentence on how no one in the Palace of Rest knew that the birth poem of the prince "was an imitation of Swinburne because Swinburne wasn't born, and if he had been born no-one would have heard of him there, whereby you may perceive that the Palace of Rest was in a country where it was always Summer and always Afternoon as Lord Tennyson (of whom you may have heard) has remarked about the Lotus Eater's district."[25] This is an elaborate variation on one of the traditional fairy tale formulas, "Once upon a time in a land far away," which itself is a framing statement that sets a story off from the everyday world. But Chesterton hyperbolizes this element by bringing in two Victorian poets, who—as the narrator admits—have no relationship to the fantastic world other than to draw attention to its artificiality.

MacDonald, interestingly, places a similar sentence at the beginning of "The Wise Woman." The speaker—in what is probably MacDonald's longest sentence—interrupts the jesting narrative also to comment upon his imitation of a poet:

> While [the rain] fell, splashing and sparking, with a hum, and a rush, and a soft clashing—but stop! I am stealing, I find, and not that only, but with clumsy hands spoiling what I steal:—
> *"O Rain! With your dull twofold sound,*
> *The clash hard by, and the murmur all round:"*
> —there! take it, Mr. Coleridge;— [...] while the rain was thus falling, and the leaves, and the flowers, and the sheep, and the cattle, and the hedgehog, were all busily receiving the golden rain, something happened.[26]

MacDonald's irony is slightly less forceful than Chesterton's, but the effect is the same. The reader is made acutely conscious of the artificial nature of the story. MacDonald produces a similar effect in other fairy tales by placing them within frame narratives such as *Adela Cathcart* and *At the Back of the North Wind.*[27] Framing in this way demarcates the boundaries between the fictional and the everyday. It establishes a congenial distance between the work and the viewer, like placing someone on a hilltop from which they can safely and clearly observe a tournament taking place below.

It should be pointed out that for both Chesterton and MacDonald artificiality does not make something less true. Though both men have Platonic leanings, they do not agree with Plato that art is less connected with ontological reality because it is an imitation of an imitation.[28] On the contrary, Chesterton says that "the image has the power of both opening and concentrating the imagination," and MacDonald adds that reflections are "lovelier than what we call the reality" and that "this feeling is no cheat" because it involves truth.[29] Here they both point to the way that art (and the fairy tale in particular) simultaneously expands and focuses vision.

The clarity of the fairy tale leaves the eye of the imagination unblocked by crowds of distracting details and speculations. Rather than blurring moral distinctions or drawing attention to how deep and conflicted individuals tend to be, as modern novels often do, the fairy tale delights in sharp, bold lines and firm boundaries. It uses bright primary colours like red and white rather than mixed colours such as chartreuse or turquoise.[30] Resplendent materials such as gold and glass are everywhere in fairy tales because they accentuate contrasts, setting things apart from the commonplace. Max Lüthi calls this the "abstract style" of the fairy tale:

> The abstract stylization of the folktale gives it luminosity and firm definition. Such stylization is not the product of incapacity or incompetence, but of a high degree of formative power. [...] The diagrammatic style of the folktale gives it stability and shape; the epic-like forward progression of the plot gives it quickness and life. Firm form and effortless elegance combine to form a unified whole. Pure and clear, with joyous, weightless mobility, the folktale observes the most stringent laws.[31]

What is interesting is how obeying "stringent laws" leads to "joyous, weightless mobility." The laws end up bearing the psychological burden of life, thereby allowing the fairy tale and its audience to play safely within their boundaries. The mind relaxes from the arduous task of abstraction because the fairy tale has already done it. Hans Gadamer explains that "the structure of play absorbs the player into itself, and thus frees him from the burden of taking the initiative, which constitutes the actual strain of existence."[32] In other words, the highly structured form of the fairy tale is precisely what makes it light and liberating.

Chesterton, of course, is highly sensitive to this paradox. Speaking about his childhood, he says:

> All my life I have loved edges; and the boundary-line that brings one thing sharply against another. All my life I have loved frames and limits; and I will maintain that the largest wilderness looks larger seen through a window. To the grief of all grave dramatic critics, I will still assert that the perfect drama must strive to rise to the higher ecstasy of the peep-show.[33]

Frames and limits put objects in perspective and in the process highlight the true greatness of a thing. The enlarging effect occurs as objects are put into relationship with each other, but also because the imagination is given space to operate. Were the wilderness not limited by the window, imagination would have no room to colour in the edges. The peep-show is an ecstasy because it leaves one longing for more and imagining what else there might be. But these limits also concentrate one's attention. The brevity of the peep-show hones and orients the senses exclusively on the performance. The picture frame excludes vastly more than it includes. Exclusion calms the tumult of the everyday world, where the senses are continually befuddled by clamouring sights and sounds.

Chesterton not only uses these principles to structure his stories, he also frequently makes clarity a central theme. In "A Crazy Tale" (1896), for instance, the narrator claims that he has "a lost knowledge" sealed within him but that once "the veil was lifted" and he knew it all. It is for this reason that he wants to tell his story:

> I am profoundly convinced that if I tell to another all the circumstances that led up to that instantaneous revelation to

him also, as he studies them, the words will suddenly give up their meaning, and their simplicity strike him with an awful laughter.[34]

He is hoping, in other words, for a moment of clarity, an instant where the truth will flash forth in brilliant simplicity. He then relates a surreal story of journeying to a land of giants where "everything was clear cut in the sunlight, standing out in defiant plainness and infantile absurdity" and "all was in simple colours."[35] Not surprisingly, Chesterton frames this story with another narrator who is the sole hearer of the tale at a restaurant. In this way Chesterton dramatizes the clarifying experience of receiving fairy tales. The climactic moment of revelation comes not from the internal narrator but from the frame narrator who realizes with a flash of insight "what was the greatest event of my life: the event I had forgotten," that is, "being born."[36] This revelation results in the creation of "a new animal with eyes to see and ears to hear; with an intellect capable of performing a new function never before conceived truly; thanking God for his creation."[37] Clarity leads to worship. The swiftness and brightness of the vision is so mellifluous that it overflows in thanksgiving.

In one of his early notebooks, a draft of the story shows that Chesterton originally intended this to be the first chapter in a book entitled "A Mystic on Holiday."[38] For Chesterton the "new animal with eyes to see and ears to hear" is the mystic. Meanwhile in a notebook from the same period, Chesterton began an essay entitled "George MacDonald, The Mystic" by saying that "a mystic is one who sees round every object a halo from the hidden sun."[39] Chesterton's later essays on MacDonald reiterate this same point, saying MacDonald made "a space and transparency of mystical light" around himself and that he saw "the same sort of halo round every flower and bird" and thus was a kind of "St Francis of Aberdeen."[40] Both mystics and fairy tales are concerned with perceiving the clarity of being, and it is thus George MacDonald's true mysticism that makes him such a great writer of fairy tales. Chesterton opposes the "true mysticism" of MacDonald to the "mixed and vague" mysticism of Yeats, saying "true mysticism is entirely concerned with absolute things" and that "the only person in the world who can be really exact and definite is the Mystic."[41] Vagueness and convoluted complexity in literature are not necessarily more sophisticated and mature ways of depicting human existence; they might just reflect muddled modes of thought. More than this, the simple clarity of fairy tales can, according to Chesterton, actually be a truer and better means of displaying the beauty and diversity of life; fairy tales, like mystics, believe "that a rose is red with a fixed and sacred redness, and that a cucumber is green by a thundering decree from heaven."[42] In other words, they believe in *claritas*, that objects have integrity and proportion and that they radiate these attributes to perceiving subjects in a way that can be joyfully received. To put it slightly differently, there is ultimate meaning in every rock and insect, if only we have eyes to see it and ears to hear it.

By Abundant Clarity Invisible: Polish, "The Golden Key" and Waking Meaning

Like Chesterton, MacDonald associates mysticism with a certain mode of vision, as he explains in his sermon "The Mirrors of the Lord":

> What has been called [St Paul's] mysticism is at one time the exercise of a power of seeing, as by spiritual refraction, truths that had not, perhaps have not yet, risen above the human horizon; at another, the result of a wide-eyed habit of noting the analogies and correspondences between the concentric regions of creation; it is the working of a poetic imagination divinely alive, whose part is to foresee and welcome approaching truth; to discover the same principle in things that look unlike; to embody things discovered, in forms and symbols heretofore unused, and so present to other minds the deeper truths to which those forms and symbols owe their being.[43]

The mystic is the intermediary between humanity and the ultimate meanings present in every created thing. In this way, mystics perform the same function as *claritas*—they "present to other minds the deeper truths to which those forms and symbols owe their being."

This seeing "by spiritual refraction" involves a process of clarification. MacDonald describes this activity in his rarely studied essay "On Polish," written in 1865 in the middle of the decade in which he wrote the majority of his fairy tales. Polish is a "condition of surface," and in art it is "the removal of everything that can interfere between the thought of the speaker and the mind of the hearer."[44] "The most polished style," he says, "will be that which most immediately and most truly flashes the meaning embodied in the utterance upon the mind of the listener or reader."[45] To achieve this, anything that distracts from the main idea or confuses observation "must be diligently refused" and "all cause whatever of obscurity must be polished away" thereby "calming the surface of the [reader's] intellect to a mirror-like reflection of the image about to fall upon it."[46] The artist must polish their work to a bright shine so that their audience can more easily drink the clarity of being. Depth is not an excuse for vagueness or bewildering complexity for says MacDonald, "simplicity is the end of all polish, as of all Art, Culture, Morals, Religion, and Life."[47]

Perhaps the most polished of MacDonald's own fairy tales—indeed of any of his works—is "The Golden Key," published in 1867 (though likely written earlier) less than two years after "On Polish."[48] Unlike most of his other fairy tales, which often have chapter divisions despite their brevity, "The Golden Key" offers a seamless narrative.[49] MacDonald manages to reduce the number of transitions between the characters to only two, the first of which is a sentence, "and now I will go back to the borders of the forest," and the second of which is a single word, "meantime."[50] Each episode in the story is smooth, crisp and radiant; not one word seems misplaced or extraneous. The various images—though strange and startling—harmonize well with each other so that nothing disturbs but rather "[calms] the surface of the [reader's] intellect to a mirror-like reflection" of the story. "The Golden Key" radiates *claritas*, allowing readers in a flash and without mental strain to delight in the images and the truth it embodies.

As with Chesterton's fairy tales, clarity is not just a structural principle but also a central motif in MacDonald's stories.[51] Mossy is "a keen-sighted" boy who "could see almost as far as the sun," whereas Tangle "could not see much, because of the ivy and other creeping plants which had straggled across her window."[52] It is in fact the extreme clarity of Mossy's vision that allows him to see the rainbow (it appears "far among the trees, as far as the sun could shine") and thus find the golden key.[53] The rainbow itself is a vision of *claritas*—Mossy is drawn to it because of its bright colours and intense brilliance that "is not dependent upon the sun." He stands "gazing at it till he [forgets] himself with delight," much as if he were drinking the clarity of being. Moreover, the golden key is the physical manifestation of the rainbow's clarity; it is "the rainbow's egg."[54] Throughout his journey Mossy sees things clearly and distinctly where others do not. The Old Man of the Sea notes how his sight "is better than that of most who take this way," and Mossy is able to discern the rainbow across the sea and know "this indeed is my way."[55]

Tangle's journey, meanwhile, could be seen as a quest to polish or clarify her vision. When she first sees The Old Man of the Sea she sees him as "an old man with long white hair down to his shoulders," but after bathing in his pool she sees him "as a grand man, with a majestic and beautiful face."[56] When she comes to the Old Man of the Earth, she again has a moment when she thinks he is "bent double with age," but this time her vision corrects itself more swiftly and "the moment she looked in his face, she saw that he was a youth of marvellous beauty."[57] Finally, just before she meets the Old Man of the Fire she experiences perfect clarity such that "all was plain: she understood it all, and saw that everything meant the same thing, though she could not have put it into words again."[58] The result is that she sees the Old Man of the Fire correctly the first time as "a little naked child." Tangle's descent into the very heart of the world functions as a purgatorial journey that teaches her how to see clearly.

With this progressive clarification of vision, MacDonald draws attention to the subjective aspect of clarity. No matter how resplendent an object of beauty is in itself, it cannot be seen in its essence unless the subject has clarity of vision. The same thing can mean different things to different people (the Old Man of the Sea is terribly frightening to some people) depending on their upbringing, circumstances, and experiences. The brighter and more full of vitality something is, the more likely it is that different people will see different things in it for "there is layer upon layer of ascending significance" in all that God has made. [59] Extreme clarity oddly results in a multiplicity of meaning. MacDonald was fond of quoting Sir Walter Raleigh's phrase "by abundant clarity invisible" to describe this effect.[60]

Criticism of "The Golden Key" itself demonstrates this point nicely. Whilst scholars have long agreed on the simple beauty of "The Golden Key," they have rarely agreed on interpretations.[61] Amongst the possible meanings of the golden key itself are: a phallus, faith, the imagination, kindness, love, the keys to the kingdom, and the promise of heaven, to name only a selection. [62] Similar lists could be given for almost every image. The point is not that any particular scholar has the right or wrong interpretation—although some are undoubtedly more "keen-sighted" than others—but that the story lends itself to multiple meanings, not because it is vague but because it is abundantly clear. The images are so polished that they have become slippery, and trying to pin down certain meanings is a bit like trying to climb a giant mirror—without rough edges climbing to the heights of certainty is nearly impossible.

For MacDonald, as for Chesterton, such certainty is not the purpose of fairy tales. Like Mossy drawn on by the bright colours and beautiful radiance of the rainbow, fairy tales arrest and attract people by their radiance and simplicity, and in so doing awake meanings. "The best things you can do for your fellow," says MacDonald, is "not to give him things to think about, but to wake things up that are in him."[63] Clarity in an object catalyses clarity in a receptive subject, as in Chesterton's "A Crazy Tale." MacDonald's great hope is that his fairy tales might function as "radiant mysteries," inviting his readers to drink the clarity of being thus facilitating the unveiling of their own *claritas*.[64]

Fairy tales, then, are clear and simple, but clarity and simplicity are themselves stranger and more nuanced than we first expect. According to Chesterton and MacDonald, within the highly framed and structured form of the fairy tale readers gain a sense of perspective on everyday life. Distracting phenomena are excluded so that the bright colours and sharp contrasts between absolute things can be accentuated and wonderingly reflected upon. All extraneous detail is polished away to create a lucid brevity of style. This shining clarity then flashes upon the calmed mind of the reader and brings to light or "wakes" meanings within them. Whilst they may not have divine *claritas*, fairy tales nonetheless manifest characteristics of radiant mysteries, hinting that reality beyond its present shattered guise might actually be whole and harmonious.

Bibliography

Aquinas, Thomas, St. *Summa Theologiae.* Translated by the English Dominican Fathers. Charlottesville: InteLex Corporation, 1993.

Chesterton, G. K. *Autobiography.* London: Hutchinson & Co, 1950.

—. *Collected Works XIV: Short Stories, Fairy Tales, Mystery Stories, Illustrations.* San Francisco: Ignatius, 1993.

—. *The Common Man.* London: Sheed and Ward, 1950.

—. "George Macdonald. The Mystic." *VII: An Anglo-American Literary Review* 28 (2011): 42-44.

—. "George MacDonald." *The Daily News* (September 23, 1905): 6.

—. "Introduction." In *George Macdonald and His Wife*, by Greville MacDonald. London: George Allen & Unwin, 1924.

—. *Orthodoxy.* London: John Lane, 1927.

—. *Twelve Types.* London: Arthur L. Humphreys, 1902.

—. *What's Wrong with the World.* London: Dodd, 1910.

Coleridge, Samuel Taylor. *Specimens of the Table Talk of the Late Samuel Taylor Coleridge.* Vol. 2, London: John Murray, 1835.

Eco, Umberto. *The Aesthetics of Thomas Aquinas.* Translated by Hugh Bredin. Cambridge, MA: Harvard University Press, 1988.

Gaarden, Bonnie. "'The Golden Key': A Double Reading." Mythlore 93 (2006): 35-52.

Gadamer, Hans-Georg. *Truth and Method.* Translated by Joel Weinsheimer and Donald Marshall. New York: Continuum, 2004.

Hein, Rolland. The Harmony Within. Chicago: Cornerstone Press, 1999.

Lewis, C. S. Experiment in Criticism. Cambridge: Cambridge University Press, 1961.

Lüthi, Max. The European Folktale: Form and Nature. Bloomington & Indianapolis: Indiana University Press, 1986.

MacDonald, George. At the Back of the North Wind. London: Blackie and Son, 1900.

—. *The Complete Fairy Tales.* Edited by U.C. Knoepflmacher. New York: Penguin, 1999.

—. *A Dish of Orts.* Whitethorn: Johannesen, 1996. 1893.

—. *Miracles of Our Lord.* Whitethorn: Johannesen, 2000.

—. *Phantastes.* Whitehorn: Johannesen, 2000.

—. *Unspoken Sermons.* Whitethorn: Johannesen, 2004.

Manlove, C. N. "Not to Hide but to Show: The Golden Key." *North Wind* 22 (2003): 33-41.

Maritain, Jacques. *The Philosophy of Art.* Translated by John O'Connor. Ditchling: S. Dominic's Press, 1947.

Plato. *Republic.* Translated by G. M. A. Grube. Indianapolis: Hackett Publishing, 1992.

Raleigh, Sir Walter. *The History of the World.* Oxford: Oxford University Press, 1829.

Wolff, Robert Lee. *The Golden Key: A Study of the Fiction of George Macdonald.* New Haven: Yale University Press, 1961.

Notes

1 This seems to be the typical scholarly approach to fairy tales, as in Vladimir Propp's classic text *Morphology of the Folktale* (Austin: University of Texas Press, 2003), which aims at analyzing and classifying the various structural elements.

2 This phrase is taken from the following passage: "With his divine alchemy [Jesus] turns not only water into wine, but common things into radiant mysteries, yea, every meal into a eucharist, and the jaws of the sepulchre into an outgoing gate." George MacDonald, *The Miracles of Our Lord* (Whitehorn: Johannesen, 2000), 245.

3 George MacDonald, *A Dish of Orts* (Whitethorn: Johannesen, 1996), 316.

4 John Keats, "Ode on a Grecian Urn"; Coleridge, Samuel Taylor Coleridge, *Specimens of the Table Talk of the Late Samuel Taylor Coleridge*, vol. 2 (London: John Murray, 1835), 18.

5 Even if MacDonald never read Aquinas, he was undoubtedly powerfully influenced by his ideas through Dante and medieval mystics such as Eckhart.

6 Thomas Aquinas, St., *Summa Theologiae* (Charlottesville: InteLex Corporation, 1993), I.39.8.

7 Umberto Eco, *The Aesthetics of Thomas Aquinas*, trans. Hugh Bredin (Cambridge, MA: Harvard University Press, 1988), 84.

8 Ibid., 98.

9 The semantic shift seems to have occurred in the eighteenth century, perhaps as a result of changing the dominant theory of optics.

10 Aquinas' understanding of optics is essentially that of Aristotle and so obviously very different from a modern understanding of how light works. Significantly, however, both Aristotle and Aquinas rejected Plato's theory that light emanated from the eye.

11 Eco, *The Aesthetics of Thomas Aquinas*: 119.

12 Jacques Maritain, *The Philosophy of Art*, trans. John O'Connor (Ditchling: S. Dominic's Press, 1947), 47.

13 MacDonald, *A Dish of Orts*: 316.

14 MacDonald would undoubtedly have also said, like Aquinas, that it is good. The emphasis on truth is probably both for the allusion to Keats and because MacDonald is trying to emphasize that intellectual knowledge is not the only form of truth.

15 It is truth in this sentence that is delightful, but it is beauty that gives it.

16 MacDonald, *A Dish of Orts*, 322.

17 G. K. Chesterton, "Introduction," in *George MacDonald and His Wife* (London: George Allen & Unwin, 1924), 9; ————, *Orthodoxy* (London: John Lane, 1927), 85.

18 G.K. Chesterton, *Autobiography* (London: Hutchinson & Co, 1950), 48.

19 Ibid., 49.

20 Ibid., 54.

21 Chesterton, *Orthodoxy*, 87.

22 G.K. Chesterton, *The Common Man* (London: Sheed and Ward, 1950), 57.

23 Ibid., 59. Elsewhere Chesterton says "there was never anything in the world that was really artificial," but by this he only means that everything has "some motive or ideal behind it, and generally a much better one than we think." *Twelve Types* (London: Arthur L. Humphreys, 1902), 201.

24 C. S. Lewis, *Experiment in Criticism* (Cambridge: Cambridge University Press, 1961), 56.

25 G. K. Chesterton, *Collected Works XIV: Short Stories, Fairy Tales, Mystery Stories, Illustrations* (San Francisco: Ignatius, 1993), 581.

26 George MacDonald, *The Complete Fairy Tales* (New York: Penguin, 1999), 225.

27 The frames also frequently discuss the stories as works of art as when the narrator comments about "Little Daylight" that he thought Mr Raymond "was somewhat indebted for this one to the old story of The Sleeping Beauty." George MacDonald, *At the Back of the North Wind* (London: Blackie and Son, 1900), 257.

28 In book X of *The Republic* Socrates says that artists are "by nature third from the king and the truth, as are all other imitators." Plato, *Republic*, trans. G. M. A. Grube (Indianapolis: Hackett Publishing, 1992), 268.

29 Chesterton, *The Common Man*, 58; George MacDonald, *Phantastes* (Whitehorn: Johannesen, 2000), 123.

30   Chesterton often used the image of mixed colours to depict the muddled nature of modern thinking, as in G. K. Chesterton, *What's Wrong With the World* (London: Dodd, 1910), 270-74. He also wrote a fairy tale about the meaning of colour called "The Coloured Lands."

31   Max Lüthi, *The European Folktale: Form and Nature* (Bloomington & Indianapolis: Indiana University Press, 1986), 36.

32   Hans-Georg Gadamer, *Truth and Method*, trans. Joel Weinsheimer and Donald Marshall (New York: Continuum, 2004), 105.

33   Chesterton, *Autobiography*, 32.

34   Chesterton, *Collected Works*, 70.

35   Ibid., 71.

36   Ibid., 74.

37   Ibid.

38   Other chapters included: "A Book of Strange Trades," "An Omnibus to Elfland," "Fairyland for Sale" and "A Farce Under the Stars." BL Manuscript 73333A.

39   This essay has recently been published for the first time: G. K. Chesterton, "George Macdonald. The Mystic," SEVEN 28 (2011): 42.

40   Chesterton, "Introduction," 12, 14.

41   Chesterton, "George MacDonald," *The Daily News* (September 23, 1905), 6.

42   Ibid.

43   George MacDonald, *Unspoken Sermons* (Whitethorn: Johannesen, 2004), 448.

44   MacDonald, *A Dish of Orts*, 184.

45   Ibid.

46   Ibid., 188.

47   Ibid., 192.

48   Chesterton seems to have thought that *The Princess and the Goblin* was MacDonald's most perfect work: Chesterton, "Introduction," 9-11. Among the shorter fairy tales a case could also be made for "The History of Photogen and Nycteris" on account of its simple yet radiant symmetry and the lucid brevity of its episodes.

49   "The Light Princess," "Cross Purposes," "The Carasoyn," "The Wise Woman" and "The History of Photogen and Nycteris" all have some sort of marked divisions within them.

50   MacDonald, *Fairy Tales*, 123, 41.

51   Some of the more obvious examples of this in other fairy tales include Richard and Alice in "Cross Purposes" having their vision not only puri-

fied but also illuminated by love and Ralph Rinkelmann returning home from his time with the shadows to find "common things [disclosing] the wonderful that was in them." Ibid., 64.

52 Ibid., 121, 23. Oddly very few critics have noted this contrast. Colin Manlove is the prominent exception who speculates that MacDonald keeps these distinctions relatively subtle because "he wants readers to acquire some of Mossy's penetrating insight for themselves." C. N. Manlove, "Not to Hide But to Show: The Golden Key," *North Wind* 22 (2003): 35.

53 The reason for the difference between Mossy and Tangle is never discussed, and it does provide an open door to feminist criticism. Yet as Roderick McGillis says, "the conundrum is to remain unexplained" because MacDonald does not intend to give social commentary but symbolic images that are full of paradoxical meaning. Roderick McGillis, "'A Fairytale is Just a Fairytale': George MacDonald and the Queering of Fairy," *Mavels & Tales: Journal of Fairy-Tale Studies* 17.1 (2003), 95.

54 MacDonald, *Fairytales:Fairy tales*, 121.

55 Ibid., 141, 42.

56 Ibid., 134, 37.

57 Ibid.

58 Ibid., 139.

59 MacDonald, A Dish of Orts, 320.

60 He quotes this at least three times in his works: twice in *The Miracles of Our Lord* and once in the third series of *Unspoken Sermons*. The quotation is from the opening sentence of *The History of the World*: "God, whom the wisest men acknowledge to be a power uneffable, and virtue infinite; a light by abundant clarity invisible; an understanding which itself can only comprehend; an essence eternal and spiritual, of absolute pureness and simplicity." Sir Walter Raleigh, *The History of the World* (Oxford: Oxford University Press, 1829). 1.

61 Robert Wolff's view is typical: "in suggestiveness and pathos, in brevity and point, in simplicity and beauty of language, "The Golden Key" is a little masterpiece, the best thing MacDonald ever did." Robert Lee Wolff, *The Golden Key: A Study of the Fiction of George MacDonald* (New Haven: Yale University Press, 1961), 148.

62 Ibid., 138; Manlove, "Not to Hide But to Show: The Golden Key," 36; Bonnie Gaarden, "'The Golden Key': A Double Reading," *Mythlore* 93 (2006):

38-39; Rolland Hein, *The Harmony Within* (Chicago: Cornerstone Press, 1999). 191.

63   MacDonald, *A Dish of Orts*, 319.

64   Aquinas lists clarity as one of four attributes of the saints after the resurrection, along with impassibility, subtlety and agility. He argues that "clarity will result from the overflow of the soul's glory into the body" (III.85.1). MacDonald echoes Aquinas when he speculates in his chapter on the Transfiguration (which begins with the Raleigh quotation "by abundant clarity invisible"): "If the soul be radiant of truth what can the body do but shine?" MacDonald, *Miracles of Our Lord* (Whitethorn: Johannesen, 2000), 439.

Chapter 13

The Land Without Stories: A Threefold Tale

Eric M. Pazdziora

You should be asleep. What do you mean, you can't sleep? Of course you can; I've seen you do it every night.

You want another story? All right. You want three more stories? I'm not sure you're lucky enough for that. But I'll tell you what. I know one story that has three stories in it. So I'll tell you that story if you promise to go right off to sleep at the end. Not in the middle of it like last night. Now, unless I'm forgetting, I think it goes like this:

Once or twice upon a time, in a faraway land that was just round the corner, there was not a princess. If there had been a princess, there wouldn't have been this story, you see. But the king and queen had no children, even though they wanted to very much.

The queen knew all the old stories and the old fairy tales, and she knew that most of them began the same way her story did. So she followed them all and tried to make them come true. She plucked three snake leaves and a rampion-flower and she wounded her hands with nettles; she pricked her finger on a spinning-wheel and let three drops of red blood fall on the snow. Still she didn't have a child.

"You mustn't put so much stock in those old wives' tales," said the king. "You know they're just stories."

"I don't care if they are," said the queen. "I'd do anything to have a little girl. I'd slay a dragon with a golden sword. I'd climb the mountains of glass in iron shoes. I'd weave seven sweaters from flax and tears. I'd walk through seven miles of steel thistles. I'd—"

"What's the good of talking? There's no such things as those," said the king.

"I don't care!" said the queen. "I want a baby! I don't care if she's no bigger than my thumb. I don't care if she looks like a pea in a pod. I don't care if she's made of gingerbread or marzipan or porridge!"

"Who ever heard of a baby like that?" said the king. "You're talking nonsense."

"All I want is a child," said the queen. "Is that so wrong? I'd love her even if she was twisted and crooked and homely and little and—"

"Hush!" shouted the king, in a rage. "What kind of daughter is that for a king? Don't even speak such things."

But sometimes wishes do come true, even if they go wrong in the wishing. A while later the queen had a child, her first child, a little daughter. And sure enough, she was a twisted and crooked thing, too small and too sickly even to cry. But oh, when she smiled, such a smile it was, and the queen thought her heart would burst for the love of her, even while she cried at the sight of her.

The king was not so happy as the queen. He called for the doctors. "Do whatever you like, only get me a strong and healthy daughter. I'll have no withered child for my heir. Think what the people would say. That's what science is for, so use it, even if you have to change this one with a doll."

Ah! That was the second wish that went wrong, as wishes do. For not just the doctors but the Good Folk were listening, as they always are, through cracks and corners and crevices. By night, when the doctors were away, the Good Folk came and took the twisted child away with them, for they delight in all things uncomely and broken. In its place they left a perfect baby, with bright blue eyes and golden hair.

The next morning the king saw the golden-haired child in his daughter's cradle, and he was pleased. He shook the doctors' hands and gave them bags of gold, for, he said, "That's what comes of science and medicine! That's proper book learning! No need for these fairy tales and stories when we have men of letters like you." The doctors departed immensely richer, though privately perplexed.

But the queen knew the difference, as a mother always will, and she pined for her stolen daughter. The golden-haired changeling could move and walk and grow like a child, but for all her beauty she was just a clever doll made by the Good Folk in mimicry of life.

"You're mad," said the king. "That's your own daughter, and she's as hale and healthy and fair as a king's daughter should be."

"Don't you have eyes?" said the queen. "The child is a changeling, a cheat. It's the wicked elves at work. They steal from the cradles and leave their own young ones behind. I've heard it in all the old stories—"

"That's enough!" yelled the king. "No more of your stories and lies. They poison your mind with that nonsense. I'll not have my daughter growing up with a mind full of madness. Forget them. They're dreams. Forget them all. There'll be no more stories in my kingdom."

That day the king made a decree and outlawed the telling of tales. No more stories, no more rhymes, no more fairy tales or nursery songs. And the king was content, and the changeling child grew, and the queen pined away in silence, never daring to show her tears.

As the years went by, the queen spoke less and less, and finally stopped talking altogether. She sat by herself at the top of a tower, waiting by a spinning wheel and staring at the sky. All her stories were still there, but only in her head and in her heart. And she wished with no words and she wished with no songs that one day her child would come back.

Yes, it is a sad story, isn't it? Don't go to sleep yet. It has another story inside.

Ten years went by like this. Ten silent years, for the changeling child couldn't speak, couldn't cry, couldn't laugh or even blink. She walked graceful and fair through the halls and the gardens, always silent and unsmiling, taking no interest in the flowers or the trees. When anyone tried to talk with her or teach her, she would fix them with an indifferent stare that left them feeling uncanny. The servants whispered among themselves that the withering had left her legs to go to her head, and what kind of queen would that be?

But one day, as she was alone in her royal nursery staring at the blank white wall, she heard a rustle and a pop and squeak. She turned around and saw a little man, no bigger than an owl, with a wrinkly old face and a spark in his eye and a cap made of paper and leaves.

"Hullo," said the man. "What luck. I got here as quick as I could, though that's slower than it should have been. What's your name? I mean, what do they call you?"

The false princess stared at him, not smiling or frowning. She just looked.

"Can't speak?" said the little man. "Goblin got your tongue? Oh, oh, oh. I see how it is. Well, this will take some special work. I suppose you can't sing a song. I can. 'Tra la liddily loddy lay, and it's hey and it's ho and it's nonny nonny nay.' No good? Well."

The little man paced the floor, stumping back and forth on his red shoes. "Well, then," he said. "I don't suppose anyone's ever told you a story."

The changeling's eyes got a little bit wider, and she said, "Who are you?"

"Oh ho!" crowed the man. "Hip hooray, it's your very first words, and they're a question. It's one I can't answer, even. I fit through locks and I squeeze through keys. I get in people's heads and I make them sneeze. I'm the little fellow who tells tall tales. Unless I'm among the gnomies, when I'm the tall fellow who tells little tales. And they'll have my heart on a silver platter for it, but I've got a story for you."

The changeling's face didn't move. "The king says stories are bad."

"Hip hooray, it's your very second words!" said the man. "And I have to disagree with them. The king only thinks that because he's never heard this story. Ready?" And he started to sing:

A shoe and a pig and a crow and a dog
  All made their bed in a hollow log,
  They lived in a day that was far away
  Through the mist and the hill and the fog.

A dog and a shoe and a pig and a crow,
  Said, "All a-traveling we will go!
  "We'll go to the sea and the poddleby-tree,
  "To find out what we don't know."

A pig and a crow and a dog and a shoe
  All went to sea in a purple canoe
  And there they found gold in a bucket, I'm told,
  So that's what we all should do.

A crow and a dog and a shoe and a pig,
  Found out at last that the world was big,
  And the boat went down, and all of them drowned,
  And the angels danced a jig.

The changeling princess listened to the story with wide eyes, not saying a word, hardly breathing. When it was finished, she was silent for a moment. Then she smiled. Then she laughed. Then she cried. Then she cried some more and laughed some more. Then she laughed some more and cried some more.

The little man smiled. "I thought you would," he said. "Anyone can walk and move and be pretty, but it takes a person to laugh and cry. You're more real than you ever knew."

"A crow and a dog and a shoe and a pig!" cried the princess. "And they were all happy and then they all died! I've lived a thousand years and never heard something like that. Is that what a story is?"

"Exactly so, no less, no more," said the little man. "Now you remember that story and I'll be back for another. Ta-taa." And with a rustle and a pop and a squeak he was gone.

Now there was another little girl, far away, living in clearings and thickets. She had a crooked back and a twisted leg, and her hair was all matted and tangled. She wore leaves and moss for clothes, but she had a golden circle around her wrist, because she was the plaything of the Good Folk. (We call them the Good Folk, you know, because it wouldn't do to offend them.) She was the queen's own daughter, the one that was stolen away ten years before.

Life among the Good Folk does strange things to a person. When all your playmates are goblins and elves and burnie-trows, you grow up with a sadder eye that thinks it's wiser, if you ever grow up at all, which is seldom. Even when they're with you, you're always lonely. And you have no knowledge of time. Sometimes the girl's keepers would come just to stare at her. Other times they would make her dance, or give her a sweet, or pinch her to see the water come out of her eyes. They would seldom speak, and they would never stay.

Today she sat alone by a hollow tree, searching for drops of dew. Then she heard a rustle and a pop and a squeak, and out tumbled the little man in a rush of leaves and paper.

"Hullo," said the little man. "My, you're a hard one to find. Lovely to meet you. Strange and wonderful things are happening, and I think they're mostly about you."

The girl did not look surprised at all. "Oh," she said. "Well, who are you, then?"

The little man looked a bit deflated. "You don't even know? All that and you don't even know? Suspender buttons, now I'll never find out. I have got the right one, haven't I?" He pulled an acorn out of his pocket and shook it around in the palm of his hand, consulting it carefully. "Yes, yes. How long have you been here?"

"A day or so," said the girl. "Forever. I don't know."

"Well, that's what you think, so it's probably true. So I'm going to tell you a story. Second story of the day or so, or forever. A story! A thing of danger and delight, of wonder and surprise! The king could have my head next!"

"What for?" said the girl. "It's just a story."

The little man blinked. "Just a story? Just a story? Who says that? Nobody says that. They're usually surprised. Unless they're missing something. What could you be missing, I wonder."

"I don't surprise much," said the girl. "I don't care."

"You don't care? About what?"

"Anything. Why should I?"

"You don't care about mollusks? You don't care about fleas? You don't care about honey or rabbits or peas?"

"No," said the princess. "They're just there."

"Rumpety-bow!" said the little man. "I know they call your keepers the Good Folk, but I've a mind to call them what I think of them. But one more thing I must know. Do you care about love?"

"I've heard of that," said the princess. "What is it?"

"That explains it," said the little man. "The world's more full of weeping than you can understand. Well then, I'll tell you the story you're in. It goes a bit like this."

She sits all alone in an empty chair,
    (Sing nettles and spindles and snow, poor thing)
    Her true love is gone and she knows not where.
    Nettles and spindles and snow.

She lights seven candles alone every night
    (Sing nettles and spindles and snow, poor thing)
    And sets up a bottle to capture the light,
    Nettles and spindles and snow.

    She plucks seven petals and presses them dry,
        And wishes inside what she never can cry,
        And blows on her fingers and watches them fly,
        Over nettles and spindles and snow.

The light from the bottle will water her tears,
    (Sing nettles and spindles and snow, poor thing)
    Tucked up in the weeping that nobody hears,
    Nettles and spindles and snow.

    Her heart has a sorrow that nobody knows,
        And she's weaving a wish into seven black crows,
        And she's holding the image that blossoms a rose,
        Nettles and spindles and snow.

"Is that what love is?" said the princess. "Nettles and spindles and snow? I never knew. I always wondered."

"Of course you did. Everyone does. More to the point, there's someone who loves you precisely like that."

The princess blinked. "Then why am I here all alone?"

The little man sighed. "That," he said, "is the question I've asked for a thousand years. Some wishes are trickier than others. Some wishes come true in a day, and some wishes don't come true in forever. But I think I can tell you the answer now. As a matter of fact—" And with a rustle and a pop and a squeak—

That was the second story. Now there's one more.

The king sat on his throne, glowering and looking grave. The queen was still silent, and that put him out of temper. But he never asked her anymore what she was upset about, because that only made her sadder, and she wouldn't ever answer.

It was quiet in the throne room, dull as a bank. In the old days there would have been a lute-player or a singer or a storyteller, but there had been none of that for ten years. The king liked it that way, staid and stolid and respectable. No nonsense.

Suddenly the silence was broken with a rustle and a pop and a squeak, and into the throne room rolled the little storytelling man in a somersault. He sprang to his feet and clicked his heels and danced a little jig, leaving behind him a trail of dust and cobwebs and bits of broken leaves.

"What's the meaning of this?" said the king. "Who are you? Speak, or I'll have your head."

"I crave your indulgence, much as you indulge your cravings," said the little man. "In fact, I'm a person who adores that very question, 'What's the meaning of this?' Because, you see, most of the time it hasn't got one."

"If you're looking for a position as a court jester, you've been sadly misinformed," said the king.

"Oh, gracious no," said the little man, and did another dance for good measure. "I'd rather be the court storyteller."

There was a gasp from all of the nobles and courtiers and guards, and the king narrowed his eyes and glowered. Even the queen looked alarmed.

"I do hope you know what you're saying, because if you're not careful those words will be your last," said the king. "Hold your tongue or you'll lose your head."

"Heads are cheap. Everyone has at least one of them somewhere," said the little man. "It's using it that's the tricky part. But never you fear, I know too much about words to just throw them away. So I'll tell you a story without any words."

"Oh," said the king, with a nasty smile that made the noblemen shudder, "now this I must hear. You come to me talking about stories and now you're not going to use any words? What story do you think could change the decree of the king?"

"This story," said the little man, and he laid his finger on his lips.

From down the marble hallway came the clatter of running feet, and into the throne room charged the little golden-haired princess, laughing and crying and dancing. "Mother! Father!" she shouted. "There was a pig and a dog and a crow and a shoe, and they were so happy but then they all died! There was a shoe and a crow and a dog and a pig, and they all died but they were so happy! It's a story, Mother! It's a story, Father! It's my very own story and I'm so happy I think I've never been alive before!"

The king's face fell in astonishment and the queen gripped the arms of her throne to steady herself. "What?" said the king. "She's never said a word before now. Who's been telling her stories? What nonsense is this?"

In reply the little man smiled, shook his head, and put his finger to his lips again. Then he pointed down the other hallway into the throne room.

Into the throne room, more quietly this time because her feet were bare, and more slowly this time because she could only limp, came the tangle-haired princess in moss and leaves. She stopped when she reached the middle of the room and looked around slowly.

"I know you," she said to the story-telling man. "You're the man who tells the stories and the songs. And I think I know you"—she looked at the golden-haired child, still laughing and capering—"you remind me of my sister. And I don't know you"—she looked away from the king—"and you—oh!"

She was looking at the queen now, looking straight in her mother's eyes. "You were the lady from the song, lighting your candles at night and making wishes on the flower-petals because you lost what you loved. And you didn't think anyone knew you were crying. It was such a sad story you were in. What were you wishing for? What was it you lost that you loved?"

The queen's eyes were as wide as the wonder and the doubt and the dreams that had been trapped inside her for so long, and now they filled with tears. She stretched out her hands to her lost child, slowly, as if she was afraid she would fade away. "It was you," she whispered. "My little baby. It was you."

Then the lost princess smiled, for the first time in ten years, and she ran toward the queen, and her sister came too, and they held each other close and cried and laughed and laughed and cried until their hearts were full again. And the king cried too, and he looked around for the little man who told stories, whether to thank him or shout at him or apologize nobody ever knew, because he was nowhere to be seen.

And that was the end of the story, though I think the third story went on for quite a while longer than the story itself, really.

Why do you want to know how it ended? I just told you. I could say "They all lived happily ever and after," if you like. I think that might even be a wee bit true. The queen still sends me a bundle of clover and honey and gold every Michelmas, any rate. That counts for something. And oh, those two weddings, you should have been there, with a faery hand in hand. But that's another story and I just told you six. So you rustle and pop and squeak off to sleep, there's a love.

Part IV
Fairy Brides

Chapter 14

In the Midst of Metamorphosis: Yōko Tawada's "The Bridegroom Was a Dog"

Mayako Murai

The heroine of Yōko Tawada's "Inumukoiri [The Bridegroom Was a Dog]" (1993) says to the children she tutors at the cram school: "Maybe the only story you know about a human being marrying an animal is 'The Crane Wife,' but there's another one called 'The Bridegroom Was a Dog.'"[1] She then goes through a catalogue of variants of this now rather obscure folktale, whose title is also the title of the story she is in.

This chapter looks at animal bride and bridegroom tales in Japanese folklore and explores the ways in which the motif of marriage between different species is represented in contemporary Japanese fiction, particularly Tawada's "The Bridegroom Was a Dog." Tawada's rewriting of this tale type, which has long existed in many cultures, radically departs from traditional tales by subverting conventional narrative expectations at multiple levels.

Animal Bride and Bridegroom Tales in Japan

Traditional Japanese animal bride and bridegroom tales are characterised by their tragic ending, in which the animal partner leaves the human protagonist for good, whereas Western tales of the same

281

type tend to end with a happy marriage after the animal bride or bridegroom is successfully transformed back into her or his original human form. The Japanese folklorist Toshio Ozawa summaries Japanese animal bride and bridegroom tales as follows:

> In Japanese animal bride and bridegroom tales, animals visit the human world from the undefined world of Nature and establish some kind of relationship with human beings. There are three patterns of development, in which the animals eventually 1) leave on their own accord, 2) are expelled by the human beings and return to the undefined world of Nature, or 3) are killed by the human beings.

Ozawa also observes that stories about animal brides usually follow either pattern 1) or 2) whereas animal bridegroom tales almost always follow pattern 3). He deduces that female animals are generally considered to be harmless once they return to the world of Nature, whereas male animals are seen as a threat even after their ejection from the human world and must be killed (242-43). In either case, Japanese tales about human-animal marriage end by re-establishing the clear boundary between the human and the non-human which, at the beginning of the story, had been broken down by marriage.

This definitive dissolution of the human-animal union seems to contradict the closeness between the human and the non-human depicted throughout the story. In Japanese folktales, transformations into and from animals are rarely explained in terms of magic and seem to be taken for granted as a natural course of events. In "Kitsune Nyōbō [The Fox Wife]," for example, the woman simply turns her back to her husband and assumes her fox form. In "The Dog Bridegroom," which will be discussed in detail below, the princess marries the dog in his original form, and the dog neither transforms himself into a handsome prince in the end nor is he expected to do so.

Ozawa attributes this closeness between humans and animals in Japanese tales to the traditional animistic view that every organism in Nature has its own meaning and power and that human beings are also part of Nature (194). At the same time, the final ejection of animal partners in these tales also shows the strong awareness of the demarcation between the human world and Nature (245). Ozawa suggests that Japanese animal bride and bridegroom tales reflect a world view located between animistic cultures—he cites as an example those Inuit tales in which human beings accept their animal partners in their original form and live happily ever after—and the anthropocentric Christian culture in which humans are clearly distinguished from animals.[2] In Japanese tales, animals remain animals till the end of the story as in Inuit tales, but they inevitably leave the human world after revealing their original animal identity. Many non-human partners in European tales, on the other hand, turn out to be human beings temporarily turned into animals by a curse, and, after recovering their original human form, they live in the human world happily ever after.

Among various animal bride and bridegroom tales, the story of "Tsuru Nyōbō [The Crane Wife]" has become canonised in Japan. especially since Junji Kinoshita adapted it for the stage mainly for an adult audience in 1949, giving it the tile Yūzuru [Twilight Crane]. "The Crane Wife" is now one of the most widely-known folktales in Japan and has also been adapted for other media including film, opera, contemporary dance, and commercial advertisements, not to mention children's books and animations. In one variant, recorded in Niigata and published in 1932 in a tale collection edited by Kunio Yanagita, the founder of Japanese folklore studies, a poor man rescues an injured crane and releases it. A couple of days later, a beautiful woman appears at his doorstep and asks him to marry her. The wife offers to weave a cloth if he promises never to watch her making it. He takes the fine brocade to the emperor, who pays a huge sum for it. The husband begs her to make another cloth and, while she is weaving, he peeks in and finds a crane plucking her own feathers and weaving them into the loom. Seeing his betrayal, the crane flies away, never to return.[3]

"The Crane Wife" contains the tale type of "Grateful Animals" (AT554), in which animals repay the kindness offered by human beings. In some variants, an elderly couple rather than a single man help the crane and adopt her as their daughter, which is the form often considered appropriate for the child readership today; it removes marriage, an element which seldom appears in Japanese folktales except for animal bride and bridegroom tales, and emphasises the theme of requited kindness instead. In all variants of "The Crane Wife," kindness is rewarded only temporarily until the protagonist discovers the true identity of the visitor. The magic spell is broken at the end of the story, but unlike "Beauty and the Beast" the husband in "The Crane Wife" ends up losing his beloved wife, who turns back into her original animal form and returns to her realm for good.

The tragic separation of the couple is caused by the husband's violation of the taboo against viewing. This Forbidden Chamber motif, classified as C611 in Stith Thompson's *Motif-Index of Folk-Literature*, can be found also in "Bluebeard" tales, but "The Crane Wife" is closer to the legend of Melusine in European folklore. Melusine is a pre-Christian water spirit who marries her husband in the disguise of a human girl and asks him not to spy on her in the bath. She disappears when he peeks in and discovers her original form as a serpent from the waist down. Unlike the Melusine legend, however, "The Crane Wife" stresses the themes of female gratitude and self-sacrifice, an emphasis which functions to obscure the dominating and destructive nature of the human husband's violation of the taboo against viewing her private self.

In their analysis of Japanese folkloric representations of non-human brides, Jason Davis and Mio Bryce claim that Japanese animal bride stories are often about the victimised female Other:

A non-human bride's permanent marriage to a human is only possible through the total suppression of her non-human identity, in other words, the necessity for her total social conformity; the total domestication of her as a resource. This means that there is no place for her to authentically live as she truly is. Despite the animistic closeness between humans and non-humans, which is often seen as a characteristic of Japanese culture, the stories expose an inability to recognise and deal with Otherness (e.g., Nature/female) as a respectable partner. [4]

The contrast between male desire and female self-sacrifice is made more explicit in Kinoshita's play. The protagonist of *Twilight Crane* is portrayed as a man who becomes so obsessed with money that he does not even notice his wife's increasingly failing health as he demands her to weave more and more cloth. The play is intended and generally interpreted as a criticism of post-war Japanese society which is driven by greed and materialism and which exploits and disregards the power of love and nature. In this context, however, the story can be read as a patriarchal society's nostalgia for nature, represented here as a female animal, from which the "civilised" human world receives benefits but remains ultimately immune.

Dog Bridegroom Tales in Asia

Unlike "The Crane Wife," the story of the dog bridegroom did not enter the modern canon of folktales in Japan. A typical Japanese dog bridegroom tale begins with the mother promising the dog that he can marry her daughter if he licks the girl's bottom clean after she defecates. When the daughter grows up, the dog interferes with her marriage to a man. She goes away with the dog to live in the mountains. A huntsman passes by, kills the dog in secret, and marries her. After having seven children, he confesses the murder to her, upon which she kills him out of revenge.

In his comparative study of the dog bridegroom tale in Japan and other Asian countries, the folklorist Akira Fukuda relates this tale to a clan origin myth found among the mountainous regions of southern China, Vietnam, Laos, and Thailand. In this story, which is generally referred to as the *Pan Gu* legend after the name of the dog and which Fukuda calls Type A, the emperor promises to give his daughter's hand in marriage to anyone who can kill the hostile leader and bring back his head. A dog returns with the leader's head and marries the emperor's daughter. Their children marry each other and become the progenitors of a clan. In the variant Type B, found among the Moken, sea nomads who inhabit the areas on and near the west coast of Thailand and the Seediq, a Taiwanese aboriginal people, the woman and the dog marry and live on a desert island, and, after the dog's death, she tricks her son into marrying her without revealing her identity. Type C, a variant found in Indonesia and on Hainan Island in China, is similar to Type B but includes the motif of patricide by the hybrid son. In Type D, found in Okinawa, a region in southern Japan which was originally part of an independent kingdom called the Ryūkyū Kingdom until the late nineteenth century, a fisherman kills the dog, marries the woman, and has seven children. When she learns about the murder, she dies of sorrow among the dog's bones.

The most notable difference between the Japanese and Okinawan variants and the other variants may be the absence of the motif of bestiality in the former. Fukuda assumes that Types A, B, and C first reached Okinawa and then spread to and diffused throughout Japan. The Okinawan tale replaces the interspecies reproduction with the marriage between humans as in all Japanese dog bridegroom tales, but it does not include the wife's murder of her human husband out of revenge, a motif characteristic of the Japanese variant. The Okinawan tale (Type D), therefore, can be regarded as a transitional form between Types A, B, and C and the Japanese variant, in the latter of which the motif of bestiality seems to have left its curious trace in the episode of the dog licking the girl's bottom.

Another interesting difference is that the Japanese and Okinawan tales end with a moral absent in the other Asian variants: "Never trust your wife even after having seven children with her." Fukuda points out that this moral is originally derived from an old Chinese poem and became a popular saying in Japan as it was considered to be an incisive description of the complex relation of the sexes. The reason why this odd moral—which puts an unfair emphasis on the revenge murder at the end over the initial murder—came to be attached to the dog bridegroom tale may be explained by the tale's older form as an origin myth which ends with the mother's seduction of her son by deception. Nevertheless, this misogynous moral was incorporated into the tale as a kind of folk wisdom and reinforced the tale's folk authenticity. As Fukuda's tautological dictum has it, "the legitimacy of the folktale is proved by the 'saying' while the authenticity of the 'saying' is proved by the folktale."[5]

The most significant difference between these dog bridegroom tales in Asia and the typical European animal bridegroom tales would be the absence of a transformation or revelation scene in the former. "Beauty and the Beast," classified as sub-type C of "The Search for the Lost Husband" (AT425) in the Aarne-Thompson tale type index, ends with the non-human husband's transformation into a human. The most widely known version of "Beauty and the Beast" was written by Madame Jeanne-Marie Le Prince de Beaumont and published in *Le Magasin des Enfants* in 1756. In her version, Beauty stays in the Beast's palace in order to save her father, whose life is threatened by the Beast when he plucks a rose from the Beast's garden for his beloved daughter. Beauty grows fond of the kind-hearted Beast, but she keeps refusing his nightly marriage proposal. While Beauty is visiting her sick father, her two evil sisters conspire to keep her longer to enrage the Beast. Upon returning, she finds the Beast on the verge of death out of despair. She begs him not to die and promises to marry him. The Beast turns into a beautiful prince, which is revealed to be his original form. They marry and live happily ever after. In the much older sub-types, "Cupid and Psyche" (AT425A) and "East of the Sun, West of the Moon" (AT425B), the heroine marries either an animal or an invisible bridegroom, who reveals himself to be a handsome youth at the end of the story.

There are also similarities, however; both Asian and European versions of the animal bridegroom tale end with the disappearance of the animal. The dog is ultimately replaced with a human in all the versions of the dog bridegroom tale in Asia just as the non-human bridegroom in "Beauty and the Beast" stories always turns into a human. In either case, the boundary between human and non-human is re-established, with the protagonist remaining on the human side.

Recent fairy-tale studies and rewritings have questioned the seemingly straightforward happy ending of "Beauty and the Beast" stories. Cristina Bacchilega, for example, claims that the Beast's transformation into a handsome prince "betrays [Beauty's] desire and decision-making" and calls it "a magic trick which leaves *almost* no trace of Beauty's desires and losses."[6] In Angela Carter's "The

Tiger's Bride" in her *The Bloody Chamber and Other Stories* (1979), it is not the animal bridegroom but his human bride who goes through a metamorphosis at the end of the story. In what follows, I will show how Tawada's revision of the animal bridegroom tale allows for new interpretations of possibilities regarding desire, narrative, and difference which this tale type may open up.

Yōko Tawada's "The Bridegroom Was a Dog"

In her own essay on "The Bridegroom Was a Dog," Tawada states that her story was inspired by Fukuda's article on the comparative analysis of the dog bridegroom tales discussed above.[7] While expressing her intense dislike for the kind of "wholesomeness" and "cleanliness" glowing on the face of the conquering hero of the story of "Momotarō [Peach Boy]" (18), a canonical Japanese folktale which praises feudal heroism and which was widely used for war propaganda in the first half of the twentieth century, Tawada claims that she found the dog bridegroom tale interesting due to the motif of the close physical contact between the princess and the dog, which is repeated in many other stories throughout Asia. In other words, she was attracted by this obscure folktale because it shows how the same motifs, peculiar as they seem, can be found widely among diverse cultures. The motifs she likes best are the dog licking the girl's soiled bottom and the wife's murder of her human husband in revenge for the killing of her dog husband, both of which can be found in the Japanese versions. On the other hand, Tawada deplores the absence of the motif of mother-son incest in the Japanese tales. She then states: "I put together only the elements that appealed to me and made up a version of my own" (19-20). Tawada's version, therefore, is intended as a structural variation on the traditional dog bridegroom tale which, as we have seen above, has maintained the same pattern however variable its details may be. This patchwork of the variants of the old tale type, however, begins to take its own course when woven together with Tawada's creative imagination. She describes this process as follows: "While I was writing a novel last year, this version vividly sprang into my mind, sneaked up from behind, took over the novel, and transformed it into 'The Bridegroom Was a Dog'" (20). This description captures the irresistible structuring power of age-old narratives, which, as I will show below, also creates and shapes the narrative desires of the characters in Tawada's story.

As I stated at the beginning of this essay, the heroine of Tawada's story, called Mitsuko Kitamura, tells different folk versions of the dog bridegroom tale, presumably taken from Fukuda's article, to her pupils at her cram school. These variants told by Mitsuko are disseminated throughout the town by the children who go home and try to reproduce the stories which they have heard, but they can only do so in a fragmentary form. Their frustrated mothers exchange the fragments with each other, and two versions of the tale emerge which they call the "forest version" and the "desert island version," roughly corresponding to the Japanese variant and the Asian variant Type B respectively (14). To the children listening, the motif of incest "seemed perfectly natural," and it is the episode about the dog licking the princess's bottom clean that leaves the most vivid impression, so that they start imitating the licking dog when they eat ice cream, for example, which disgusts their mothers. To the mothers, on the other hand, the folk origin of the story gives Mitsuko's retelling some kind of moral authority: "someone who was taking a class in folklore at the Culture Center swore she'd seen that story in one of her books, so it must be authentic, which was a comforting thought to the other mothers" (15-16). Although they seem disturbed by the episodes about the licking dog and the mother-son incest, the mothers feel reassured by the knowledge that it is just another version of the same old story, just like "The Crane Wife."

Mitsuko also tells her pupils her eccentric opinion about the use of tissue paper, which they report to their mothers as follows: "Miss Kitamura says wiping your nose with snot paper you've already used once is nice, because it's so soft and warm and wet, but when you use it a third time to wipe yourself when you go to the bathroom, it feels even better" (11-12). This real-life episode about Mitsuko and the "snot paper" becomes mixed up with the folkloric episode about the dog licking the girl's bottom and begins to haunt the mind not only of the children but also of their mothers: "no matter how determined they were not to imagine their child's beautiful teacher sitting on the toilet wiping herself with that lovely moist tissue, Miss Kitamura's smiling face invariably rose before them" (12). As the strange motifs of the folktale begin to take on lives of their own, the boundary between reality and fantasy becomes blurred in Tawada's story.

"The Bridegroom Was a Dog" revolves around various other binary oppositions. The story is set in a town made up of two distinct areas. The northern area consists of public housing complexes developed about thirty years ago while the southern area is said to have prospered as a rice-growing area along the river since ancient times until the 1960s and still has the remains of "human dwellings that dated back farther than you could imagine" (19). It is in the south side of the town that Mitsuko arrives on her mountain bike from nobody-knows-where and opens a cram school for elementary school children in an old house which she rents from a farmer. Her pupils come from the new housing complex in the northern district populated mostly with young couples who have seldom stepped into the southern area themselves. As her family name Kitamura (*kita* means "*north*," and mura means "village") indicates, Mitsuko is an intermediate figure between the archaic south and the modernised north.

Mitsuko crosses not only spatial but also epistemological boundaries. Upon finding out from their children about her age, the mothers face a categorical question: "when a woman doesn't have any children, the age of thirty-nine—past youth yet not quite over the hill—makes it hard to know what category to put her in" (18). Mitsuko is perceived by the mothers as an in-between being, neither young nor old, educated but uncivilised, and beautiful but not feminine in a conventional way. In other words, she is seen as a fantastic being who does not belong to their clean and clear-cut "reality" and therefore comes to function as a kind of safety valve for their repressed desires. Tawada's story plays with Gothic narrative conventions in that what follows in the story can be read as a fantasy arising from the unconscious of these housewives living their obsessively hygienic and decorous lives in the standardised housing complex. It also shows the process in which a little known version of the animal bridegroom stories stirs up their forgotten or repressed desires and drives them to spin stories around those whom they consider as different or not quite as "human" as themselves.

Mitsuko resists being classified as a traditional beauty such as those who appear in popular tales like "The Crane Wife."[8] The head teacher of the elementary school expresses his bewilderment: "It's unusual for a beautiful woman to look that happy. I thought traditional beauties were supposed to be sad and lonely" (12). According to the Jungian psychologist Hayao Kawai, the wife's disappearance in "The Crane Wife" serves to complete a "sense of beauty with sorrow" called aware, an aesthetic quality valued in Japanese cultural tradition.[9] In this view, the male protagonist's eventual loss of his beloved wife is not perceived as a punishment for him as the story achieves an aesthetically satisfying effect through the realisation of the pathos of nature, which is valued above the realisation of a harmonious marital union. This "sense of beauty with sorrow," however, is achieved at the cost of the animal wife who represents such feminine virtues as self-sacrifice, obedience, diligence, and beauty, which are also valued in the heroine of de Beaumont's "Beauty and the Beast." The heroine of Tawada's story, on the other hand, pays no attention to any of the gender stereotypes endorsed in canonised tales.

The story takes a magical turn when an immaculately groomed man in his late twenties suddenly arrives at Mitsuko's house and, to her complete bewilderment, invites himself in, saying, "I'm here to stay" (25). He then introduces himself: "You can call me Tarō. Under the circumstances, it mightn't be advisable to use my real name, but I can't think of any other" (25). Since Tarō, like Tom or Jack in English tales, is a generic name for male characters in traditional Japanese tales such as "Momotarō," this revelation of his "real name" self-reflexively confirms his fairy-tale status.[10] His family name "Iinuma," which includes "inu," the Japanese word for dog, also confirms his identity as the dog in the folktale. He then initiates a bizarre kind of sexual intercourse during which he licks Mitsuko's bottom in a manner evocative of the dog in the folktale:

[T]he man slipped off her shorts as easily as drawing a handkerchief out of his sleeve, laid her on her back, and very politely, still in his shirt and pants, fitted his body on top of hers, then gently pressing his canine teeth against the delicate skin of her neck, began sucking noisily, with Mitsuko's face growing paler all the while until she suddenly flushed crimson and the beads of sweat standing out on her forehead got sticky from the shock of feeling a thing with both the flexibility and indifference of a vegetable slide into her vagina, but as she writhed, struggling to get away, he flipped her over and, easily grabbing her thighs, one in each hand, raised them up and began licking her rectum, now poised precariously in midair. The sheer size of his tongue, the amount of saliva dripping from it, and the heavy panting were all literally extraordinary... (26-27).

This breathtaking description of their sexual intercourse, with one verb followed by another in rapid succession, parodies the sexually charged narrative thrust of Gothic fiction by juxtaposing his vampiric act of sucking her neck with the non-climactic insertion of his "vegetable"-like penis followed by his dutiful licking of her bottom. Every day, after performing this "canine" sexual ritual, he runs into the kitchen, cooks a scrupulous meal, "wolf[s] it down," and starts rigorously cleaning her house (28). This self-invited handsome bridegroom, who impeccably performs all the housework for the heroine, can be seen as a parody of the beautiful and resourceful crane wife. By thus bringing another variant into focus, Tawada's story rewrites the canon of animal bride and bridegroom tales. At the same time, Tarō's over-fastidiousness echoes the mothers' obsession with hygiene and decorum, which makes us suspect that this dog-like Prince Charming may be born out of their conflicted fantasies or at least partly embroidered by them.

In Tawada's story, the transformation works only one way, from humans into dogs. Tarō's habit of smelling Mitsuko's body for over an hour every day begins to make her aware of various subtle nuances of her body aromas changing according to the mood of the moment, so that she begins to smell her body to check her own feelings. Her newly developed sensitivity to smell seems to indicate the beginning of the process of her transformation into a dog. This possibility becomes more likely when Tarō's history is revealed.

One day, Mrs Orita, the mother of one of Mitsuko's pupils, recognises Tarō as her husband's ex-colleague—"one of my husband's favourites" (38), she explains to Mitsuko—who disappeared three years ago. Mrs Orita then informs Taro's wife Ryōko, "a thin, soft-spoken woman who looked like a fox" (43), where Taro lives, and Ryōko invites Mitsuko to her flat in a housing complex in a neighbouring town which looks exactly like the one where Mitsuko's pupils live. There, Ryōko reveals to Mitsuko that she has been "training" to make herself as physically fit as Tarō and, just as Tarō did when he first met Mitsuko, suddenly lifts Mitsuko's body, lays her flat across the table, and starts sucking her knee, saying, "I feel I'm gradually turning into Tarō somehow" (50). Ryōko then tells the story of how Tarō changed completely after being attacked by a pack of stray dogs in the woods and carried to a hospital in a police car. His grandmother arrived at the hospital "with wild look in her eye" and uttered a sinister warning: "The boy's lost. An evil spirit's got him now" (52), adding a flavour of the werewolf legend to this episode. After this accident, he stopped talking to Ryōko and soon left her and his company. He was still to be seen in the neighbourhood park, and every time she saw him, he looked fitter and more muscular, which made her envious of his doggishness. However, this almost dog-woman, who seems to offer the Gothic double to both Tarō and Mitsuko, leaves the story at this point, probably because she is considered by Mitsuko's pupils and their mothers to be just an outsider living in the next town.

Mitsuko also learns from Ryōko that Tarō has started to "play around" at night with Toshio, the father of the girl called Fukiko, who is Mitsuko's favourite pupil and is bullied by the other children (48). Fukiko's name includes "fuku," the verb "to wipe" in Japanese, indicating the connection with the motif of the dog licking the princess's bottom. When asked by Mitsuko why they bully Fukiko, the children explain that it is because she is "strange," "fat," "never washes her hair," and sometimes "doesn't even wear socks" (24), which all indicate the girl's otherness, placing her on the side of the "not-quite-human." Mitsuko feels protective about this motherless nine-year-old girl, who is left alone in the evenings with enough money to arrange dinner for herself. Mitsuko per-suades Fukiko to come to her house every day after school and have the dinner which Taro has cooked. Watching this quiet and absent-minded girl, "Mitsuko often felt a love akin to irritation well up in her, so strong it hurt" (57). They develop an intimate relationship, echoing the motif of mother-child incest absent in the Japanese variants of the dog bridegroom tale:

> [W]hen, for example, Mitsuko took Fukiko's blouse off so she could sew on the buttons that were hanging by a thread, the girl would sit there beside her, naked to the waist, in-tently watching the movements of her fingers, and after a while her head would be leaning against Mitsuko's shoulder, and when Mitsuko was sure she must have fallen asleep, she'd look over to find the child still gravely following the needle with her eyes, so Mitsuko would say:
> "You like sewing on buttons better than reading, don't you?"
> "That's because I'm not 'smart' like you."
> This cheeky sort of remark only made Mitsuko angry again. (57-58)

After Mitsuko becomes Fukiko's protector, the children stop bullying her openly, but instead start spreading a malicious rumour about her father "'swinging his hips' at the Game Center" with Tarō (58). Although the elementary school children seem to be using the expression "swinging his hips at the Game Center" without knowing exactly what it means, the mothers infer that it refers to a homosexu-al relationship. Hearing this rumour, Mrs Orita visits Mitsuko and desperately tries to persuade her to marry Tarō; Mitsuko, however, has no desire to marry, which itself thwarts any attempt at a respect-able ending. Fukiko's father, who might be expected to play the role of the huntsman in the Japanese variant of the dog bridegroom tale, is of course no help here, as his desire is clearly oriented towards men. In trying to make sense of the relationships between those whom they consider as different from them, the mothers struggle to make them fit into some kind of frame they can recognise, that is, heterosexual marriage between Mitsuko and Tarō and proper family bonds between Fukiko and her father.

At the end of the story, however, all the four "not-quite-human" characters escape from this frame; Tarō disappears with Fukiko's father, and on the same day Mitsuko elopes with Fukiko. It is as if they were conveniently kicked out of the story to be banished to somewhere remote—preferably a desert island or mountains as in the folktales—when it looked as if they were deviating too far from the conventional pattern. With their disappearance, order is now apparently restored to the community with the boundary between the human and the non-human firmly re-established: "The house where Mitsuko had lived was soon torn down to make room for some apartments, and by the time construction began, the children were all going to new cram schools, and hardly ever ventured into that part of town again" (62). This ending, however, opens up rather than closes the narrative possibilities as none of the characters has either revealed his or her true identity or transformed into something with a fixed form. We are not even told what becomes of the heroine, who seems to be still in the process of turning into a dog-woman. The four characters exit the story in the midst of metamorphosis, in a state of fluidity, pregnant with infinite variations. Tawada's "version," therefore, structurally departs from traditional narratives by definitively resisting the desire for stability and closure usually fulfilled at the end of the story.

Conclusion

As its self-referential title indicates, Tawada's "The Bridegroom Was a Dog" is a variant of the dog bridegroom tale as well as a story about this tale type. It shows how certain plot patterns and motifs in traditional tales may generate new variants while at the same time shaping them into recognisable patterns. The conflicted narratives of the mothers reflect their desire to deviate from *and* conform to what they already know. The story, therefore, is also about the difficulty of stepping out of the old patterns without becoming just another variant that does not radically subvert our expectations. Like its heroine, Tawada's story departs from the old pattern and instead opens up the possibilities of creating new narratives and desires out of old. Although apparently back to their familiar reality, the children and their mothers in the north of the town will be occasionally haunted by the story of Mitsuko, especially when they are sitting on the toilet.

Bibliography

Bacchilega, Cristina. *Postmodern Fairy Tales: Gender and Narrative Strategies*. Philadelphia: University of Pennsylvania Press, 1997.

Carter, Angela. *The Bloody Chamber and Other Stories*. London: Gollancz, 1979.

—. *Fireworks: Nine Profane Pieces*. London: Quartet, 1974; repr. London: Virago, 1988.

Davis, Jason, and Mio Bryce. "I Love You as You Are: Marriages between Different Kinds." *The International Journal of Diversity in Organisations, Communities and Nations*. 7. 6 (2008): 201-10.

de Beaumont, Madame Le Prince. "Beauty and the Beast." 182-95. *The Classic Fairy Tales*. Edited by Iona Opie and Peter Opie. London: Oxford UP, 1974.

Fukuda, Akira. "Inumukoiri no Denshō." In *Mukashi-Banashi: Kenkyū to Shiryō 4*, edited by Mukashi-Banashi Konwa-Kai. 36-69. Tokyo: Miyai Shoten, 1975.

Kawai, Hayao. *The Japanese Psyche: Major Motifs in the Fairy Tales of Japan*. Translated by Hayao Kawai and Sachiko Reece. Woodstock: Spring Publications, 1996. (Mukashi-Banashi to Nihonjin no Kokoro. Tokyo: Iwanami Shoten, 1982.)

Ozawa, Toshio. *Mukashi-Banashi no Kosumoroji: Hito to Dōbutsu tono Kon'in-Tan*. Tokyo: Kodansha, 1994.

Tawada, Yōko. "*The Bridegroom Was a Dog.*" The Bridegroom Was a Dog. Translated by Margaret Mitsutani. Tokyo: Kodansha International, 2003 (1998). 7-62. ("Inumukoiri." *Inumukoiri*. Tokyo: Kodansha, 1993. 77-137.)

—. "'Inumukoiri' ni tsuite [On 'The Bridegroom Was a Dog']." In *Katakoto no Uwagoto*. Tokyo: Seidosha, 2007, 17-20.

Yanagita, Kunio, ed. *Zenkoku Mukashi-Banashi Kiroku: Sadojima Mukashi-Banashi-Shū*. Tokyo: Sanseido, 1942.

Notes

1   Tawada, Yōko, "*The Bridegroom Was a Dog.*" The Bridegroom Was a Dog. Translated by Margaret Mitsutani. Tokyo: Kodansha International, 2003 (1998). 7-62, 13.

2   Ozawa's idea here seems to be influenced by nineteenth-century theories of cultural evolutionism represented by comparative anthropologists such as E. B. Tyler, Andrew Lang, and James Frazer. I am grateful to John Patrick Pazdziora and Defne Cizakca for bringing this connection and other helpful points to my attention.

3   Yanagita, Kunio, ed., *Zenkoku Mukashi-Banashi Kiroku: Sadojima Mukashi-Banashi-Shū,* Tokyo: Sanseido, 1942, 64-65.

4   Davis, Jason, and Mio Bryce, "I Love You as You Are: Marriages between Different Kinds," *The International Journal of Diversity in Organisations, Communities and Nations* 7.6 (2008): 201-210, 204.

5   Fukuda, Akira, "Inumukoiri no Denshō," in *Mukashi-Banashi: Kenkyū to Shiryō 4,* edited by Mukashi-Banashi Konwa-Kai, Tokyo: Miyai Shoten, 1975, 36-69, 64.

6   Bacchilega, Cristina, *Postmodern Fairy Tales: Gender and Narrative Strategies,* Philadelphia: University of Pennsylvania Press, 1997, 81.

7   Tawada, "'Inumukoiri' ni tsuite [On 'The Bridegroom Was a Dog']," In *Katakoto no Uwagoto,* Tokyo: Seidosha, 2007, 17-20, 18; my translation.

8   The name Mitsuko recalls the tragic beauty in Claude Farrère's *La bataille* [The Battle] (1909), a novel about a British Navy Officer and his Japanese mistress called Mitsouko, as well as the 1919 perfume by Guerlain, which is said to have been named after her.

9   Kawai, Hayao, *The Japanese Psyche: Major Motifs in the Fairy Tales of Japan,* translated by Hayao Kawai and Sachiko Reece, Woodstock: Spring Publications, 1996, 122.

10 It is interesting to note in this connection that the first-person narrator of "A Souvenir of Japan," Angela Carter's semi-autobiographical short story, calls her Japanese lover "Tarō," rendering visible her fantasisation of their relationship. See Angela Carter, *Fireworks: Nine Profane Pieces,* London: Quartet, 1974; repr. London: Virago, 1988, 5.

Chapter 15

A Gothic Fairy-Bride and the Fall: A Lecture on "The End of the World" in Kenjirō Hata's *Hayate no Gotoku*

Joshua Richards

There are all kinds of literary loves. There is the courtly love of a Dante or Milton—distant, idealized, and inspirational. There is the infatuation of youth that makes a young man of nineteen fawn over the collected works of Yeats and the mature affection that lends a touch of *frisson* to the reading of Tennyson. There is also the deep, placid spousal love of the scholar, in which there is no rapture but a fondness and familiarity. But the love that inspired not only my long poem *Dante* but this lecture is the most insidious kind—that strange, instantaneous nexus with someone just met, the kind where you stay up all night conversing with them; it fades, it always does, but there is the memory of that frantic, wondrous sensation of connection. I encountered Kenjirō Hata's *Hayate the Combat Butler*[1] in a long stretch of convalescence in the spring of 2010. At that juncture, I'd been reading manga for hours every day, for several weeks on end, so I was frankly rather inured to the assorted emotional ploys of manga, but I was absolutely awestruck and nearly moved to tears by the flashback storyline "The End of the World." It simply wouldn't leave my mind, and slowly, the story fused with an idea which had been lying inchoate for several months—what eventually became my long poem *Dante*.

The difficulty in writing on such a work is avoiding eisegesis, *i.e.* I want to write on Hata's work, not my response in Dante. While I realize that the initial impulse will be to apply what I have written here to that work, I would ask you to refrain, although I also realize this request is futile. However, please go read Hata's work at some point—it deserves your love.

As something of a disclaimer, let me note that I am no manga scholar—my area of research is religious and mythological intertextuality, focusing on T.S. Eliot currently. Japanese manga is my favorite "pulp" reading, and I come to you as an enthusiast—I admittedly know little of the history and development of the art form, but I am here to discuss something I love, not provide a full, critical reckoning of Hata's work. As such, I have foregone the chilly austerities of the full, academic style and treatment for the posture of a lecture—and accompanying cavalier approach.

Nonetheless, that impulse also leaves this the purest of all literary inquiries. I'm not interested in assessing the biographical implications of this work, the effect of *shōnen* manga[2] on the youth of Japan, the way the story simultaneously subverts as it establishes female hegemony, or even the appropriation of the manga aesthetic by the American literary scene—what I want to know is this: why, of all the manga I have read, did this little flashback story pull at my heartstrings?

It moved me, and I want to find out how it did so.

The answer I came to, however, is anything but simple. By defying the expectations of his own story and genre and appropriating the conventions of the Gothic, Hata transforms "The End of the World" into a new fairy tale, specifically into a fairy-bride story; however, the framing and location within the overall narrative combined with the tragic ending results in mythopoesis—in short, his fairy-bride tale becomes the Fall of Man.

Now, this may seem overly involved for a series entitled *Hayate the Combat Butler*; however, I think the following examination will vindicate this. Although the manga may initially seem to be in the same absurdist, parodic vein as *Bobobo-bo Bo-bobo et al.*, even the most cursory examination of *Hayate* will justify my assertion that Kenjiro Hata is one of the great sad clowns of literature—in the words of a great contemporary poet, he (and, incidentally, his main character) is a court jester with a broken heart. Throughout all the absurdity and comedy, there's a vein of smiling sadness to the work, and this overtone comes to the forefront in "The End of the World."

Before I begin discussing the work itself, let me explain "The End of the World."[3] The story occurs in Volume XVII and XVIII (deep into the manga's run); it is a flashback relating the main character Hayate's past. In his author's note, Hata explains that

> This volume includes a story line about Hayate's past that's a bit different from the usual comedy plots. In video game terms, these flashbacks are like cut scenes that can't be skipped. They contain elements of the original plot I developed for the story before it started serialization. I've been thinking for some time that I ought to reveal Hayate's backstory, but when the time came I really had to give it serious thought. Because the final version of *Hayate* was so different from my original concept, I was afraid that the flashback was too much of a downer to work. I put it off for a long time. After giving it a lot of consideration, I decided the manga couldn't move forward until I told this story. (Hata qtd. in *Hayate* XVII:186).[4]

As few of you will be familiar with the content of the manga or the story, let me give a lengthier summary of both the manga as a whole and "The End of the World" than I might otherwise be inclined to do. Now, this is a fairly long story, and so there are any number of elements that will not be discussed, and some elements mentioned later that will not be in this summary. We are interested in this story as a new fairy tale, and thus, it is the morphology that interests us the most; the individual details are somewhat ancillary.[5]

Hayate opens with 16-year-old Hayate Ayasaki, by the virtue of his superhuman physique and work-ethic, supporting his deadbeat, crooked parents. However, on Christmas Eve of that year, his parents sell his organs to the Yakuza to cover a 150 million

301

yen gambling debt and leave town.⁶ Desperate to find the money, Hayate attempts to kidnap a girl he meets in the park, Nagi Sanzen'in, and hold her for ransom. Unfortunately, Hayate botches the attempt royally, being a fundamentally good person, and Nagi believes that his poorly-worded kidnapping attempt is actually a bumbling confession of love. He wanders away in defeat, but at that very moment, she is kidnapped by another group of criminals (as Nagi is fabulously, plutocratically wealthy)—he saves her and is subsequently hired as her butler—and that's just the manga's first issue.

"The End of the World" opens after a chapter where Nagi gets a camera and walks around taking pictures with all of the characters; however, she fails to get a picture with just her and Hayate. When asked about this, she says that they'll have plenty of opportunities—"Hayate, you and I are going to be together forever ♥" (*Hayate* XVII.68.1, 69.1). "The End of the World" begins with Hayate lying in bed at night, and he thinks "I had a dream; it was about a long time ago. A golden dream engraved in my deepest memories. A dream about the day I found out that the world contains terrible things. A dream about the first time I thought I wouldn't mind death. And..." (*Hayate* XVII.69.3-4). Here, the page turn reveals a "splash" double-page spread showing Hayate as a little boy on his hands and knees in a field of flowers with a little girl in Victorian clothes, a parasol hiding her face, offering him her hand—"...About the girl with whom I once vowed to remain forever" (*Hayate* XVII.70-1).

The story flashes back to when Hayate is six years old and runs away from his parents in disgust at their dishonest and generally awful behavior. He runs and runs and runs, finally collapsing in exhaustion in a field of flowers, wishing for death. However, the aforementioned girl awakens him and helps him. Her name is Athena Tennos,⁷ and it is, in her words, "the name of the world's greatest goddess," and "the perfect name for someone like me, unique in this world" (*Hayate* XVII.89.1).

She tells him that he is in The Royal Garden and pointing to a Western-style castle perched precariously, impossibly on a precipice says, "That's the center of the universe. It's said that the

God who dwells on Calvary hill[8] dwells in that castle" (*Hayate* XVII:93-5). It is, in Hayate's words, "full of wonderful things. Things everyone longs for. Sparkling jewels. Delicious meals. Beautiful, spacious rooms. A big garden that's always in bloom. A playtime that never ends. Divine powers and magical tools" (Hayate XVII:172.6-173.1-2). Athena invites him to become her butler and teaches him to be the perfect servant, and "what it takes to be a perfect boyfriend"—in his words, "she told me I needed to be stronger and more considerate... ...and financially dependable so she'd never have to suffer hardship... and on and on..." (*Hayate* XVII:165.2-3). They pass the days happily until Hayate gets homesick for his parents. He leaves The Royal Garden but is disappointed in them, as usual. He works hard and purchases a small ring as a way of making his absence up to Athena—at which point, she berates him for getting one that's too large and for not getting a matching pair; however, smiling softly, she gives him a large, jeweled ring, saying "someday... let's grow up to be adults... ...and wear these together"[9] (*Hayate* XVII:183.6). Hayate leaves the castle again to ask his parents if they'll take in Athena so that she can leave the Royal Garden. However, they trick him into giving them the ring, then pawn it and take the money. Athena is furious and tells him to leave his parents—he replies that "[i]t's easy for you to talk! You don't have parents"—here, the older Hayate's narration says, "when you commit a sin... ...you'll pay for it sooner or later" (*Hayate* XVIII:17.3,5). In her towering fury, Athena tells him to leave and he does. Yet, when he wants to return to apologize, the path to The Royal Garden has disappeared, the woods that hid it cut down as part of a construction project, and Athena is left alone in the castle—"I didn't mean what I said, Hayate. [...] Alone again. I'm trapped here again... all alone..." (*Hayate* XVIII:34.4, 35.5). The final scene shows Athena, now sixteen herself, standing in the Parthenon at Athens[10] indicating that she, by some unexplained means, has escaped the castle but still dreams of Hayate—and now, in her words, "must open the way to my Royal Garden" (*Hayate* XVIII.58.2).[11]

Summary is a fool's errand, and this one does justice to none of the story's desperate sweetness and little of its sadness; however, it needed to be done.

Now, at this juncture, let me reiterate my contention regarding "The End of the World" and the mechanism of its effect, which will be the answer to my question—by defying the expectations of his own story and genre and appropriating the conventions of the Gothic, Hata transforms "The End of the World" into a new fairy tale, specifically into a fairy-bride story; however, the framing and location within the overall narrative combined with the tragic ending results in mythopoesis—in short, his fairy-bride story becomes the Fall. First, I will discuss how "The End of the World" is atypical both for *Hayate* and for the *shōnen* genre. Second, I will discuss in what ways the story is Gothic. Third, I will show how by adapting the Gothic to Hayate creates a fairy-bride tale. Finally, how the frame causes the fairy-tale to become a Tolkienian fairy-story and attain to mythopoesis, specifically, a story of the Fall. This will, I believe, provide something of an answer to the riddle of Hata's "The End of the World."

In terms of norms of the genre, what is unusual about "The End of the World" is its size and tone. Generally, in a weekly publication like *Hayate*, flashbacks are a single issue or if unusually large and important, they are two or three issues. "The End of the World" is ten. That is over two and a half months of publication time, and it would fill an entire *tankōban*.[12] For perspective, the entire run of *Hayate* to date is only 31 *tankōban* (a sumptuous length for a manga). That Hata was aware of the exorbitant length is highlighted at several points. First, in the *omake* pages[13] for Volume XVII, Nagi and Maria (Nagi's maid) state, "Hello, I'm Nagi Sanzen'in, the main heroine of this manga. Likewise... ...I'm Maria, the *main heroine*." Nagi, glancing over her shoulder to Hayate, "for some reason or other... ...most of this volume has been wasted on some stupid flashback that doesn't feature us" (*Hayate* XVII.185.1-2). In the author's note to the next volume, Hata states, "In this volume, I wrapped up the flashback arc with Hayate and Athena. It took longer than I expected. As an author, I'm pleased I was able to write such a long story" (Hata qtd. in *Hayate* XVIII.185). It seems obvious that he is aware of the unusual size of the work. As for the unusual nature of the content, it will suffice to note that the stories surrounding "The End of the

World" feature Hayate's underage charge Nagi attempting to rent a pornographic movie but ending up with a scary zombie movie instead and suffering nightmares, and a multi-issue arc where the ghost of a Catholic priest (don't ask) sends Hayate a stalker-like love letter and so Nagi devises a plan to have Hayate and Maria go on a pretend-date to dissuade the stalker (*Hayate* XVII.5-20; *Hayate* XVIII.69-118). Those episodes were by no means uncharacteristic of the series, so it seems clear that "The End of the World" is subverting the reader's expectations for the both the genre and series.

A reader who is not familiar with the series might be inclined to ask why the repeated mentions of the Gothic, and a reader who is might be inclined to ask why this is a new fairy tale and not a latter-day Gothic romance. For the former, let me simply say that "The End of the World" is steeped in a Gothic aesthetic; even the most cursory examination of the art will render this point beyond debate so let me simply ask the reader who has not yet read the story to take me at my word. Now to the latter: possessing the visual trappings alone does not make a story Gothic, so let us turn to Horace Walpole's seminal prefaces to *The Castle of Otranto*. He asserts in the second preface that *Otranto* "was an attempt to blend the two kinds of romance, the ancient and the modern" *i.e.* the supernatural romance of the old world and the 18th century realist fiction.[14] In practice, what this amounts to is the characters "think, speak, and act, as it might be supposed mere men and women would do in extraordinary positions."[15] I will deal with this position in a moment, but it is, at least, not implausible for "The End of the World." Additionally, Walpole advises for an infusion of the comic to "artificially [exalt]" the serious, and this is accomplished quite effectively in "The End of the World"—again, this is patently obvious to even the casual reader.[16] Finally, the first preface indicates that the moral of *Otranto* is that "the sins of the fathers are visited on their children."[17] In practicality, what this means simply that the past haunts the present; however, in "The End of the World," this, though less than a moral, is definitely a palpable theme—Hayate is abused at school because of his parents' reputation as crooks, and Athena is a lost child—in one panel, a newspaper is shown with the headline "Tennos Family daughter—still missing" (*Hayate* XVII.74-5, 180.4).

Now, it would seem that this story is indeed a Gothic romance; however, while this is *theoretically* true, it is not so practically. A story where the principle actors are young children simply cannot be classically Gothic—this may seem a rather arbitrary assertion, but please follow my logic. Walpole states that the key to this Gothic aspect of his story is that the characters behave as "real people" might when confronted with the supernatural.[18] In practice, this amounts to fear, horror, and incredulity—a practice which *Hayate* maintains. Many of the series' more fantastic elements, such as the aforementioned ghost-priest and Tama the talking tiger, are largely met with doubt and incredulity. However, realistically, small children (like the six-year-old Hayate) would not be overly bothered by a magic castle or other supernatural occurrences, treating them as any other. Hayate admits that "something about the castle made me a little uneasy," and this is the whole extent of his response to a place as magical as Tír na nÓg—time even slows within the boundaries of The Royal Garden[19] (*Hayate* XVII.125-6). In other words, portrayed realistically, children do not respond realistically, and what would be realistic for adults is unrealistic for children; thus, it is a practical impossibility for a story with young children as the primary actors to meet the requirements of the classical Gothic, and so "The End of the World" is not merely a Gothic romance. According to Walpole's analysis, the lack of a realistic response to the supernatural is the province of the "ancient romance"—fairytale, folklore, and mythology.

This brings me to the most complicated aspect of my argument: how "The End of the World" is transformed from the Gothic into a new fairy tale. In short, what occurs is this: "The End of the World," like many works, has, in Kate Ellis's schema, "masculine" and "feminine" Gothic plots at the same work but each embodied in a separate character. This is not particularly uncommon—consider *The Castle of Otranto* or *Wuthering Heights*. What is unusual is this: in response to the over-arching master/butler dynamic in Hayate, the genders of these positions are inverted—Athena carries the masculine plotline and *Hayate* the feminine. This causes the story to fit neatly into the morphological Fairy-Bride category. This may seem far-fetched, but Hayate is often forced into the female position. When Nagi imagines their wedding, it is with her as the groom and Hayate as the blushing bride including the white dress and bouquet.

Now, I will here be presenting a kind of summation of the masculine and feminine Gothic plots triangulated from Kate Ellis's *The Contested Castle* and Anne Williams' *Art of Darkness*. Both of these works are focused particularly on feminist and Marxist interpretations of pulp Gothic women's literature, especially the Gothic romances of the 1960's. This has little bearing on the work at hand, so I will not weary with the derivation.[20] Besides, the gender inversion applied to the roles in "The End of the World" complicates their analysis immensely. These are morphological features and are best presented in chart form so that the reader might easily see the features

Essentially, the masculine Gothic[21] is the story of the exile from the family, tragic in form with a more open-ended narrative, and a focus on the suffering of the primary character. Additionally, the supernatural is taken as a reality in the masculine Gothic and there is frequently an unspecified curse driving the action. The feminine Gothic, on the other hand, is a story of domestic integration—the heroine is forced into a hostile household and by her virtue and persistence transforms it into the family she desires. The supernatural is either explained away or ultimately irrelevant. The narrative is closed and the focus on the romance. Again, the character who embodies the former in "The End of the World" is Athena, and the latter, Hayate.

How does this heap of broken Gothic images become a fairy tale? Let's examine this tale morphologically. The Gothic elements produce the following scenario: An ordinary boy wanting a family finds a supernatural girl under a curse in a magic castle. He agrees to become her butler, and they fall in love and "marry" due to his persistence and virtue. However, Hayate misses his parents and, in doing so, causes the argument that leads to his exile from The Royal Garden. Let us see how this fits the overall pattern of the fairy-bride story.

Masculine Gothic	Expression in Athena
Reality of the Supernatural	This needs little justification—Athena even mentions when she is enhancing Hayate's body (the apparent source of his seemingly superhero physique throughout the manga) that here in the Royal Garden, she has learned to "play God" (*Hayate* XVII.115.5).
Exile	Athena mentions that she has no parents and is all alone in the enormous castle (*Hayate* XVII.100-1). Additionally, it seems that she cannot leave—a permanent exile from the world.
Tragic Form	The tragic aspect is most apparent in the destruction of her own happiness by banishing Hayate in a fit of fury, consigning her to the loneliness she experienced before.
Uncertain narrative closure	The final scene featuring Athena, now age 16, at the Parthenon, re-opens what is, to Hayate, a simple flashback.
Focus on suffering	The primary thread in Athena's story is her loneliness instead of any kind of explanation of her circumstances or nature.
The Curse	It is, of course, not explained why Athena is trapped in The Royal Garden, but the ghost of King Midas who appears, responding to her wrath, from within the coffin held in the basement, which Hayate is forbidden to touch, strongly hints at some kind of curse. (*Hayate* XVII.122.4).

Feminine Gothic	Expression in Hayate
Lack of Supernatural	Outside of the events within The Royal Garden, there is nothing particularly magical in "The End of the World."
Reclamation of Domestic Unity	Hayate's goal throughout is the assumption of Athena into his own family. When another character asks what concerns him, he says, "how to financially provide for the woman I love... ...and the issue of cohabitating with her and my parents" (*Hayate* XVII.177.1). He continues to believe that he can change his parents for the better and rejects Athena's request to abandon them.
Persistence by virtue	Hayate decided to live by the words, given to him in a dream by Santa Claus (seriously), "The earnest and the honest are the ones... ...who deserve the last laugh (*Hayate* XVII.73.2). He requires help from others, from Athena and Nagi, but it is on account of his virtue.
Closed narration	Although it ends tragically, he sees it as a closed event—something in the past which he can move beyond—"I never... ...saw her again" (*Hayate* XVIII.46.1).
Focus on Romance	Hayate, especially his narration, focuses on the romantic aspect. Cf. *Hayate* XVII.134.1, XVIII.42.5

Well, first, is it a fairy-tale at all? If we use Propp's morphological analysis, it certainly would be: Hayate lives at home impoverished (a^5) with awful parents (β^2), he runs away from home ($\uparrow$), wishing to die (B^7). After collapsing in a field of flowers, he meets Athena, who helps him up and offers him a job (D^2). Hayate is pleased by the prospect (E^2) and the two fall in love. While there, Athena uses her magic to give Hayate an incredible, invincible physique (F^1). Hayate decides to get a present for Athena and works hard, availed by his newfound power, to buy her a ring (K^6). He presents it to her, and there is an exchange of rings (w^1). After their fight, he returns home to live with his awful parents again ($\downarrow$). It follows the morphology to an extent. The real difficulty here is that this type of fairy tale (AT F302), a fairy-bride story, is somewhat unusual in Western folklore;[22] however, it is seemingly quite common in Japanese folklore. I am certainly no expert in the topic, but even my meager knowledge turned up a number of fairly prominent tales of this type: most importantly, the story of Tanabata,[23] the tale of *Tsuru no Ongaeshi*, better known as "The Crane Wife" in English—a story that I remember encountering as a child—and the story of Itō Norisuké.[24]

Synthesizing the aforementioned tales, we can see the basic pattern—a man (or in the case of "The End of the World," a small boy) meets a goddess of some form. In some cases, it is in the form of an animal as in "The Crane Wife" and the related Urashimo Tarō. Due to some service on his part, he marries the girl. In the case of "The End of the World," it is due to Hayate's persistence and pure heart and the result is a marriage promise, as they are children. However, things go wrong. In the Tanabata tale, the couple neglect their duties, and in "The Crane Wife," the husband violates the interdiction: here I think, the most germane one is in the story of Urashimo Tarō, concerned for his mother, desires to leave the palace of the Dragon God to his own demise. Regardless, a line is crossed, and the couple is separated: in Tanabata, the lovers are separated only to be reunited once a year; in "The Crane Wife," the husband sees the wife's true form and she flies away; and in "The End of the World," Hayate leaves the garden and can never find a way back.

The justification for its being a "new" fairy tale rather than a retelling is the presence of the Western Gothic elements. Athena's imprisonment in a magic castle, the classic princess in the tower, has no place in the original fairy-bride schema. Additionally, the desire for domestic unity, to restore his fallen family and integrate

Athena into it, is rather peculiar. Although it does not interfere with the fairy-bride morphology, it certainly is not a component thereof. This, to me, suggests that "The End of the World" is not simply a rehashing of a previous folktale, but a new fairy tale of the fairy-bride type.

That brings us to the final component of my assertion: the transition of "The End of the World" from new fairy-tale to mythopoesis. It is my (somewhat incendiary) belief that not just "The End of the World," but all new fairy tales, when they are unqualified successes, make this self-annihilating transition to *mythos*. Justifying this theory is beyond the scope of this lecture; however, I ask the reader to entertain at least the possibility of "The End of the World" attaining to mythopoesis. Tolkien, in his seminal essay "On Fairy Stories" provides the theoretical criteria for this transition.

For Tolkien, the fairy-story requires a "magic of a peculiar mood and power, at the furthest pole from the vulgar devices of the laborious, scientific magician" and with the qualification that the magic itself must "be taken seriously, neither laughed at nor explained away" (Tolkien 43). By the "laborious, scientific magician," I take Tolkien to mean the magic of something like Robert Jordan's *The Wheel of Time* where the supernatural is supported by a dizzying edifice of schematics—it may have an ineffable source, but the utilization of the One Power is explained in great detail. This is, of course, not the case in "The End of the World" where the nature of The Royal Garden and Athena's place in it are left mystifyingly vague; this may irritate the reader, but it is a key aspect of the story's mythopoesis. On the other hand, in a work as comic and parodic as *Hayate*, the reader may suspect that it would violate Tolkien's injunction against laughing at the magic. However, the magical aspects of "The End of the World," as part of its Gothic trapping, are not played for comedy—there isn't a single joke about it in the story's roughly 200-page span. The comedy that is present comes from the romance between Hayate and Athena, which, though sweet and sad on the large scale, is treated comically in any number of smaller vignettes.

Now, there is one more issue to deal with, and that is Tolkien's objection to the visual portrayal of Fantasy.[25] I cannot imagine that the idea of a fairy-story in comic or manga form ever occurred to Tolkien—what with his infamous dislike of Disney films. Generally, I think his objections stand, and that had Hata portrayed The Royal Garden as a traditional fairy-land or, indeed, as a garden at all, it would have been artistically a failure. However, this is where the story's Gothic aesthetic supports it. As E. J. Clery notes, in his introduction to *The Castle of Otranto*, "[t]he effect of the story as a whole depends on vivid, static images, rather than a gradual build-up of suspense."[26] Thus, the use of singular, visual images is useful in portraying a Gothic tale—this is, of course, exactly what a manga is, but more than this, Hata does not actually attempt to portray The Royal Garden—there's no sense of layout, of structure, of place but rather a kind of collage of realistic, Gothic images—hallways, candles, clocks, esoteric symbols carved into floors—that all point to an ineffable reality. In this way, Hata creates a fantasy world, a fairy-land in images, without truly depicting it, so the medium is no bar to it being a fairy-story; I think "The End of the World" is very much one.

What do I mean when I say that "The End of the World" is mythopoeic? Let me first assert two things that are probably true, but that I do not intend. The first is that "The End of the World" is a Campbellian hero-story. It would be easy to demonstrate: Hayate's terrible family life is the call, and he runs from the world, crossing the threshold into the dream-world of The Royal Garden. Then, there is the encounter with the goddess, Athena. His powers are enhanced, and there is the Sacred Marriage (or at least the promise thereof), and then the departure back into the real world with a heavy heart and the strength to survive his forthcoming trials.[27] The second item I don't intend is Athena as the archetype that Haggard touches on in She as C. S. Lewis delineates in "The Mythopoeic Gift of Rider Haggard."[28] Is Athena, the child-goddess—no, the goddess-child, it makes all the difference—another incarnation of that ineffable feminine archetype yet divested of the sensuality of Haggard's Ayesha? Maybe, but that's a matter for another lecture.

When I say "The End of the World" is mythopoeic, I mean something far less technical, at least here: that "The End of the World" touches on one of the fundaments of stories and, thus, achieves a universality beyond its initial scope. And the way it does this is by its framing and place—I have had to, for this whole discussion, sidestep the bitter ending of the work. What gives the story its tremendous power is that Hata takes the Gothic-decked fairy-bride story and uses it to reenact the Fall of Man. This is done through the intervention of Hayate as narrator reflecting upon the experience. At the start of the experience, he describes it as "a dream about the day that I found out the world contains terrible things"—in other words, of innocence lost (Hayate XVII.69.4). Consider the structure: a boy and a girl are in a garden where God dwells—with prohibitions, it is a place where "you have to be careful what you touch" (Hayate XVII.123.4). It is an Edenic place—"it was nothing but joy... ...and every day shone like gold" (*Hayate* XVII.145.2). Recall the summary: when Hayate says, "[i]t's easy for *you* to talk! You don't *have* parents," here the older Hayate's narration states, "when you commit a sin... ...you'll pay for it sooner or later" (*Hayate* XVIII:17.3,5). The result of the sin is exile; Hayate is banished from The Royal Garden, and he cannot return. Though stronger, he is haunted even ten years later by the consequences of his actions. Is this not The Fall of Man?

Tolkien, though, adds one more requirement to mythopoesis: that is eucatastrophe, "the sudden joyous 'turn'" that "denies [...] universal final defeat and in so far is *evangelium*, giving a glimpse of Joy, Joy beyond the walls of the world, poignant as grief."[29] Where is the eucatastrophe in the bitter vision of the Fall in "The End of the World," which is, in Tennyson's words, "deep as first love, and wild with all regret?" Yet there is eucatastrophe in "The End of the World" and it is in the context of the work. "The End of the World" contains numerous, heavy-handed parallels to the opening of *Hayate* as a whole, and the entire matter is triggered by the echoing of Athena's words in Nagi's mouth. Hayate even invokes the same image of sin and retribution at the beginning of the flashback—the reader sees his failed attempt to kidnap Nagi in the background of his comment that "[i]f someone who committed a crime... ...knows he's going to be punished someday, will it still happen when he least expects it?" In short, Hayate is anticipating that history will repeat itself, and the loss of Athena in "The End of the World" will be reenacted with Nagi as the punishment for his crime. However, when he gets up the next morning at the end of the flashback, Hayate's train of thought is interrupted by Nagi who grabs his hand and says, "Today, you're going... ...To play with me all day, right?" The coming retribution for his sin never takes place, and the final image in the story with Hayate is one of play, and the reader is then treated to the image of the grown Athena and her desire to return to The Royal Garden—and above all, the echoed hope that the bitter confrontation was not the end, that Hayate and Athena will, indeed, meet again one day. This is the eucatastrophe of "The End of the World"—at the end of this fairy-tale of the Fall, we are, in Evelyn Underhill's words, given "the great swing back into sunshine which is the reward of that painful descent into the 'cell of self-knowledge.'"[30] Is this not a joy poignant as grief—poignant because of awful grief?

That is my answer to how "The End of the World" managed to touch my heart—it recreates the Fall of Man for the reader and suggests that this fall will recur—and then denies it for joy. And yet a direct expression of this would not have been successful. It is the concatenation of effects—the way the Gothic aesthetic transforms this unusual manga flashback into a fairy-bride tale, and the way, in turn, that Hata's mythopoeic power and the subtle touches and position within the overall narrative transform "The End of the World" from fairy-bride tale to Fall of Man, and then from justice to mercy—and this myth is what gives it the power that might seem out of place in a work entitled *Hayate the Combat Butler*. Yet, let me remind the reader of what C. S. Lewis says about Haggard's work that "the most 'popular' fiction, if only it embodies a real myth, is so very much more serious than what is generally called 'serious' literature. For it deals with the permanent and inevitable."[31]

Bibliography

Bayer-Berenbaum, Linda. *The Gothic Imagination*. Rutherford NJ: Fairleigh Dickinson UP, 1982.

Botting, Fred. *Gothic*. London: Routledge, 1996.

Bradley, F. H. *Appearance and Reality*. 2nd ed. London: Swan Sonnenschein, 1897.

Bloom, Clive. *Gothic Histories*. London: Continuum, 2010.

Campbell, Joseph. *The Hero with a Thousand Faces*. Princeton, NJ: Princeton UP, 2004.

Ellis, Kate Ferguson. *The Contested Castle*. Urbana: University of Illinois, 1989.

Jones, E. Michael. *Horror: A Biography*. Dallas: Spence, 2002.

Hata, Kenjiro. *Hayate the Combat Butler*. Trans. Cindy H. Yamauchi and Yuki Yoshioka. Vol. XVII. San Francisco: Viz Media, 2011.

---. *Hayate the Combat Butler*. Trans. Cindy H. Yamauchi and Yuki Yoshioka. Vol. XVIII. San Francisco: Viz Media, 2011.

Hearns, Lafcadio. *The Romance of the Milky Way and Other Studies & Stories*. New York: Houghton Mifflin, 1905.

Horner, Avril, and Sue Zlosnik. *Gothic and the Comic Turn*. Houndmills, Basingstoke, Hampshire: Palgrave Macmillan, 2005.

Lewis, C. S. *On Stories and Other Essays on Literature*. Ed. Walter Hooper. New York: Harcourt Brace Jovanovich, 1982.

Lüthi, Max. *Once Upon a Time: On the Nature of Fairy Tales*. Trans. Lee Chadeayne and Paul Gottwald. Ed. Francis Lee Utley. Bloomington: Indiana UP, 1976.

Propp, Vladimir. *Morphology of the Folktale*. Trans. Laurence Scott. Ed. Louis Wagner. 2nd ed. Austin: Texas UP, 1968.

Smith, Andrew. *Gothic Radicalism*. New York: St. Martin's, 2000.

Tolkien, J. R. R. "On Fairy-Stories." *Essays Presented to Charles Williams*. Ed. C. S. Lewis. Grand Rapids: Eerdmans, 1966. 38-89.

Underhill, Evelyn. *Mysticism*. New York: Doubleday, 1990.

Walpole, Horace. *The Castle of Otranto: A Gothic Story*. Ed. W. S. Lewis. Oxford: Oxford UP, 2008.

Williams, Anne. *Art of Darkness: A Poetics of Gothic*. Chicago: University of Chicago, 1995.

Notes

1   This is the English title of *Hayate no Gotoku*—the two titles have an independent and seemingly authorial existence as *Hayate no Gotoku* contains an untranslatable pun on the character's name. Both phrases appear in the title of the Japanese version and anime. I follow Hata's habit of referring to the work simply as *Hayate*.

2   Manga is divided into several categories/genres based on its intended audience and the kind of publication. *Hayate* is a *shōnen* manga *i.e.* its primary target audience is younger males (˜ 12-17); however, it frequently satirizes the expectations of the genre.

3　This is not a translation—the title is rendered in English even in the Japanese version. There are a number of possible sources for this, including the cryptic use of this phrase in *Revolutionary Girl Utena* as well as, intriguingly, a short story by G. K. Chesterton. While Hata is strongly influenced by early Twentieth Century literature, particularly Francis Burnett, there's no evidence of him having read Chesterton, to my knowledge. On the other hand, while there are numerous allusions to *Utena* in *Hayate*, this connection is not elucidative at all. In short, I know of no conclusive allusion behind the title beyond the work itself.

4　As a procedural note, the citations from *Hayate* are in the form of volume:page.panel. In cases where there would be no confusion about the text, the panel number has been omitted. The typesetting in the English edition uses a font that does not differentiate between capital letters and employs bold text for emphasis. I have silently inserted capitalization at appropriate junctures and altered the latter to italics throughout. Additionally, the somewhat idiosyncratic use of ellipses as a way to mark speech continuing across multiple "speech bubbles" and panels has been retained throughout.

5　Cf. Propp 19-24

6　This rather ghastly turn of events is toned down for the anime version—as something of an aside, the anime, which is admittedly rather different, never does "The End of the World," to my knowledge.

7　Her last name seems to be some kind of play on the word *Tennō*, emperor, *lit.* "Heavenly Sovereign," which is the title used for the Emperor of Japan.

8　While his personal religious inclination is unknown to me, Hata is clearly better informed on Christianity than many other *mangaka*, which is admittedly faint praise. Nonetheless, this rather cryptic comment is never really explained, and a full exploration of Christian symbolism in *Hayate* is beyond the scope of this lecture. Let me, rather baldly, assert that the use of Western Christian symbols is roughly analogous to the appropriation of Catholic imagery in the classical British Gothic, which will suffice for this lecture.

9　Like first kisses, a childhood marriage promise is taken very seriously in Japanese romantic comedy—in fact, it is the driving element of Ken Akamatsu's classic *Love Hina*.

10　Apparently, the name Athena and the city Athens are identical in Japanese.

11　The reunion of Hayate and Athena has yet to be published in English and as such is beyond the scope of this lecture.

12 A brief word on the eccentricities of manga publishing—most manga, especially *shōnen* and *shōjo*, appear in weekly or monthly compilations which feature over a dozen different titles. After several months, these are repackaged into tankōban—small, separately published works that feature about three months of a single, weekly comic, what would be analogous to "trades" in American comics. These are often, as here, referred to as volumes, although they are generally a little less than 200 pages.

13 These "outtake" or bonus pages feature at the end of volumes or occasionally issues for monthly comics. For serious comics, they often show the characters in lighter moments, but for comedic series, such as *Hayate*, they are generally extravagantly metafictional.

14 Walpole 9.

15 Ibid. 10.

16 Ibid. 11.

17 Ibid 7.

18 Walpole 10.

19 This element is most likely drawn from *Ryūgū-jō* in the classic Japanese folk-tale of Urashimo Tarō—there's a great deal of resemblance between this folktale and "The End of the World" but that is beyond the scope of this lecture.

20 The interested reader should consult Ellis ix-xvi, Williams 99-114 for further information.

21 For my models of the masculine Gothic, I am focusing on *Rime of the Ancient Mariner*, *Manfred*, and the character of Manfred in *Castle of Otranto*. The choice of M. G. Lewis's *The Monk* as the exemplar in Williams and Ellis seems uncharitable, to say the least.

22 The more common Sleeping Beauty tale is a related version, but it distinctly features an enchanted, ordinary girl rather than a supernatural girl; the medieval German tale of Melusine is the only actual fairy-bride tale I can recall.

23 This is the folktale that forms the basis of the Japanese Tanabata festival. For a rather poetic version of the story, Cf. Lafcadio Hearns *The Romance of the Milky Way* 1-49.

24 Cf. Hearns *The Romance of the Milky Way* 141-66.

25 Tolkien 68-70.

26 Clery qtd. in Walpole xv

27 Cf. Campbell 227-33.

28 Lewis 97-100.
29 Tolkien 81.
30 Underhill 233.
31 Lewis 100.

Chapter 16

Dante

Joshua Richards

Eternity is
    Children beautifully at play
    Theirs is the Kingdom

Once upon a time, a little boy
    Found himself alone in a dark night,
    The right road lost
    In fog and frost
    That stifled streets to gloomy circles   5
    And caverned lanes to lairs;
    The streetlights hung like gallowed ghosts,
    Burning in starless air.
    The cars were corpsed by crooked roads;
    The houses stood as tombs,   10
    But were there shadows moving in
    Those cold and empty rooms?
    The shipless oceans soundless as
    They marred the shores of night,
    But what disconsolate chimera   15
    Cried from out of sight?

What was that sound
High above the trees?
Were those footsteps
20　Or just dying leaves?
The night had closed before;
The night had closed behind;
The phantoms of the fog
Were grasping through his mind.
25　　　The way was wide; it was not steep,
　　　　The dangers hidden well.
　　　So walking destitute of day,
　　　　He turned then slipped and fell.
　　　But there, on hands and knees, he heard
30　　　　A low and solemn bell.

I

There was a dead sound
   Upon the final stroke of nine.
   There was a haunt of myrrh,
   As darkness fell across the boy,
   But he forgot the cold   *35*
   That drank his strength away,
   And he forgot the hunger
   That lead his heart astray
   When he saw a pretty, little girl
   Standing over him with grace.   *40*
She wore an antique dress a shade of blood,
And golden ringlets framed her ghostly face,
Cascading downwards in a wanton flood
Over tiny shoulders shrouded in lace.
Her fairy grin was cold, feral, and free.   *45*
Her feet were bare; her eyes wild with light,
The color of the January sea
And gleaming like the dark intent of night.
The damp adorned her shawl with pearled mist.
The lights above were writhing in thin flames   *50*
Along her gown, but did the shadows twist
About her into black shapes without names?
Her eldritch voice, no matter what was said,
Gave him a chill as if he were long dead.
What a stupid boy you have to be   *55*
To lose yourself on this, the darkest night
Of all the year, she said.
       A shock of tears brimmed in his eyes
           At her reprimand.
       She licked her lips and laughed at this,   *60*
           But when he could not stand,
       The little girl sighed then smiled
           And offered him her hand.

II

Like thunder in sunshine,
65 She stood amid the night—
But did the streetlights flicker
With the wind in her hair?
He saw the streetlights flicker,
And her hair dancing—
70 The leaves clinging crimson
On the trees were still,
Still as the mist burning
Beneath the yellowed lights,
Still as the standing water
75 On the blackened cobbles—
Still, still, still, still, still,
There was no wind.
Take my hand, she said to him.
Even this night is not so long
80 That I can dawdle on your whim.
Her hand was small; her hand was cold,
And yet, he rose and walked again,
Inspired by the girl's touch.
Come play with me, she ordered him
85 It's what I want. Not here, but there.
She gestured past the gathered gloom,
Down a deep road, pointing to where
A chapel as a mist rose into spires
At the ever-silent limits of the East.
90 It's what I want. Promise you will.
He did, and she was gone.
    He could not see the chapel either,
        Yet, the path was there.
    It was a dark, ominous tract
95   That tightened like a snare.
    Though he was scared, it was a promise,
        So he went with care.

III

Empire of screech-owls whose silent cries
   Sound the thousands of ghost-roads
   Invisibly rending the fog—   *100*
   The boy shivered; savage tangles
   That must be trees were sifting murk
   Through finger-bones that must be branches.
   A rustle that was not the wind,
   Not here, there was no wind here,   *105*
   That must be roots ripping themselves
   From rotting soil just out of sight,
   So out of sight, were the trees moving?
   Something was moving in the mist,
   Could they move? The rattle through   *110*
   The fog of wood on wood or bone.
   The snap of roots cracking the bones
   That once were cheeks they snaked between.
   He thought the alders were coming closer.
   Were they coming? Were they closer?   *115*
   They were closer—they were coming.
   The town was gone. The road was gone.
   The trees were everywhere around him,
   Branches reaching, damp and dripping,
   Blood in dying light, reaching   *120*
   Closer and closer about the path—
       He ran and ran and ran until
           He crumpled to the ground.
       The little boy was soaked with dew
           As vapors snaked around,   *125*
       Lending an awful form to fears
           That shrieked without a sound.

IV

Through the grand waste of mist and trees,
   The little boy could see a shape—
130   Whether a shade or living man,
   He could not tell but cried for help.
   A voice, weak from a lasting silence,
   Said that he had been commanded
   Here to help him down the bitter
135   Road to where she is. The boy
   Shrunk back, reciting all the forest's
   Terrors in his mind. The man
   Knelt down and said he would not make
   The boy go with him, but the girl
140   Really wanted to play with him.
   Though she would never say it to
   His face, the girl was lonely there.
      Taking the offered hand, the boy
        Was once more on his feet.
145   Though dark before and dark behind,
        There was someone to meet,
      Making the black miles before
        The little boy seem sweet.

V

Thousands of eyeless gazes stared from every hollow,
    Empty sockets glinting bloodied glass and rusted blades, *150*
    Mangled piles of mutilated toys,
    Slews of safety pins splaying sewn mouths to smiles,
    A lipstick rictus painting every frozen face,
    Fishhooks barbed and bent for fingernails,
    Fleshed with each other's stuffing. *155*
    Cobwebs coiled into braids,
    Torsos split and emptied,
    Soulless little bodies torn and bruised,
    Smiling from the puddles—
    So many, so many heaps of broken playthings. *160*
    The little boy was so afraid
    He fixed his gaze ahead until
    He saw a teddy bear beside the path,
    A little thing missing its eyes,
    Perhaps the best sort of present *165*
    For her—but the man knocked his hand away
    And prodded the toy bear with a long stick—
    Hidden in its belly-fluff bristled
    Bright and broken hypodermic needles.
    They left it lying on the grass. *170*

Ahead lay gnarled, lightless regions,
Fields and fields and fields of babies' hands
Reaching from the fetid murk
Porcelain fingers filed down to points
175   Flexing with their automatic pleas
Playplayplay
Bubbling through the mire
Play with me
A rustling Babel
180   *Play with me*
Sown like sacrifices
Play with me
Beneath the savage slough
Playplayplay
185   The man hoisted the little boy
Onto his back to ferry him
Above the immense arc of swamp.
      Cascades of shrieking filled his ears
        From every sunken doll;
190   They stretched their china talons,
        Praying he would fall,
    But still, the boy remained above
        Their clutches and their thrall.

VI

There was a little light
   Amid the gorgon-black,   *195*
   A single, silver taper
   Burning in the back
   Of a lone house inside
   The blankness of the night.
   There was a little light,   *200*
   Above a girl at play,
   Alone in white, upon
   A silent wedding day.
   An eyeless congregation
   Made of smiling toys,   *205*
   A little eyeless groom,
   Sewn for bridal joys,
   All standing in their service,
   Solemn in his sight.
   There was a little light   *210*
   To see her lift the veil
   And kiss the cotton lips,
   Then with a sigh curtail
   The phantom matrimony.

215   Would you stop here and play
        With her instead, he asked.
        It's still such a long way,
        And she looks just as lonely.
        Will you end it here?
220   The boy wondered how—
        How they might play together,
        How she would smile and smile,
        How her damp fingers
        Would feel smoothing his hair...
225   A face lanced through his mind—
        You promised to play with *me*.
        Was that not what you said?—
            He shook his head for onward through
               The spaces of the dark
230   Someone was still expecting him.
               The road ahead was stark
           And growing colder, but he steeled
               His spirits to embark.

VII

Those bones could harm no one
   Not now, not now, not now   *235*
   Or so he told himself—
   Skulls sunk to the brow
   With silt staring from sockets
   Emptied by hand or tide,
   And though their throats were choked   *240*
   With mud, their mouths gaped wide
   With horrid warning under
   Veils of brackish fen
   That spread a sea of slime
   Across the rotting horizon—   *245*
   The man could walk upon
   The water of the world
   And carried him above
   The deeps where decayed fingers
   Curled a winter's welcome.   *250*
   The fog, nothing but fog,
   Was all that could be seen
   Upon that haunted bog.
   St. Elmo's fire simmered
   Like a writhing plume,   *255*
   Serpentine, fairy flickers
   Dancing through the gloom.

   —Then they were gone.
   Slowly, the fog rolled away.
260 There, on the far bank, the little boy
   Could see the little girl sitting by
   An older, taller boy. She laughed and bit
   Her lip; her eyes danced to his face then darted
   Back to what was lying in her hands—
265 A rose her little fingers slowly twirled.
   His breath staggered, and smile splayed to
   Nothing; the man began to sink into
   The mire, and yet he made a promise and
   A promise hauntingly fulfilled was all
270 That he could do—with a despairing sigh,
   The little boy ushered the man forward.
   The vision fled. The fog was deeper now,
   And on the bank, a tree,
275 The tyrant of the slough,
   Wretched, gnarled, palsied
   By its colossal weight,
   Arrayed with votive candles
   Whose flames, colored like slate,
280 Were dancing in death-fires;
   Cascades of wax had stooped
   The oak into a willow;
   The hobbled branches drooped
   To finger the old bones
285 Wreathed by the downward smoke,
   Heaped through long roots that looked
   Like they could clutch and choke.
     His spirits now refreshed, the boy
      Was set upon the shore
290   And now he led the man ahead
      Until they came before
     A tall cast-iron wall with only
      One small wicket-door.

VIII

It was a cosmos filled with crypts,
   A fatal universe of crimsoned fog—   *295*
   A soft, sulfurous rain of sand
   Spending itself against the scattered tombs,
   And all throughout the yawning catacombs
   Burned watch-fires of the deeps.
   Through the blackened air stood steeples   *300*
   Burnished like a bloody sun,
   The church was farther now
   Than when he had begun,
   And all between the shadows fell
   Like ash and human embers, there   *305*
   Between the gargoyles and the pits
   Between wide streets and hillside doors,
   Unangeled graves and mausoleums
   Furnaced from within, but there
   Where the occluding fog was thin,   *310*
   A little light was glinting on
   The monumental capitals
   In the pale courts of empty kings.
   Was this sepulchral tract, was this
   The only road to where she is?   *315*
   A face lanced through his mind. This was
   The only road to where she is.
      Above the wicket-gate, there hung
         A mutilated crest.
      Vera perennanda sola—   *320*
         Reliquum nebula est.
      Heedless, the little boy went through
         With only a breath's rest.

IX

Beyond the gargoyles and the pits,
325   Beyond wide streets and hillside doors,
The citadels like hollow skulls
Sunk in the red, miasmal mist,
Loomed the old church at last but now,
Swollen to a vast cathedral,
330   A stone sermon in cruciform,
Immense, magnificent, terrible,
And every block a monument.
The boy smiled before the door and knocked.
No answer—all was still,
335   Cloisters, chapels, undercrofts.
Is anybody there, he asked
And knocked the door again.
No answer—all was still,
Steeples, buttresses, and bells.
340   Half in tears, the boy looked to the man
Who said nothing, his face impassive.
I came, but no one answered—I kept my word!
The man said nothing, face impassive.
Turning to the door again, he read
345   A phrase knife-etched into the wood:
Si bene calculum ponas,
Ubique naufragium est.
Is anybody there, he asked
And knocked again; then, with a snarl, he pushed
350   And the black gate opened,
        But when he entered, it was empty.
           No one greeted him.
        Only the wind sentineled by
           The marble seraphim,
355   And all throughout, black candles burned
           Invisible and dim.

X

There, in the throat of the night
    Where the pale flames like parched tongues,
There, beyond the pews
    Shattered in ancient desecration,   *360*
There, upon the altar lay
A corpse,
The body of a knight.
What must have been his daunted blood
Guttered in darkness down the altar's sides.   *365*
The boy recoiled and turned,
But he was gone—the man was gone.
The little boy was all alone,
Alone in the black church.
And then, the wind.   *370*
The flames quivered and bowed
Towards the altar.
Were the haggard features of his guide
Impressed upon the corpse?
Three swords caked with blood or rust   *375*
Driven through palms and feet,
St. Elmo's fire dancing on the hilts.
There, above the heart,
An ashen veil on the knight's chest.
The wind began to howl.   *380*
Was the veil the way?—
It's mine. I want it.
For me, get it for me—
Surely, it was the way.

385   He took a step,
        What must have been a hidden hand
        Suddenly snuffed a candle on his right.
        Put out the light
        Was there a voice upon the wind?

390   Another step—
        Put out the light
        Another flame was gone,
        But myrrh lingered in darkened air.
        Again,

395   Put out the light
        Again,
        Put out the light
        Again,
        Put out the light

400   *Put out the light*
        Put out the light
        The candles' ghosts enwreathed the altar
        Cloying all the timeless black within
        The still and silent chapel,

405   Yet, it was not silent.
        Was it the wind that gibbered curses?
        tagaropsoniateshamartiasthanatos
        The little boy covered his ears and screamed
        But could not hear himself.

410   *eitisecheiotaakoueinakoueto*

It would not stop. It would not stop.
tomedunonpoteposantislathoi
Groping for the veil,
Seizing a blade instead,
hothenoudheprotechorishaimatosegkekainistai   415
He cried—*haima*
Blood dripping from his palm
haimahaimahaima
Closing his eyes against the dark
haimahaimahaimahaimahaima   420
　　　His bloodied fingers felt the cloth
　　　　　Upon the corpse's chest.
　　　A voice hoarse from a lasting silence
　　　　　Whispered to arrest
　　　His hand as a breath passed with horrid   425
　　　　　Warning to suggest—

XI

All was light.
   His sight seasoned in night
   So long was quenched in a moment.
430   There was a haunt of myrrh,
   And far above, a bell
   Rang in the third watch.
   Slowly, slowly, the hours sounded
   Slower than the boy had ever heard them sound before.
435   Opening his stricken eyes, he saw her face
   Smiling slightly, sadly through a veil
   Of his own blood staining the once white lace.
   His wounded hand was bandaged with a pale
   Lady's kerchief scented with myrrh and wine.
440   The girl wore an old, white satin dress
   With matching stockings and no shoes, but fine
   Clothing could not belie the golden mess
   Of curls beneath the crown of hellebore
   That held her veil—she seemed a tiny bride
445   To him. Though everything the girl wore
   Had frayed, she dolled herself with scorn and pride.
   You promised that you would, and you still came.
   Thank you, and then the girl pronounced his name.
   The boy smiled at her,

And then she slapped him hard across the face. *450*
How dare you make a lady wait,
And come in here all wet and filthy,
Look at you, and, and you're hurt.
How can we play if you're like this?
You're just so selfish, aren't you, boy? *455*
Making me wait and wait and worry
That you wouldn't come—it was so long...
 A shock of tears brimmed in his eyes
  And prickled down his cheeks
 Even as laughter teemed within *460*
  At her boundless critiques.
 His sheepish grin twitching with pride
  Provoked her into shrieks.

XII

It was a holy thing,
465   A chalice hewn from stone
And taller than the girl,
The base a shade of bone,
The stem was like bruised flesh,
All cracked and fire-flaked,
470   The bowl was like blood fresh
From severed veins, and all
Across the water, light
Like flames on oil writhed
In green and blue and white.
475   Around the rim was scrawled
In dark incarnadine
ΝΙΨΟΝΑΝΟΜΗΜΑΤΑ
ΜΗΜΟΝΑΝΟΨΙΝ·
Her hand was pulling him
480   Towards the crimsoned font,
Bruising his wrist with little
Fingers tight with want.
What are you, stupid? Come!
His feeble hindrance drew
485   Her nails and nearly blood.
Stop it! What's wrong with you?

And she recoiled, red
As the dark stain upon
Her veil. The girl looked
Askance—her features drawn   490
With sibylline umbrage.
I brought you here to play
With me, why won't you just
Play right? Do what I say!
He silently relented,   495
And she released his wrist.
Take off those filthy clothes,
She said and don't resist.
Off, off, she said and laughed—
And then produced a brittle   500
Bough of mistletoe.
On her tip-toes, the little
Girl immersed it in
The font, and once it steeped,
She aspersed him, saying   505
In silence sown and reaped.
　　His body quaked as frigid hands
　　　　Began to wash him clean,
　　And as she dressed the boy in ancient
　　　　Robes of white and green,   510
　　He gazed around the dim cathedral,
　　　　The girl's shadowed demesne.

339

XIII

The Word made bones instead of flesh—
It must have been so dark outside,
515   He thought, because the vast cathedral
Seemed devoid of any light,
Though far above were glimmers. Through
A southern window, Naos sailed
Beyond the night's horizon to
520   The ever-hidden pilot-star,
But in the north, the weaving princess
Rose before her spectral loom,
Still with half a year of waiting
For the ebb in Heaven's tide.
525   Above the altar screen, the erring
Lord of war rested between
The lion's paws and virgin's breasts;
Over a western lintel, Jove
Had spread his throne upon the shore
530   Of Aries and the northern cord.
Beneath an ancient, tattered arras,
Candles feebly flinging shadows
Against the spectral umbrage stood,
Like broken columns, six feet high,
535   Bleeding pools of wax, like blood
In dying light, but there was dust,
As if of ages, over all.
The candles burned, and yet the wicks
Were not consumed—who kept them lit?

The church's sole parishioners,   540
The sculptured dead, were all in white,
But they had mutilated faces—
It looked as if someone had tried
To savage out the eyes of eyeless statues,
And there, beneath his feet, a sea   545
Of graves—every flagstone and
They were so young, all of them,
No one even lived till nine.
Only children were buried here.
He must have started breathing fast   550
Because the little girl threw
Her arms around his throat.
Shhh... shhh... dry bones can harm
No one, she said, then laughed.
    They lingered for a moment till   555
        She squeezed his hand and fled,
    Loosing a minxish grin beneath
        Her bloodied veil, which said
    That he should chase—her feet soundless
        As she scampered ahead.   560

XIV

The cathedral was filled with the laughter of children,
    Ringing the hollow cloisters,
    Running beneath the stained-glass saints
    Aching in their restraints,
565   Footfalls echoing through chapels
    Steeped in centuries of silence.
    Catching his breath, the little boy stopped
    Again, again, she giggled,
    Chase me, chase me, he heard her say,
570   And laughing himself, he did.
    Past the confessionals marred with the words
    θεῶν ἰότητι μόγησαν
    Past countless doors to endless halls,
    Cobweb-clotted walls,
575   Memorials buried in a black past,
    Pageants of decay,
    And through them all ringing laughter
    Sounding the emptiness.
    Catching his breath, the little boy stopped
580   Again, again, she said,
    Chase me, chase me, he heard her say,
    And laughing himself, he did.

Gliding like phantoms, the children ran
Past chapel aisles heaped
With shattered golden censers and severed   *585*
Coils of silver chain,
And ravaged curtains faintly billowing
Or was it shadows flitting across
The spidered gossamer
Through cloisters where cold candles flickered   *590*
Like summer fireflies
Lost in coffined winter
Catching his breath, the little boy stopped
Again again she insisted
Chase me chase me she said again   *595*
And he began to run,
    But past the rotten pulpit-fall
        And ashes of the psalter,
    His haggard breaths guttered in white;
        His steps began to falter,   *600*
    And soon, the little boy slipped
        And fell before the altar.

XV

Look, look, flowers, look there, look there.
    There are flowers where
605   The swords, the corpse, the candles heralded the night,
    And all around the altar lay
    Armfuls of Easter lilies,
    A floral pyre of white.
    Yet for a cloth the altar had a little cerement,
610   And above was blooming an array
    Of lilacs in a silver chalice of wine
    The only other ornament
    Upon the vernal shrine
    Was a broken spear.
615   Get up, get up, why are you stopping here?
    Can't you see
    I'm tired? he said.
    So... so you don't want to play with me?
    Shaking his head,
620   That's not it at all,
    That isn't what I said.
    It's what you meant!
    Even through the crimsoned pall
    Of her white veil,
625   Her ghostly face grew pale;
    Her eyes began to frost with insolent
    Fury before the slow descent
    Of tears in silver strands
    Across quivering cheeks.
630   Don't cry, don't cry, he said with fluttering hands
    I really want to play.
    Smearing the streaks
    Across her face with tiny fists,
    She sniffed then seized his wrists.

With me, the girl implored, with me?   *635*
Well, yes, of course, with you, the boy replied.
Crossing her arms, she turned aside,
Well, are you blind? Can't you see
You've hurt my feelings? Make it up to me!
Go on, I'm waiting.   *640*
Seizing some lilacs from the altar-piece,
He thrust them forward—
And how like blood and water
Wine is dripping from the stems—
See, see, black streams across the firmament.   *645*
The girl paled in stupid shock,
Disarmed of every guile.
Her lips, curled to mock,
Just quivered to a simple, joyful smile.

650 Snatching the flowers from his hands,
The girl straightened her white dress and lifted
Her veil, tucking any errant golden strands
Behind her ears; the little boy shifted
Uneasily at this display.
655 With her eyes closed and her lips pursed, she leaned
Forward and waited—sometime today,
The little girl growled.
Ummm... I don't think I know this game,
So she whispered to him, her face aflame
660 Oh, he said, *Oh*! As the girl scowled.
And with tremulous hands over her waist,
The boy suddenly froze.
So it's... really okay?
She glowered to insist,
665 And when their noses bumped,
The children laughed, and then, they kissed.
   The little couple cast a single
     Shadow upon the light.
   The glassy image of the Lord
670   Observed from out of sight,
   And rusted bells now rang in solemn
     Tolls through the cold night.

XVI

A crown of vows and woven Easter lilies,
   Green shadows upon his curls twined
   By tiny fingers—lilies, as she was   675
Too small to reach the lilacs on the altar.
Come on, come on, she said, with arms spread wide,
We kissed before an altar
Now we have to dance.
—Who makes these rules?   680
And when the girl looked askance,
He sighed and half agreed
But wavered as she took her stance.
I... I don't know how.
Insistent hands on his,   685
Pressing fingers to her waist
Like this, like this, no, no, no! ...Keep them there.
With what taut softness underneath his palms
And all the lilac as she laced
Her arms behind his neck,   690
Unwilling to release her flowers.

Resting her head upon his shoulder sadly,
The girl gazed away, as if she prayed,
And so they gently swayed
695 With timeless steps,
Small toes gravely tracing
Over the names inlaid
In the cold slate.
Then she began to sing faintly
700 In that high voice, like frozen chimes,
The war three kings intae the East,
Frae heichest Camelot,
An' they hae sworn an aith to seek
The Lady o' Shalott—
705   Yet as she sang, the arms around
        His throat slowly drew taut.
    Three gaed to fell the witchlin bann'd
        The Lady o' Shalott,
    But anely twa retour to quate,
710   Unco-like Camelot.

XVII

The lady chapel, now a lady's chamber
    Filled with an immense canopy bed,
    Heaped with all the toys a little girl
    Could ever want: stuffed bears and dolls but all
    Without their button-eyes and thick with dust,   *715*
    As if of ages—so many, so many forgotten playthings.
I'm not tired yet—I'm *not*!
The little girl said,
Arms crossed and bolt upright in bed.
Well, I am—we can play some more tomorrow,   *720*
If... if that's alright with you...
Leaning over, the girl kissed his cheek.
Tomorrow and tomorrow and tomorrow
You and I will be together forever...
The little boy simply, joyfully smiled.   *725*
Goodnight... *princess*. Goodnight, you silly boy.
Goodnight steeples.
Goodnight gargoyles.
Goodnight bells, tolling the hours.
Goodnight altar. Goodnight flowers.   *730*
Goodnight statues.
Goodnight saints.
Goodnight candles gasping in the deep.
Goodnight children buried in quilted sleep.
Goodnight. Goodnight. Goodnight.
    As the fourth watch was rung above,   *735*
        They slept in the dead nave,
    The boy holding the girl, she
        The flowers that he gave.
    Each of his breaths faintly shivered
        To fog grave after grave.   *740*

XVIII

Did a rooster crow
  Far into the distance?
Did the angels glow
  In glass renewed with light?
745 No—all was night,
  Frigid, dark, and deep.
The little girl lay in dreamless,
  Uninvaded sleep,
Yet the little boy arose
750 And sought to rouse his drowsing friend.
But then he stopped—girls love the sunrise.
  He would carry her
  Down the way to the East Sands—
It would be a great surprise.
755 They could watch the dawn
  Beside the realmless ruins
Before they went to play.
  Donning the lily-crown
  And hoisting her onto his back
760 He carried the girl, still clutching her lilacs
  Into the empty chapel's black,
Down the wide stairs
  Beneath the marmoreal pairs
  Of blinded seraphim.
765 One by one, the dead bolts slide,
  And then the great doors groan aside—
      To a warm breath upon his face,
        Wind that had lost its sting.
      The ground was white but now with flowers
770   Fully blossoming,
      And all about the cold cathedral
        Was long-wintered Spring.

XIX

In the east, the stars who heralded the newborn Sun,
   Waiting to begin his year within the Ram,
   Were quired as they had been when the Divine Love   *775*
First counted off the Heavens' fairest things.
Bright Mars was fleeing with the Lion to the west,
while gray-haired Saturn rested with the Maiden,
but even now, through the deep dusk, a little light
Was glinting on the peak of St Salvator's.   *780*
The slow, ineffable ascent to fulgent May
Had dawned all the grayed oaks with greening leaves
—Yet the boy saw undelighted those delights.
What happened? I... I just don't understand.
It wasn't even Christmas, how can it be Spring?   *785*
And yet, the childhood of the year was soon
To fade, the flush of early flowers to green gowns
Of summer grass. Wake up, wake up, he said,
Something magical has happened while we slept.
Come on, come on, who knows what we could miss,   *790*
And as the little girl was rubbing her hushed eyes,
Lightly, the boy gave a good-morning kiss.
She giggled, blushed, then sticking out her tongue, she said,
I would have had to hit you, if you hadn't
Done that soon... it was just what I wanted—   *795*
But then she saw the heavens' ashen edge
Kindling rosy shadows over the dim sea
And the slow crimson creep across the waves,
Then far away, they heard the rooster crow again.
    Her features paled at the announced   *800*
        Arrival of the sun.
      The girl glanced to the old church
        And turned as if to run,
    Whispering No—you stupid boy,
        What- What have you *done*?   *805*

XX

Shadows stretched into the west
  In long fingers of night
  Across the tumbled graves like burning
  Blood in rising light.
810 Fury and tears brimmed in her eyes,
  Twisted and upset,
  How could you do this? Stupid! Stupid,
  Ever since we met!
  The boy just stood in stupid shock
815 And then began to wring
  His little hands. What did I do to
  Deserve this?—Everything!
  —Like in a story... I wanted it
  To be—be a surprise.
820 I wanted us to be together
  Watching the sunrise
  You see, I just... Well, I don't,
  Don't want that—not at bit!
  I thought that girls loved the sunrise.
825 No, you little twit!
  Come on, we need to play inside,
  She said and seized his wrist,
  The girl pulled him to the door
  And then began to twist—

Stop it, he said and tore away.   *830*
Why can't we play outside?
Look, it's so warm out here, like Spring;
Why would we stay inside?
Because... because it's what I want.
Come on, we can't delay   *835*
I called you here to play with me,
So just do what I say!
No. Why do we always do
What *you* want? Can't I pick
For once? We'll play inside later   *840*
After we—No!
No. No. No. No!
The girl brandished the flowers
In her hand—then stopped and slowly turned
Away, and with her back to him, she whispered   *845*
I... don't want to play with you, not anymore...
Hot tears dewing the lilacs clasped against her heart.
     Then, nearby, a rooster crowed;
         The night, at last, was gone.
     Yet as the boy began to speak,   *850*
         He was left looking on—
     The girl and the church dissolved
         With the first light of dawn.

XXI

The peals of owls instead of bells sounded the hours.
855   There was green grass
Amid the broken walls, the crumbled roof and towers,
Windows emptied of stained glass.
The weight of ages stooped the wreck—
A couple walls of wild stone,
860   A haggard eastern gable,
And now a little boy alone
With arms outstretched,
Echoing an embrace.
No... no... no...
865   I- I'm sorry...
Please, please come back,
I'm so, *so* sorry!
The ruined shells of hollow cloisters
Echoed his late-repenting cries—
870   *...I'm sorry...*
Only the wind whispered among
Steeples and broken stone.
Only the gulls were singing; all
The choirs were overgrown.
875   But- But I said I'm sorry!
Nothing replied from cruciform remains
Blighted by seven hundred years of wear and waste.

Then looking down, he saw
His old and ragged clothes
Instead of the green robe.   *880*
Was it... was it just a dream?
Did I imagine all of it...
Did I imagine *her*?
Then with his wounded hand,
He felt lilies unwithered on his curls—   *885*
The scar and crown remained.
The boy sat down and wept, wild with all regret.
But then he heard the noise of life
And the distant growl of cars—
The fog had lifted, Spring had come,   *890*
A damp gust stirred in rubbled fields,
And as he slowly walked the aisles
They had run—the graves covered
With flowers—the little boy looked up and saw
    Where the warm sky was once obscured   *895*
      By stone and iron bars
   And where the smoke from censers and
      From candles made dark scars,
   The rosy ceiling of the church
      Was filled with fading stars.   *900*

Part V
Fairy Tale Pedagogy

Chapter 17

Footsteps in the Classroom: "The Little Mermaid" and First-Year Writing

Katharine Wolford

Shock and anger are the predominant responses when students discover the "truths" about "The Little Mermaid." The little mermaid who is not named "Ariel." The little mermaid who does not get married at the end of the story. The little mermaid who is, when the story is nearly done, a suicide for love. Disney's 1989 movie based on Andersen's fairy tale, while charming, is remarkably different from the story. Eventually, most students like both the story and the movie a great deal, after the shock subsides. Then my students discover that the "real" little mermaid, as written by Hans Christian Andersen, is all too real as a person—mermaid status notwithstanding. She is headstrong, clueless about how romantic love works, and filled with a touching yearning. She is very human. Human enough for my students to identify with her. They shake their heads over her, they think she is a fool for love, and they empathize with her. What they tend not to do is forget her—the "real" little mermaid. Of all the Andersen heroines my students have studied over the last six years, the mermaid is the one who raises the most passion and compassion. Hers is the story I still use most semesters, because the tale demands an emotional and critical response. It gives students something to write about.

Writing is what my students do, and it is what I teach. I have taught many first-year writing classes with both a little and a lot of focus on writing about fairy tales, but the work and art of writing is always the main point of each course. One of the toughest tasks a writing teacher faces is helping students discover something to write about, and that something needs to take each student beyond the first person. Andersen's stories, especially "The Little Mermaid," are effective as classroom texts because they are full of description, they return students to the original, often shocking versions of beloved fairy tales, and most importantly, they give students a chance to write about a universal experience: suffering.

Biography and Caveats

Then there is Hans Christian Andersen himself. His story, as Maria Tatar has noted, is of an "upwardly mobile" writer.[1] Like many of my students, Andersen came from a working-class background. He was a first-generation educated professional who faced years of painful obstacles to success, and, like the little mermaid, never truly fit in the world he had so ardently desired. To understand why Andersen's heroines appeal so strongly to my students, it is useful to examine his life and struggles.

I always begin reviewing Andersen's biography with a strongly-worded caveat: Be very careful about using a writer's life in interpreting his or her work. Every story he wrote has bits and pieces of Andersen in it, because all writing contains elements of any author's self. Yet all reading is also an act of interpretation, because each reader brings his or her self to a text. Communication always involves bending, folding, twisting, and mutilating on both ends. How can biography overcome that? Biography is just another opportunity to renew the process of interpretation for both writer and reader. No text or interpretation, then, is "reliable" in the sense readers often want to believe it is.

Fortunately for students inclined to use biography when analyzing his work, Andersen himself is on record as identifying with the suffering of many of his characters, most notably the little mermaid. As Terri Windling, founder of the Endicott Studio, wrote, "He would draw upon this experience [personal rejection] years later when creating tales such as *The Little Mermaid,* in which the heroine submits to loss and pain in order to cross into another world— only to find she'll never be fully accepted, loved, or understood."[2] A writer willing to go on record as identifying with a specific character is inviting the reader to interpret the writer's life and stories both together and through one another.

Andersen was also a very public figure throughout his life. He may have felt out of place in the rarified social and literary circles he came to inhabit, but he was ambitious and knew his achievements were far from ordinary. Andersen saw himself as an outsider in some ways, but he knew his own worth as well. His sense of self both as achiever and as outcast can be found in the mermaid's intense sense of determination as well as her genuine inability to recognize that she had set her sights on the wrong candidate for love: the human prince.

In publically connecting himself to the suffering of characters like the little mermaid, Andersen helped illuminate his life and his writing. And while over-focusing on his life to understand his work has its hazards, Andersen provides students with useful points of entry to do so—with caveats in place. To my everlasting delight, Andersen's stories, especially, "The Little Mermaid," help writing students move beyond themselves.

Son of a Cobbler

Most Andersen fans know he began life in Odense, Denmark, as the son of a cobbler. His footsore heroines, like the little mermaid, and the nasty (but hideously punished) Inger in "The Girl Who Trod on the Loaf," probably do reflect his keen understanding that aching feet are one of the human body's meanest tortures. In the classroom, students delight in tracing the larger outlines of Andersen's biography and "the son of a shoemaker" theme is irresistible. The tragic loss of his father when Anderson was only eleven-years-old makes him even more sympathetic to them; the possibly apocryphal story that Andersen was depantsed by cigarette-factory coworkers bent on determining his gender is deeply compelling to classes filled with post-Freudian youth.[3] Their reactions are something like this:

"Poor dude!" they exclaim.

"That's awful!" they cry.

"You don't get over that!" they observe.

The fact that Andersen tended to fall in love with both men and women he could not have, as well as the tricky social class barriers in place during Andersen's lifetime, usually leads students in my classes to feel profoundly sympathetic toward him.[4] The depantsing is seen as barbaric hazing and the lack of love as tragic. Whether he preferred men or women tends not to concern students. The lack of genuine romantic love does, because Andersen himself so clearly believed that true love exists—like the little mermaid.

As people living in the United States today, the social barriers of Denmark in the 1800s shock them. Students do not come to school unaware of social history, nor do most of them seem to believe the popular fiction that the US is a classless society. What does often stir their sympathy is that the origins of a self-made, talented writer could matter once he or she has become successful. The idea of a man rising from poor circumstances to achieve greatly appeals to them whether they're native-born Americans or not. Even students from comfortably middle-class circumstances buy into the idea that a person's origins should not matter. In fact, overall, students seem to like Andersen *more* as a person and a writer because of how humble his life was at the beginning. Many of my students like the notion of the great achiever. True, they are mostly Hoosiers, and self-promotion is not an accepted Hoosier attitude, but the Danish concept of "don't think you are too special or at all unique" or *jantelov*, a term I have not specifically used in class, seems cruel when applied to a man who was, manifestly, special.[5]

The idea that men and women should not think too well of themselves and should not rock the boat is at odds with who the little mermaid essentially is and how Andersen lived his life. Both burst through the restraints of their childhood worlds. The little mermaid was born into a life of privilege and beauty, which Andersen enthusiastically describes. In setting the mermaid ball scene, Andersen writes, "In the great ballroom, walls and ceiling were made of thick but quite clear glass. ... [E]normous shells, rose-red and grass-green, were ranged on either side, each with a blue-burning flame which lit up the whole room and [...] lit up the sea outside as well."[6] Yet the mermaid's world is clearly, in Andersen's eyes, an inferior one, for all its pleasures. A dedicated Christian, but not harshly committed to dogma, Andersen often inserted his religious beliefs into his stories, and the mermaid's is no different. He adds a quest for a human soul to her tale as her journey progresses. As she ascends to the human world, the mermaid moves toward (but stops short of) Christian heaven. She casts aside her family and her world in a quest for human romantic love. Love that might, after a marriage ceremony that Andersen suggests could confer a soul upon her, lead her to salvation after death. Andersen left behind his lower-class life and the superstitions of the working class that initially fired his imagination for the greater riches to be found in success as a writer. Both he and the mermaid rise above the crowd, defying social expectations that suggested they stay in the places society assumed they would inhabit for life.

Suffering for Love

Students recognize Andersen and the mermaid as class travelers who suffered for their ambitions. The Christian themes that show up in "The Little Mermaid", "The Red Shoes", and numerous other Andersen stories may or may not resonate with them personally. Christianity is the predominate faith of most of my students, I suspect, but I do not poll them and individual spiritual testimony is not part of classroom discussion. What might surprise people who do not live in Northern Indiana is the rapidly increasing minority of students who practice no faith or are Muslim or Buddhist or Jewish – amongst others. Yet no matter what a student's faith or lack of faith, they know that everyone suffers. Assignments involving Andersen's stories give practicing Christian students a chance to write about faith in a nonproselytizing manner and allow students of other faiths or no faith to discuss human anguish free of the trappings of Christian teaching. Yes, Andersen wrote as a Christian, and yes, the little mermaid seeks a traditionally Christian form of spiritual salvation, but some students take the story beyond a dominant faith's traditions, and find a universal message in passages like the following, in which Andersen describes how the mermaid's feet and self feel pain. "Never had she danced so brilliantly. It was as if sharp knives were wounding her delicate feet, but she never felt it; more painful was the wound in her heart."[7] Overblown? Perhaps. But love is usually intensely painful in some way. And the physical body, even for the mostly young and fit inhabitants of my classes, is a vessel of misery from time to time.

The trials of the mermaid and Andersen are compounded by a sense of being an outsider, a feeling both share. Andersen seems to understand, in writing the character of the little mermaid, that those not born to a certain social station have trouble comprehending the codes of its inhabitants, and even if they do, do not respond to them in ways that help the outsider's fate. For example, the prince who is the object of the mermaid's passions allows her to sleep "on a velvet cushion outside his door."[8] This passage never fails to arouse discussion in the class. Students readily comprehend that Andersen must have known that his heroine will look like a dog to readers. It seems unlikely that someone as in love with description as Andersen could have used a passage like that unwittingly. Yet the mermaid persists in her quest, when a human-born girl who voluntarily sought a place in the prince's heart and life would probably have recognized that she had no chance with a prince who sees her as a cushion-sleeper, velvet comfort notwithstanding.

Realizing that Andersen identified with the mermaid, that his descriptive powers were in full force in her story, and that he felt like an outsider much of his life, no matter how celebrated he became, often leads classroom discussion back to his love life (or lack of it). Almost as often, I find myself talking about the sometimes awkward and painful relationship Andersen had with the Collin family. In my brief outlines of his connections to the Collins, I always warn classes, once again, that readers should not overanalyze Andersen's work in light of his life. Yet the fact that the Collin family helped Andersen while keeping him at arm's length might explain why he mined biography when describing emotional pain.[9] Never belonging fully to any group can be excruciating, and very few people make it as far as college without feeling like an outcast in some way. The intense emotional separation Andersen felt from the Collin family is explained by Windling, who writes that while the family was generous and kind to him, "Andersen was never allowed to forget that he was not entirely one of them, for he was not a member of their class."[10]

Worse, Edvard Collin, who may have been the person who Andersen loved most in his life, always kept the writer from Odense at a distance. Like the rest of his family, Edvard was an educated, upper-class Copenhagen native, and he appears to have been kind to Andersen, while keeping the writer away from any profound emotional intimacy. Edvard Collin never, for example, preferred "Du," rather than the more relaxed and intimate pronoun choice of "De," when addressing Andersen.[11] The passionate, ambitious Andersen keenly felt the rejection. When reading that the little mermaid refuses to kill the prince in order to regain her life under the sea and, instead, kisses both him and his bride before allowing herself to die with the rise of the sun, it is easy to suppose that Andersen was voicing his own sense of loneliness and self sacrifice. After all, he lived, unwillingly, at the edges of Collin family life, for several generations. Like the mermaid, ultimately, despite his ambition and his gifts, he never fully made it into the charmed circle.

Students understand that. They too are travelers, outsiders even. No matter what their socioeconomic circumstances, they are in transition themselves, because they are at a university. By attempting a degree, they are risking failure, perhaps failure at a profession they may wish to join or failure to obtain the diploma that entitles them to be a member of the educated class. And who knows? Even if they, like Andersen, attain their career goals or even become famous, they may not find a sense of belonging any more than he did. Like the mermaid, they are swimming toward a vision upon the shores, but what will it mean, when, and if, they get there? The same could be said of any reader of Andersen's works, university student or not, but it is the gambling nature of the undergraduate experience that may, in part, make Andersen's studies in suffering so easy for them to relate to, for Andersen's personal ambition involved risk as well. With higher education marketed (oversold?) as a chance to leap up the ladder of success in the US, reading the life and works of a man who dared and won in career and dared and lost in love makes for heady writing material.

In the Details

Not all class work with Andersen involves serious topics like love and faith and failure. A great deal of the writer's appeal is that he lends himself to gossipy discussions about the beauty of the mermaid's palace, the dreadfulness of the sea witch, and whether or not the mermaid officially qualifies as a stalker. Usually, the consensus is that the mer-people are mighty lucky to live where and as they do, the sea witch is perpetually cool in an evil way, and the mermaid is a stalker who would be subject to a restraining order should she live in the Midwest.

Why bother with such a discussion? After all, education is supposed to elevate the mind. Should students dwell on the disturbing grossness of the sea witch's home? Yes, because Andersen shows his best descriptive powers when he writes about the witch. He writes: "She called the horrible fat water-snakes her little chicks and allowed them to sprawl about [on] her great spongy bosom."[12] In one sentence, he paints an unforgettable image of a gross, terrifying woman who cloyingly sentimentalizes nasty creatures. His stories of physical torture and disgust translate well after nearly two hundred years because he understood that horror fascinates us. Students who think people have moved beyond such dubious amusements need only be reminded that slasher entertainment is alive and well. More importantly, Andersen provides me, as instructor, with an opportunity to teach students that details and description matter, as do examples. When students write about

Andersen's stories, I encourage them to emulate his eye for explanation and detail. One of the toughest hurdles student writers face is fully explaining to the reader what they actually mean. Andersen shows them how.

The fact that Andersen describes the beauty of the mermaid's first life in glorious detail provides me with the opportunity to show students how much like us people of the nineteenth century actually were. Current-day people delight in reading about the scandal, homes, jewels, clothes, and transportation of the wealthy just much as their nineteenth century counterparts. Andersen shows a deep understanding of how people crave this information. For instance, he writes with zeal about how the little mermaid suffers a painful beauty treatment when her grandmother has eight oysters snap onto the mermaid's tail. What's more, the reports of her early good fortune not only entertain us, they draw us deeper into caring about the princess. Like some sort of underwater movie star, the mermaid's fabulous and strange lifestyle bewitches us. Imagine the headline: "Mermaid Undergoes Gruesome Oyster Procedure!" We want to know more and are gratified to learn about the mermaid's lovely voice and her nearly-as-gorgeous sisters. Drawing readers in is the responsibility of every writer, and student writers are just as obligated to entice and entertain the reader as anyone else. Andersen shows them how.

On the face of it, dwelling on the mermaid's extreme fascination (to put it mildly) with the prince seems a bit unkind, and not entirely important to a story rife with issues about social class and religion. After all, Andersen very much reflects the unloveliest aspects of his times in his stories—gender, parental authority, race, and so on—and the level of torture his protagonists endure is stunning. The little mermaid is right at the top of the misery index of Andersen heroines. Yet students seek to identify with the mermaid as a person, and a person who is unbalanced by love is one who can be examined easily by each reader. That does not mean they believe the mermaid's willingness to hide in the shadows and stare at the prince is anything less than stalking. Some, as has been said, see her as possibly criminal in that regard. They are not even sure what the mermaid feels is true love until the end of the tale, and neither am I. Obsessive pursuit of a goal does not love make. Yet the urge to love someone romantically is near-universal and even if the mermaid and Andersen yearned foolishly, they did feel, and who cannot identify with that?

The actual process of writing is spurred on by the opportunities Andersen's stories offer to analyze human joys and trials in the simple structure of the fairy tale. Even literary fairy tales have easy-to-comprehend narratives. When it comes to actually producing several short papers in a semester, the idea that fairy tales are for children and are therefore "easy" subjects of analysis, gives students confidence. Most students actually use the sense of being in charge, as a reader, to dive into complex ideas about romantic love, parental expectations, religion, and suffering. Because characters like the little mermaid seem childishly unthreatening, students feel safe moving beyond "I" stories and personal experience when writing about the texts. They feel up to writing about a nameless little fish-girl with some sense of authority. First-year students are tentative writers. They seldom think they have any real "right" to analyze or interpret a text, but if they begin with a fairy tale, they can move on to reading complex analyses about fairy tales, and, in turn, use both kinds of sources to produce solid writing that goes beyond just their own, individual experiences.

Love, stalking, horror, lifestyles of the rich and royal, sacrifice, pain, and shock all come together in reading about Andersen's life and work. In the classroom, both become real and useful to inexperienced writers who need to examine the personal in both biography and fictional characters in order to find out what they want to say. The self Andersen provides allows writers to move beyond themselves as essayists. In doing so, they learn how to appeal to readers. Footsore heroines like the little mermaid show them the way.

Bibliography

Hanford, Juliana. "Hans Christian Andersen." *Literary Traveler.* June 1, 2002. http://www.literarytraveler.com/articles_search.aspx?term=Hans+Christian-+Andersen.

de Milius, Johan. "Hans Christian Andersen: A Short Biographical Introduction." Hans Christian Andersen Center. Dec. 5, 2011. http://www.andersen.sdu.dk/liv/mini-bio/index_e.html.

Tatar, Maria. "Introduction: Hans Christian Andersen." In *The Classic Fairy Tales*, edited by Maria Tatar. New York: Norton: 1999.

Windling, Terri. "Hans Christian Andersen: Father of the Modern Fairy Tale." *Endicott Studio Journal of Mythic Arts*. Summer 2003. http://www.endicott-studio.com/jMA03Summer/hans.html.

Notes

1 Maria Tatar, "Introduction: Hans Christian Andersen," in *The Classic Fairy Tales*, ed. Maria Tatar (New York: Norton: 1999), 216.

2 Terri Windling, "Hans Christian Andersen: Father of the Modern Fairy Tale," *Endicott Studio Journal of Mythic Arts* (Summer 2003). http://www.endicott-studio.com/jMA03Summer/hans.html.

3 Juliana Hanford, "Hans Christian Andersen," *Literary Traveler*, June 1, 2002, http://www.literarytraveler.com/articles_search.aspx?term=Hans+Christian+Andersen.

4 Johan de Milius, "Hans Christian Andersen: A Short Biographical Intro-duction," Hans Christian Andersen Center, Dec. 5, 2011, http://www.andersen.sdu.dk/liv/minibio/index_e.html. *Jantelov* is, of course, more complex than suggested here and continues to be debated on many levels. A quick Google search demonstrates that it is still a topic of dis-cussion among citizens of Northern Europe. The search will also produce far better information than what I have presented here. What is more, some form of *jantelov* is found in all cultures, and certainly in the United States.

5 de Milius.

6 Tatar, "Introduction: Hans Christian Andersen," 224.

7 Tartar, 230.

8 Tartar, 228.

9 Windling, "Hans Christian Andersen: Father of the Modern Fairy Tale."

10 Windling.

11 Windling.

12 Tatar, "Introduction: Hans Christian Andersen," 225.

Chapter 18

Dragons in Hereville: Comics as a Vehicle for Fairy Tales

Orlando Dos Reis and Emily Midkiff

On Eclectic Forms

Readers of different texts learn the codes inherent to them. The study of semiotics, as summarized by Barbara Postema, specifies that "meaning is transferred through signs, using codes. Signs thus form an arbitrary code which users learn to apply and interpret by convention."[1] Some art forms, such as the fairy tale genre and the medium of comics, are largely defined by how they use systems of signs and codes. Echoing Propp's 31 narremes in his seminal *Morphology of the Folktale*, Anna Tavis suggests that fairy tales are a secondary language that, like written language, contains a set series of signs which are rearranged based on predetermined rules.[2]

The signs and codes that make up fairy tales have been long gathered into indices such as Stith Thompson's motif index and the Aarne-Thompson collection of story types. For Tavis, the originality and creativity of fairy tales comes from their ability to construct these same structures and motifs in ways that inspire new individual interpretation and comprehension.[3] Similarly, Scott McCloud describes comics as a language consisting of words, pictures, and icons unified in one purpose.[4] Postema, following McCloud, specifies that "the form of comics as a whole can be viewed as a system that utilizes a number of codes that are based on convention and that the reader must learn, to understand comics fully."[5] In other words, comics are defined by their consistent use of familiar signs and codes, just as are fairy tales.

When comics become the medium for a fairy tale, the overlap of their similar semiotic systems creates a perfect playground for the signs, codes, and styles of each genre to interact and build new interpretations. Comics already employ multiple codes (visual, verbal, iconic); with the addition of fairy tale codes the resulting art becomes layered. The original semantic codes of fairy tales perform in the same way, but with extra access to the codes of comics. For instance, Max Lüthi says fairy tales have "the tendency to make feelings and relationships congeal into objects, so to speak, and become outwardly visible."[6] Through the medium of comics, the "objects" to which Lüthi refers become literally visible. Comics artists may build on Lüthi's concept of fairy tales by including an actual visual representation in the text. The artist takes an abstract concept and transforms it into something more concrete than a word: a visual representation of the artist's own interpretation of that abstraction. Through the codes of comics, these visual representations need not lose the "precision and brilliance" that Lüthi finds in the simplicity of European fairy tales.[7] Lüthi explains that fairy tales are not meant to portray individual or specific stories or locations, but are meant to be made of "abstract stylization" upon which the reader or listener can layer their own interpretations.[8] Similarly, McCloud explains that the typical drawing style of comic books is intentionally simple to perform as "a vacuum into which our identity and awareness are pulled...an empty shell that we inhabit which enables us to travel in another realm."[9] The overlap between the two categories of literature makes them well suited for collaboration.

The structure of each system enables the artists to intersect and juxtapose signs and codes from one system into the other at will, producing a commentary on both fairy tales and comics. The narrative itself may employ familiar fairy tale structures but expand upon the possibilities for interpreting those traditional story types through the corresponding visual art codes of the comics. Karin Kukkonen asserts that "comics quite clearly cut across the categorical distinctions between words and images and their functions."[10] So comics are a semiotic system, containing the multimodal tools to comment upon that system. Fairy tales expressed through the medium of comics also acquire the ability to produce a visual commentary upon their own semiotic systems. Not only does this add greater diversity of creative interpretation to fairy tales, it also provides the field of comics with an opportunity to experiment with the visual incorporation of the same material.

This emerging combination of comics and fairy tales can be viewed as a beneficial step in the progress of both fields. Kukkonen explains that new media develop in order to overcome the shortcomings of the old in a specific culture and that emerging "storytelling practices both shape and are shaped by the media in which they unfold."[11] Fairy tale comics are capable of improving upon both traditional fairy tales and the medium of comics when they make use of their combined potential. In his foundational text on fairy tales, Jack Zipes argues that in order to make a mark on society, contemporary fairy tale writers must "interject themselves into the fairy-tale discourse on civilization first by distancing themselves from conventional regressive forms of writing, thinking, and illustrating."[12] While he primarily means moving away from the happy endings and otherwise meddling with the usual tropes of fairy tales, his suggestion could just as easily be applied to transferring fairy tales over to the medium of comics.

The combination of fairy tales with comics may potentially produce a result that fluidly maximizes their semiotic potentials. Kukkonen describes the process of reading the various storytelling modes within a comic as "a dynamic process of narrative cognition, rather than a piecemeal combination of non-commensurable semiotic resources."[13] To serve as an example of this combined artwork of the fairy tale told through the medium of comics, we will examine Barry Deutsch's *Hereville: How Mirka Got Her Sword* (2010).

Hereville

Hereville tells the story of Mirka, a young Jewish girl living in an isolated Orthodox Jewish community, and her quest to become a great dragon slayer someday. In an attempt to evade a pair of bullies, Mirka follows an unfamiliar path, discovering a strange house in the middle of a forest. The house belongs to a witch and is guarded by a talking pig that Mirka angers. Although the pig terrorizes Mirka, she later defends and saves it from the bullies; the witch, believing she is indebted to the girl for saving her pig, tells Mirka where to find a sword with which she may finally become a dragon slayer. Mirka must seek out a troll and conquer it, a task that requires the help of Mirka's highly logical and protective stepmother, Fruma. Mirka sneaks out one night to find and battle the troll despite Fruma forbidding her to do so. The troll challenges Mirka to a sweater-knitting battle: whoever knits the better sweater, wins. If the troll wins, he will kill Mirka and eat her for breakfast. If Mirka wins, she claims the sword as her prize. The troll's sweater is perfect, but Mirka's sweater is disproportionate and has three arms and several neck holes. Although the troll thinks he has clearly won, Mirka unleashes a long but logical argument that lasts until sun rise. The troll turns into yarn; Mirka finds an unfinished end and threatens to unravel the troll if he does not admit defeat and provide her with the sword.

Throughout the tale, Deutsch employs several known fairy tale motifs such as the wicked stepmother, the ogre, the talking animal, and the sword quest. We will focus on these important examples in *Hereville* to discuss the semiotics of comics and fairy tales.

The Nurturing Stepmother

One example from *Hereville* regarding how the two types of storytelling can interact occurs in Mirka's relationship with Fruma. Traditionally, stepmother figures in fairy tales are portrayed as being in competition with their stepdaughters; also common is the witch-stepmother, a combination that only strengthens the character's cruel nature within these tales. While examples of the opposite do exist, readers have come to accept these conventions given the overwhelming number of story types that utilize the wicked stepmother character: according to the Aarne-Thompson tale- and motif-type indices, there are over twenty story types and over sixteen specific motifs wherein the stepmother is unnaturally cruel to her relatives.[14] In Deutsch's *Hereville*, however, Fruma both reinforces and defies traditional fairy tale motifs through the juxtaposition of text and image—a defining characteristic of the comics medium.

From the very beginning, Deutsch pits Mirka and Fruma against one another by presenting Mirka as a curious girl who questions her religion and Fruma as a very logical and overwhelming master of argumentation. After Mirka expresses her desire to slay dragons, Fruma plays devil's advocate by listing several logical counter-arguments to Mirka's claim that dragons are evil and eat people:

> That's just *nature*. *Owls* eat other animals, but we don't call *owls* evil. *Don't* tell me "eating humans is different." Try telling *that* to a *chicken's* mother sometime! For that matter, you eat fish and beef and chicken, but you don't suggest killing *yourself* in revenge! Why not hold yourself to the standard you judge dragons by?...Isn't killing a *dragon* attacking a *symptom* while ignoring root ecological causes? And if you're *not* dealing with the root, are you solving *anything*?[15]

And yet it is useless for Mirka to engage in the argument because Fruma changes sides as soon as Mirka concedes: "*Mirka!* You mean you'd let a dragon devour me and the whole town? How *could* you?" (4, italics in original). Deutsch's consistent use of italics helps to convey some emphatic emotion, but readers can form an accurate interpretation of the text and Fruma's character only when considering both text and image. The text by itself characterizes Fruma as rational but detached from her stepdaughter; when read alongside the images, however, Fruma is depicted as very emotive and passionate about her argument. Not only do her facial expressions indicate her fervor, but the proliferation of speech bubbles indicates that the argument is being visually piled on as Fruma rattles off. In another way, when Fruma abruptly switches sides in the last panel on page four, her accompanying visual reaction turns the scene from purely ironic and preachy to humorous as well—a fact that would have been more difficult for readers to understand based simply on the text provided. (See Fig. 1: Fruma's argument with Mirka.)

Fig. 1: Fruma's Argument with Mirka. Barry Deutsch, *Hereville* (detail), 2010. Copyright Barry Deutsch. Reproduced with kind permission.

A similar scene occurs later in the novel, to the same effect. When Fruma learns that Mirka has skipped school, Fruma facetiously undermines the severity of the situation in order to teach her stepdaughter a lesson by allowing Mirka to develop her own answers. Similar to the spread on page 4, the spread on page 89 shows Fruma lecturing through logic while the accompanying images suggest her kidding nature. She ultimately concludes,

> Tomorrow I'll tell your little sisters they can do whatever they want, with no supervision. Don't say it's a bad idea—who are *you* to say five-year-olds need supervision? What give you that right, just being older and wiser? *I'm* older than you, and we've already agreed that *I* shouldn't tell you what to do, right? (89, italics in original)

In response, Mirka counters by admitting that "society will break down if no one learns! Children *need* to go to school!" (89, italics in original) At this point in the images Fruma changes her emotions drastically: at first she appears agreeable, then mocking, and finally, in the first panel on page 90, she suddenly looks very stern. Although readers may be able to understand Fruma's intentional irony through reverse psychology in the text, the images of familiar emotions help exemplify it more clearly. Furthermore, a scene such as the former or latter would likely involve much more verbal description in a written text, whereas the images provided are capable of achieving the same effect in considerably less time.

Although Fruma's and Mirka's relationship echoes the common stepmother-stepdaughter feud found in traditional fairy tales, readers may question Fruma's motives. Wicked stepmothers in fairy tales are typically motivated by jealousy or fear; stepdaughters are too often oppressed by their stepmothers or view them as usurpers who have taken their birthmothers' place. Fruma, on the other hand, tests Mirka through argumentation in an effort to teach her, not suppress her; this is portrayed primarily through the accompanying visuals. One code of comics at play here instructs readers to interpret speech bubbles and visuals as complementary forces rather than focusing on only one or the other. By using this code to his advantage, Deutsch demonstrates that Fruma's stern logic is a constructive force. Accordingly, it is not surprising that although Mirka does miss her birthmother, she clearly accepts Fruma as a mother surrogate. In the most tender moment between the two, Mirka passionately tells Furma about seeing her mother's ghost.

In the center of the page is a small dark image of the ghost as she imagined it, holding her when she was distressed. The image is surrounded by small panels depicting Mirka's expressions and is obstructed by a long chain of speech bubbles. On the other side of the spread, Fruma holds Mirka in a similar way in a large, clear, simple and borderless image. The two mother-daughter embraces are mirrored across the centerfold, putting Mirka between the two mother figures, receiving comfort from each. Yet the relative clarity and boundlessness of the image with Fruma makes it more real—the current, accepted mother rather than the remembered, past and limited mother.

Furthermore, Fruma is well aware of her title as stepmother and would seem to accept it: "I live in the family your mother made, surrounded by her children and under her roof" (96). Fruma does not seek to hide or erase the fact that she is not biologically Mirka's mother. For Fruma, the title of stepmother is an honorable inheritance, not a badge of shame; she is not threatened by her predecessor or her stepchildren, like readers of fairy tales might expect a stepmother to be. Instead of a figure that represents a rift within a family, Fruma has kept Mirka's family together. By presenting the visual impression that Fruma was being nurturing in her own way Deutsch has effectively taken traditional fairy tale motifs and codes and revised them through the comics medium. Without the visual stimuli, the text may not have been able to portray Fruma and Mirka's relationship clearly.

Trolls and Social Norms[16]

Mirka's encounter with the troll in the latter part of the novel is similarly enhanced by the juxtaposition of fairy tales and comics. A troll is a type of fairy tale ogre, usually humanoid in form with exaggerated or extra features and generally huge, strong, and ugly. Through the comics medium, Deutsch is able to create a troll different from the norm but without losing its ambiguity, which Lüthi says defines a fairy tale.[17]

This portion of *Hereville* plays on tale type The *Small Boy De-*

feats the Ogre (AaTh 327B). *Hereville* diverges from *The Small Boy Defeats the Ogre* most obviously in that Mirka is a girl, not a small boy. This simple change accentuates gender stereotypes not only in older fairy tales, but also in Mirka's community. Mirka struggles with the social expectations on young girls in Orthodox Judaism. Her desire to gain a sword and slay a dragon counters what normal adolescent girls in Hereville are supposed to be concerned with, which is, as Gittel keeps reminding her, to find a husband and start a family (41-42). Given that the visual context lets the audience see and understand how Mirka functions, or sometimes fails to function, in her society through the comics and fairy tale codes involved with the troll, Deutsch can focus on how Mirka negotiates her place within the society.

The visuals in this part of the comic are used to comment on the original motifs, such as G519, "Ogre Killed through Other Tricks." Mirka does not technically win the sweater knitting competition, but is able to keep an argument going long enough until the sun comes up. The troll is not killed, merely defeated and transformed following motif F455.8.1, "Trolls Turn to Stone at Sunrise." Instead of turning to stone, however, the troll turns into something like a knitted sock. By evoking the "Trolls Turn to Stone at Sunrise" motif Deutsch uses the transformation into yarn to produce not only a humorous turn to the fairy tale code, but also to comment on the substance of the troll in a way that words do not. By turning to messy knitwear, Deutsch implies that the true substance of this troll is not stone, but poor knitting. Furthermore, the troll's many awkward limbs and flaccid nose and ears resemble the awful sweater that Mirka knit in the competition. In other words, the troll is made of Mirka's weaknesses. She defeats it and symbolically solves the conflict of her struggle with womanly arts. In this way, the visual aspects of comics serve the narrative through customizing the motif to specifically suit Mirka's development.

In the comics medium, Deutsch brings Mirka's nightmare to life while retaining the vagueness which Lüthi describes as an essential aspect of fairy tales. Lüthi specifies that "genuine" fairy tales give minimum detail; particularly, he mentions that in fairy tales "the word 'monster' suffices. [...] The fairy tale indicates the action and does not get lost in the portrayal of scenes and characters."[18] Of course in comics the images depict these aspects for the reader, giving them detail and substance. While style and simple cartooning still leave much undefined, Deutch also addresses this need for ambiguity through absences in the narrative. In the beginning, Mirka does not even know what a troll is until Fruma explains that it is a monster. Mirka performs the role of the fairy tale listener and imagines the creature from the name alone. In a nightmare, she sees a monster with six eyes, seven fingers on one hand, a huge warty nose, and massive pointy teeth. But it also has a beard like her father and a hat like Mirka's brother (103). Mirka creates a monster that exaggerates physical characteristics, making it fearsome, while keeping characteristics that are known to her and common in the world around her, just like a listener to a fairy tale. In this way, Deutsch acknowledges the fairy tale codes that allow the reader to construct their own vision of a monster.

Yet, in the visual text, the troll must eventually be portrayed. Deutsch accomplishes this without losing the indistinct qualities of fairy tales. When Mirka finds the troll in the woods, many elements of its appearance are surprising and out of place. Most startlingly, it is an effeminate creature. Whereas the monster of Mirka's imagination had masculine characteristics of muscled forearms, a beard, and wore only jeans, the actual troll carries a purse and is skilled in knitting. In most fairy tales, trolls bear masculine pronouns when they have pronouns at all, and they are always fierce and strong. Deutsch's alterations retain the necessary vagueness that Lüthi requires of fairy tales, if in a different way than Lüthi imagined; the book does not attempt to inform the reader how to construe the troll's purse or choice of battle. The displacement of the masculine stereotype leaves this scene just as open for interpretation and self-application as are the indistinct scenes and monsters of traditional fairy tales.

The yarn also functions as a visual but metaphorical canvas for the battle, something that would be entirely impossible in a written tale. On the first page of the battle the yarn creates a vortex through which Mirka appears to be falling (124). The yarn creates a funnel, much like a tornado, with the skein at the eye of that tornado. As the yarn encircles Mirka, it visually indicates that it could become loose and free her, or it could become tight and trap her. What Deutsch implies here is that the troll forces her either to accept the challenge and succeed, and by extension accept the traditional role her community expects from her, or to fail and perish, and also be considered an outcast by her society. The text does not expressly say that Mirka battles for the sake of her place in society, but the visuals show how important her grasp of knitting is to her success as an Orthodox woman as well as to her survival of the contest.

The medium of comics has allowed Deutsch to embrace and expand on the preexisting troll story types. He is able to bring to life that which was previously left to the imagination, using the medium of comics as the tool with which to do so. He breaks convention, giving us a new means of interpreting what trolls look like, while retaining the malleability of fairy tales by using the interpretive codes of comics. He creatively employs known story types and motifs in his visual art to open new possibilities for fairy tale codes.

The Talking Pig[19]

The pig is another important example of the beneficial combination of fairy tales and the comics medium. As a talking and perhaps enchanted animal, the pig represents a classic fairy tale element that is also changed and enhanced by its visual representation. The pig fits nicely into tale type AaTh 2075, *Tales in which Animals Talk,* and also incorporates motifs N774 "Adventures from Pursuing an Enchanted Animal," Q482.2 "Magic Swine Causes Robbers to be Drowned," B211 "Animals Using Human Speech," B211.1.4 "Speaking Hog," and B360 "Animals Grateful for Rescue from Peril of Death." However, unlike many talking animals in folklore and fairy tales, the pig serves as more than just a sidekick or helper. In *Hereville,* the pig functions as quest-giver, a trial, and most importantly, as an initiation to a world outside of Mirka's Orthodox upbringing. The pig functions as a symbol of the *goisch* (non-Jewish) world.

Although animals in folklore often serve the function of benevolent helper or guide, the pig does not begin as a benevolent force at all. Roger Sale describes the stereotypical enchanted animals as "the kindest, the most patient, the most gentlemanly or ladylike, the most civilized creatures in the stories," but Deutsch's pig utterly defies this description.[20] On the contrary, when the pig first enters the story as the guardian of a magical garden hidden in the middle of the woods, he is best described as Mirka's adversary, since he swears eternal enmity against Mirka for stealing grapes. In order to protect her life from a grudge that, according to the pig, will last until her funeral, Mirka sets out to change her fortune by catching the pig to put an end to the pig's "merciless" harassment (36, 49). After tricking the pig, lassoing it, riding it throughout the town and nearly drowning, Mirka wins her peace. But it is not until she shares a near-death experience and sympathizes with the animal enough to save it from bullies that it finally relents. Thus, the pig is not so much an animal helper as a trial that Mirka must overcome in order to find a sword. Once the feud has ended and the pig has been freed, the witch grants Mirka a favor and provides that help.

By seeing the image of the pig on the page, the reader is able to experience the creature both as common livestock, a typical character from European fairy tales and fables, and as the fantastical creature Mirka sees. Mirka, who was raised in an Orthodox Jewish community, has no context within which to interpret the pig. While Mirka and her siblings are scared of the pig because they have had no exposure to a creature like it, Rochel, who is Fruma's daughter and has lived in other towns, jadedly explains that the pig is *only* a pig, an animal often kept as a pet by Gentile children (21). In this way, the pig is both a symbol of the world outside of Hereville and a reminder of the differences between Mirka's culture and the others surrounding her town. Throughout her story, Mirka is called upon to confront the world outside her culturally isolated home, and in order to achieve her goal of becoming a dragon slayer, Mirka must use the tools Hereville and its people have given her to defeat a foe that exists entirely outside of her world. With its connections to a world outside of Jewish culture, the pig becomes the first real symbol of a world outside of Hereville, the world that Mirka must choose to join or ignore. The reality of this world and the importance of this decision are only emphasized by the ways in which the pig is visually rendered. Here the medium of comics lends credibility and weight to the creature's existence.

Through comics, the reader is able to experience the scale and consequence of a creature that, while magical, is undeniably real and unavoidable. While at some points the reader may question the pig's authenticity, especially when it begins to wreak havoc on Mirka's schoolwork, the very act of seeing the creature manipulating objects and scenery in the real world, speaking in speech bubbles, and interacting with secondary characters serves as proof of the pig's authenticity. In terms of visual cues, color saturation and pigment often aid the reader in determining any given situation as authentic or imaginary. When the pig first appears on page 19, it is shown from a low angle that implies a domineering and threatening presence; Mirka and her siblings appear underneath the pig as if diminished. The pig itself is presented in much more detail than the human characters (at least in this spread): there are at least three different pigments used to represent light and shadow. Deutsch similarly uses intricate shading to show depth and thick outlining to suggest a very real presence. The human characters, by comparison, lose much of their detail; in fact, it is not until Mirka and the pig confront one another, conveniently in the absence of her siblings, that the two appear together in equal detail. Deutsch thus discourages skepticism and signals to the reader that the pig really has a physical, visible, and linguistic presence in Mirka's world, without disrupting the structure of legitimacy of the tale itself.

Spinning and Swordplay

A final aspect of the story enhanced by the combination of fairy tales and comics is Mirka's quest for a sword. The visual confusion between the sword and knitting needles that occurs near the end of the book intensifies the story types and motifs that relate to the sword quest. This part of the plot plays on the tale-types *The Dragon Slayer* (AaTh 300) and *Cinderella* (AaTh 510A), and incorporates several motifs, most notably Q114.3 "The Sword as Reward," and A1459.1 "The Acquisition of a Weapon."

The Dragon Slayer and *Cinderella* tale types frame the book with the conflict of Mirka figuring out her generational and gender identity, expressed through her desire to slay a dragon. As Francisco Vaz da Silva argues, these two tale types parallel one another along the axes of the father/son continuity in the former and the mother/daughter connection in the latter. Vaz da Silva states that because of this comparison, the daughter in *Cinderella* can be expected to "perform some sort of mother-slaying with ophidian overtones."[21] He explains that many fairy tale daughters will through some action or even just their birth cause the death of their mothers. The involvement of snakes is unsurprising given their mythic associations with fertility. The mother passes on her fertility powers to the daughter, who in receiving them kills the mother. The daughter essentially must slay the previous dragon-serpent before she can have her powers. Vaz de Silva emphasizes that often these ritual or literal mother-slayings happen through a domestic, maternal activity such as cooking, or involve domestic objects such as spindles.[22] The daughter may not always be aware of what she is doing, and often the mother dies at the daughter's birth, but the daughter's role is to grow into the mother's place.[23]

Mirka's argumentative relationship with her stepmother and struggle with female responsibility seem to mirror these fairy tale mother-daughter conflicts. She does not want to accept any conventional feminine roles, as demonstrated by her distaste of knitting. On the first page, the narration seems to sympathize with Mirka, calling it "unreasonable" for Fruma to want Mirka to learn "womanly arts" (1). Later Gittel yells at her for her disinterest in marriage. These scenes intensify Mirka's incongruity with Hereville (41-42). Yet her rebellion against womanly chores is at odds with her longing for her dead birthmother. She does not even necessarily dislike Fruma, only her maternal teachings. Her desire to slay a dragon first appears as an example of Mirka's argumentative relationship with Fruma, as discussed above, and as such is entangled with her desires to come to terms with her maternal figures (3). Her dream of slaying a dragon may be seen as the expression of her own need to vanquish her psychological distress over mothers and also to embrace her own femininity.

Of course, Mirka never actually slays a dragon. Instead, Deutsch displaces the conflict onto the quest to get a sword from a troll. Heroic dragon slaying is often immediately preceded by the motifs of forging or finding a sword.[24] Locating a suitable sword enables the dragonslaying, and in this case encountering the feminized troll to receive the sword appears to replace the need to slay anything at all.

The sword becomes a site of visual displacement leading the reader to combine the Cinderella and *The Dragon Slayer* tale types. On the second two-page spread of Mirka's knitting competition with the troll, knitting needles cascade down in the background. The foreground reveals Mirka wielding the sword in various poses within the same frame (126-127). The codes of comics here signify that all these versions of Mirka are imaginary duplicates, depicting different times rather than multiple Mirkas. The needles in the background, on the other hand, portray Mirka's own blurring of the distinction between sword and needle. Despite the real world differences between a sword and knitting needles, Deutsch depicts them as the same size and color. (See Fig. 2: Mirka's knitting obstacle.) The two objects become easily confused. The needles are even granted little nubs on the end that resemble a stubbed version of the handle and hilt of the sword. Furthermore, the words accompanying the images provide the opportunity for semantic blurring as well. Mirka chants to herself the movements of knitting: "Insert! Loop! Push through!" but the images closest to those thought bubbles portray her doing those activities with the sword (127).

Fig. 2: Fruma's Knitting Obstacle. Barry Deutsch, *Hereville* (detail), 2010. Copyright Barry Deutsch. Reproduced with kind permission.

The confusion of wielding a sword with wielding knitting needles directly juxtaposes the heroic killing of a dragon with the homely responsibilities that her stepmother wishes to teach her. Deutsch implies through similar drawings that the reader should discard their differences and regard what the two signify together. The meeting of the phallic sword and the domestic needle visually represent the *Cinderella* and *The Dragon Slayer* tales combining.

It is possible to understand how Mirka successfully comes to defeat her own reluctance to be like her mother/stepmother through the interplay of visual signs in the art of the comic. Vaz da Silva points out that often the daughters in the *Cinderella* tale come to replace their mothers after killing or indirectly causing their deaths.[25] Once she achieves her quest, Mirka does not kill anyone, but she embraces the traditionally feminine chore of knitting and takes her place as a future mother. On the last page of the book, the narration reads, "Knitting was easier to get through now. In Mirka's mind, she held an entirely different needle" (139). Even here the sword is referred to still as a "needle" and not a weapon. The sword has become a feminine tool of house-making; as if to affirm this use of her slaying skills, a picture of Mirka's birth mother smiles over her as she knits in this final frame. Vaz da Silva also explains that in a number of tales within the *Cinderella* type the mothers' doom is directly related to their daughters' spinning or weaving, but this also results in the rejuvenation of the daughter and a continued cycle of mother-daughter replacements.[26] In the style of the Greek Fates, cutting the thread of the mother's life means that the daughter's life may then be spun from the same thread.[27] Similarly, Mirka's own knitting ties her to both Fruma and her birth mother and prepares her for future roles as wife and mother.

In literary fairy tales, *The Dragon Slayer* and *Cinderella* stories have often met before, but in this incarnation of the tale types, the comics medium in which they appear grants them further opportunities to merge the slaying/spinning that determines the daughters' relationships with their mothers. The visual blurring allows the reader to interpret the objects for which Lüthi praises fairy tales and further exemplifies how comics and fairy tales can complement one another well.

Conclusion

Traditional fairy tales have withstood the test of time and influenced contemporary literature in part because of their adaptability to new forms of storytelling. They first began as oral stories and were then recorded. Between the fifteenth and seventeenth centuries, these recorded tales became important markers of European values, morals, and beliefs; in the meantime, these tales developed their own conventions that constitute the genre.[28] For these reasons, they became associated with children, which prompted a more visual narrative (illuminated collections and picture books, for instance). Today we see them adapted into film and television. Kristeva's idea of intertextuality suggests that this is a natural progression.[29] Modern fairy tales work well within the comics genre because of their adaptability and reliance on signs and codes. Perhaps combining the modern fairy tale story type with the comics genre is merely the next step in their evolution.

Bibliography

Aarne, Antti, and Stith Thompson. *The Types of the Folktale: a Classification and Bibliography*. 3rd rev. ed. Helsinki: Suomailainen Tiedeakatemiia, 1961.

Chandler, Daniel. *Semiotics: The Basics*. New York: Routledge, 2010.

Dégh, Linda. "Folk Narrative." *Folklore and Folklife, an Introduction*. Ed. Richard M. Dorson. Chicago: University of Chicago Press, 1972.

Deutsch, Barry. *Hereville: How Mirka Got Her Sword*. New York: Amulet Books, 2010.

Kukkonen, Karin. "Comics as a Test Case for Transmedial Narratology." SubStance 40.1 (2011): 34-52. *Project Muse*. 13 November 2011. http://muse.jhu.edu/.

Levy, Gertrude Rachel. *Sword from the Rock: Investigation into the Origins of Epic Literature and the Development of the Hero*. Westport: Greenwood Publishing Group, 1977.

Lüthi, Max. *Once upon a Time: on the Nature of Fairy Tales*. Translated by Lee Chadeayne and Paul Gottwald. Bloomington and London: Indiana University Press, 1970.

McCloud, Scott. *Understanding Comics: The Invisible Art*. New York: HarperPerennial, 1994.

Postema, Barbara. "Draw A Thousand Words: Signification And Narration In Comics Images." *International Journal Of Comic Art* 9.1 (2007): 487-501. *Art Full Text (H. W. Wilson)*. 30 Mar. 2012. http://web.ebscohost.com.

Sale, Roger. *Fairy Tales and after: from Snow White to E. B. White*. Cambridge: Harvard University Press, 1978.

Tavis, Anna. "Fairy Tales from a Semiotic Perspective." *Fairy Tales and Society: Illusion, Allusion, and Paradigm*. Ed. Ruth B Bottigheimer. Philadelphia: University of Philadelphia Press, 1986. 195-202.

Thompson, Stith. *Motif-index of Folk-literature*. Bloomington: Indiana University Press, 1955-58.

Vaz da Silva, Francisco. *Metamorphosis: The Dynamics of Symbolism in European Fairy Tales*. New York: Peter Lang, 2002.

Zipes, Jack. *Fairy Tales and the Art of Subversion: The Classical Genre for Children and the Process of Civilization*. Second Edition. London: Routledge, 2006.

—. "The Changing Function of the Fairy Tale." *The Lion and the Unicorn* 12.2 (1988): 7-31. Project Muse. 13 November 2011. http://muse.jhu.edu/.

Notes

1 Barbara Postema, "Draw a Thousand Words: Signification and Narration in Comics Images" 2007, *Art Full Text*, 488.

2   Anna Tavis, *Fairy Tales and Society: Illusion, Allusion, and Paradigm* (Philadelphia: University of Philadelphia Press, 1986), 196.

3   Tavis, 197-198.

4   Scott McCloud, *Understanding Comics: The Invisible Art* (New York: HarperPerennial, 1994), 47.

5   Barbara Postema, "Draw a Thousand Words: Signification and Narration in Comics Images" 2007, Art Full Text, 489.

6   Max Lüthi, *Once upon a Time: on the Nature of Fairy Tales* (Bloomington and London: Indiana University Press, 1970), 51.

7   Lüthi, 52.

8   Lüthi, 50.

9   Scott McCloud, *Understanding Comics: The Invisible Art* (New York: HarperPerennial, 1994), 36.

10 Karin Kukkonen, "Comics as a Test Case for Transmedial Narratology" 2011, *SubStance*, 37.

11 Kukkonen, 41, 35.

12 Jack Zipes, *Fairy Tales and the Art of Subversion: The Classical Genre for Children and the Process of Civilization*, (London: Routledge, 2006), 177.

13 Kukkonen, 39.

14 Stith Thompson, *Motif-index of Folk-literature* (Bloomington: Indiana University Press, 1955-58), 300.

15 Barry Deutsch, *Hereville: How Mirka Got Her Sword* (New York: Amulet Books, 2010), 4 (italics in original). Further citation given in the text.

16 The authors gratefully acknowledge the contributions of Samantha Purdy to this section of the paper.

17 Lüthi, 50.

18 Lüthi, 50.

19 The authors gratefully acknowledge the contributions of Allison Shufelt to this section of the paper.

20 Roger Sale, *Fairy Tales and after: from Snow White to E. B. White* (Cambridge: Harvard University Press, 1978), 78.

21 Francisco Vaz da Silva, *Metamorphosis: The Dynamics of Symbolism in European Fairy Tales* (New York: Peter Lang, 2002), 195.

22 Vaz da Silva, 198.

23 Vaz da Silva, 198.

24 For examples of this, refer to the Northern European tale of Sigurd and Fafnir, as it was disseminated from legend into fairy tale through Andrew

Lang's *Red Fairy Book* (1890), or the "Tale of Two Brothers" as collected by the Grimms.

25 Vaz da Silva, 198.

26 Vaz da Silva, 198.

27 Vaz da Silva, 198.

28 Jack Zipes, "The Changing Function of the Fairy Tale" 1988, *The Lion and the Unicorn*, p.7-8.

29 Daniel Chandler, *Semiotics: The Basics* (New York: Routledge, 2010), 198.

Chapter 19

Little Sparrow

Kristin Zhang

Long ago, when Japan was still ravaged by bandits and civil war, the Emperor died suddenly and there were rumours that he had been poisoned by his son. The noble lords put aside their differences to meet with the Lord High Chamberlain. Regicide was one thing, they argued, but patricide was another. They agreed that they would sleep much better in their beds with a Princess on the throne.

Perhaps these eminent men thought the Emperor's daughter would prove a placid and malleable ruler. Certainly Princess Aito wore the wasted look which was fashionable amongst court ladies of the time, slim as a willow, white as the snow on the mountain. Beneath the muted silk and shaved eyebrows, however, was a woman of wisdom and more than a touch of wilfulness.

"She has joined the Tendai sect and believes women can achieve enlightenment," complained Lord Entsu. "She is talking of national days of reflection and schools for the poor, so that they too might write poetry."

"What can we do about it?" asked Lord Gento.

"Nothing," replied the Lord High Chamberlain, "unless we want to admit we have made a mistake. We must simply bide our time."

And so the capital grew in fame as a centre of wisdom and beauty.

In the spring children flew flags painted with the sun and the moon to celebrate the equinox, and in the autumn the farmers lit incense to honour the souls of the insects that had perished as they ploughed the fields or harvested the crops.

But while the common people prayed for their ruler's health and happiness, the courtiers grew restless. "When will she marry?" "Another suitor rejected, you say?" "I hear Lord Gento has arranged a spectacular firefly party to introduce his son." "Ahhh, perhaps he will have more luck than Lord Entsu. He sold his estate at Hara to pay for the entertainment and she sighed only at the sight of the moon."

In truth, the Empress longed for a husband, but her dilemma was this—which of the young lords should she choose? For as the memory of war receded, so the great families began once more to jostle and jockey for power, and rumours of intrigue and insubordination grew daily.

Finally, after a period of fasting and devotion, an answer seemed to be delivered. The second son of the Chinese Emperor sought her hand in marriage.

According to the ambassador he was a sincere young man and a scholar of the earliest Buddhist teachings. "The prince has written you a poem," said the Ambassador presenting her with a little scroll of silk. "He is not sure if it is any good, but he hopes that you will like it."

Slipping the scroll from the Prince into her purple-edged sleeve, she called together the heads of the great families and ordered them to meet her prospective groom on the beach at Hamamatsu at the time of the next full moon.

Now, among the crowd who watched the noble party ride out a month later was the daughter of the Imperial Gardener. A tiny creature, she strained to catch sight of the pageantry. "Oh, oh, if only I was a great lord with a golden crest upon my robes," she cried and in her excitement stepped on toes and prodded her neighbours with her sharp, little elbows.

"What a bothersome child," the people around her complained, "hopping about like a bedbug."

The little girl fled their hurtful words and climbed into the branches of a maple tree on the edge of the forest.

Her mother had named her Chieko which means "Great Wisdom." But after her mother's death people began to call her "Susume" or "Little Sparrow" instead. "Look," they would titter as if they were witnessing the antics of a simpleton, "there goes Little Sparrow talking to the birds again." For it was true, that everywhere that Susume went she was followed by birds.

"Dry your tears," said the hawk, lighting in the maple tree, "I have great stamina and excellent sight. I will follow the noble party and bring you back a full account."

Off he flew.

As she waited for his return, Susume tried to keep busy. She ran errands for the sick and elderly, planted cucumber and eggplant seedlings under her bedroom window, played hide and seek in the forest with the birds. Sometimes she would see the Empress sitting alone under a linden or a larch tree reading the Prince's poem. Her painted lips moving silently and her face, usually so pale, flushed pink.

One afternoon as Susume helped her father pull ivy from high on the castle walls she caught sight of the coloured pennants of the nobles. "They're coming. They're coming," she called. "I see their horses kicking up a great cloud of dust."

The city was soon abuzz with the news. The ladies of the court began their beauty preparations, painting their faces white and blackening their teeth; the musicians tuned their lutes, and the servants hung cages of fireflies from the trees. Finally, the gates of the city were opened to allow the riders to enter. But where was the Prince?

The Empress, who was watching their arrival from a small tower, looked anxiously up and down the line of richly-dressed, if rather dusty, lords, but none of them resembled the prince she saw in her dreams.

The High Lord Chamberlain soon prostrated himself at her feet and told a sorry tale. The Prince and his retainers had climbed into a smaller boat in order to reach the shore more easily. But a violent storm had blown up. It had tossed them about and finally thrown them into the sea. "What could we do your majesty? We are forbidden to touch the imperial person. We wept and prayed, but the Prince and his men were lost."

Without a word the Empress retired to her private chapel and the crowd dispersed to discuss the tragedy.

When the courtyards were empty the hawk spoke up for the first time since his return. "Oh indeed it is a terrible story, but I saw no storm, only a gang of treacherous nobles, who chopped and hacked at the Prince and his men and threw their limbs into the sea for the sharks to devour."

Susume flinched in horror. "If only I was a great lord or a lady-in-waiting, I could warn the Empress."

Trilling prettily, the nightingale, said, "Don't fret, Little Sparrow, I sing each night by her window. I will tell her of the deceit."

And so, that evening, as the Empress lay unable to sleep in her dark chamber, she heard the nightingale sing. Was there ever a song so sad? She wept and thought her heart would break. In the morning she arose and found her heart not broken but only hardened. Dressed in the rough, hemp robes of mourning she composed an edict and commanded her Master-In-Arms to deliver it throughout the capital. *Every man, woman and child was to leave the city by noon and the gates were to be locked forever.*

Many years passed. The country descended once more into civil war and lawlessness. Without the gardens and woods of the castle to tend Susume's father grew increasingly despondent. But what could she do?

One evening her father limped into their tiny cottage bloody and bruised. On his return from market, where he sold the flowers and fruit of their little garden, he had been set upon by brigands.

Susume bathed her father's wounds and wept. "If only I had a bright shining sword, I would cut off their hands and cut out their tongues."

"No, no," cried the Crane, shaking her elegant head, "not more blood and violence. You must make a petition to the Empress and somehow soften her heart."

So the next morning, putting on a pair of her father's old *hakama* (the divided skirt worn by men over kimono) and tying back her hair, Susume set off to the castle, the hawk flying ahead as a lookout.

At the drawbridge the little group looked up in dismay. The walls, now completely covered in ivy, seemed impossibly high and the great wooden gates impenetrable.

"If only..." began Susume.

But before she could finish, the raven, hungry and irritable snapped. "Oh no, not more "ifs." Let's eat those rice balls you packed earlier and think about what you can do rather than what you can't."

For a while they sat in silence nibbling at their lunch, lost in their thoughts and memories of the past.

"Remember the day you hung from the walls in that basket pulling ivy from the castle walls?" said the hawk. "You seemed quite fearless."

"Yes," agreed the nightingale, "Your father always complained about the damage the ivy did to the mortar."

"Of course," cried Susume. Then taking hold of one of the ivy vines she tugged. The walls began to crumble.

"Oh, oh," wailed the crane. "We'll all be killed."

But once the dust had settled they saw that they were all quite well and where once there had been solid stone there was now a great gaping hole.

The Empress was sitting on a bench, beneath a pear tree, the peonies and nettles brushing against her skirts.

"I'm so glad to see you Little Sparrow," she said. "I've been so lonely." And she made the girl sit next to her and tell her all the news of the world outside.

Some months later, the Empress called together the noble lords and asked them to put aside their differences. And they did. For who amongst them had not lost a son or even a daughter to these dark times? Then touching the poem from the prince which she still kept in her sleeve, Empress Aito said, "I have been alone too long now to marry. Therefore, I wish Susume to be my heir, for she is everything a ruler should be; humble and brave, compassionate, but, most importantly, wise."

Once more the capital flourished and people often saw Susume walking among the cherry blossom in her imperial robes, deep in counsel with her ministers: the hawk, the nightingale, the raven, and the crane.

Chapter 20

Beedle's Moral Imagination

Travis Prinzi

The *Harry Potter* series (1997–2007) is a lengthy fantasy fiction story, the final story of which turns on a fairy tale: "The Tale of the Three Brothers." This little nursery story tells of three brothers who were given gifts by Death, who was trying to ensnare them. Near the final book's climax, Harry Potter's mentor, Albus Dumbledore, gives Harry an important bit of wisdom about his enemy, Voldemort: "Of house-elves and children's tales, of love, loyalty, and innocence, Voldemort knows and understands nothing. Nothing."[1] Given the weight that Dumbledore places on children's tales at the story's key turning point, we should give close attention to *The Tales of Beedle the Bard*, the small collection of fairy-stories with which every Wizarding World child is believed to have grown up. While this little volume may not have been planned from the beginning of Rowling's career, it does not mean it is an accidental byproduct of the *Harry Potter* creation. These tales are to the Wizarding World, the magical, hidden world of Rowling's series, what stories like Cinderella, The Frog Prince, Narnia, and even *Harry Potter* are to our world. Rowling wrote *Harry Potter*, and then gave this world its own ancient fairy tales.

I have argued in *Harry Potter & Imagination* (2008) that Rowling's *Harry Potter* series follows in the tradition of fairy tale writers and thinkers like George MacDonald, G.K. Chesterton, and J.R.R. Tolkien, whose works point both to morality and to a certain philosophy of life which sees the world as being more than what the physical senses perceive. In other words, there is a spiritual reality to the world, and mythical thinking is not to be rejected as old superstition with no relevance to our enlightened modern living. Fairy tales continue to be a protest against modernism's strict rationalism and naturalism. Chesterton writes:

> I am not concerned with any of the separate statutes of elfland, but with the whole spirit of its law, which I learnt before I could speak, and shall retain when I cannot write. I am concerned with a certain way of looking at life, which was created in me by the fairy tales [...][2]

Chesterton suggests that fairy tales are not mere morality stories., They teach us about *reality itself,* and this interpretation of reality comprises their morality.

That Rowling shares Chesterton's view can be seen at several instances in the Harry Potter series. For example Hermione and Ron, Harry's best friends and allies against Voldemort, get confused while trying to decipher the meaning of "The Tale of the Three Brothers." Hermione thinks it is "a pile of utter rubbish,"[3] "nonsense" and just "a story."[4] Ron dismisses the story's underlying reality by calling it "just one of those things you tell kids to teach them lessons [...] Don't go looking for trouble, don't pick fights, don't go messing around with stuff that's best left alone."[5] When Harry, who has not been raised on the Wizarding World's tales, stands by Dobby's grave, faced with the meaning and power of death, he learns the lesson of "The Tale of the Three Brothers, and he knew to destroy Horcruxes, Voldemort's wicked magical inventions that kept his soul bound to earth, rather than to pursue Hallows, the three magical gifts Death had given to the brothers. Harry's understanding of reality is informed by the philosophy of a fairy tale.

But is reality truly understood through these quaint little tales about "Babbity Rabbity" or pus-spewing cauldrons? Surely, the great mythologies would give us more insight into reality than little stories for children, meant to teach them to behave. Tolkien would argue in the opposite direction:

> The nearer the so-called 'nature myth', or allegory of the large processes of nature, is to the supposed archetype, the less interesting it is, and indeed the less it is of a myth capable of throwing any illumination whatever on the world. (337)[6]

The smaller and more local the story, the more potential it has to communicate mythic truth. This is precisely how it was for Chesterton:

> My first and last philosophy, that which I believe in with unbroken certainty, I learnt in the nursery. I generally learnt it from a nurse; that is, from the solemn and star-appointed priestess at once of democracy and tradition. The things I believed most then, the things I believe most now, are the things called fairy tales. They seem to me to be the entirely reasonable things. They are not fantasies: compared with them other things are fantastic.[7]

Compare this with Richard Dawkins's wish to write a children's book to teach them "how to think about the world "in contrast with mythical thinking":

> I would like to know whether there is any evidence that bringing children up to believe in spells and wizards has a pernicious effect. So many of the stories I read allowed the possibility of frogs turning into princes and I'm not sure whether that has a sort of insidious affect on rationality.[8]

Dawkins believes that the magic found in *Harry Potter* and other fairy-tales is "anti-scientific." All three thinkers demonstrate in different ways that fairy tales do more than convey a moral message; they teach us a way of understanding the world.

Moral Imagination

I have argued in *Hog's Head Conversations: Essays on Harry Potter* (2009) that the *Harry Potter* stories are written with "moral imagination.[9]" Expounded by eighteenth century British philosopher-statesman Edmund Burke, the literary and politico-philosophical concept of the moral imagination has been given more recent explanation by his American student, Russell Kirk. Kirk was a conservative political philosopher who also wrote imaginative fiction, most notably ghost stories. In 1981, he wrote an essay on the moral imagination for *Literature and Belief.* He writes of Burke's concept:

> By this "moral imagination," Burke signifies that power of ethical perception which strides beyond the barriers of private experience and momentary events "especially," as the dictionary has it, "the higher form of this power exercised in poetry and art." The moral imagination aspires to the apprehending of right order in the soul and right order in the commonwealth. This moral imagination was the gift and the obsession of Plato and Virgil and Dante. Drawn from centuries of human consciousness, these concepts of the moral imagination—so powerfully if briefly put by Burke—are expressed afresh from age to age.[10]

Let's examine the definition, to begin: "The moral imagination aspires to the apprehending of right order in the soul and right order in the commonwealth." It's a fantastic summary of what I believe is the heart of the *Harry Potter* books: inward personal transformation leads to outward societal change.[11] Rowling quoted Plutarch in her 2008 Harvard commencement speech: "What we achieve inwardly will change outer reality." Plutarch's quotation contains the same idea as Kirk's, but with a specific trajectory: the inward achievement ("right order in the soul") leads to the outward ("right order in the commonwealth"). This is not a theoretical elaboration, but rather a statement about reality itself.

Right Order in the Soul: Humanity in Beedle

With the right ordering of the soul being the overarching narrative in *Harry Potter*, one would expect to find at least hints of this in even the smallest of tales within the Wizarding World, those of Beedle the Bard. And that is precisely what we find. Let's start backward in the little volume published in December of 2008, beginning with the story most relevant to the *Potter* books. "The Tale of the Three Brothers" is key to the plot of *Deathly Hallows*, because it addresses the central motif of human encounter with death. The story turns out to be more than simply a morality tale, for the Hallows themselves were real, although Dumbledore believes the story's events—the brothers meeting Death on a bridge—are not factually accurate. Most importantly, what it teaches about being human—its philosophy of reality—is true.

The truth of the Hallows tale is not in any representation of historical facts, but in Ignotus Peverell's willingness to accept death as inevitable, and to die well. He chooses the Invisibility Cloak because it allows him the opportunity to live his life peacefully—avoiding the power temptation of the Elder Wand and the death-defying temptation of the Resurrection Stone—and to greet death calmly when his time comes. It is this truth about reality—human goodness being found in a willingness to die well—that works its way into Harry's heart and finally strikes home while he stands in the grave of his friend, Dobby, who has demonstrated the power of dying well.

Its thematic place in the *Harry Potter* story is clear enough, but what about Dumbledore's commentary in *The Tales of Beedle the Bard*? Here's the great irony of what the old wizard wrote on "The Tale of the Three Brothers": the man who knows the dangers of temptation to power, particularly the temptation of deathlessness, uses his authority as a well-respected, even revered, member of the Wizarding community, to convince the Wizarding World that the three Deathly Hallows have no basis in reality.

This is not Dumbledore enumerating the real dangers of the Hallows and the reasons they must be abandoned or destroyed. It is Dumbledore burying the story further in the aura of legend and fable, or perhaps under scholarly dismissal—and in doing so, attempting to accomplish, by the deception, the philosophical and moral point of the story for the entire Wizarding World.

First, Dumbledore writes concerning the Cloak of Invisibility: "Throughout all the centuries ... nobody has ever claimed to have found Death's Cloak."[12] This is likely true, in and of itself. We can't even be sure James knows what the Cloak really is. Having written this commentary just eighteen months prior to his death, Dumbledore both possessed the cloak and knew its present location. What this means, in conjunction with his gift of the Beedle tales to Hermione, is: he trusted Harry to keep the secret.

Second, regarding the Resurrection Stone, he states that it's never been found. We should note that eighteen months before his death, this was probably still true in Dumbledore's mind. If he discovered the stone in the summer between Harry's fifth and sixth year, then he must have written this line approximately six to eight months before he discovered the Stone. His commentary then reverts to the lesson of Babbitty Rabbitty (no magic can raise the dead) and the fifth tale's point that the Stone is Death's trick to lure the second brother to his death. We can assume, of course, Dumbledore believed the Stone to exist.

Lastly, we get more of Dumbledore's clever trickery regarding the Elder Wand. He is obviously the wand's possessor at this point, but he simply recounts the "bloody trail of the Elder Wand," seemingly dismissive of the idea that there is one true Elder Wand passing from hand to hand ("the so-called history of the Elder Wand," p. 106).

On the whole, Dumbledore reinforces his lesson to Harry from *Philosopher's Stone*: That humans choose precisely the wrong things for themselves.[13] Very few are those as wise as the brother who chose the Invisibility Cloak. Dumbledore's final lesson to Harry about the Hallows is the very first lesson he taught him in the first book, and it was taught by Beedle centuries before. The final line of Dumbledore's commentary is chilling: "Even I, Albus Dumbledore, would find it easiest to refuse the Invisibility Cloak; which only goes to show that, clever as I am, I remain just as big a fool as anyone else" (107). So Dumbledore, with knowledge of the

Hallows in hand, chooses to use his authoritative voice in the Wizarding World to put a stop to any future seeking of the Hallows.

As long as we've started at the end, let's move backward toward the beginning. "Babbitty Rabbitty and Her Cackling Stump" is a delightful little story, but perhaps the most mundane of the five. Dumbledore explains why: this is the only story of the five that almost completely plays by the rules of real Wizarding World magic. Magic in Wizarding World fairy tales has got to take a different place in the fairy-tale genre than it does in our own Muggle world. Magic in our fairy tales immerses us in a dynamic world where things are changing, not everything can be explained by science and reason, and supernatural events can invade and change history.

Wizards and witches, on the other hand, will not be taken by surprise when encountering magic in the same way that we are when we encounter it in a story. For us it's unfamiliar. This was fundamental to Chesterton's understanding of the power of a fairy tale; it has to present something *different*, something startling. Through the wild nature of fairy tales, we are supposed to learn, philosophically, that the world we live in is similarly unpredictable and magical. But how would this work in a world that is already full of transformational magic? Beedle answers by writing four out of five tales using a *different kind* of magic—magic that didn't behave in the same way as "real" magic does. In other words, the element of difference—creating an "other" world in which to explore problems in our own—is still a fundamental part of the Wizarding World's fairy tales. "Babbitty Rabbitty" is the exception.

Even so, it's from this simple story that Dumbledore claims most witches and wizards first learn that no magic can raise the dead (78-79). Again, this is more than a moral lesson; it's a claim about reality itself. The dead cannot be raised by any means. Dumbledore is giving us big statements about the very nature of the world from a story called "Babbitty Rabbitty," which confirms Chesterton's belief that children's stories can make up a philosophy of life.

Any discussion of life, love, death, and the soul has to contain symbols of tarnished, tainted, and ruined souls. Enter the Gothic tale, "The Warlock's Hairy Heart." This story, the most gruesome of Beedle's tales, draws more directly from a tradition Rowling has already tapped for the creation of Horcruxes: the magical ability to remove one's heart and keep it in a safe place. Horcruxes seem to bear certain similarities to George MacDonald's story, "The Giant's Heart." Dumbledore makes the point clearly, commenting on the young warlock's magical removal and locking away of his own heart: "The resemblance of this action to the creation of a Horcrux has been noted by many writers" (58).

This story provides the best space for considering the use of the gruesome in children's stories. Many object harshly to this, because of fear that children will be frightened. Rowling parodies this brilliantly in Dumbledore's commentary for "The Wizard and the Hopping Pot" and in a footnote for this story with the character Beatrix Bloxam, whose goal it is to remove all gross elements from fairy tales and replace them with "happy, healthy thoughts" (17-18). For the former story, Dumbledore describes her rewriting of the tale, taking out all the warts and bodily fluids spewing from the cauldron and inserting instead exceedingly cute language ("WeeWillykins," "hoppitty pot," "poorly tum-tums," "dollies," "teethy-pegs," and "grumpy-wumpkins"); this re-write causes the children, ironically, to actually *do what the original hopping pot did*, which Dumbledore describes as "uncontrollable retching" (18-19). Dumbledore tells a story about Ms. Bloxam, noting that, having overheard "The Warlock's Hairy Heart," she never fully recovered (55).

Why the satirical portrayal of someone concerned about filling the minds of children with wholesome instead of gruesome thoughts? Rowling has been asked about this before, and she has displayed the wisdom of a true fairy tale philosopher in response:

I feel very strongly that there is a move to sanitize literature because we're trying to protect children not from, necessarily, the grisly facts of life, but from their own imaginations.

And also, what are we saying to children who do have scary and disturbing thoughts? We're saying that's wrong, that's not natural, and it's not something that's intrinsic to the human condition. That they're in some way odd or ill.[14]

Protecting children "from their own imaginations" is not a good thing if we're talking here about the importance of cultivating a moral imagination. And the moral imagination must take into account symbols and depictions of that which is less than human. Evil, in the *Harry Potter* books, is symbolized in dehumanization, the most clear example of which is Voldemort's descent into snake-like appearance and manner as he divides up his soul to keep himself alive.[15] When the man locks his heart away for fear of falling sway to the foolishness of love and family, his heart begins to grow black hair all over it. His heart has become a beast, and when he returns his heart to his chest, he can only act like a beast. He has dehumanized himself, and so become evil in the process. This is how many great fairy tale writers of the past have depicted evil. Consider, for example, George MacDonald's *The Princess and Curdie* (1884), in which humans through evil choices can become less than human; or C.S. Lewis's *Narnia* stories (1950 - 1956), in which the Talking Beasts can choose to act like brute beasts and eventually become like them, unable to speak.

The symbols of the Gothic point to the reality of broken, fallen humanity. Depictions of monstrous humans, ghosts, and gruesome creatures are all pictures of dehumanization. Dr. Ann Blaisdell Tracy concludes the following:

> [N]ovels with Gothic overtones might best be identified not as those which contain some superficial trapping like a ruined monastery or the rumor of a ghost, [...] but as those [...] which contain imagery or action pertinent to the Gothic/Fallen world., *i.e.*, wandering, delusions, temptation.[16]

Her thesis is that "the Gothic world is above all the Fallen world, the projection of a post-lapsarian nightmare of fear and alienation."[17] This places the Gothic very much within the sphere of the moral imagination, giving it an essential role: to depict with supernatural and stark symbolism, the consequences of evil, of having disorder, rather than right order in the soul.[18]

The Warlock's choice of wooing methods when finally confronted with the perceived need to marry is telling: he quotes "words of tenderness he had stolen from the poets" (49). Recall from our earlier discussion that Burke had argued that the moral imagination's "higher form ... [is] exercised in poetry and art." The Warlock employed the tools of the moral imagination, but sadly, "without any idea of their true meaning" (49). He was captive to a diabolic imagination—one which sought his own pleasure above all and used that which was beautiful, poetry, only for his own ends. There is, of course, the obvious moral lesson: if you lock away your own heart for fear of love, you will turn into an evil person. But deeper than this is the philosophy of life and humanity espoused by the story: You cannot separate from yourself what is essential to humanity—and that includes pain and death. "To hurt is as human as to breathe," Dumbledore writes (56).

Perhaps the philosophy of "The Warlock's Hairy Heart" is best summed up by C.S. Lewis in *The Four Loves* (1960):[19]

> Love anything, and your heart will certainly be wrung and possibly broken. If you want to make sure of keeping it intact, you must give your heart to no one, not even to an animal. Wrap it carefully round with hobbies and little luxuries; avoid all entanglements; lock it up safe in the casket or coffin of your selfishness. But in that casket—safe, dark, motionless, airless—it will change. It will not be broken; it will become unbreakable, impenetrable, irredeemable.[20]

As in the *Harry Potter* series, Rowling does not shy away from employing the Gothic imagination and the use of the grotesque in Beedle to define humanity by the negative example: a distorted, dehumanized heart.

"The Fountain of Fair Fortune," the tale which Dumbledore calls "a perennial favorite (35) and "probably the most popular" (39), is a story of three women searching for a magical answer to their ailments. Three witches, and the very non-magical knight, Sir

Luckless, find themselves on the quest for the legendary fountain that will cure their various problems. In the story's conclusion, it is not magic, but their own human resourcefulness that cures them (though the three witches and the knight are never aware of this.) This story is also probably the most fascinating and complex as far as fairy tale philosophy goes. It is the story which illustrates the point J.K. Rowling made in her Harvard commencement speech: "We do not need magic to change the world, we carry all the power we need inside ourselves already: we have the power to imagine better." Chesterton's belief about the place of magic in the fairy tale was that as the young person learns about magical worlds, he or she also believes that our own world is magical. One of the lessons learned from fairyland is this:

When we are asked why eggs turn to birds or fruits fall in autumn, we must answer exactly as the fairy godmother would answer if Cinderella asked her why mice turned to horses or her clothes fell from her at twelve o'clock. We must answer that it is MAGIC.[21]

This is in contrast to the "scientific fatalist," who finds no wonder in the world, because everything supposedly operates by fixed laws, which cannot have been anything other than they are. But paradoxically, the fairy tale effectively teaches this philosophy precisely because there are *not* magic wands and spells used on a daily basis in our own world. It's the fairy tale that *reminds us* of these things, because they are harder to see in our world, and quick to forget.

But what of magical tales in an already magical world? One might have imagined that fairy stories in the Wizarding World would be tapping into the peculiar oddness of the Muggle world, treating things like electricity and motor engines as fascinating glimpses of another world—much like Neil Gaiman's story, "Forbidden Brides of the Faceless Slaves in the Nameless House of the Night of Dread Desire," and in another way, like Arthur Weasley. But there's a fundamental difference: the Wizarding World has no reason to flat-out disbelieve in Muggles and their technology, because they have encountered Muggle technology, and they are in hiding because of it.

So, then, back to the question: what of magical tales in an already magical world? We've already observed that only one of the five tales follows the rules of the magical world as we know it. So, Beedle, with his other tales, created *different kinds* of magic. Imagination is still a fundamental part of the tales.

But it must also be remembered that in true fairy tales, the magic itself is a supernatural context in which the real activity takes place. There is no fairy tale whose moral is, "Magic solves everything." Indeed, as Rowling notes in her forward, "In Muggle fairy tales, magic tends to lie at the root of the hero's or heroine's troubles" (viii). Beedle's tales take the lesson a step further than that: even when the heroes can do magic, it does not solve problems, and often complicates them. In other words, fairy tale philosophy teaches us that "the world is wild" (as Chesterton says). It does not simultaneously teach us that there are easy magical solutions to problems—just like the philosophical belief in a spiritual reality underneath, around, and in the physical world does not automatically lead to the belief that one can manipulate the gods to make one's life easier.

This brings us back to "The Fountain of Fair Fortune," and we find we've summarized its message. There is no magical fountain that could cure anyone; the magic lies within the three women and the knight themselves. But it is no easy magic to be tapped into. It's a spiritual journey, and the road to the end is filled with suffering. Asha is desperately ill, and by the end of the journey is in mortal agony so that she cannot be touched. Altheda is robbed of home, gold and wand, so that she is powerless and poor. Amata is betrayed and left by her lover, and so is heartbroken. Sir Luckless, as his name describes, has no good fortune in life, no magic, and no skill as a knight. The tests they have to pass on the way to the fountain demonstrate the great pain they've suffered. Much like Harry Potter himself, the heroines of this story must face pain on their road to redemption.

This is, once again, a Gothic tale, with a knight and damsels on a journey (though the women lead, not the knight—see below), a gothic "white worm" (Bram Stoker's last novel was *Lair of the White Worm*), medieval symbolism, and representations of broken humanity. This story, more than the others, needs consideration of Rowling's artwork. The depiction of the fountain at story's end is covered in symbols. At first glance, one sees sparkles in the fountain which look like crosses, which fits well the thesis that the story is filled with spiritual themes about redemption found on a suffering road. This is not the first time, by the way, that cross imagery has been paired with water. In *Deathly Hallows*, when Harry finds the sword of Gryffindor, it is described as a "silver cross" at the bottom of the pool.[22]

Each of the four basins in the fountain contains two images: one on the bowl itself, and one on the rim. The first basin has a familiar symbol to *Potter* fans—that of the Deathly Hallows; and above it on the rim, the symbol for Saturn. Why this pairing? Readers will recall that the triangular eye represented the pursuit of deathlessness—the possession of the three Hallows which would make one Master of Death. And yet the eye has a second and deeper meaning, as explained by John Granger in *The Deathly Hallows Lectures*: the eye represents the Coleridgean transformed vision, the ability to rightly see spiritual reality.[23] Harry achieves this not in his successful finding of all three Deathly Hallows, but in his abandoning of them, choosing self-sacrificial death instead.

Why Saturn? In the first place, as a Roman god Saturn was portrayed as an old man with a sickle—an image which later morphed into the mythical character of "Death," portrayals of which are still quite popular at Halloween. The pairing of Saturn, then, which the Deathly Hallows symbol, is appropriate; it was Death, after all, who gave the three brothers those Hallows. More than that, Saturn is a rather harsh symbol, dealing with the difficulties of reality and the consequences of living out of accord with reality. It symbolizes suffering, with which our story is most concerned, and its metallurgic parallel is lead, the base metal which is the subject of the alchemical process. Saturnine symbolism is that of sorrow, Michael Ward argues, but not that of lasting sorrow; it is the sorrow of repentance that leads to joy (if Saturn's symbolism is heeded) (196). Much like the triangular eye, the symbolism of Saturn can point to dread for the unrepentant seeker of that which is not truly real and human, or transformation for the one who embraces reality. As Harry abandons deathlessness and walks into Saturn's cold reality, he emerges with joy, able to see (even physically see without glasses in the heavenly King's Cross) and to change outer reality in the defeat of Voldemort.

The All-Seeing Eye on the next highest bowl probably parallels the triangular eye symbol, and if we're looking at the bowls as spiritual steps upward, we might assume Rowling intends us to see that as the triangular eye being "opened," the vision being transformed. In other words, confronted with the choice of the Hallows, and the right choice being made (Harry's choice), one's eye is opened, and one can see. Above that eye is the symbol for Mercury, or quicksilver in the alchemical process—again, a pointer to the process of spiritual formation.[24] On the next bowl, we have the Omega symbol, the last letter of the Greek alphabet; the rim of that bowl contains a number 4, which is the symbol for Jupiter. On the highest bowl, the sun/moon combination is a symbol for platinum which points to the resolution of opposites, while the rim bears the symbol for Mars, or sulfur in the alchemical process. In other words, all these symbols have astrological and alchemical meanings, and all point to the spiritual process which enables the resolution of opposites and the inward achievement of the transformed vision.

The careful reader will notice two omissions from the symbolism on the fountain. In the first place, the Omega is not paired with an Alpha, as John Granger pointed out on his website.[25] Secondly, only six of the seven planets of medieval cosmology are symbolically represented—Saturn, Jupiter, Mercury, Mars, Sun and Moon; Venus is missing. Why these omissions?

They are explained by the characters themselves—or, more properly, the heroines. John Granger notes that Asha, Altheda, and Amata all have names that both begin and end with "a"—in the Greek alphabet, *alpha*. There's the alpha to your omega. Furthermore, Venus is missing because the three women *are* the representation of Venus.

This is a depiction of the human interaction with story and symbol at a mythic, transformative level. This is no mere "morality tale," but a stark portrayal of the power of story and symbol to produce inward change in a human being. The symbols of the fountain are incomplete without the three heroines. Human story and mythic symbol work together to bring about redemption.

Finally, we have "The Wizard and the Hopping Pot." Beneath the story's moral about treating people kindly and not being hard-hearted is a philosophy of humanity which teaches equality—even equality with one's oppressors. Dumbledore notes in his commentary that the person who thinks this story a "heartwarming fable" (*i.e.*, a nice morality tale) is "an innocent nincompoop" (11). Beedle wrote this story when Wizards and Witches were being routinely persecuted and burned at the stake. This is the story of an old man who continues to love his enemies, even if he has to do it stealthily. We could make the right conclusion about the story's moral—love your enemies—but we dare not get there without the fairy-tale philosophy that gets us to the moral: we are all humans, and the pain that other humans feel is a shared pain. The young wizard needed a hexed pot to see that.

Right Order in the Commonwealth

"What we achieve inwardly *will change outer reality*." The power to "imagine better" is the power to "change the world," according to Rowling. Each Beedle story has a moral that flows from the fairy-tale philosophy. Eugene Peterson says this about the soul:

"Soul" is a word reverberating with relationships: God-relationships, human-relationships, earth relationships…. "Soul" gets beneath the fragmented surface appearances and experiences and affirms an athomeness, an affinity with whoever and whatever is at hand.[26]

This understanding of soul is right at home with the *Harry Potter* stories; after all, Voldemort, the one who cares so little about his soul he splits it in eight pieces, has no friends and no relationships, while pure-souled Harry Potter knows he needs his mentors and friends and embraces them.

Right order in the commonwealth is characterized by souls rightly connected to one another. Built on spiritual realities, each Beedle tale conveys an allegorical lesson which finds its parallel in an issue of social justice. The very interesting thing about *The Tales of Beedle the Bard* is that they were written by J.K. Rowling, a twenty-first century woman writing to a twenty-first century audience, but they are also written by Beedle the Bard, a fifteenth century wizard writing to a fifteenth century audience of British witches and wizards. This means we need to be looking for a double moral meaning in each tale: one for fifteenth century magical folks, and one for twenty-first century Muggles like ourselves.

We will take the stories from beginning to end. We've already touched on the moral meaning of "The Wizard and the Hopping Pot": love your enemies. We haven't pressed the profundity of the lesson, nor its difficulty. In the case of the fifteenth century Wizarding World as Rowling depicts it, Muggles were not just bullying and deriding the magical community; they were persecuting and attempting to kill it (though Dumbledore points out in his commentary that magical escape was the norm, and very few were ever hurt or killed). This is before the Statute of Secrecy (which was enacted in 1689), so the Wizarding World had not yet gone into hiding. As persecution of the magical community continued, anti-Muggle sentiment grew stronger, and this story was re-written, keeping its gruesome elements (which children like), but rejecting its pro-Muggle message in favor of an anti-Muggle message. Dumbledore notes that "to this day" (Dumbledore's time), the anti-Muggle story is the one that is read to young witches and wizards (14).

Beedle, in short, was a radical for his time. He was willing to love even those who hated him, and for that his story was cast into the fire and re-written. Looking back on a fictional story like Beedle's, we can see the wisdom of his moral, but what could have been on Rowling's mind for twenty-first century readers? Surely, we are more adept at seeing the obvious mistakes of the past than discerning our own in the present time. Perhaps the most obvious parallel for Western civilization, of which Rowling is a part, is its current ideological and wartime enemy, radical terrorism. A modern day version of this fairy tale might tell the story of a terrorist—or perhaps someone who we would think of as a terrorist—coming to the door for help, like the Muggle did.

One political commentator recently wrote that what is lacking in all the rhetoric surrounding foreign affairs and violence in our time is moral imagination: politicians and people do not go through the difficult task of imagining what it would be like to be in the position of another nation.[27] This is at the heart of how moral imagination works toward right order in the commonwealth. And this is exactly what is encouraged in Beedle's first tale. It is a radical position, to be sure, but perhaps only radical because it is so rarely practiced.

"The Fountain of Fair Fortune" is a feminist tale. Rowling prepares us in the introduction for the strong female characters we would find in Beedle's tales (viii-ix). As already noted, the three women are the completion of the story's symbolism, and they, far more than Sir Luckless, are the story's heroes. But in addition to and trumping the feminist themes in this story is the matter of a Witch-Muggle marriage. After an amusing story about an attempted theatrical version of the play to celebrate Christmas at Hogwarts (who ever thought we'd get backstory on Silvanus Kettleburn?), Dumbledore explains that this story has been challenged in the school library by Lucius Malfoy, because it contains a Muggle-Witch union. This was the original source of Dumbledore's longstanding conflict with Lucius, and the impetus for the latter's frequent attempts to oust the former from his position as Headmaster.

We have, then, our fifteenth century Muggle allegorical meaning. But what of its twenty-first century counterpart? Once again, I think John Granger has unveiled the correct meaning: given the little cultural battle surrounding Rowling's pronouncement that she'd always thought of Dumbledore as gay, which battle is a small part of a greater culture war on the issue, it's quite likely Rowling intended this to be a subtle, thematic look at gay marriage ("Dumbledore Votes for Gay Marriage").[28] The Muggle/Magic divide in *Harry Potter* is an allegory for racism; but mixed-race marriages are hardly the social controversy they once were. At present, the biggest social battle surrounding marriage is gay marriage, and if Rowling has injected both fifteenth century Wizard and twenty-first century Muggle meanings into these fairy tales, then one does not need to look further than the gay marriage political battle for a modern-day meaning.

The final three stories are easy to access, because they all address the same themes from different angles. "The Warlock's Hairy Heart," "Babbitty Rabbitty," and "The Tale of the Three Brothers" do not seem to touch directly on one particular social justice issue, but they do get to the root causes of all social justice issues: the quest for power and invulnerability, and the lack of love. As such, their double-applicability to fifteenth century magical folks and twenty-first century Muggles is more obvious and generalized, though no less potent.

At the heart of the *Harry Potter* stories is the difference between Harry's ability to love and embrace death without fear, and Voldemort's rejection of love and quest for deathlessness. Voldemort is a symbol of evil and of oppression, and we see very clearly in *Deathly Hallows* how social evils are increased exponentially when Voldemort takes over the Ministry. "The Warlock's Hairy Heart" is one story of a woman being murdered by a powerful man who has rejected the capacity for love. The same story could be told from long before the fifteenth century up until the current day, in both Muggle and Wizarding Worlds, both on personal levels and on larger scale levels. The rejection of love in order to make one invulnerable, as Dumbledore says, is a "foolish fantasy" (56). "Babbitty Rabbitty" teaches the simple yet profound lesson of the finality of death: there is no raising of the dead. While this is a lesson quite specific to the Wizarding World—no *magic* can raise the dead—it touches on the human quest for invulnerability so often seen in power grabs which result in the oppression of others.

"The Tale of the Three Brothers" gives us three stories of human interaction with power and death. The oldest brother seeks deathlessness through power—the ability to defeat any witch or wizard with the Elder Wand; his result is death, because another person on that same selfish quest for power kills him. The second brother seeks deathlessness through the supposed raising of the death with the Resurrection Stone; since no magic can truly raise the dead, the summoning of his deceased lover's spirit from the place she truly belongs drives him to suicide, because she cannot bear to be where her spirit is not at rest. The third brother does not seek deathlessness, but invisibility—which is to say, humility and peace until the time comes when he must die. It is only the third brother who lives a life that brings no harm to others. His invisibility is in a sense a death-to-self, a willingness to give up power and notoriety in favor of a peaceful life.

Conclusion

If Kirk was right that "the end of great books is ethical—to teach us what it means to be genuinely human," then *Harry Potter* and their accompanying *The Tales of Beedle the Bard* are great books. *The Tales,* in particular, will likely never reach the status of a "Great Book" at the academic level, simply because they are dependent upon the *Harry Potter* stories for their existence. They are "great" because the *Harry Potter* books are great, because the Beedle tales succinctly summarize the themes of the *Potter* books. If the moral imagination is the quest for right order in the soul and right order in the commonwealth, then the *Harry Potter* books and the Beedle tales are possessed of a moral imagination. In an age of scientific fatalists, idyllic and even diabolic imagination, their fairy tale philosophy is quite welcome, and represents, as Kirk said, a groping "toward the springs of moral imagination."

Bibliography

Chesterton, G.K. *Orthodoxy.*

Dawkins, Richard. "Interview with Richard Dawkins on Fairy Tales and Retirement," *The Richard Dawkins Foundation*, October 26, 2008. http://richarddawkins.net/videos/3278-interview-with-richard-dawkins-on-fairy-tales-and-retirement.

Fry, Stephen. "Living with Harry Potter," BBC Radio4, December 10, 2005. http://www.accio-quote.org/articles/2005/1205-bbc-fry.html.

Granger, John. *The Deathly Hallows Lectures*. Zossima Press, 2008.

—. "Dumbledore Votes for Gay Marriage?" *Hogwarts Professor*, December 5, 2008. http://www.hogwartsprofessor.com/rowling-votes-against-proposition-8/.

—. "The Esoteric Meaning of 'Fountain of Fair Fortune,'" *Hogwarts Professor*, December 14, 2008. http://www.hogwartsprofessor.com/the-esoteric-meaning-of-fountain-of-fair-fortune.

Lewis, C.S. *The Four Loves*. New York: Mariner Books, 1971.

Peterson, Eugene. *Christ Plays in Ten Thousand Places*. Grand Rapids: Wm. B. Eerdmans Publishing Co., 2005.

Rowling, J.K. "The Fringe Benefits of Failure, and the Importance of Imagination." *Harvard Gazette*, June 5, 2008. http://harvardmagazine.com/2008/06/the-fringe-benefits-failure-the-importance-imagination.

—. *Harry Potter and the Deathly Hallows*. New York: Scholastic, 2007.

—. *Harry Potter and the Sorceror's Stone*. New York: Scholastic, 1997.

—. *The Tales of Beedle the Bard*. New York: Scholastic, 2008.

Tolkien. J.R.R. *Tales from the Perilous Realm*. Boston: Houghton Mifflin Harcourt, 2008.

Tracy, Ann Blaisdell. *Patterns of Fear in the Gothic Novel, 1790-1830*. Ayer Publishing, 1980

Wright, Robert. "The Greatness of Ron Paul." *The Atlantic*. January 3, 2012. http://www.theatlantic.com/politics/archive/2012/01/the-greatness-of-ron-paul/250827/

Notes

1   J.K. Rowling, *Harry Potter and the Deathly Hallows* (New York: Scholastic, 2007), 709.

2   G.K. Chesterton, *Orthodoxy*, ch. IV.

3   *Hallows*, 414.

4   Ibid, 426.

5   Ibid, 414.

6   J.R.R. Tolkien, *Tales from the Perilous Realm* (Boston: Houghton Mifflin Harcourt, 2008), 337.

7   Chesterton.

8   Richard Dawkins, "Interview with Richard Dawkins on Fairy Tales and Retirement," *The Richard Dawkins Foundation*. http://richarddawkins.net/videos/3278-interview-with-richard-dawkins-on-fairy-tales-and-retirement.

9   Travis Prinzi, ed., *Hog's Head Conversations: Essays on Harry Potter* (Zossima Press, 2009), chapter 5.

10 Russell Kirk, "The Moral Imagination." *The Russell Kirk Center for Cultural Renewal*, http://www.kirkcenter.org/index.php/detail/the-moral-imagination/.

11 See *Harry Potter & Imagination: The Way Between Two Worlds* (Zossima Press, 2008), chapters 11-12.

12 J.K. Rowling, *The Tales of Beedle the Bard* (New York: Scholastic, 2008), 97.

13 J.K. Rowling, *Harry Potter and the Sorceror's Stone* (New York: Scholastic, 1997), 297.

14 Stephen Fry, "Living with Harry Potter," BBC Radio4, December 10, 2005, http://www.accio-quote.org/articles/2005/1205-bbc-fry.html.

15 For more on this, see chapter four of *Harry Potter and Imagination: The Way Between Two Worlds* (Zossima Press, 2008).

16 Ann Blaisdell Tracy. *Patterns of Fear in the Gothic Novel, 1790-1830* (Ayer Publishing, 1980), 327.

17 Ibid, 313.

18 This is why there appears to be a strong link between Calvinism, which holds a strong view of human depravity, and Gothic literature. Victor Sage first explored this in *Horror Fiction in the Protestant Tradition* (New York: Macmillan, 1988), and others have explored it since.

19 J.K. Rowling, "The Fringe Benefits of Failure, and the Importance of Imagination." http://harvardmagazine.com/2008/06/the-fringe-benefits-failure-the-importance-imagination

20 C.S. Lewis, *The Four Loves* (Mariner Books, 1971).

21 Chesterton.

22 Rowling, *Hallows*, 367.

23 John Granger, *The Deathly Hallows Lectures* (Zossima Press, 2008, 156-159.

24 For lengthy discussions on alchemy in *Harry Potter*, see John Granger's books, *The Deathly Hallows Lectures* (2008)and *Unlocking Harry Potter* (2006), and *How Harry Cast His Spell* (2008).

25 John Granger, "The Esoteric Meaning of 'Fountain of Fair Fortune,' *Hogwarts Professor*, December 14, 2008, http://www.hogwartsprofessor.com/the-esoteric-meaning-of-fountain-of-fair-fortune.

26 Eugene Peterson, *Christ Plays in Ten Thousand Places* (Grand Rapids: Wm. B. Eerdmans Publishing Co., 2005), 37.

27 Robert Wright, "The Greatness of Ron Paul." *The Atlantic*, January 3, 2012, http://www.theatlantic.com/politics/archive/2012/01/the-greatness-of-ron-paul/250827/.

28 John Granger, "Dumbledore Votes for Gay Marriage?" *Hogwarts Professor*, December 5, 2008, http://www.hogwartsprofessor.com/rowling-votes-against-proposition-8/.

Chapter 21

The Sea in the Hat

Tori Truslow

They said she was the best fishwife in the market. Not the loudest, or the strongest, or the sharpest-tongued: simply, her fish were the best. She only came once a week, and when she did, you couldn't get them fatter, couldn't get them fuller-flavored. What was her secret? She had given her nights over to studying the sea, straining to understand the waves. The waves speak a flummoxing language, their slip-slap voices always folding over, one into the next. But the fishwife sat up, under the moon, listening until she recognized certain strands of their chatter. Where to fish and when to fish—that's what she heard, between the fall and the drag. When she slept, the waves muttered on, and she dreamed the things they spoke of: deep fish, ones she would never catch, fish with lights in their mouths, fish with horns and antlers, fish of shadow, fish of glass.

They knew her in the city by her wave-black hair, her night-dark eyes. Rising early, people would flock to those eyes, fill up their baskets, ask her how she got such a good catch. "By listening," she would say, as she hacked off a great fish's head, as she slashed away its scales, her thick arms bronzed with sweat. She would pack up early, always the first to sell clean out, and take her cart out of the city and home, to a tiny village by the sea. As she passed over the fields and through the narrow streets she heard people call out, asking what the sea said. "Oh, chit-chat," she mostly told them, sometimes adding, "But watch out for the wind tonight."

Now, one market day she was shaking chipped ice all a-glitter with fish scales into the gutter, when she got a straggling customer. Dressed like a fine gentleman in a high hat, he had dripping wet hair tied in a graying tail, running like a stream down his back.

"You're the one they say has golden nets, then?" he said, in a tall, handsome voice. "Would you like to catch fish that no-one's caught before? You'd have to go down to the very heart of the sea."

"And how would I do that?" asked she.

"I'll give you my hat," said he. "If you take it home and put it upside-down on the floor, just wait till high-tide, then you'll see. It will look to you like a deep well, and if you only jump down it, you'll land on the furthest sands from the sun. There are forests of oyster-trees there that drop their fruit straight into your mouth. There are terrible things there, too, shining monsters and hidden ones and creatures that wear the faces of the dead. But take my watch and show it to them. They don't know time, so it frightens them. Then walk out and see what you can find. If you keep to the shelter of the trees you'll be safe enough. The fish there are the kind you see in dreams, and they'll swim right into your nets."

The fishwife narrowed her gaze. "Why would you give me something like that? What do you want from me?"

"Nothing at all," said he, "save my old lobster-pot—I left it in a clearing in the oyster forest long ago and it must be bursting full by now. I'm getting too old to go jumping down there myself, but you're young and strong, and I can hear the sea on your tongue. Now, listen: when you jump, you'll find the bottom all right, but discovering the way back is a different matter. Just tie a long rope to your bed-post and hold onto the end, and you can pull yourself and anything you catch up with no trouble. Just do the same every week, and bring me my lobster-pot, and you'll have all the wonders you can dream of." He took off the hat and held it out to her.

"Well, I'll have a look," she said. And she put on his hat and went home. It was somewhat large, and felt light on her head, ready for one of the sea's bounding breezes to knock it off. It didn't feel like a hat to perform the kinds of tricks the man had said. No, not at all. But when she got home she laid it on the floor of her cottage, next to the bed, just as he had told her. Then she set about mending her nets, washing her shirts and sweeping her floor.

The afternoon rolled along its course, day ebbed from the sky, and she had just put the stove on to make a broth of fish bones and seaweed, watching out of the window as the tide flowed up the shore, when she heard something change behind her. It sounded like a rising silence, far away at first, so great and so heavy that it bloomed up and up and up. She turned, and saw that the hat had gone very wide, the shadows inside it very dark, and the thick nothing-noise was pealing out of it.

When she looked down into the well, she could see nothing but black and cold. But, thinking of what the man had said, she gathered her nets, tied a long rope to her bed-post, took a long breath, and jumped.

There was no splash, but she was falling through water. She could feel it on her skin, yet she could breathe well enough. Down, down, down, thick salt sea wrapping tight around her. She realized she had left the broth on, but there was no doing anything about that now. Down, down and then soft sand under her feet, and scant light shining through trees, a slow beating weight of water against her ears.

Looking up, she saw there were pale things swimming above, shining and flashing, strange stars. Under their light the fruit shone on the trees: huge oysters, open and full. She pulled on a branch and sucked one down. How sweet it was! She pulled the branches down hungrily, swallowed every oyster she could reach until she was almost sick with their sweet, salty savor. Then looked around her.

Beyond the closest branches, all was black. She saw fish with eyes like gleaming buoys—she hoped they were fish and not just eyes—peering out of the dark. "I could do with eyes like that," she said, and her voice was pressed flat into nothingness by all the water. She stepped forward and found herself walking through a grazing shoal of the best fish she had ever seen, tall as foals and round as hogs, with gleaming antlers on their heads. They watched her go by, placid as anything, not startling even when she reached out to stroke one. She walked on, keeping a firm hold on the rope-end, gazing up and around at everything that swam through the trees—and nearly stepped into some great gaping thing's mouth. She only caught herself thanks to a fleeting light above that illuminated a row of wicked curving teeth. Stepping back and letting the pale glimmers outline it bit-by-bit, she saw a hill-sized creature rearing up in front of her as clear as glass, jaw and maw and eyes and all. Her first thought was to turn and go back, but she squared her shoulders and stared straight into one of its enormous empty eyes.

"What are you looking at?" she asked, and pulled the gentleman's watch from her pocket. The glass monster shuddered with phosphorescence, snapped and backed into the black, bumping its way away through the trees.

The woman carried on her way and soon the trees thinned out into open space. Beyond the scudding lights, the black sea looked huge without branches to cage it off. And there, in the middle of the clearing, was the lobster-pot, big as a greenhouse. Around it clustered more fish. These were like lanterns, mouths wide and beaming. They were green and blue and yellow, joyfully swallowing anything that swam into them. She opened her nets and called softly and—ah, it was just as he said—in they swam! She jumped to the top of the lobster-pot, grasped its handle, and hauled herself up the rope. Up, up, up, and then she was bursting out of the hat, heaving out the fish and the lobster-pot behind her.

Just like that, the hat was a hat again, and the world burst into noise. The wind walloped about the house, the surf beat a frothing retreat down the shore, the fish in the nets slithered and flapped and clattered their lantern-mouths, and something—somethings—rattled inside the lobster-pot. The broth on the stove seethed. It had only just come to boil. But she was still so full from the oysters that she took it off and poured it away.

Next morning was market day in the heart of the city. The word spread fast: the fishwife was selling something new. Fish with lantern mouths that shone—but only if they were kept alive, so she had them beaming their colors in a barrel. Men and women of the city towers, who would never normally risk getting their shoes briny, left their offices to see for themselves. She got a good crowd. Everyone looked and talked, but not many wanted to buy. By the end of the day, she had sold a few fish to the curious, but with most of her customers it was the same: "Lovely, but you wouldn't put them on your plate, would you?"

The owner of the hat was nowhere to be seen.

He came as she was packing up. "Did you bring me my lobster-pot?"

She took him to her cart, which was groaning under the weight of the chattering greenhouse-sized trap. "The things inside it," she said, "they muttered all night, and it sounded like language. I hardly slept for wanting to know what they were saying. What are they?"

But he wouldn't answer until he had clicked open the latch and pulled out the creatures inside. Not quite lobsters, not quite eels, but something like both, with stony bodies and claws of glass. When the last one had gone into his coat pockets, he said, "They are my secrets, and I am going to take them apart so no-one will know them. Now throw the pot back down tonight, and bring it back to me in a week's time. And between now and then you can jump down as many high-tides as you like. Whatever you met down there, I promise the next time will be even better." And off he went.

Well, she went back over the fields, through the village and home, and looked into the hat like she had looked into the glass-beast's eye. She thought of all the things that could be down in the sea's heart, of walking among them and calling them to her nets. Only—not today. Today she was tired. She hung the hat up on a hook by the door, and went about her evening. But as she was eating her supper and watching the tide roll in, a great silence washed down over the cottage. She turned to see that the hat had fallen to the floor, and once again was yawning widely, waiting to be leapt into.

"No," she thought, "I'm not ready for another adventure." She threw down the lobster-pot, which had got quite small on the journey home, and carried on as best she could, stepping around the hat-hole and looking elsewhere, until the high tide had passed and it was a simple hat again. It was the same again the next day, and the next, no matter where she hung it. "It's not that I don't want to go down again," she thought, "and I'll have to, or what will I tell the gentleman? But I'm not in the mood for stepping into monsters' mouths tonight."

In the end, it seemed the only way to make the hat behave itself was to keep it on her head. Then, when the tide was due, her hair would seep with saltwater, but the world continued as normal. No silence rolled down, no well appeared. As the week trickled out, she told herself she should be getting ready to go down again. But every time she thought of it, she thought of the silence, and the glass leviathan, and of how she needed to tend her boat and go out on the sea, because lantern-fish got her next to nothing at market. She mended her nets and caught fish for the village and wore the hat until her hair was all brackish tangles, and market day came and went.

"Well, I've been busy, he surely won't mind me being a little late," she thought. "Perhaps I'll go down tonight." But she kept the hat on as she prepared the broth for her supper. When it was just starting to boil, a knock came at the door. She jumped at the sound, and the hat sailed off her head. She heard it land with a thud on the floor behind her. "Who's that?" she called.

"Have you got my lobster-pot?" came a voice, tall and perfectly courteous and just a little hungry-sounding—how had he found her? A knock again, and "Have you got my lobster-pot?' again. As she stepped backwards, away from the door, she heard the silence roll down behind her. There was nowhere else to go. She took hold of the rope and leapt into the hat's wide well.

Down she plunged, down and down, with lightlessness wrapping thick around her, until her feet hit the deep soft sand. The forest glimmered around her as it had before, but now the oyster-shells were half-closed, and it was harder to get the sweet flesh out. Still, she sucked her fill as best she could, for she had left her supper half-made again and the fall had made her hungry. Then out she went into the black. Big-eyed fish sat in the trees, like owls, watching her. She had not gone far when a crowd of faces seemed to jump out from behind the trees, and the depths took her voice as she cried out in joy. People she'd not seen in years, and here they all were, smiling and nodding and waiting for her to come and join them. But how pale! She steadied her step and looked closer, and saw that they were the faces of the dead, worn like masks on the snouts of jostling, toothed things.

"Who dreamed you up?" she said, and waved the man's watch. The crowd shook its many-masked heads and blundered backwards into the dark, jouncing and jumbling against one another. The woman carried on and came to the clearing. This time she saw that the lobster-pot was the size of a doghouse, and around it were fish with long trailing nets for mouths. She summoned them into her own nets, took hold of the pot, and pulled them all up.

In her cottage the broth was boiling and the man was still knocking. She opened up the door and he stood, polite as ever, on the step. "Here," she said, pushing the lobster-pot against the doorframe. Inside, things were sliding and sighing. "What are they this time?"

But the man was wordless as he unlatched the trap and pulled out the creatures inside. He slipped them one by one into his trouser pockets: pale tentacled things with rills of colored lights pulsing up and down their bodies. "They are my dreams," he said when the last one had been put away, "and I am going to dry them in the sun, cut them to strips, and study them, so that I can know myself. Now, throw my pot back down, and bring it to market next week. Don't tarry next time, or it will be the worse for you." And off he went.

"What does he think he means by that?" she asked herself. And she turned off the stove, for the exchange had left her with no appetite, and turned to look at her catch. The fish had folded up their net-mouths and were looking at her with wide rolling eyes. "You might be useful," she told them, and went to fill a basin with seawater to keep them in.

Now, the woman had all the fish she could want, without needing to pay attention to the whispering waves as she used to. All she had to do was throw one of the net-fish into the sea and it would return to fling itself onto the shore, filled up with a bright slippery catch. She boiled and fried and dried them, put them into stews and soups and pies, ate and ate her fill and shared them with all the village, and still had fish to spare. "I'll never need to brave the water again," she said. And she told herself that all was well. As for the lobster-pot, she tied a glass buoy with a long rope tightly to its top, threw it down and then pulled the hat firmly onto her head. "The ocean's heart is too much bother," she said. "I'll bring the pot up one last time and then that man can have his hat right back."

She kept busy: making star-gazy pies, cleaning the house, giving her boat a new coat of paint. Her hair was always wet. With each night the tide came later, so she sat up to wait for it, and when it came later still and she could not keep her eyes open, she pulled the hat down until it was good as stuck, and slept in it. Her dreams rolled full of shining fish in all kinds of shapes. She chased them, always into the waiting jaws of enormous looming things. The sea ran out of her hair and made the bed cold and salty, and when she woke she found that small creatures had slipped through. A shower of translucent fish fell from her hair as she rose. A cuttle-fish had its tentacles tangled in her locks. When she looked into the mirror she saw a sea-star clinging to her neck. There were only a few at first, but with each passing morning there were more until she was waking to find herself raised up on a bed of tiny gasping things. There were marvels among them: seahorses with real kicking hooves, globe-like jellies with whole worlds of color and light inside them, shrimps of bright silver and crabs of burnished gold. Most of them turned to sea-foam when the sun touched them, and even though they were impractical, the woman was sorry to see them splash away into the floorboards.

As the week wore on she noticed that the net-fish weren't faring well, floating sadly in their basin. She tried to feed them and realized too late that she had never known how they nourished themselves—their nets had no throats. When they had starved she dried them out and cut the nets from their bodies, to fold and keep.

This time, at least, she had tied the pot to a buoy, and would not have to go down unless she wanted to. It would be enough to turn the hat upside-down, wait for it to open out, and haul the thing up. But even that, she thought, would bring down the awful waiting silence. Not for long, but still, but still...

She took the hat from her head, ready to place it on the floor and wait, when a wonderful thought occurred to her. Nothing really good, nothing safe and stable could come of these adventures, so better to be rid of them altogether. Lobster-pot man be damned, she would throw the hat into the sea.

She rowed her newly painted boat out on a calm afternoon, dropped the thing into the water, and went home. But that evening she looked out of her window and saw the tide nudging it back up the shore towards her. A horrible thought came to her mind, of someone wandering along the beach and falling unprepared into the hole, to be eaten by glass monsters. Or, worse, capturing them and bringing them back to sell in the market instead of her. No, she couldn't let that happen. She ran outside. When the tide reached its high point, she had hat firm on her head again. Even waking, now, things slipped through. She saw them, shoals of color, fins and tails turning the evening to a kaleidoscope as they fell and foamed away.

In the night, she dreamed of a fish with a hollow back, a dorsal fin like a mast, beacon eyes. A boatfish, with bands of pretty green and blue scales like swathes of paint along its sides. She chased it all through the night, and woke with the certainty that she would find it there, if she went back down. Seahorses pounded their hooves on her skull as they coursed through her hair, then burst into foam with the sunrise. It was market day, and she hadn't got anything to take—and no lobster-pot.

Well, she locked her door, and put the hat on the floor, and waited. "I'll put up with the silence," she said, "just to pull up his idiotic pot, and I won't let him leave without his hat, this time." Her hair, at last, started to dry.

In the evening, when she had lit the stove to boil up her broth, when the tide was lapping up the shore, she sat and watched the hat. She wanted to see how it changed, but while she was watching a knock came at the door, and she turned her head away. "Who's there?"

"Have you got my lobster-pot?" came the voice, and just a heartbeat later came the silence. She turned to the hat and it was wide and waiting. Her buoy bobbed on top of the darkness inside. She pulled it up. It came away all too lightly, the rope nibbled through.

"Oh," she said.

And looking to the door, she saw the handle turning. How had he unlocked it? Well, there seemed to be one place where he wouldn't follow her. She turned; she jumped.

Down, down, down. She realized she had forgotten to grab the rope, but it was too late to worry about that. The water caught her and held her tight. She landed on the deep sands, and looked up. The oysters in the trees were all tightly shut. She pulled a branch down and tried to pry one open until her fingers were sore and bleeding, to no avail. She looked about her, but there was nothing else to eat, so she set out into the forest with hunger swimming in her belly.

Though she followed the same path as before, she found the way blocked by some brooding hill-like form. In the pulses of light from above she made out its shape bit-by-bit: an enormous whale, dead, fallen from the sea above. Holes in its sides, a jagged sear where its jaw had been ripped off, nibbled-out eye sockets, all pale as dirty ice. The descent had sucked the color out of it. The sight made her want to slump to the ground—that something so mighty should come to this, in the end. But no, she would climb over. She was about to set her hand on its side when she noticed, in a flash from above, the ends of bones sticking out of its skin, bones too small to be its own. She stepped back and watched an eel coil up to the great beast's side, latch its mouth to it. The dead flesh puckered, and began to draw the eel into itself. She lifted the man's watch and waved it, but the thing was dead and didn't care about time; when the watch brushed its side it, too, was caught and swallowed. The thing's skin was glue, was white tar, eating everything that touched it.

How to get past?

Well, she was in water, wasn't she? The man had told her to keep to the shelter of the trees, but what could be out there that was more terrible than this? Up she swam, and over. The ocean was immense, above and around her. She was swimming with the star-things, looking down on the forest and the all-consuming dead whale. The water gripped them all, tight and tighter, making her bones ring. She realized the thing pressing all around her wasn't silence, but a sound too deep for her to hear. It shook her, it made her slow, but she saw the clearing up ahead. There was the lobster-pot, and now it was the size

430

of a dollhouse and, waiting beside it, her boatfish. It wasn't exactly as she'd dreamed it. Stony-coloured, barnacle-brindled; its eyes like beacons, yes, but muddied green and brown so that their glow was mottled. But its tall proud dorsal-mast was already rigged with a billowing fin, and glimmering fishing-lures hung from its lip. She dived down to it, and it bucked away from her. She calmed it as if it were a horse, and it still seemed skittish—but it allowed her to haul the lobster-pot, and sail up, up, up.

"But wait here," she told the boatfish, when they neared the top. Pulling herself and the lobster-pot out of the hat, she stood once more in her cottage with the door just opening and the broth just boiling. She held the pot in both arms, and could hear something beating inside.

"What's this?" she asked the man. He came to her with one hand stretched out. She did not give it to him.

"I'll tell you when it's safe in my keeping," said he.

But she had an idea what it might be, and unlatched the door to look. Inside was a deep-sea fish, all spines and grimace and teeth, and every bit of it a dark, bloody red. She took it in her hands—her fingers already covered in oyster-cuts, what were a few more?—and looked in its eyes, which bulged and sank, bulged and sank in a nervous rhythm.

"Come, give that to me," the man said.

She held the thing's glare a moment more, and then turned to the man, and smiled. "But I haven't had my supper," she said, "and this looks like it'll make a hearty soup." And she dropped it into the merrily boiling pot.

And the man burst into a mess of blood and foam and bone, and fell and splashed away into the floorboards.

The woman tutted, and turned to stir the soup. "That'll be hell to clean," she sighed.

The next week, in the city, she once again had the finest wares in the market. Her regular customers told her how glad they were to see her again, but she shook her head, and told them that she was going away for a time.

When they asked why, she only said: to learn the sea, to catch better fish.

Author Biographies

Colin Cavendish-Jones studied Classics at Magdalen College, Oxford, and subsequently practiced as an international lawyer in London, Dubai, and the USA. After working as a teacher, lecturer, journalist, and theatre director in numerous countries throughout Europe, Asia, and the Americas, he has returned to academia and is now completing a PhD at the University of St. Andrews, on Art as a counterforce to Nihilism in the works of Oscar Wilde. His research interests include the nineteenth century religious unsettlement, Romanticism, Aestheticism, and the reception of nineteenth century British writers in Europe.

Defne Çizakça is currently completing a creative writing PhD at the university of Glasgow where she is writing a historical novel about 19th century Istanbul. Her creative work has appeared in such journals as DECOMP, Fractured West, Sein und Werden, In Between Altered States, Spilling Ink Review, and Time Out Istanbul among others. Her critical work focuses on the Ottoman storytelling tradition and its linkage to coffeehouses and has appeared in *Anti-Tales: The Uses of Disenchantment* (2011) and *Navigating Space and Place* (2012).

Gaby Cohn is lecturer in children's literature at The Open University of Israel, Department of Literature, Language and the Arts, and a member of the *Yemima Center* for the Study and Teaching of Children's Literature, *Beit Berl* Academic College.

Orlando Dos Reis has a BA in English from Virginia Tech and is currently working toward a MA in English and Children's Literature at Kansas State University. His primary research interests include 19th century English literature, film adaptation, narratology, comics, and picture books.

Daniel Gabelman teaches English at Eastbourne College in East Sussex. He recently completed his PhD at the University of St Andrews on the fairytale levity of George MacDonald. Daniel's current projects include: a series of interconnected fairy tales, an investigation into how Victorian culture understood and narrated biblical miracles, and a book on literary doodling in the nineteenth century (with Jeremiah Mercurio).

Katherine Langrish is a British author of children's and YA fantasy. Titles include her critically acclaimed Viking trilogy, *Troll Fell, Troll Mill and Troll Blood*, recently republished in one volume as *West of the Moon* (HarperCollins), as well as *Dark Angels* (US title *The Shadow Hunt*, HarperCollins), a tale of elves and ghosts on the Welsh border in the twelfth century, nominated for the ALA's Best Fiction for Young Adults 2011, and *Forsaken*, (FranklinWatts/EDGE), a short re-imagining of Matthew Arnold's classic poem "The Forsaken Merman." Her writing is strongly influenced by British, Celtic, and Scandinavian folklore and legends, and has been compared with that of Alan Garner. She has a story appearing in the Windling/Datlow anthology *After* (DisneyHyperion, October 2012), and is currently working on a YA post-apocalyptic fantasy. Katherine's website is www.katherinelangrish.co.uk , and she blogs about folklore, fairytales and fantasy at *Seven Miles of Steel Thistles* www.steelthistles.blogspot.com.

Hanna Livnat is lecturer in literature at Tel Aviv University, Department of General Studies, Culture and Children's Education Cluster; *Beit Berl* Academic College; and Seminar *Hakibbutzim* Academic College; she is also head of the *Yemima Center* for the Study and Teaching of Children's Literature, *Beit Berl* Academic

College. She is the author of *Jews and Proud – Shaping Identity for Jewish Children in Germany, 1933-1938* (Institute for the Study of the holocaust, Yad Vashem Press, Jerusalem, 2009 [in Hebrew]) and the translator of literary works from German, English, and French into Hebrew.

Catriona McAra studied for her PhD in the History of Art at the University of Glasgow, and is now Research Assistant in Cultural Theory at the University of Huddersfield. She is particularly interested in contemporary uses of taxidermy, narrative art, and Surrealism. Catriona has published articles on Joseph Cornell (The Apothecary's Chest, 2009), Dorothea Tanning (Postmodern Reinterpretations of Fairy Tales, 2011 and Anti-Tales, 2011), Lewis Carroll (Papers of Surrealism, 2011), the Cottingley fairy photographs (The Inklings Yearbook, 2012) and has an essay on Brian Froud and The Dark Crystal forthcoming (McFarland). She is currently working on an essay collection about Tessa Farmer and a monograph on Dorothea Tanning.

Christopher MacLachlan is a Senior Lecturer in the School of English at the University of St Andrews. His main teaching and research interests are in eighteenth-century and Scottish literature. He has published essays on Dryden, Ramsay, Hume, Burns, Scott, Hogg, Stevenson, Buchan and Spark, co-edited a book of essays on Edwin Muir (1990), and edited *The Monk* by Matthew Lewis (1998) and Stevenson's *Travels with a Donkey* and *The Amateur Emigrant* (2004) for Penguin. He also edited *Before Burns* (2002), an anthology of eighteenth-century Scottish poetry excluding Burns, and, with Robert Crawford, a selection of the poetry and prose of Robert Burns, *The Best Laid Schemes* (2009). He recently authored *Tolkien and Wagner: The Ring and Der Ring* (2012).

Claire Massey is a writer and editor. Her short stories have been published in *The Best British Short Stories 2011, Murmurations: an Anthology of Uncanny Stories about Birds, Cabinet des Fées, A cappella Zoo,* and as chapbooks by Nightjar Press. Claire is the founding editor of online magazine *New Fairy Tales* and co-editor of *Paraxis*. She lives in Lancashire with her two young sons and keeps a blog called Gathering Scraps.

Emily Midkiff has a MA in English and Children's Literature from Kansas State University. She focuses on topics including myth, fairy tales, and fantasy and also studies the dynamics of visual storytelling as appear in comics, picture books, and children's theatre.

Mayako Murai is Associate Professor in the English Department at Kanagawa University, Japan. She received her PhD in Comparative Literature from University College London. Her research interests include contemporary recastings of fairy tales in literature and visual arts, the transformation of European fairy tales in Japan, and the framing strategies of multicultural fairy tale collections in English. Her recent writings appeared in *Anti-Tales: The Uses of Disenchantment* (Cambridge Scholars, 2011) and *Postmodern Reinterpretations of Fairy Tales: How Applying New Methods Generates New Meanings* (Edwin Mellen, 2011).

Eric M. Pazdziora is a composer and author. His writings have appeared in publications including *Enchanted Conversation, Quivering Daughters, Precepts for Living, Urban Faith, and Journal of Ethnodoxology*. As a composer, his music has been performed by orchestras, instrumental ensembles, choirs, and soloists, recorded on several CDs, and published by GIA and Alliance. He performs as a pianist, songwriter, and multi-instrumentalist with the folk / Americana band Thornfield (www.thornfieldmusic.com). Eric holds a BMus in Sacred Music Composition from Moody Bible Institute, and is currently pursuing a MM in Composition from the University of North Carolina at Greensboro. He lives in Greensboro with his wife Carrie and cat Eloise. For more information, visit his website at www.ericpazdziora.com.

John Patrick Pazdziora is a writer, editor, and doctoral candidate at the University of St Andrews, researching Scottish Children's

Literature. His articles have appeared in *VII: An Anglo American Literary Review* (2012) and various collections including *Anti-Tales: The Uses of Disenchantment* (Cambridge Scholars, 2011) and *Harry Potter for Nerds: Essays for Lit Geeks, Academics, and Fans* (Unlocking Press, 2011). Together with Ginger Stelle and Christopher MacLachlan, he is the co-editor of *Rethinking George MacDonald: Contexts and Contemporaries* (ASLS, 2012). He lives in Scotland with his wife and daughter.

Travis Prinzi is an author and speaker on the intersection of fantasy and politics, myth and culture in J.K. Rowling's Harry Potter novels. He is the author of *Harry Potter and Imagination: The Way Between Two Worlds* (Zossima 2008), and editor of two essay collections on the *Harry Potter* series. He has been a featured speaker and led panel discussions at five Harry Potter conferences and has lectured on everything from *Harry Potter* to religion to education to hit TV shows like *The Office*, at university campuses and libraries in the United States and Canada.

Elizabeth Reeder is a novelist and essayist, and also writes for radio. She teaches on the Creative Writing Programme at University of Glasgow. Her debut novel, *Ramshackle* (Freight Books), was published in April 2012 and her second novel, *Fremont*, will be published by Kohl Publishing. Her website is ekreeder.com.

Joshua Richards (Palm Beach Atlantic University) recently completed his PhD at the University of St Andrews in Scotland, researching T.S. Eliot and asceticism. His research interests include not only T.S. Eliot but also religion in literature, mythological intertexuality, and Japanese manga. He oscillates between scholastic penury in Scotland and scholastic penury in south Florida.

Jesse David Sharpe recently completed his PhD in seventeenth century devotional poetry at the University of St Andrews. He has published articles and presented papers about Philip Sidney, George Herbert, Robert Herrick, and Aemilia Lanyer. In addition to this, he is also involved in several digital humanities projects relating to English Renaissance literature, most notably digitising works for the John Donne Society's Digital Donne project.

Fiona Thackeray's stories have won awards including the Macallan/ Scotland on Sunday and Neil Gunn competitions, been broadcast on BBC radio, and published in anthologies and journals including Polygon/Birlinn 'Shorts' and Markings magazine. In 2007, she was a guest reader at the Bydgoszcz International Book Festival. Her work has been published in translation in Polish and Brazilian Portuguese and her short story collection "The Secret's in the Folding" (Pewter Rose Press) was long-listed for the Edge Hill University and Frank O'Connor Prizes. Her first novel, a work in progress, tells a story of cake makers, bewitching recipes, and sugar planters.

Tori Truslow is a fiction writer based in the south of England. Her stories have appeared in the *New Fairy Tales webzine, Polluto, Paraxis, Clockwork Phoenix 3, Verge 2011, Breaking the Bow: Speculative Fiction Inspired by the Ramayana*, and elsewhere. Her work received a Special Commendation in the 2011 James White Award. A graduate of the Warwick MA in Writing, she is currently working on a novel, and does her best to spread her story-addiction by running workshops in schools, universities and beyond. Find her online at http://toritruslow.com.

Kate Wolford is a senior lecturer in writing at a small university in Indiana. She is also editor and publisher of *Enchanted Conversation: A Fairy Tale Magazine*, at www.fairytalemagazine.com.

Kirstin Zhang spent her childhood in Papua New Guinea. Following periods in America and Japan, she attended the School of Oriental and African Studies in London and took a MLitt in Creative Writing at the University of Glasgow. Her short stories have been appeared in various publications, including the Scotsman, Soho House Magazine, and GQ. She now lives in a village on the west coast of Scotland, where she is the writer-in-residence to *Creative Communities (www.creativekilmacolm.org)*.

Lightning Source UK Ltd.
Milton Keynes UK
UKOW04f0739120716

278170UK00013B/415/P

9 780982 963388